Christmas Runaway

HAPPILY EVER AFTER SERIES SECOND NOVEL

DEBORAH KULISH

Christmas Runaway
Happily Ever After Series Second Novel

ISBN-13: 978-1519213969 (Paperback)

This book is fictional and is a product of the author's imagination. Any resemblance to actual persons, names, places, events, or locations is entirely coincidental.

Library of Congress Control Number: 2017919088

Cover Photography by iStockphoto.com, Getty Images

From Book To Market
Minden City, MI

Praise for the

Happily Ever After Series

Life Changing

"I enjoyed reading the book." - Jennifer, 4 Stars, Goodreads

Moonlighting Bride

"Great read! The plot was suspenseful, and kept me wanting more." - Amazon Reviewer, 5 Stars

"Great pool side reading." - Amazon Reviewer, 4 Stars

"Moonlighting Bride's protagonist Jan is a new bride who seems to have it made: she has a good job and a lifestyle with many perks, and now she's snagged the man of her dreams. Or is it the man of her nightmares?" - Diane, 5 Stars, Goodreads

"A good read." - Brenda, 4 Stars, Goodreads

"Lots of exciting scenarios, with several twists/turns & a great set of unique characters & facts to keep track of. This could also make another great family drama movie, an animated cartoon, or better yet a mini-TV series. There is no doubt in my mind this is an amazingly easy rating of 5 stars." - Tony, 5 Stars, Goodreads

Christmas Runaway

"This story was amazing! Going from corporate high roller with big bucks, to trying to save her husband's company! Even trying to make both sets of parents happy at Christmas, by visiting with his and then taking off by herself in a snowstorm to visit with hers without telling anybody and almost freezing to death when her truck breaks down!"
- Amazon Reviewer, 5 Stars

"A lot of this sounds like rejuvenated, as in all the compromising husbands and wives do when joining two families. I hope there's a 3rd book coming, want to know what's going on with the financial books, the Detroit issue." - Amazon Reviewer, 4 Stars

Add your review for the Happily Ever After series on Amazon, Kobo, Goodreads, or any of your other favorite bookstores.

CONTENTS

1   Party Supplies   1

2   Everything Old is New Again   14

3   Working Conflicts   22

4   The F-Word   39

5   The Bet   50

6   Monica's List   61

7   Doppelgänger   68

8   Thanksgiving Day   76

9   Gift Lists   85

10 Meat Me   93

11 Rob Bashing   103

12 Hedge Corp Christmas Party   111

13 She's Baaack   122

14 Work, Work. Work   129

15 Intervention   140

16 Power Struggle   149

17 NCC Christmas Party   160

CONTENTS

18 Christmas Shopping   173

19 Parental Therapy   183

20 Conspiracy   192

21 Dinner with Friends   204

22 Gift Wrapping   215

23 Run-In   222

24 First Night   230

25 King of the Hill   240

26 Shopping for One   248

27 Christmas Eve   255

28 Merry Lonely Christmas   265

29 Rescue   273

    Epilogue—The Gang's All Here 282

    Next Book in Series Preview

    Reading Group Guide

    Happily Ever After

    About the Author

CONTENTS

For Clarence and Vivian. Thank you for the many wonderful, loving Christmases we shared together on our family farm for so many generations. Whether it's on the road or in our hearts, we will always come home to you for Christmas. *Love you like beer!*

1 PARTY SUPPLIES

Jan Nichols couldn't help staring at his hard body. His ripped chest, muscular arms, and six-pack abs made her mouth water. She licked her lips and ran her hand across his shiny torso. She took a deep breath. "I haven't read one of these books since college. Maybe I should buy one?"

"C'mon, honey. We don't have all night to get the grocery shopping done. The store closes in a couple of hours," Rob's voice carried from the next aisle over. "We've still got half the list to go."

"On my way." She set the book back on the shelf, stopped, picked it up again, and threw it into the front of the shopping basket, burying it under a bag of apples. Swiftly, she shoved the cart to catch up with her husband.

A successful career woman, Jan Nichols accomplished every goal she had ever set for herself. Being tall and slender with light, golden brown hair and blue eyes, she had no shortage of choices for a husband. But it was love at first sight when she met Rob. And, with everything else checked off her list at twenty-nine, marrying him seemed like the natural course of events for her life. That had been just six months earlier.

As she strolled about the store, she marveled at the glistening red, green, gold, and silver decorations. The smells from the bakery mingling with the hot deli food service gave off a delicious aroma, making her think of holiday meals. Memories from her childhood flooded her mind, and her eyes brimmed with tears. This year was going to be her best Christmas ever. Her first Christmas together with her husband at her grandparents' farm, where she has celebrated every Christmas so far. Merry Christmas, she smiled at the thought.

"Jan? Do you?" Rob stared questionably at his wife.

"Do I what?" Awoken from her musing, she beamed back at her husband but saw him watching her patiently.

"Have a coupon for this detergent?" Her husband gave her an odd look. "Are you crying?"

"No," Jan denied, blinking away the moisture in her eyes. "I'm probably allergic to something here."

"This is on sale." He held up the gallon container and tapped the side with his left hand. "With a coupon, it'd be a helluva deal." Holding the product at arm's length, he continued examining it.

"Just a minute," Jan grumbled as she removed her red leather gloves. "Let me check." She forcibly dug into her large, brown canvas satchel. She huffed as she pulled out a thick stack of glossy slips of paper. Licking her thumb, she then swiftly shuffled through the sheets. Until a few months ago, she didn't even know what a coupon was.

Pausing to stare off into the distance with her memories, she rested her hands on the child's seat while still holding onto the coupons. Deciding to put aside the logistical frustration of grocery shopping, she lovingly looked at her husband. "I want you to know, Rob, how excited I am about us having our first Christmas together. This will be so much fun being with you at Busha and Jaja's," Jan said as she stretched her hands through the air. "Sharing that huge farmhouse with the rest of my aunts, uncles, and cousins. Busha will be so surprised when we—

" Jan's smile dropped. "What?" Her voice turned icy. "Why are you looking at me like that?"

Rob shifted his weight to his other foot while running his hand through his hair. "Jan, we're not going to your grandparents for Christmas." He waited, standing there watching her.

Jan winced as she tried to process what her husband just said. She slowly shook her head. "Whaaat? Nooo!"

"The Nichols family has always spent the holidays at their cottage in Caseville. You're part of the Nichols family now." He shrugged. "So, that's what we'll do for Christmas."

Jan's jaw dropped as her arms fell to her sides. One of the coupons escaped the pack and fell, twirling down to the floor with her emotions. "Rob, you can't be serious. I've always spent my Christmas with my family. I just assumed we would—"

"Well, you assumed wrong." Rob firmly replied. "Maybe we can make a day trip some weekend before Christmas to visit your grandparents."

Rob Nichols was the manager of Nichols Construction Company, a business owned by his family that specializes in commercial building. He took pride in making contacts and getting new customers. But he would also get right in the trenches with his crews at the job sites, lifting heavy material and handling equipment and tools. At six foot four and with a muscular physique, Rob's dark, wavy hair and brown eyes made him the tall, dark, and handsome man who completed Jan's life.

"A day trip?" Jan threw the coupons in the cart and placed her hands on her hips. "A day trip? There's no way Busha and Jaja, much less my parents, will accept a day trip. I—we," she pointed at herself, then at him, "need to be on my family's farm for Christmas." Jan held her arms open to Rob. "I have so many wonderful memories, tobogganing down the barn hill, eating Busha's fresh-baked cookies, golumpki, angel wings, and other delicious foods. Throughout the year, we would help Jaja in the garden—"

"Oh man," Rob sighed loudly. "Do you have a coupon or not?"

"It's right there." She snapped and pointed down to the gray linoleum floor.

"Thanks a lot." Rob stooped to pick up the piece of paper.

Jan noticed a woman at the end of the aisle watching them. She stared back at the stranger, who seemed curious about their behavior. The woman was tall with shoulder-length black hair that fell in waves on her scarf-covered shoulders. Spike heel fashion boots started where her mid-length, gray wool coat ended.

When Jan's eyes met the stranger's, the woman's lips curved into a knowing smile. "Can I help you?" Jan shouted down the aisle for her to hear.

"No, thanks. I've already got it." Rob stood up.

"No, not you. Her." Jan directed her husband's attention behind him.

He turned from the waist to see. "Who? There's nobody there." The corners of Rob's mouth started to turn up. "You okay?"

"Yes. I'm fine." Jan narrowed her eyes at him, annoyed by what he was implying. "A woman was standing there watching us for a while. As soon as you went to turn around, she dashed away."

"Dashed . . . away?" Rob smiled wide. "Like Dasher? Or maybe Prancer? How about Vixen? Or, maybe—"

"Ha-ha."

"She was probably just looking to see what all the commotion was about," Rob said as he glanced over a box of dishwasher detergent and then set it back on the shelf. "Come on. Let's grab some extra paper plates and plastic forks for Thanksgiving dinner while we're here. The store brand is fifty percent off." Rob continued to chuckle as he walked to the next aisle, shaking his head. "Dashed away.

Still funny."

"But Ed doesn't like plastic," she shouted after him.

"Ed, I mean, Dad, can have regular silverware, and the rest of us will use plastic. Problem solved." He kept walking.

Jan gave the cart a push, but it didn't budge. She dug in with her heels using all her weight, but it hardly moved. Quickly, she stuffed all the slips of paper back into her canvas bag and grabbed her purse.

Jan followed her husband, trotting in her two-inch heels to catch up with him. What a way to spend a Saturday night. This would be so much easier to do myself, she thought. But I'll be damned if the groceries are coming out of my budgeted money.

"Are you trying to avoid an argument? Because if you are, it's not going to work," she said while walking over to the paper products aisle, leaving the heavy, overloaded cart behind.

He picked up one package after another with one hand while already holding several items in his other arm. "Here, take these. Okay, is that everything on the list?" Rob looked twice at Jan. "Where's the cart?"

Jan stood there with her arms crossed. "It's too heavy. I'm leaving it in the middle of the store and walking the groceries over to it until we're done."

Jan followed as Rob returned to the cart and dumped his armload on top of the other groceries, catching a couple of boxes that almost slid off the heap created from meats, cheeses, snacks, beer, and wine.

"Oh honey, put that back on the shelf." Jan removed a box of snacks from the cart and stuck it in his chest.

"Why? I like those."

"Because if you look at the ingredients list on this product, it's so long, and it reads like a parts list for an old truck."

"I know. That's why they taste so good."

"Rob, you need to start eating healthy."

"I'll push the cart," Rob said. "Especially if it will get me away from this conversation." He gave it a push. "Huh, this is pretty heavy." He leaned into it and shoved it with all his weight.

"Did you come along because you don't trust me to get the Thanksgiving Day groceries and party supplies?"

"Honey, I can take an hour or two out of my busy schedule to spend time helping my wife with the grocery shopping. Besides, I don't want you lifting those heavy bags."

"Why now?" She grimaced. "Since we were married last June, I either did it myself or with your stepmom."

"Okay." He leaned his head back with a sigh, then turned his attention to Jan. "This meal is a big deal to my dad."

Jan looked at her husband strangely. "Every meal is a big deal to your dad."

Rob shrugged and leaned on the cart handle with his elbows. "Yes, that's true. But Thanksgiving Day, well, it has to go perfectly. That's why I'm saying we should just call Denise and concede to her cooking dinner."

Jan took in a deep breath and looked away from Rob momentarily. "No." She looked at her nails on her right hand, then buffed them on her chest. "I always succeed at everything I want, and I want this."

"Why? She's not your competition."

"Denise? My competition?" Jan snorted. "Of course, she isn't. I mean, you know."

Rob straightened his posture and headed toward the front of the store to the checkout lanes. Using all his weight, he pushed the cart as fast as possible. When he gained momentum, he glided past the rows of products as other shoppers dodged out of his way.

Jan ran past Rob just as he was getting in line. "Ha-ha, beat 'cha." She grinned, catching her breath. "I win. And we're going to Busha and Jaja's for Christmas," she said, leaning against the checkout counter, her chest heaving.

Rob shook his head. "This isn't a contest. There's no prize. This is family a tradition," Rob said, his voice bored with the subject. He started placing the items from the cart onto the conveyor belt. He watched Jan from his tilted head. "And the tradition is the Nichols go to their family cottage in Caseville for Christmas." Rob focused on the groceries, occasionally glancing back to Jan.

She knew he considered the case closed. Nothing she could say right now was going to change his mind. It would only make him more determined to stand his ground. She quietly shuffled the coupons and readied them for the store associate.

Rob reached into his back jeans pocket and withdrew his wallet. He thumbed through the contents and selected three one-hundred-dollar bills. He watched as Jan fiddled with the handles on her purse.

She returned his stare with a smile. "Everything okay, honey?"

"Yeah, I guess it is." He started reading the magazine headlines from where he was standing.

"That'll be three-hundred and ten dollars and seventy-six cents," the store associate announced.

"On second thought, everything's not okay." Rob turned his attention to the person behind the counter and leaned forward.

"Listen, mister, don't blame me. I don't set the prices. I just work here," the young man announced, visually concerned by Rob's aggressive stance. "I'm trying to save some money for college next year."

"I did the math as we shopped, and the total should be less than three hundred. What did you do wrong?"

"I . . . I . . . didn't do anything wrong," he pleaded. "My job is to scan the products. That's all. I swear."

Jan's attention turned to the strange woman again. This time, she was watching them from several aisles over. She stared back, but the stranger didn't flinch. Jan fixed her gaze on her and shrugged.

The stranger smiled and shrugged back at Jan.

"Jan, are you giving me the silent treatment?" Rob lamented. "Listen. I know you're upset, but let's talk about the holidays when we get home."

"What?" Jan dazedly pointed her finger in the direction of the other woman. "No. I was just watching—"

"The coupons. Where's the coupons?"

Jan dropped her arm as she stared at the spot where the other woman had been.

"He won't pay for the groceries, ma'am, until we take off the coupons," the store associate said apologetically.

"That's okay. I understand." Jan smiled at Rob. "I live with him."

Rob smirked at her, fanning himself with his money.

"Whoa, you saved a bundle," the young man said as his face changed from fear to amazement.

"So now, what's the total?" Rob handed over his money to the clerk.

Jan looked back to where the woman had stood, but she didn't return. She wondered if the stranger knew them somehow. Why would you watch someone for that long in a grocery store, of all places?

"Ma'am, can you let the next customer get through?"

Jan startled. "Oh sure, of course." She curiously looked around. "Where's my husband?"

"He went out the door with the groceries, ma'am."

"What?" Jan took off running. "Rob, wait up."

Jan slammed her truck door extra hard, determined to send a message that this wasn't over.

"Real mature," Rob muttered, starting the engine.

"Oh, I'm sorry. Is that not how the Nichols family closes car doors?" The words tasted bitter on her tongue.

"You knew who I was when you married me. You knew about my family's business, our traditions—"

"Your traditions." Jan turned in her seat, tugging at her safety belt to look at him. "What about mine? What about the family I've had my whole life? Do they just stop mattering because I changed my last name?"

Rob gave her a stern look, then started the drive home.

"Why were you being such a jerk to me in the grocery store?" She raised her open hands in the air.

"Because once again, Mrs. Nichols, you're forgetting that we're married, and you're making plans for the both of us without talking to me first."

"Me? What about you?" Jan scrunched her chin to her neck and used her deepest voice. "We're the Nichols family. We have traditions. Rah, rah, rah."

"Well, you were all," Rob increased his pitch, "Oh Rob, I can't wait to be with you at Busha and Jaja's. Oh, Rob, I love you. Oh Rob, mwah, mwah, mwah."

There was an awkward silence until they both busted out laughing.

"That wasn't a very good impersonation of me," Rob said as he glanced at Jan while driving.

"No, but you were spot on when you did my voice."

They continued laughing, and Rob sighed. "Listen, let's just get through this holiday. Then we can start planning for the next one. Compromise doesn't mean giving up what matters. It means creating something new that we both cherish. Besides, this is turning out to be a lot of work, and this is only for grocery shopping. I thought we learned our lesson from the Fourth of July party, which included everybody and their brother."

Jan pressed her lips together, turned her head away to look out the window, and quietly sat for the rest of the ride home.

"I can call Denise," Rob said smugly.

Denise was married to Rob's father, Ed. Not having any children of her own, she delighted in preparing meals and parties for her husband and his three sons. They, in turn, showed their appreciation for her culinary skills by never being late for a meal.

Jan's husband carried in the heavy bags from the truck.

"This is the last one," Rob said as he stood in the middle of the kitchen, holding the paper sack. "Where do you want it?"

"Over there." Jan pointed at the island as she put the groceries away. She took in a deep breath, then sighed. She contemplated how to convince him that spending Christmas day at her grandparent's farm with her family instead of his would be so much more fun. She loved Rob and couldn't imagine being without him. But why does it always have to be his family that we spend time with, she pondered. He doesn't give my family enough consideration.

"Where does this go?" Rob held a bottle of salad dressing in the air, twisting his hand back and forth as he looked through several cupboards for similar items.

"In the fridge," Jan replied softly.

"Okay, now what's wrong?" Rob walked across the kitchen to put the product away.

"What are you talking about?"

"You. You're sulking. I can tell by how you press your lips together in a little pout." Rob removed a new bag of potato chips from the brown paper bag. Opening them, he shoved a stack of several chips into his mouth. He watched Jan as she busied herself putting things away. "Is it about Christmas still, or something else I did?"

Struck by his question, Jan turned quickly, her mouth opened in disgust. "I'm not sulking. So, stop making assumptions about me." She frowned, turned away from him, and gripped the edge of the granite counter. But I am upset, damn it!

"Fine. You're right. Something's bothering me," Jan said as she turned toward Rob. Not ready to have this conversation, she paused momentarily to see if he would say something first.

Her husband busied himself with the next potato chip selection, giving the bag a couple of gentle tosses.

"Just because I took your family's last name doesn't

mean I take all your family traditions. I have family traditions too. You already get Thanksgiving dinner with your family. But do you have to have Christmas too?"

Rob leaned back against the island and popped another chip into his mouth. He went back to the task of putting the groceries away. Grabbing the next item in the bag, he removed the book. He studied it briefly, then showed it to Jan. "Is this your new boyfriend?"

"What? How did that get in there?" She feigned disgust.

"Yeah, I saw your drooling in front of the erotica book rack when we first entered the store." Looking at the cover, he ran his hand over his chest and stomach. "I look as good as this guy, right?"

"You look better than that guy, honey. I just bought it to keep me in touch with reality. You know, the lower standards all the other women are putting up with."

"No problem. Less work for me," he said, moving on to the next shopping bag.

Jan opened her mouth to dispute but stopped. Instead, she wanted to focus on winning the family holiday argument. Rob could have this one. And, besides, he was right.

"First of all, Thanksgiving dinner is with your family, and only my parents are coming," Jan countered.

"Monica is coming."

"She's your brother's girlfriend." Frustration surging through Jan's veins caused her to raise her voice.

"She was your friend first. Their relationship is all your fault."

"Oooh."

Their attention was diverted when they heard a muffled ringtone.

"That's your phone. You better answer it," Rob said as he looked inside the potato chip bag to make his next selection. He gave it a couple of tosses, looking for the good ones to surface to the top.

"What? That can't be my phone. Who would call me at this hour on a Saturday night? It has to be your phone." Jan walked over to her handbag sitting on the island and started digging through it.

"It's your phone. It's got that muffled sound from being buried at the bottom of your purse," Rob said as he patted the back pockets of his jeans. He dug into his front shirt pocket, then took off running. "Oh shit, where's my phone?"

Jan smiled sarcastically as she held up her silent phone, twisting it in the air.

Rob grabbed his bomber jacket hanging in the mudroom. He came stomping back into the kitchen. "Shit! It's Brian. Now what?"

"Rob, don't answer it," Jan begged.

"It's probably about Pete again. He's a grown man. He should take care of himself. Or, maybe I should say grown child."

Jan listened and watched her husband carry on the phone conversation. With her busy career and his family's company, the two struggled to make time together.

"Well, then maybe Ed and Denise should start going out at these odd hours of the night to find him." Rob stood up straight. "Hey, Dad. Didn't know Brian was at your house." He shook his head to Jan. "I know he's my brother, Dad, but—" Rob rolled his eyes and shifted his weight to his other foot.

"Fine. If it'll make you happy, then Brian and I will go down to the job site and check it out."

"Of course." Jan's laugh held no humor. "Another Nichols family crisis right on cue." She felt an emptiness coming over her. "Saturday night, and I'm alone again?"

"You heard the conversation." Rob picked up his jacket. "I don't know why Pete doesn't leave work when we do."

"Did they check with Monica?"

"She hasn't heard from him either. She's the one who

called Ed and Denise." Rob's expression softened.

It appeared to Jan that her husband appreciated Monica's concern for Pete's whereabouts. But it didn't help her situation, and she disliked what this meant for her tonight. "How soon do you have to go?"

"The sooner I leave, the sooner I get back," he said, putting on his jacket. "I'll be as quick as I can. Will you wait up for me?" He smiled.

"We didn't even have dinner yet. At least have a sandwich or something before you go."

"That's a great idea. I'll take one with me." He went to the pantry and came back with bread and mustard. He brought out the smoked turkey and pepper cheese to the island. Setting a paper towel down, he assembled a thick sandwich and wrapped the paper towel around it. "Sorry about leaving you with this mess to put away," he said as he walked toward the mudroom.

"But what about cleaning the house and watching a movie afterward?"

Rob stopped, then turned to look at Jan. "I didn't ask for this. Do you not want me to go and check on my brother?"

Jan said nothing and crossed her arms.

"Listen. I'm sorry my family's company takes me away so much, but this is what pays our bills." Rob held out his arms, walking toward his wife.

"Your family's company?" Jan glared at her husband. "What about my work? You think I'm not contributing anything?"

He stopped in his tracks and dropped his arms to his sides as his shoulders slumped. "Again," Rob mumbled under his breath, then cleared his throat. "I know you make a lot of money. I'm sorry."

Jan's icy exterior melted. "Rob, why can't we both slow down our careers and spend more time together?"

"Sounds great, honey." Rob wrapped his arms around her. "But I don't have time to talk about it now. Do you want a kiss before I leave or not?"

"No." Jan folded her arms across her chest, creating a barrier between them.

Rob rolled his eyes and sighed. "Fine then." He stomped out of the kitchen and disappeared into the garage, leaving behind a loud bang as he slammed the door shut.

Jan picked up Rob's remnants from his sandwich and set them into the sink. She dragged her feet to the great room and punched the decorative pillow. Plopping down on the couch, she let her arms drop to her sides and sat limply, brooding.

"Yes, I want a kiss," Jan whimpered, pouting, as tears filled her eyes.

2 EVERYTHING OLD IS NEW AGAIN

The front doorbell rang, and Jan grinned wide. He's back, she thought. He's playing games with me. Running through the great room, she pulled the ends of her sleeves into the palms of her hands and used them to dab her eyes.

"I knew you'd be back," she shouted. Throwing open the heavy, cherry wood doors, she closed her eyes and protruded her puckered lips into the air with arms stiffly aligned by her sides.

"Um, excuse me," a woman said. "I was looking for—"

"Oh my God!" Jan stumbled backward as red ran through her face. "I thought you were . . . I was just . . ." she mumbled and stared at the stranger. "Hey, aren't you the woman from the grocery store?" She shouted out in an icy tone.

"Yes." The woman expressed amusement. "You surprised me. I thought you were being overly affectionate for just having exchanged glances." She smiled and held out her hand. "Hi, I'm Marissa."

"Uh, okay. Hello, Marissa." Jan limply accepted her greeting.

"I can tell you're wondering why I'm here. May I come

in?" She took a step forward.

Jan didn't budge. "Well, my guard dog doesn't like strangers in the house and . . ."

Marissa pushed past her.

Jan stumbled backward. "Hey." She ran after her into the house.

Marissa looked around the foyer, peering into the other rooms and turning in all directions. "Not bad." She slowly nodded her head in approval.

"Not bad what?" Jan huffed. "Why are you here?"

Marissa didn't reply and continued to visually inspect the house.

"I'm calling the police," Jan said as she went to get her phone.

"No, stop." Marissa turned her focus toward Jan. "I'm just very impressed with the house. May I sit down?"

"Who are you?" Jan raised her voice.

"Yes, I'm sorry. I should explain myself," Marissa said as she walked into the great room, removing her coat. Folding it times, she laid it next to herself on the sofa. "It's just that when I see what I want, I go after it. You know what I mean, misses?"

Jan stood with her arms folded across her chest, glaring at the other woman.

"Well, my name is Marissa Mankowski and," she paused momentarily and tossed her hair off her shoulders, "I'm with Michigan Homes. It's a magazine that features beautiful homes in, of course, Michigan."

Jan continued to glare at her.

She cleared her throat. "I take it you haven't heard of our magazine?"

"I have. I'm listening."

"I was given your name and address from a contractor who recommended I check out your house. Apparently, he worked on it for a while and was very impressed," Marissa said, folding her hands on her lap. "So, how would you like to have your home featured in one of the finest magazines around?"

The tension in Jan's face eased as she lifted her chin, regarding Marissa with newfound interest. "Well then, let me ask you this," Jan sat down across from her. "Will I be in some of the pictures too?" A smile tugged at her lips.

Marissa's chest heaved as she blew out a breath. She relaxed, draping her arm across the back of the couch. "Of course, you will be in the pictures. A beautiful woman like you, we wouldn't want it any other way."

"Seriously? Oh, this is so exciting. I can't wait to tell Rob." She perched herself on the arm of the couch, crossing her legs. "What do you think of this pose. I see this pose a lot in different magazine articles and even advertisements. I think this will . . . be . . . uh . . ."

"There'll be plenty of time for deciding on poses." Marissa rose smoothly, guiding Jan back to her seat on the couch with a gentle but firm touch. "We'll need to schedule time for a crew to come in to take pictures, an interview with the chief editor, and review and approve the layout before going to publication. So, what do you think? It's a lot of commitment. Are you up for it?"

"Absolutely!" Jan leaned forward on the edge of her seat. "My friends are going to be sooo jealous."

The slam of the garage door cut through their conversation. Both women turned their heads to watch the entryway to see who it was. Heavy footsteps approached, and they sat quietly.

Rob walked into the room, his attention fixed on his phone while he spoke. "Hey, hon. Pete's fine. Dad just texted me that he had just got home." He didn't look up as he continued, "Did you make anything for dinner because I'm starving? That sandwich was only an appetizer."

"Hi, honey." Jan jumped up and went to her husband, lightly kissing his cheek. "There's someone I want you to meet." She gestured toward their visitor. "Rob, this is Marissa. And, Marissa, this is my husband, Rob."

Rob's hands dropped to his sides as he finally looked

up. The color drained from his face as he stared at the woman across the room.

"Nice to meet you, Rob," Marissa said enticingly with a slight tilt of her head.

Jan looked at her husband. "Rob? What's wrong with you? You're pale as a ghost." Jan grasped his arm. "Rob? Are you coming down with something?

Rob didn't say anything and continued to stare.

Jan moved closer to him, pulling on his arm and speaking softly. "Honey, are you okay. Can you at least say hello?"

He jerked his arm away from her and stumbled backward. "Uh, yeah, hello."

"Rob, what's wrong with you tonight?" His cold, distant tone shocked Jan. "Be polite and come sit down." She nodded toward the great room.

"Yes, Rob, I would love to talk to both you and your wife about your home. We're going to—"

"Nope. Don't have time." Rob turned and walked out of the room. "Jan, I'm going back to work," he shouted as he walked away.

"What? But you just got home. Rob, come back," Jan pleaded as she ran after him. The sound of the door slamming echoed through the house. Jan returned to the great room, looking down at the floor. "Well, I guess he had to go back to work. He works a lot." She forced a smile as she met Marissa's gaze.

"That's okay. We can plan this ourselves." Marissa waved off Rob's departure. "Husbands usually get in the way anyhow."

"Okay then. Where do we begin?"

"I'll have my office contact you first thing Monday, and we can schedule some time for interviews and photos. Sound good?" Marissa stood, draping her coat over her arm. "Do you have a business card with your phone number?"

"Yes, I'll get it." Jan briskly walked into the library and

grabbed a card from her portfolio. Before returning to the great room, Jan watched the other woman. The woman was still visually inspecting the house. She had concerns about this woman admiring her home and wondered if that's all she was up to? She fanned the business card in her hand as she walked into the great room. "Here you go." Jan held her hand out. "I'll look forward to hearing from you or one of your assistants."

"Great." Marissa threw on her coat. "I'm really looking forward to working with you." She gave a menacing smile and walked to the front door.

Jan closed the door behind her and made sure it was locked. From the side lights, Jan could see her getting into her car and driving away.

"Is she gone?"

"Rob?" Jan quickly turned to meet him in the kitchen. "I thought you went to work?"

"I was just hanging out in the garage until I saw her leave."

"So, what do you think? Our home in a major magazine?" Jan flashed a big smile at him but quickly pressed her lips together when she saw he was giving her a smug look. She had a gut feeling that he knew something he wasn't telling her.

He sighed and turned away from her. "Sure, if you want everybody to easily case our home for robbery." Rob grabbed a beer. "Is that what you want?"

"Rob, they feature a house every month. That doesn't make them more or less vulnerable to robbery. Come on. This is going to be fun."

"How do you women say that?" Rob squinted, looking upward. "Something about having a bad feeling about a person." His gaze locked onto hers. "Well, that's me. I've got a bad feeling about her, and I don't trust her."

Astonished by his immediate dislike for someone they just met, Jan sat quietly for the moment. "Well, it's late. And I'm tired. Do you want a cold sandwich for dinner?"

"Do you want to go over to Ed and Denise's?"

"No." Jan grabbed several items from the refrigerator and brought them to the island.

"Okay, so I guess we're not having a hot meal tonight for dinner?"

"There won't be anything hot for a long time if you keep that up."

Rob's laughter carried a hint of surrender.

"I was looking over the bags of groceries and decorations, and that's a lot of stuff, but is it enough?" Jan said, setting down the plates of food in front of each of them.

Rob focused on his food, avoiding her question.

"I was thinking." She paused and waited for him to look at her.

Rob turned his head her way.

"I would like to add more to the menu. I think we need more appetizers."

He tossed down his napkin. "Why don't you just give it up already. You're giving yourself a lot of extra work that you don't need."

"I've always excelled at everything I've gone after, and I'm going to show Denise that she's not the only party planner in town."

"Why? You're great at everything else. But this isn't what you want to do. So, why are you doing it?"

"I do want to do this.." Her voice rose. "It sounds like you don't want to have a family party. So, why did we have a Fourth of July party?"

"Because I had Denise's help. Otherwise, it wouldn't have happened."

Jan glared at him, hurt spreading across her face. "Wow. So, you don't believe in me."

Rob fell back in his chair, dragging his hands over his face. "I do believe in you. I know you. I love you. And I know that you don't want this. You want to be the host while the staff does all the work."

"You're wrong. I do want this. And it's going to be a huge success. Just like everything else I do."

"Okay then." Rob pulled out his phone and checked his calendar. "Thanksgiving is only four days away. We better start divvying up the work between the two of us."

Jan picked up her phone and opened her calendar app. "Wow. I am so busy at work." Using her thumb, she scrolled back and forth between the days. "I can make room for us on Tuesday afternoon."

"Not Tuesday. I'm meeting with Mr. Daniels at the project site. How about Monday or Wednesday?"

"After work only. We have staff meetings all day Monday and a new client coming Wednesday afternoon."

"How about," Rob looked at his wife, "I schedule Denise to come over, and we'll get it done while you're at work?"

She winced. "And miss all the fun? Honey, this is what family traditions are made of. I want to have some influence on the Nichols family holidays."

"Jan, you are. You're just as much a part of this family as the rest of us."

"You say that. But I don't think the others feel that way." Her voice softened. "I'm not sure you feel it either. I always feel like an intruder. Being an only child weighs the family dominance in your favor with your two brothers."

"You're being unreasonable." Rob stood up and held his hands open to her. "We only have four days. So, what's it going to be?"

"I'll get it done." Jan walked away, hunching her shoulders and studying her phone. Suddenly, she brightened and turned back to her husband. "Okay, here it is. You do what you can on Monday afternoon and evening. I'll handle Tuesday in the late afternoon and evening. And then," she moved closer to her husband, warming to her plan, "we can finish up whatever is left to do on Wednesday together." Jan threw up her hands. "So, what do you think? See? I've got it all worked out."

Rob's gaze drifted around their usually pristine kitchen, now cluttered with shopping bags, party supplies, and scattered decorations. "Honey, your plan sounds great. Count me in," he said, his tone carefully neutral.

"I appreciate you believing in me." Jan stepped closer to her husband, toying with his shirt buttons. "It's important to me to be a great hostess and throw dinner parties for our friends and family."

"I know. And I want to support your plans." He wrapped his arms around her, drawing her closer.

"What about finishing our dinner?" Jan whispered in his ear.

"I'm hungry for something else." His kiss was deep and passionate. "Something hot." He took her hand, leading her upstairs.

3 WORKING CONFLICTS

Sleepily, Jan reached over for her husband, searching the sheets and covers with her hand. Stretching her arm across the comforter covered in a taupe, silky duvet, she patted the fluffy down. When her grasp came up empty, her eyes snapped open. She rolled over and stared at the place where he should be lying next to her in their king-size bed.

Not again, she thought. She sighed, grabbing a handful of the down comforter, raising it up, and slamming it back onto the bed. She picked up the covers and threw them to the opposite side, watching as the encased feathers settled in their wake. "Take that," she muttered.

She slid out of bed, her mind racing with questions. Though she was a married woman, she contemplated what she would do today if she weren't married. She started to question whether she needed to be with Rob all the time, even when she wasn't working or busy with friends. She had a life before she met him. What happened to her ability to be alone? She used to enjoy time alone, reading, writing in her journal, or just relaxing while listening to music.

While tying the sash on her robe, Jan's thoughts wandered to her life before marriage. She used to spend

Sundays curled up with a good book, jotting down dreams
in her journal, or simply enjoying the quiet. A pang of
longing struck her. She missed the ease of those days, the
freedom of not having to check if her plans fit someone
else's schedule. A familiar ache of loneliness threatened to
overwhelm her, but something else sparked inside, a tiny
flame of possibility.

She sat on the edge of the bed, staring across the room.
Is this what my life has become? Waiting for Rob to make
time for me? The thought stung, and tears pricked her
eyes. But before they could fall, a wave of determination
washed over her. I don't need to feel this way, she thought,
fingers tightening on her robe's soft fabric. I used to be
whole on my own.

And, if this was how it was going to be, then married or
not, she needed to get back to living her life without him.
The realization hit her like a shaft of sunlight breaking
through storm clouds – she'd been waiting for permission
to live, permission from someone who couldn't even be
bothered to spend Sundays with her.

No. She stood abruptly, brushing the tears away. I
don't need to wait around for anyone. I used to thrive on
my own, and I can do it again.

"I'm free," she declared aloud, her voice filling the
room with possibility instead of absence. Throwing her
hands in the air as she realized her renewed independence.
She spun in a small circle, her robe flaring around her like
a victory flag.

"I'm going to plan my time, with or without Rob." Her
tone grew steadier, more confident. She caught her
reflection in the mirror and straightened her shoulders.
"Most importantly, I'm going to be happy because I
deserve it." The words felt like a promise to herself, one
she intended to keep. For the first time in months, the
silence in the house didn't feel heavy. It felt like a blank
canvas, waiting for her to fill it with whatever she chose.

A spark of excitement ignited inside her. Ideas for how

she could fill her day emerged. For the first time in a while, her loneliness faded, replaced by the realization that she could reclaim her joy, starting now.

After a deep breath, she stepped lightly down the stairs. Unable to stop smiling with her innovative disposition, she poured a cup of coffee, took a quick sip, and set it on the breakfast nook table. She looked around the kitchen. "Hmm, no paper." She shrugged and headed for the front door. "No paper, no problem." Her silky pajamas and robe were street-worthy, so she opened the door and took several steps outside. The late November Michigan air bit her skin as she retrieved the paper, sending her scurrying back into the warm house.

Settling into her seat at the table, she took another sip of her hot beverage and snapped the front section into place. "Let's see today's headlines. Hopefully, there's something juicy, maybe give me some marketing ideas," she murmured. She scanned the front page. "Wow, a law enforcement agency is looking into the dealings with the city of Detroit contracts." Jan snapped the paper again and took another drink. "Sounds serious for the city." Her eyes drifted to the chair where her husband should be, and she felt a pang of loneliness. She drew in a deep breath, refusing to let it upset her. Leaning over the table, she rested on her crossed arms and continued reading.

After a couple of hours of reading the paper and making notes in her journal for prospective clients whose advertisements could use improvement, Jan lifted her coffee cup and started to take a drink. Empty again, she thought, frowning. She stretched her legs under the table and arms far above her head. "Oh, that felt good." She went to the kitchen sink and set her cup down. Turning around, she leaned a hip against the counter and looked out at the expansive home. "This is one big place for one person," she murmured. "One lonely, big place." Her phone rang, and she ran back to the breakfast nook table to answer.

"Oh, it's only you," Jan said. "Yes, Monica, of course, I'm happy to talk with you. I just thought you were somebody else. Yes," she coughed, "Rob's here." She closed her eyes and pressed her lips tight.

She listened as she removed her right sleeve from her arm while walking up the stairs. Switching the phone to her other hand, she proceeded to remove her other sleeve. Holding her pajama top to her chest, she entered the room and closed the door. In her bedroom, she tucked the phone between her shoulder and ear, then prepared for her shower. "Oh wow, that's very generous of them to give you tickets. Well, you and Pete have a fabulous day at the football game. I have . . . I mean, we have some things of our own to do, and I need to get ready now."

After hanging up, she couldn't help but feel a bit of jealousy towards her friend Monica. She and Pete always went on exciting adventures and had a seemingly perfect relationship. Sighing, Jan shook off the feeling and focused on getting ready for the day. Her day, alone. It'll be fun, she told herself.

"You don't need Rob," she told herself firmly. "You're an independent woman who can handle anything on your own."

After showering and getting dressed, Jan left home to spend the day at the Detroit Art Museum. She loved immersing herself in the beauty of different works of art. It has always helped her with her creativity and marketing projects. And she had meant to visit this exhibit for some time, but Rob was reluctant to go with her. But now she didn't need his approval.

Walking through the museum halls, Jan couldn't help but feel inspired by all of the vibrant paintings and sculptures around her. She took out her notebook and jotted down ideas for potential clients and some personal goals she wanted to achieve.

Jan reflected on how amazing art can spark creativity and evoke emotions as she made her way to the exit. Lost in her thoughts, she didn't realize how much time had passed until her stomach started growling with hunger. Glancing at her watch, she realized it was already late afternoon. Rather than stopping to dine somewhere, she decided to pick up some dinner at a nearby cafe to take home.

During the drive home, Jan couldn't help but feel grateful. She couldn't stop smiling, thinking about the vibrant colors and thought-provoking sculptures she had just experienced at the art exhibit. The afternoon had been more than just relaxing; it was truly memorable. Realizing that sometimes taking a break from work, friends, and family and doing something for herself can lead to unexpected opportunities. Jan felt motivated and inspired as she headed home.

"What a great time I had by myself," Jan thought, thinking back through the hours before on how she spent her Sunday. She hung her coat in the mudroom and took her purse and restaurant carryout to the kitchen island. She emptied the carryout bag and set out her plate. When she heard the garage door open, she paused momentarily before continuing with her food.

"Hi," Rob said softly, setting down his briefcase and removing his coat and boots.

"Hi," Jan replied, feeling the awkward tension in the air. "I was hungry and decided to have an early dinner. I have enough for you, too, if you're interested?"

"Yeah, sure," he said, walking to the kitchen sink. He washed his hands. "I'm starved."

Jan gave him a curious look. "Why didn't you eat if you were hungry?"

"I was too busy with work and," he shrugged, "just didn't take the time for it."

Jan pressed her lips in a slanted line. She grabbed another plate from the cupboard and prepared it for her husband.

The awkward silence filled the room. Jan wanted to talk

about something, anything. But it felt like she didn't have the strength to argue again about how he puts his company first.

"I missed your text messages today," Rob blurted out, looking at Jan, then turned to take another bite of food.

"I . . . I don't understand." She gave him a puzzled look. "I never sent you any messages today."

"I know." He laughed quietly. "I actually had my phone with me," he cleared his throat, "close by the entire day thinking Jan is going to send me a message, so I'd better be ready to answer it." He watched her, waiting for a reaction.

Jan set down her spoon and leaned back in her café stool. "Rob, I love you, But" she stammered for the words. "I'm not going to wait around for you. If you're not here, then I'm going to do whatever I want to do. I deserve to be happy. Not stood up every weekend by my husband, of all people." She looked down at her food, trying to hide the pain in her expression as she stirred her soup.

Rob stood up abruptly and walked away from the island. With his back to her, he held his forehead in one hand and placed the other on his hip. "You're right. You do deserve better. Better than what I can give you. It wasn't supposed to be this way after I landed the Daniels Tech Center contract." He slapped his hand on his thigh and turned to face her. "But Jan, I'm not sure about Nichols Construction Company anymore. I'm trying to manage the books myself, but I'm not good at it. I still have to do my job of overseeing the project site, ordering the materials, and dealing with staff. The accounting and paperwork are so time-consuming. I feel like I'm starting to drown in all this stuff." He shook his head. His face wrinkled as his chest heaved with a deep breath.

"Where's your office manager? Why isn't she taking care of the bookkeeping?"

"She was sick for a while. Then, she wanted to leave

the country for a vacation to recover." He sighed heavily. "I don't think she's coming back."

"What?" Jan leaned forward with her arms spread wide open. "Rob, why didn't you tell me this? What are you going to do?"

Pacing between the sink and the refrigerator, he waved his hand through the air. "I don't know. I didn't think taking on her responsibilities would be that big of a deal, and I could handle it myself. But I can't. In the meantime, I thought about calling one of those temp agencies."

Jan moaned and rolled her eyes.

Rob's hands dropped to his sides. "Then what? Do you know anyone looking for a bookkeeping-slash-office manager job right now?"

Jan thoughtfully stared at him. I know bookkeeping. Boy, do I know bookkeeping. I can help my husband and give us a chance to work together. She started smiling at the thought.

"Are you going to say something or just laugh at me?" He threw his hand in the air.

"Rob, I can help you," she said tentatively. Holding out her arms, she stood up and started walking toward him.

"You know somebody who needs a job?"

"Yeah, well . . ."

"I knew it. You're messing with me."

"No, Rob, I mean, I can help you. Me," she said as she pointed her finger into her chest, expressing excitement at the idea. "I have an MBA. I'm pretty sure I could handle your company's finances." She picked up his hands. "So, what do you think? Am I hired?"

"Wow, Jan, that's an incredible offer. But you've already got your own career." He pulled away from her. "I'm afraid if you did this, you'd end up hating me for taking you away from what you love."

"Rob," she said, discouraged by what her husband implied. "I love you. And, I always dreamed about what it would be like to be working side-by-side with my husband." She shrugged. "I just never thought it would happen because our careers are so different. But this is an opportunity to see if it works." She beamed and went back to her seat at the island.

"I don't know." He shook his head as he looked at the floor.

"Come on, it'll be fun." She grinned. "If nothing else, at least let me help you until you can find a replacement."

He looked at her and walked back to the island. "That's not a bad idea. If you can, just help me until I hire somebody else. I don't want to take you away from your career, and you'll end up hating me for it."

"I would never hate you." Jan squinted at him.

He peered back at her. "Uh huh, you sure about that?"

"Never." She tilted her head, grinning.

"Okay, then you're hired," he said, picking up her hands and holding them. "But just until I can find someone else."

"I accept," Jan said, pulling her hand back and then holding it out to shake.

Rob accepted her gesture. He quickly picked up his phone, holding it in one hand and using the other to punch in some text. He looked at Jan with an enticing grin and hit send.

Jan could see he was proud of himself for using his phone's technology. "Oh, excuse me, honey. I've got a text message," she said seductively. She picked up her phone, and after reading what he had sent, her thumbs moved swiftly over the keys. Giving it a punch with her index finger, she set it down, smiling.

Rob pretended to be surprised when his phone buzzed in his hands. Turning it over to read, his grin grew wider.

Jan watched his expression as she bit her bottom lip.

The corners of his mouth turned up, and his eyes tapered in excitement when he returned Jan's look. "Okay. How about this?" Using his index finger, he hunted and pecked at the keys. "I'll have to work on my typing skills," he said, glancing at her.

Jan read her screen. "Mmm, I like how that sounds."

"Oh yeah," he said, getting up and taking her by the hand. "Then why don't we go upstairs, and I'll show you how it's done in person." He pulled her close and embraced before breaking it off and heading to the stairs.

They had barely reached the great room when the doorbell rang. Looking at each other, they simultaneously slumped their shoulders and sighed.

Jan shrugged and pointed to the front door. "We don't have to answer it." She whispered, giving her husband a mischievous glance.

They both looked at her phone, and it buzzed with the caller ID displaying Mom.

Jan gave Rob a helpless look. "Should I answer it?"

He flashed an inquisitive stare. "It's your mother."

She took a deep breath, picked up her phone, and put it on speaker. "Hi, Mom."

"Oh, Jan. We weren't sure you were going to answer."

Rob squinted as he listened to the distant voices coming from the front door.

They walked to the foyer, and she held the phone out for both of them to hear.

"Just because she answered doesn't mean she's home. That's why they're called mobile phones."

They heard Jan's dad say in the background.

"I know, Charles. You don't have to tell me."

Jan threw the front door wide open, and she and Rob stood there watching them.

"If you wanted to know if they'd be home, then you should have called them before we left," Charles disputed.

"Mom, Dad, it's great to see you," Jan said.

Charles and Beth Brooks were self-made millionaires and protective parents of their only child. So much so that Jan struggled with the adjustments, going from being a single woman who had no idea how to manage her own money to being a married woman whose husband held a tight grip on the budget.

Jan shared a quick hug with her parents as they entered the house, and Charles shook hands with Rob.

"We thought we'd help you decorate outside," Beth said as she laid her coat over the back of an over-stuffed chair.

"Decorate outside? Why?" Jan gave them a curious gaze.

"Yeah, what for?" Rob moved over to his wife's side.

"Christmas, you sillies. Your neighbors are getting into the spirit of things. Look," Beth said as she pointed outside while her husband opened the door for all the light to shine in.

"But we haven't even finished with our Thanksgiving decorations yet," Jan protested, feeling overwhelmed.

The four of them stepped outside onto the front porch.

"It's so dark out, but look at all those lights. It's beautiful," Jan breathed in the cool, crisp air.

"Hmmm, very nice, but that's a lot of unnecessary expense for all the materials. And not to mention an increase in the electric bill. Maybe we'll just hang a wreath or something," Rob suggested.

"What?" Jan turned and glared at her husband. "You can't just hang a wreath in this subdivision. You'd have the neighbors storming our door with pitchforks."

The four of them moved back inside the house, where it was warm.

"That's why we're here," Jan's mother interjected. "We have plenty of decorations, all kinds. We'll even have our company come here and set up whatever you want."

"That won't be necessary." Rob placed his fingers in his front pockets with his thumbs out. "Most of those houses, I mean our neighbors, have companies that do the work for them. Those companies are expensive."

"That's why—" Beth tilted her head and held out her arms.

"And, I would rather do it myself. I have some ideas."

Jan and her parents stood speechless as they stared at Rob, waiting for him to explain.

"Huh, okay then, what did you have in mind?" Jan placed her hands on her hips and walked up to her husband.

"Line the roof edge with lights."

"What color?"

"Multi."

"Okay. Go on."

"String lights on the shrubs and hang wreaths on each front window and door."

"That sounds nice," Charles nodded. "Sounds like what every other house in this subdivision and ours has. Which brings us back to the question, do you want us to have someone do it for you? Why would you want to do your own?"

"I just said why!" Taking a step back, Rob raised his voice slightly as he hunched his shoulders and spread his arms wide open.

"Fine. Do it yourself. But at least come and take a look at what we have for supplies in our car. What you don't use, then we'll donate it."

"Free stuff?" Rob shrugged. "Okay." He relaxed his shoulders and followed his father-in-law outside to the hatch of their SUV. Jan and Beth lingered behind, rubbing their crossed arms, their coats draped over their shoulders.

"I tried to offer you free services too, but you're too—"

"Okay, okay. I get it. I'll pass on the services and accept the decorations."

Charles grumbled as he opened the hatch.

"Wow, this looks like a mini Santa workshop. You've got just about everything in here," Rob said as he picked up several boxes of lights, looked them over, and then went on to some garland. "Jan? Did you see this stuff?" He yelled over his shoulder.

"I already did, honey. I lived there. Remember?" She

stepped over to his side and rubbed his shoulder.

"Oh yeah. Right," Rob said softly. "Must have been nice to have parents who outdid themselves for the holidays." He continued examining the materials.

Charles turned an inquisitive stare to his son-in-law. "Your parents, err dad, didn't decorate for the holidays?" Charles asked.

"A little. You know, things like a tree with lights inside the house but visible through the front window. When Denise came into the family, she made it homier." He stepped back and put his hands on his hips. "But this, this is like commercial stuff. This is top-grade."

"I'm glad you like it," Charles said, patting him on the back. "Tell you what, why don't we take all of this into your garage? You can pick and choose what you want. What's left over, then you can donate the stuff."

"Okay." Rob shrugged. "But I'm not sure they'll be much left to donate." He beamed, stacking one box on top of another.

They walked into the garage as the door went up.

"Kitten, I've been talking with my brothers and sisters, and we came up with a menu for Christmas. Do you want to pick something, or should I just tell you what to bring?" Beth looked quizzically at her daughter.

"I'm guessing you want to tell me?" She went along with her mother's game.

"Good," Beth grinned. "It's like you read my mind."

"You didn't tell your mother?" Rob whispered to Jan as he walked up next to her.

"Tell me what?"

Jan frowned at Rob, rolled her eyes, and then turned to her mother. "Rob thinks we're spending Christmas day at his family cottage in Caseville instead of going to Busha and Jaja's."

"I don't think it. I know it."

"Well, perhaps you two could come over for a couple of hours. Seems like there should be some kind of compromise," Beth replied firmly, glaring at her son-in-law. "It's not like Caseville is that far from Parisville."

"It's forty miles." Rob huffed.

"That's the equivalent of fifteen miles of city driving, which no one thinks twice about doing," Beth shot back.

Jan was relieved that her parents were taking her side and made a big grin at her husband.

"With all due respect, Beth—"

"Oh, it has nothing to do with respect. Once you're married, respect goes out the window, and couples need to figure out what the hell they're going to compromise on for the holidays to get along," Beth snapped.

"Beth, this is between them, and we shouldn't interfere," Charles tried to reason, placing his hand on her arm.

"It's between two families. One of them is mine." Beth placed her hands on her hips as she turned to her husband.

Jan and Rob both noticed the resemblance in her mother's behavior, and they looked at each other with raised brows.

"Beth, Jan and I will work something out. I didn't mean to upset you. Maybe we could take a day—"

"Damn right, you'll work something out. Otherwise, I'll do it for you." Beth dropped her hands to her sides. "Let's go back in the house, Kitten. It's colder out here than I thought." She glared at Rob as she put her arm around her daughter's shoulders and directed her steps into the house.

Charles took a few steps closer to Rob and mumbled. "Sometimes you just have to let them think they're in charge."

"I heard that, Charles."

"I wanted you to, dear."

Jan looked back to see Rob stare at his father-in-law, then watched her and her mother as they entered the house. He's probably thinking we're crazier than his family, she thought.

"Let me hang up your coat, Mom." Her mother

relinquished the jacket, but Jan sensed the tension she was feeling.

Beth walked into the great room and stood quietly in the center.

"It'll be okay, Mom. I'll figure out some way to get to Busha and Jaja's. You know me. When I want something, I do whatever I have to do to get it." Jan slightly laughed as she walked over to her mother. "Mom? Is everything okay?"

Beth's back was to her daughter. "Is that what you want? To go to your grandparents for Christmas?" She turned around to face her daughter. "Or, would you rather stay with Rob and his family?"

Jan couldn't believe what her mother was asking. She shook her head and held her mother's hands in hers. "Mom, I'll always want to go home to my grandparents' farm for Christmas," she said resolutely. "I didn't expect this to be an issue when I married. Is it like this for every newly married couple?" Jan dropped her mother's hands and turned to walk away, not wanting her to see the tears in her eyes. She waved her arms through the air as she spoke. "How is it that two people who love each other so much can still have so many differences about how to get along? Finances. Holidays. What's next?"

Beth sighed. "It's not always easy, and compromises do have to be made. I know it's not my place to interfere. But your grandparents' farm is where the Knowalski family celebrates Christmas. And you're a Knowalski, aren't you?"

"Yes. I am." Jan hugged her mom tight.

"What was that?"

The two women turned toward the front door when they heard a crash coming from the outside of the house.

"Let's grab our coats again,"

"Sounds like the guys are up to something," Beth said as she put her jacket on and followed her daughter outside.

They walked to the front of the house and looked up to the roof, two stories high.

"Rob, what are you doing? It's dark. How can you see anything?" Jan shouted to her husband.

"This is the best way to string Christmas lights, hon," Rob yelled back from the top of the ladder while looking over his shoulder and down toward Jan. He turned back to continue to focus on his work. "You can check your work while you're doing it."

"Rob, why don't you wait until tomorrow? It's supposed to be sunny and safe," Jan shouted up to him.

"Hey, there's our neighbor." Rob pointed down the sidewalk.

"I'm not falling for that, Rob." Jan folded her arms across her chest.

"Hi, Jan." Rich, who lived in the house kitty-corner behind theirs, held out a tray of mugs.

"Oh." Surprised, she abruptly turned and took a step backward. "Rich, hello. What happened to your hands?" They look swollen."

"These things." He held the tray higher and visually inspected the apparel. "I just forgot to take off my oven mitts. But I think I'm on to something. I can go from kitchen to outside in zero seconds. Well, as fast as I can walk outside anyway."

Rob came down off the ladder and gave his neighbor a curious look. "Forgot to take off your oven mitts again, huh." He picked up a mug, smelled the contents, and sighed. "That happens to a lot of guys. I've forgotten to take off my work gloves, golf gloves, and driving gloves. But not, uh," he squinted at Rich, "not my oven mitts." He took a drink. "Damn. This hot cocoa is good," he complimented.

"Nice decorations you got going up," Rich nodded. "Some of the neighbors were worried you wouldn't do anything decorative."

Jan and Rob exchanged knowing glances, thankful for her parents. Otherwise, that would have been the case.

Jan was the first to meet Rich while working in her

garden during the summer. Since then, he has occasionally stopped by to talk with the couple while working in the yard or taking a walk through the subdivision. Often bringing good advice as well as the neighborhood gossip, Jan and Rob enjoy their neighbor's scoop on the community.

"Every year, the Bonkowskis win the subdivision decorating contest. But you may give them a run for the money this time," Rich said. "Sometimes, weather permitting, we have an ice sculpture contest too. Watch your mailbox for the flyer."

"Oh hey, we can win that one," Rob gloated.

"Well, you have to do your own sculpture. Not bring one in like you did for the Fourth of July." Rich smirked and shook his head. "That contest is always won by the Bonkowski family too."

"Who are these people? We have to meet them," Jan said.

"You will. But not tonight. They're at the Detroit game. They're season ticket holders."

"Why?" Rob joked and looked at his wife.

"Rob, stop that," Jan interrupted the conversation. "Don't pay attention to him, Rich. He's a fair-weather fan." She turned to her husband with a righteous glare.

"He does have a good point, though," Rich replied.

The two men laughed heartily.

Jan felt small and turned from the waist to give Rich an icy stare.

"Oh, it just got a whole lot colder out here," Rob quipped.

"That's right." Jan pointed her glove-covered hand at her husband and then her neighbor.

"You should try oven mitts sometime, Jan. They're very warm," Rich teased.

"I'm not sure they would go with my wardrobe. But I'll keep that in mind." Jan slightly laughed at the notion.

"By the way, how's the Daniels Technology Center

coming along? The neighbors are talking it up quite a bit. You're kind of a celebrity here."

"Pretty good," Rob replied. "It's a big project, but so far, we're still on schedule."

"That's good. Detroit needs it. Have you seen the news lately? Whatever it is they're trying to expose is taking forever." Rich shook his head. "The city needs to improve, but it seems like something always interferes with the progress."

"I couldn't agree more." Rob threw back the last of his hot cocoa.

"Well, I'll take those mugs if you're done. Time to trade my oven mitts in for a good crochet hook and basket of yarn. Best hobby ever with the cold weather. Create and stay warm. I'm thinking about starting a blog," he joked.

Jan threw her drink back and signaled to her parents to hurry up. She gathered their mugs and set them on Rich's tray. "Thank you, neighbor. That was delicious "

Jan and Rob watched their neighbor continue on his way home.

"Who is that guy?" Rob said as he placed his arm around his wife.

"I'm not sure. Maybe a water boy for a sports team in a previous life. Because he always seems to show up at just the right time," Jan replied as she watched her husband climb up the ladder.

"Hi, sis," Brian said as he walked up the sidewalk toward them. He put one arm around Jan's shoulders and briefly hugged.

"Brian, I'm so glad you're here. We haven't seen you in a while." Jan flashed a scheming smile at him.

Walking up to where Rob was working on the roof, he shouted from the bottom of the ladder. "Hey, R-squared."

Brian was the youngest of the three brothers and had his oldest brother's good looks but with an easier-going demeanor. He was usually the one Rob called on when he needed backup to run the family business.

"Don't tell me," Rob said, giving his brother a sideways look from the ladder.

"What?" Brian looked surprised by Rob's reaction. "Oh. No. It's not . . . that." He looked around at Jan's parents and the neighbors. He flashed a smile at all of them. "I just thought I'd stop by for a brotherly visit." He shrugged and started to turn. "But if you're too busy for me, I'll leave."

"Hell no, you won't leave." Rob grinned. "I've got plenty of time for you. Now grab the other ladder in the garage and get your ass up here," he said as he waved him over.

"You called your brother-in-law? What about the other one?" Beth said quietly, standing beside her daughter and watching the men decorate the house.

"This one is Switzerland. The other one causes consternation."

Beth gave her daughter an understanding smile.

Rob walked back to the sidewalk and looked over the brightly decorated house. "Come on, everybody, take a look."

After admiring the Christmas display, Jan's parents said goodbye and left for home.

With a contented sigh, Jan entered her home with her husband and brother-in-law.

"Well, the house looks great. Thanks for helping with the Christmas decorating." Rob walked over to his brother and patted him on the back several times. "You'll be at work tomorrow?"

Brian grabbed his jacket and headed for the front door. "Of course. Why wouldn't I be at work tomorrow?" He looked curiously at his older brother.

"No reason. It just seems like you've been taking quite a bit of time off lately."

"Rob, I'm sure Brian has his own personal reasons for time off. So, thank you so much for making time to help us." Jan picked up the beer bottles and set them in the sink.

"Okay. I know. He's got a life. See you tomorrow." Rob patted his brother on the shoulder one last time, then walked into the great room.

Jan folded her hands to her brother-in-law and mouthed thank you. She grabbed her jacket in the mud room and walked with him to his car. "I'm so sorry to take you away from your friends on a Sunday evening. I know you have better things to do. But if it weren't for you, he'd still be out there on the roof."

"I know it. You know it. You have to make him think it was his idea," Brian said, getting into his truck.

Jan nodded and watched her brother-in-law drive away before going back inside the house.

"Well, for a day that started out quiet and alone, it sure turned out crazy," Jan said as she handed a beer to her husband. She sat beside him on the couch and turned to face him.

"Yeah, and it's late. Almost midnight." He took a swig of his beer. "Boy, your mom was acting a little crazy tonight. Right?"

"Are you kidding me? My mom?"

"Well, yeah. She never talked to me like that before, like a boss. It was scary."

"Rob, it's because it means a lot to her to be with Busha and Jaja for Christmas. They don't have that many years left with us. They're in their eighties. Mom is just concerned about carrying on a family tradition that's lasted generations." Jan slapped her hand to her thigh. "Rob, this a family legacy."

"Yes, but so is the Nichols family tradition."

Jan shifted in her seat and licked her lips. "Okay, it's important to my parents, or at least my mom anyway. She and her brothers and sisters are all very competitive, and it's always been that way for generations. You should hear some of the stories Busha's told over the years about how she and her siblings would get into it." Jan laughed a little at the memory.

"Maybe we take turns," Rob suggested. "This year, it's my family. And next year, it's with your family."

"I don't want to give up Christmas with my family every other year just because I'm married now."

"Well, I don't either. So now what?"

"All I can say is my mother will not agree to us taking turns. You saw her reaction tonight." She shook her head. "You're either brave or stupid."

4 THE F-WORD

Jan pulled open the restaurant door, and a blast of warm air greeted her as she stepped inside from the frigid November afternoon. She stamped her boots on the welcome mat, dislodging flecks of snow, the first of the season. Scanning the room, she spotted her friends sitting at a booth, chatting and laughing.

As she navigated through the maze of diners, Jan's mind was preoccupied with the upcoming holidays. She struggled to convince Rob to come with her to visit her family for Christmas instead of his family. His protest, claiming he needed to stay with his family and carry on the Nichols tradition. But Jan knew how much it meant to her and her parents to have the whole family together. Her mother, Beth, would be so disappointed if they didn't.

Maybe I should put my foot down, Jan thought, approaching her friends' table. Rob needs to realize that marriage means compromise. He can't avoid my family forever. We'll have Christmas morning with his side and then pack up and drive to my grandparents' farm.

Jan! There you are!" called out her friend Christie, sliding over into the booth to make room next to her. "We were starting to worry you got lost!"

Jan smiled as she sat down and picked up the menu. She pushed away her frustrations about Rob and focused on enjoying lunch with her girlfriends. The holidays are still a few weeks away, she told herself. I have plenty of time to figure out how to finally get my husband on board with my family for Christmas.

"Hi, Gina. How's the off-site conference going? I missed riding with you for lunch today," Jan said, sliding into the booth beside her. Viva Italiano's was the place where Jan and her three best friends met regularly for lunch.

Monica and Christie stopped flipping through their menus to smile at Jan.

Jan settled into her seat and shivered from the warmth of the nearby fireplace. Breathing in the delicious scent of garlic and seasonings, she waved to the others with a yellow note stuck on her finger.

The four women have been friends since childhood. They never kept secrets from one another, although talking about each other behind their backs wasn't unusual.

Monica Silverowski was a doctor of sports medicine. She used the "demands on doctors' time" as her excuse for—well, anytime she needed an excuse to get her out of a jam. Of the three women, it was Monica that Jan considered her best friend, like a sister. Monica and Rob's brother, Pete, started dating a few months earlier, which created an interesting dynamic in the Nichols family.

Gina Robbins worked as a financial analyst at a prestigious investment firm in the west tower of the Troy Professional Center. Since Jan's office was in the east tower, it was convenient for her and Jan to get together for quick coffee breaks or long coffee breaks, depending on their mood. Gina was an attractive woman who had feelings for her boss, Michael Goodson and had recently started dating him. Gina didn't care for it when Jan was moonlighting at the investment firm for a short stint because Michael gave her too much attention.

Christie Lopez was an attorney who worked in her family's law firm for two generations. She married her husband, Manny, who also worked at the family firm, in August, just two months after Jan and Rob's wedding. That left Gina wanting to get married and Monica running from it, or so she said.

"Well, I have so many things to talk about that I had to make a list," Jan said, plucking the note off her hand to read.

Christie grabbed her hand to focus on the note. "Six? You have six things you think you will share with us at our one-hour lunch today? I'll have to call my assistant to take the afternoon off."

Jan tilted her head and smirked at her friend's sarcasm.

"If we're taking the afternoon off, can we order drinks now?" Monica grinned.

"Not until I've finished discussing my list because I need your full attention."

The women turned to look at their waiter, Frank, as he walked up to their table. He had taken the women's food orders for several years and established a rapport with them. He immigrated from Italy five years ago to help his uncle run the four-star restaurant. He was twenty-nine years old then. Having learned the business well, his uncle would put him in charge and leave for weeks or months at a time.

Frank's head twisted to his left as he watched another waitress serving entrees at her table. The lack of attentiveness to Jan and her friends was uncharacteristic of him, and their expressions were a mix of confusion and annoyance.

"A new trainee, huh, Frank?" Gina asked. "And it's your responsibility to make sure she doesn't screw up?" Gina shook her head. "I hate that responsibility."

"No." Frank smiled as he continued to watch her. "No, she's not a trainee. She's just beautiful," he crooned.

The women looked at each other with hints of smiles

and quiet gasps.

"Are you two dating?" Jan timidly asked.

Frank sighed as he hung his head. "No." He turned his attention back to the table, took a deep breath, and smiled. "So, I assume it will be the usual for lunch today, ladies?"

The four women stared back at him.

"You're acting like nothing just happened, Frank," Monica said as she turned in her seat to face him, resting her elbow on the table. "You have to share some dish now."

"I will serve you any dish you want that's on the menu." He glared at her.

"Why don't you ask her out on a date?" Christie urged.

"So, what will it be today, ladies, the usual?" Frank gritted his teeth.

"Frank, we can help you. Tell us what's going on." Jan slapped her hand on the table.

"There is nothing going on," Frank said through his smile. "There never will be anything going on. Because I have nothing to offer this beautiful creature." His shoulders slumped, dropping his hands to his sides. "I'm just a lowly waiter. And, a woman like Rosie needs someone who has much money and can buy her pretty things."

"But you're a wonderful man," Gina said. "You're handsome and charming."

Frank looked sternly at her. "But no money. I've been saving to start my own restaurant," he whispered, "but it's taking forever."

"We can help you with the money if that's what's holding you back," Monica said, picking up her glass of water. "How much do you need? We'll figure out the loan terms with my accountant."

"Oh, about $500,000."

Monica choked and quickly set the glass down.

He stood up straight and smiled. "You could be my partner. Yes, you can be the money, and I'll be the brains.

What do you say, partner?"

"Uh, well, I was thinking more along the lines of twenty or thirty thousand. Are you sure you've been saving your money?" Monica gave him a distressed look.

Frank's smile dropped. "Oh, I see. It was just a . . . what do you call it, courtesy gesture. You weren't really going to invest in my restaurant," he scorned.

"No, no, that's not true," Monica leaned forward. "Frank, I want to help. But five hundred K is a lot of dough."

"I'll kick in some money," Gina said while looking at her phone. She paused to look at him. "I can probably get Michael to do the same."

Frank grinned. "Really?"

"I'll invest in your restaurant too," Christie offered. "Although not as much as Gina, but I want a piece of the action so I can have my own table. Jan, what about you?"

Frank and the other women turned their eyes to her.

Jan kept her head down, pretending to study the menu.

"Jan, you already know what you're going to order. Now answer the question," Gina demanded. "How much are you going to invest in Frank's restaurant?"

Jan looked up and gazed at the group with surprise and uncertainty. "Huh? Oh, well, I'll have to talk to Rob and—"

"Oh, brother," Monica blasted, slamming her hand on the table.

Christie and Gina moaned and rolled their eyes.

"What? You know Rob and I promised to talk to each other about money from now on and not keep secrets."

"Not keep secrets about your shared money," Gina sneered. "What about your fun fund?" She steadied her gaze. "Can't you spare a few thousand bucks from your fun fund?"

Jan cleared her throat. "Oh, that account. I almost forgot about it," she said through her teeth, giving Gina a nasty look.

Monica and Christie smirked, seemingly enjoying the challenging exchange between their friends.

Jan sighed as she looked up at him. "Frank, I'll look at my available funds this evening to see what I can do to help with investing in your company. I mean restaurant." She smiled and clasped her hands on the edge of the table.

"That's so nice of you, Jan." Frank glared. "Thank you for checking your available funds."

Jan shifted in her seat, feeling uncomfortable by his stare.

"I'll be back with your salads." Frank threw kisses to Monica, Gina, and Christie. "And, thank you, thank you, thank you so much for believing in me."

Jan's three friends turned to her with contempt.

She smiled in response, ignoring the underlying message they were trying to convey. Picking up her note, her eyes scanned the list for her first topic. "Oh," she said excitedly. "I've got some exciting news," she said as she referred to the yellow note in front of her. "My house is going to be—"

"Do you believe it's Thanksgiving already?" Gina shook her head while checking her phone's calendar. "Michael and I are going to his parents' house in Flushing. He wanted everything catered so his mother wouldn't have to work so hard. But she insisted on cooking for her children. She said it wouldn't be a family Thanksgiving if everything came in tin foil packages. What are all of you doing for the holiday?" There was a pause while she waited for someone to reply.

"My house—"

"Aww, that sounds sweet, Gina," Christie cut in after swallowing her drink.

Hey, I was talking first. Jan glared at her friends as she squirmed and grimaced, anxious for her chance to speak.

"We're going to Manny's Abuela's, but everyone is bringing something. It should be fun. I'm looking forward to—"

"My house is going to be in a magazine." Jan cut in, eager to share her news.

"Hey, I was talking," Christie admonished.

"An editor from Michigan Homes came over," Jan shrugged nonchalantly, "unannounced, and said people contacted them about my fabulous house, and they wanted to see it."

Christie picked up her phone and started scrolling through it.

"Sounds like a scam to me," Gina said as she wrinkled her nose.

"What do you know about this magazine? Did you call and ask to speak with the editor?" Monica chastised.

"It's not a scam," Jan said, looking down at her bread plate. She nervously ran her finger around the edge. "It's a real magazine."

"Is this the editor?" Christie pushed her phone into Jan's face.

"Oh, uh." She squinted, then opened her eyes wide and pushed Christie's hand away to a safe reading distance. "Uh, yes. Yes, that's her," Jan said as she continued to focus on the picture as the others watched. She shrugged. "She's changed her hair a little. But yeah, other than that," she pushed Christie's hand away to her side of the table, "that's the editor I met with. Maybe it's an earlier picture of her." Jan stared defiantly at the others.

Monica and Gina glared at Jan for several seconds without saying anything.

"Christie, you were saying?" Monica goaded.

Christie focused on her glass of water, huffed, crossed her arms, and sat back in her seat.

"Okay. Well then, Pete and I are going to Jan and Rob's place for Thanksgiving dinner."

"What? Why? Since when does Jan cook?" Christie laughed. "Oh, I get it. Jan is having Thanksgiving dinner," she said as she winked. "But Denise is going to do all the cooking and all the work? Isn't that right, Jan?"

"No, it's going to be a tailgate party," Monica interjected. "You know, to go with the football game."

Jan swiveled in her chair to face her friend. "A what?"

"A tailgate party. Come on. It'll be fun. Look, I'll even help you with the food."

"That completely changes everything I've planned though."

"It's Monday," Monica said, patting the back of Jan's hand. "You have two days before Thanksgiving to get things ready."

Gina and Christie started laughing.

Monica pointed her finger, giving them a warning look.

"Jan's father-in-law is going to expect a traditional dinner with homemade food," Gina commented. "How are you two going to pull that off."

"You better save yourself, Jan. Call Denise and tell her she can do Thanksgiving. Besides, it's so much work. Why would you want to do it anyway? Didn't you learn your lesson from the Fourth of July party?" Christie added.

"I need to do this," she said disheartened. "Because Rob is always imposing his family traditions on me. And, for once, I want it to be my family's tradition."

"Your family's tradition is to do a tailgate party?" Gina looked curiously at her.

"No." Jan's shoulders slumped. "But" she said, sitting upright, "I do like the idea of a tailgate theme for Thanksgiving. That could be our new family tradition."

"There you go. Now you're getting into the spirit." Monica beamed.

"It might create a problem though. When Rob and I were grocery shopping last Saturday, I tried to talk to him about what we'll do for Christmas since he gets Thanksgiving. But he insisted we're going to be with his family for that too." She sighed and scanned her friends' faces for their reaction, but they were looking at their phones or playing with their drinks. "Are you listening to me?"

Monica looked at her. "What are you thinking, that you're living in a fairytale and some prince charming is going to take care of your every whim?

Jan pressed her lips together and looked up. "Yeah, that's exactly what I was expecting. That's what I had all my life until I got married. Then, not so much. I know Rob's a great husband, but he can be, well, insensitive."

"Manny's not insensitive. He's perfect," Christie said.

"Oh yeah, right," Jan countered.

"Perfect, I'm sure," Gina added.

"Well, we're not arguing about whose family to spend Christmas day with because we're going to Mexico."

Jan gasped and then pursed her lips.

Monica slumped back in her seat.

Gina's jaw dropped, and she sat quietly.

"Jan, your parents spoiled you rotten," Christie accused. "You're just used to always getting what you want. And now that you have to grow up, you can't handle it, and you blame your husband."

Frank brought out a large tray and sat it on a stand. He set the first plate in front of Gina, then paused. "Is everything okay, ladies?" He paused for a response.

"Yes," Christie happily answered. "Everything is great, Frank. I won the conversation today." She clapped softly. "Hooray for me."

He continued to serve them their lunches. "I'll be back to check on you." He walked away, giving them a puzzled look and shaking his head.

Jan reviewed her list as the others started to eat. She crossed off three items. "Rob said the F-word," she blurted.

"Was it during sex? Because if it's during sex, it doesn't count." Gina teased.

"No." Jan deplored. "It was during a heated moment."

"Yeah. During sex." Monica shrugged. "So what?"

"No. Besides, that would be weird."

"Weird? Why?" Christie asked as she and Monica

scrunched their faces while picking at their salads with their forks.

"It would be weird because F is for family. It would be weird if Rob shouted 'family' during sex." Jan smirked. "I call it the F-word now because he made me mad by not wanting to spend any time with my family for Christmas. He won't even consider going to Busha and Jaja's for a couple of hours."

"Jan, I can help you with your divorce. Just say the word," Christie suggested.

"You're weird because the F-word doesn't mean family, and everyone knows it," Gina said. "Besides, if this is back to the grocery store discussion, then before we go down that rabbit hole again, I just have one question,"

"What's that?" Monica said, giving her full attention.

"Well, I've been thinking about how we're like sisters. Right? We're like family. But we won't be together for the holidays because we'll all be with our real families. So, what do you think about the four of us and our significant others getting together for dinner to celebrate Christmas? Just one night before Christmas?" She shrugged with a big smile. "Our pseudo-family."

"I like that idea. That would be fun," Monica replied.

"Me too," Jan said.

"That's a great idea. But when can we all meet?" Christie said with a puzzled look. She opened the calendar app on her phone and started scrolling.

Jan, Monica, and Gina did the same and mumbled comments as they came up short of a date.

"The only day I could meet with all of you is the Saturday before Christmas. What do you say?" Gina gave the others a hopeful smile.

"I can do that," Jan agreed. "I mean we. We can meet with our adopted family." She typed the entry into her phone.

"Pete and I will be there. Uh oh, where's there. Now we have to pick a meeting place."

"Here is good. We can get Frank to reserve a table for us," Christie suggested.

"Okay then, done. Here on Saturday, December twentieth, at eight o'clock." Gina placed her phone in her handbag.

"Well, I have to run," Monica said as she placed her receipt with cash next to her plate. She left a note on the back of the receipt for Frank to call her regarding taking the next steps toward his business.

"Wait," I'm not done yet," Jan pulled on her friend's arm, and she landed back in her seat.

"We told you there wasn't enough time," Christie said as she slid out of the booth following Gina.

"Happy Thanksgiving." They started walking away, then looked back at the table. "Jan, aren't you going back to work?"

"Um, well, my meetings were canceled for this afternoon, so I'm thinking about taking some time off to get ready for Thanksgiving. You go ahead." When they were out the door, she stood up to watch as the three women went to their cars and drove away. Sitting back down, she picked up her phone and opened the browser app. Michigan Homes, she entered and tapped on the website link. She studied the staff pictures for the magazine.

"If this is the editor, then who was at my house? Who is the woman I was talking to?" she mumbled as she looked at the editor's photo. She took a deep breath, sat back, and relaxed. It has to be that the magazine still needs to update its website, she pondered. She stared at the picture until she convinced herself that the editor she met with was new and the website needed updating.

Jan left the restaurant feeling overwhelmed with curiosity about the magazine editor. That, along with only two days left to prepare for hosting Thanksgiving dinner and her husband's stubbornness to compromise on Christmas. The issues all swirled in her head, and she knew she had to tackle one at a time to be successful with any of them. And hosting Thanksgiving had to be her first priority because she wouldn't let her husband say, "I told you so."

Only two o'clock in the afternoon, Jan thought as she walked into her kitchen carrying her portfolio, handbag, and the contents from the mailbox. I should get a lot of party preparations accomplished today. Then, with two days left to do the finishing touches, I'll be in good shape for Thanksgiving with the family.

She set the mail down on the island and went through it. "How sweet," she whispered. "Our first Christmas card as a married couple." She opened several more Christmas cards. "People are sending these things earlier and earlier. I better get going on ours."

Rob paused at the doorway and watched as Jan opened another envelope.

"Where were you? I thought you would be here getting things set up for Thursday's dinner," Jan said, surprised.

"There were a few issues to deal with. Finally, I left the foreman in charge. I felt like I should be here to help you. Especially since you'll help me with my company's bookkeeping."

"You mean work for you. Work for Nichols Construction Company, I mean."

"Uh-huh." He quickly walked over to where she was standing. "What are all those envelopes? Are those billing statements? Are you using credit cards again?" He picked up several and shuffled through them. "Merry Christmas?" He turned it over and over. "Who are all these cards from?" Rob asked as he picked one up and started reading.

"Most of them are aunts, uncles, and cousins from my Mom's side," Jan replied as she hung them on the decorative wrought iron wall hanger with other cards and pictures. She paused to look at her husband. She considered asking him about his family's Christmas card tradition but decided against it. He wasn't offering any information and what good would it do to dredge up tender memories.

"So, ready to tackle your party to-do list?" She wrapped her arms around his waist.

"Absolutely." He took a deep breath. "This party is going to be great," he said with a smirk.

"Yes, it is," she stammered. Something in his tone made Jan feel he still didn't support her idea. She tilted her head, disheartened with him. Dropping her arms, she stepped away and started fiddling with some decorations. She wished he would at least pretend to believe in her idea. She could use the extra confidence, especially since she wasn't really sure about it herself.

5 THE BET

Tuesday before Thanksgiving, and the work day went a lot longer than expected, Jan thought as she blew out a deep breath while walking into her house. Ten hours at Hedge, and now, if I'm lucky, I'll get an hour or two for myself— she stopped and stared at all the grocery bags still sitting unemptied on the kitchen counters. The contents still need to find their place in her home. Filled with party supplies and decorations, she took inventory with very little time left before Thanksgiving Day. Rob's words about leaving the parties to Denise continued to play in her mind over and over again. She continued to question, what was she thinking? She needed to leave the parties to Denise. She's good. No, she is excellent at them. And she has the time and loves to do them.

The door going into the garage closed with a thud, and Jan listened as her husband removed his boots. "Another tough day on the Daniels Technology Center project?" She called out to him.

"That and it doesn't help with the traffic on I-75," he shouted back from the powder room as he washed his face and hands.

Jan walked in, picked up a fresh towel, and handed it to

Rob.

"Thanks. Is there anything for dinner?"

"Soup and sandwiches. I stopped at the Gourmet Market since there's no time to cook."

Rob narrowed his eyes and opened his mouth while pointing a finger in the air.

"It's just soup and sandwiches," she rebuked before he could say anything. "Were you able to get the bales of straw for decorations from the farmer's market?"

"Uh-huh. And I have to say, they smell rather good. Very earthy."

"Darn."

"Darn?" Rob gave his wife a curious stare.

"I was talking with Busha on the phone today, and she said they have some bales we could have. We could have enjoyed a nice road trip to go see them and pick up the straw."

"Not between now and Thanksgiving." Rob held up his palms in a helpless gesture. "There's no time."

"We could take tomorrow off?"

"Not last minute." He shook his head. "I didn't leave any instructions for the supervisor. Besides, I thought you said you have a new client coming in?"

"Darn."

"Darn? Again?" He gave her an annoyed look.

"Yeah. It would have been nice to visit with Busha and Jaja before we see them on Christmas day," she said, testing the waters.

"Don't start that again. Not now. We need to stay focused on getting through this holiday before we start arguing about the next one."

Jan clenched her jaw. It's not over yet, she thought as she scooped the soup into two bowls. She placed the soup dish on a plate and propped half a sandwich on each side of the bowls. Taking the plates to the island, she slid her arm across the granite, pushing the bags and party items aside to make way for their food.

"Do we need these?"

Jan smiled at her husband. "Yes, thank you for the spoon. If construction hadn't worked out, you could have gone into the food service business."

"Looks like there's a lot we need to do before Thursday," Rob said as he looked at all the bags. "Maybe we could ask Denise—"

"No."

"Just saying. You could be in charge."

"You know that won't happen," Jan said as she tilted her head and frowned. "It's just that I see how much you love and enjoy Denise's cooking and parties. And I want to do that for you too."

"Honey, you do other things for me that Denise could never do," Rob looked over at her, grinning.

"We'll be okay. Look at what a great success the Fourth of July party was," Jan said as she grabbed Rob's hand and gave it a gentle squeeze.

Rob nodded and drew his spoon through his soup. "But Denise was—"

"I've got a plan."

"Does it include calling Denise?"

Jan smirked. She would have loved to do that, but she had already made her stand. So, no turning back for her now. She went to the counter by the sink, withdrew a notepad from the drawer, and returned to her seat. "See," she said, pushing the paper next to her husband's plate.

He studied it, shrugged, and looked at Jan. "Okay, let's give it a try. You're really organized."

Jan smiled as she moved the pad over so they could both look at it. "So, I was reading in one of the magazines that Denise gave me about turning Thanksgiving Dinner into a tailgating party. That way, you also include all the family members watching the football game. So, what do you think?"

"I think my dad would drop dead if he didn't have his traditional dinner with all the fixings." He set his spoon down. Picking up the bowl, he put it to his mouth and leaned his head back, drinking the last of the broth.

"But this is the year to try it because Denise isn't in charge, and you can blame it all on me." She smiled.

"You say that now, but when Ed blows his stack, then you'll be all upset and offended."

"No, I won't. I promise." She bit her bottom lip and turned to him with a pleading look. "Can we please just try it? Just this one year? Please? If you get Christmas, can't I have my way for any of the holidays?"

He shook his head and moved away from the island. "Fine. But remember, this is all on you." He paused and smiled at her, putting on his jacket. "So, you concede. I get Christmas. No more discussion?"

"No, of course not. I was just using that to get my own way." She grinned and picked up her empty dishes, carrying them to the sink.

The tone of a text message that just arrived came from Rob's jacket pocket. He withdrew it, studied it momentarily, and turned away.

Jan was puzzled as to why he didn't say what it was about. "Everything okay?"

"Yeah. Everything's fine," he forcefully shoved his phone back into his pocket and headed toward the garage door. "I'm going outside to set the bales, pumpkins, and those weird-looking things you bought around the front of the house," Rob said as he carried his dishes to the sink.

"They're gourds."

He paused and looked at her strangely.

"The weird-looking things. They're called gourds," she enlightened. "Anyway, I'll come outside and check on you in a little bit."

After fussing with some fall decorations, Jan stepped off the three-foot ladder beside the fireplace. She walked to the other side of the room and studied the arrangements on the mantle.

"Not bad, not bad at all," she said, looking at her

watch, then returned to make some adjustments. "It's nine-thirty, and with only one more day before Thanksgiving, I'm finally decorating." She moved the pine cones further apart and turned the vase of pheasant feathers and branches of Fall leaves to expose the best side. Interior decorators have all the fun, she thought as she turned to walk back for a second look.

She caught a glimpse of the straw bale through the side light window of the front door. "Oh no. That's too close to the house," she mumbled as she grabbed a jacket out of the closet.

Going out the front door to take a look from the street, she paused when she heard voices. Slowly, she strolled down to the sidewalk and was surprised to see Marissa talking to Rob. For never wanting to meet her, he sure was having a heated conversation with her now.

Jan's mind was filled with suspicious curiosity as she walked faster down the sidewalk to the driveway.

Rob stopped pointing his finger at the other woman and slacked off when he saw Jan.

Marissa startled and turned around. She saw Jan standing there, watching them.

"Honey, Marissa's here to do . . . something." He shrugged. "Whatever plans you two made. But I told her this was a bad time. Right? Honey?" He shook his head and mouthed "no" as he pointed at Marissa while her head was turned.

Jan stopped walking and stared at her husband, deepening her brows.

Marissa turned back to look at him.

Rob quickly looked away, moved his hand to the back of his head, and shifted his weight to the other foot.

"This is a bad time, Marissa," Jan said as she walked up the driveway. "We're preparing for Thanksgiving with our families." She squinted at her. "Besides, I thought we switched our meeting to next week?"

"Oh, you're right," Marissa said as she lightly touched

her temple and shook her head. She started down the driveway. "I misplaced my schedule and thought it was today." She laughed lightly.

"Uh huh." Jan stared at her with arms crossed. "I was looking at the Michigan Homes Magazine website today. The picture of the editor was someone else."

Marissa leaned backward. "Oh, yes. She moved on, and they haven't updated the website yet."

Jan relaxed her arms and put her hands in her pockets. "That's what I thought. That's what I told my friends. When will it get updated?"

"I'll get on them about it first thing tomorrow. I'm glad you brought that to my attention. Well, I'll be on my way," she said as she walked to her car. She pulled up to the end of the driveway and rolled down the window. "See you next week," she said, waving, then drove away.

"Well, that was weird, huh?" Rob said as he dreadfully watched his wife walking toward him.

Jan gave him a suspicious look, then proceeded to review the arrangements around the garage doors. "Yes, that was weird," she said as she looked over the nicely displayed bales, cornstalks, pumpkins, and gourds. "This really looks great, but can we move it closer to the edge of the grass, away from the house? It'll be more visible from the street view then." She stopped examining the props, turned her eyes off the objects, and stared at Rob.

He let out a deep sigh and laughed slightly. "You bet, honey. Anything you want," he said gleefully, sliding the bales across the lawn.

Jan tucked her chin and looked at him with amazement. "Anything I want? Where's this coming from?" She laughed. "Who are you, and what did you do with my husband?"

Rob smiled back at her while pointing at the straw. "How's this?"

"Not bad. I like it," she said, nodding. "You know, if it's anything I want, then my friends all have plans for the

Christmas holidays," Jan said as she picked up a gourd and nervously rubbed the rough texture on the palm of her hand. "So. . ."

With a sigh, Rob dropped the last bale and stood up straight, turning to look at Jan. "Tell you what, you keep telling me not to be a fair-weather fan for Detroit. So then, let's make a bet on the Thanksgiving Day game. That is if you're so confident in your team."

Jan looked down when she realized that her preachiness about supporting our teams was coming back to bite her. She pressed her lips and contemplated the outcome. "Well, okay, but—"

"I pick Tennessee."

"Wait. You can't do that." She huffed. Still holding the gourd, she placed the back of her hands on her hips. "We were supposed to talk—"

"Too late." Rob grinned. "Your team wins, we go to your grandparents for Christmas. My team wins, and we go to my parents' cottage."

"But—"

"It's a bet." Rob turned away to put the finishing touches on the outside decorations. "You may be onto something with this fair-weather fan stuff."

"Fine," Jan's icy tone seemed to amuse her husband. "If you're done out here, then let's go inside and finish up."

"Anything you want, honey." He chuckled as he followed her into the house.

"So, what do you think of the mantle?" Jan asked as she touched her warm hands to her still cold, rosy cheeks.

"I like it. It has kind of a classic cabin appeal." Rob nodded. "Nice work."

"With everything we accomplished today, we can take tomorrow off. From party preparations, that is," Jan said as she cozied up to her husband.

The front doorbell rang, and they stopped to look at each other with annoyed expressions.

"If that's her again, I'll just—"

"I'll take care of it," Rob said as he took off to the door. He threw it open. "Look here, Mari—"

Monica and Pete smiled back at him, then looked at each other before helping themselves inside the house.

"Why are you two here? It's after ten o'clock." Rob wailed.

"Because your house is nicer than my condo," Monica declared.

"And cleaner," Pete added. "The place looks great. We may never leave."

Pete was the middle child of Rob's family and had to work at getting his fair share of attention, unlike his older and younger brothers. As a result, his antics took a toll on his reputation for being responsible. He was handsome like his brothers, but unlike Rob and Brian, he was a little thicker through the middle. Time and time again, he proved himself to be an equal partner in the family business. But his older brother didn't see it that way.

Rob rolled his eyes and released a deep breath as he followed them into the great room.

"What's this?" Monica slapped a rolled-up, soggy paper into Jan's chest.

"Where did you find it? That's our newspaper. I was looking all over for it this morning." Jan walked with them to the kitchen, holding it with the tips of her fingers.

"Why don't you read the paper online like everybody else? More importantly, is drinking on the job allowed at Nichols Construction Company?" Monica stared into the refrigerator and moved some things around.

"What do you mean? We're not on the job right now," Rob gave them a curious look.

"I like a real newspaper because it's structured," Jan interjected. "You can't go off following the advertisements targeted specifically for you while reading an important article," Jan said as she laid out the damp paper on the counter. "I know this because we covered it at a conference last year. The retailers want you to read everything online to lure you into buying their products." She nodded her head once, closing the subject.

"Technically, we are on the job," Pete said, grabbing four beers from the refrigerator. "And it depends," he said, looking at Monica. "Right now, it's allowed." He turned his attention to Rob. "We have a problem with the State's Department of Environmental Quality. They tested the ground on the project site for Daniels Technology Center."

"Well, why the hell didn't you call me?" Rob demanded.

"Check your phone." Pete took a drink of his beer.

"Oh." Rob scratched his head while staring at his phone.

"You need to take this seriously," Pete warned.

"I'll take you seriously when you put in the same number of hours that I do."

Pete pointed his finger at his older brother. "Not this again."

"How extensive is it? The entire site or sections?" Jan asked, looking at Rob and then Pete.

"Might as well consider the entire site contaminated according to them," Pete replied, throwing his hand in the air.

"Is this a big problem for Nichols Construction Company?" Jan asked, leaning a hip against the counter.

"This is new territory for us." Rob sighed and looked at Pete, hands hanging from his index fingers stuck in his jeans pockets.

"You've been doing commercial construction for this long and never encountered anything like this before?" Jan gaped.

"A few small issues or two, but nothing of this magnitude." Rob leaned forward onto his elbows resting on the island. "We should probably be proactive about this. If not, it'll look like we're trying to hide something."

"I agree," Pete concurred. "We don't want the DEQ to be suspicious of us, or they could hold this project up for years."

"L & L Construction had a similar issue, and it nearly killed them," Rob added. "It wasn't their fault, though, or the DEQs. Their customer wasn't being completely forthright about the property. They knew it had issues, but didn't want to pay for the cleanup. They thought they could build a large condo complex, close the corporation, and move on."

"What would happen to the condo owners when they discovered the toxic issues?" Monica gasped.

"It would be their problem, and they would have to pay for it."

"Wow," Jan said, shaking her head along with the others. "Even after a corporation closes, there should be a law that they have to keep a reserve account for issues that arise after the fact. Too many corporations are closing and getting away scot-free while consumers are victims."

"Sounds criminal to me," Monica said as she held up her beer.

"Well, that's not going to happen with Mr. Daniels. He cares about the city, and he's not looking to get rich and get out." Rob said, glancing at the others. "I'll talk with Mr. Daniels tomorrow and see how he wants to handle this."

"No," Pete stated firmly. "You need to tell him what he should do tonight. If you leave it up to him, he could try and do the same thing as what happened to L & L."

"I just told you. He's not like that. He wouldn't avoid a problem by passing it on to somebody else. Besides, he'll remain the owner of the complex when it's finished."

"That's what he's telling you now," Pete warned.

"Still, Rob," Jan interjected, "it wouldn't hurt for you to guide him in his decisions. He probably hasn't experienced anything like this before either."

Everyone was quiet, momentarily contemplating the

issue at hand.

Jan thoughtfully nodded, then took a deep breath. "Pete, do you have the DEQ's contact information? If you give it to Rob, he can share it with Mr. Daniels." She turned her attention to her husband. "Rob, the two of you can call from your truck and get all the information you can. You'll be right there to instruct Mr. Daniels. In the meantime, Pete can hire a private company to do our own testing. We would want to do that anyway to make sure whatever the DEQ comes back with is legit. Right?" She looked around at them.

The others gaped at her by the time she finished her brainstorming session.

"You're not such a dumb blond after all," "Monica acknowledged.

"Did I say something wrong?" Jan asked with a puzzled look on her face.

6 MONICA'S LIST

"What?" Jan walked faster trying to keep up with Monica. "What? Wait up," she shouted. She knew something was bothering her friend. Her gruff behavior was a dead giveaway. The problem is what would she have to deal with now. She followed Monica to a table at the Troy Mall food court. She placed her tray of spinach lasagna down on the melanite table, removed her crossover purse, and placed it on the back knob of the chair before seating herself. "You have to talk loud. I can't hear you with all these kids screaming and yelling," Jan shouted as she leaned toward Monica pointing to her ears. "This is probably the worst place to be the night before Thanksgiving."

"What the hell kind of parents are stupid enough to take their kids to the mall a month before Christmas?" Monica shouted as she looked around the dining area with disdain.

Parents nearby turned a dirty look her way and covered their children's ears.

"Maybe they're getting their picture taken with Santa." Jan gave a gloating smile at her friend.

"Huh, well maybe," Monica huffed. "Well, when I

have—" she swallowed hard. "If," she said shaking her finger at Jan, "if I ever have kids, I'll take them to a studio. Why fight these crowds." She sneered, then quickly she took a big bite of her fettuccini alfredo. "But I'll never have kids," she muffled with a mouthful of food.

"What did you just say?" Jan gulped her bite of pasta. "You want kids?"

Monica rolled her eyes. "I said I need your help and guidance dealing with the Nichol's Family."

"Me?" Jan leaned back. "How am I supposed to help?" She looked curiously at her friend.

"I've got a list. And, I want you to know that I am quite impressed with how you're dealing with the DEQ issue to help their company. You're pretty smart."

Jan stopped chewing her mouthful of food as she stared across the table. Quickly, she finished chewing and swallowed hard. "Thank you?"

"*Tsk!* I didn't mean it like that. I always knew you were smart." She threw her hand in the air. She set her fork down and clasped her hands giving Jan her full attention. "It's just that you're doing this on top of everything else you do. You're taking on your step-mother-in-law. It's the holidays and you're contesting your husband's plans for Christmas. And, you're working more than full time at your career." She sat back. "Why do you do this? Where is all this energy coming from?"

Jan chewed and rolled her eyes upward. "Well, when I want something, I go for it. Those are all the things that I want to be successful at for the moment. DEQ because I don't want my husband's company harmed. His success is my success. Besides what would Rob do if he didn't have his construction company?"

"His company?" Monica placed her hand on the edge of the table and made a slight tilt of her head. "Don't you mean the family's company?"

"Yes. Yes, I do." She widened her eyes and patted her fingers on the table. Seeing that her friend wasn't impressed with her answer, Jan opened her hands with a pleading look on her face. "Thank you for correcting me. I didn't mean his alone."

Monica sat back looking suspiciously at Jan. "What about Denise? It seems like you got to know her quite well since marrying into the family. Do you like her? Are you two close?"

"Wow, where is this coming from?" Jan opened her eyes wide in astonishment.

Monica held her poker face and waited for her friend to answer.

"Well, I wouldn't say we're close. I do like and admire Denise. She has many endearing qualities. But her ideas and mine about how to run a household differ dramatically," Jan said with closed eyes and a slight head toss.

"It seems like she really cares for you. I was hoping you could help me have a better relationship with her. I don't think she cares for me so much."

"Oh, I'm sure she likes you." Jan thought back to some of Denise's stinging comments about Monica and cringed momentarily. "But I'm not so sure how much she thinks of me. I feel like she considers me to be a spoiled brat."

"Well, you are."

"You say that like it's bad thing."

The two women laughed, relaxing back on their chairs.

"I'm sorry did you say something?" Jan leaned forward again. "It's like a zoo here tonight."

Monica shook her head. "Maybe we should go somewhere else. We really need to have this conversation."

"But where? We need to get out shopping done too."

"Jan? Is that you?" Marissa leaned over and attempted a friendly hug.

"Marissa? What are you doing here?" Jan stood up and received the gesture. "I'll introduce you to my best friend, Monica." She held her hand palm up and directed the attention across the table.

"Nice to meet you." Marissa smiled at Monica. "Any friend of Jan's is a friend of mine."

"Hi." Monica turned to look in the other direction. "Don't count on it," she mumbled.

"Monica, this is Marissa," Jan said. "We met last Saturday at the . . ."

The two women looked at each other with amusement.

"Well, kind of the grocery store?" Jan gave Marissa a puzzled look.

"Yes, I would definitely say the grocery store." Marissa firmly nodded once. "Well, I saw you here so I thought I'd stop by and let you know that things are progressing for your interview with *Michigan Homes*."

"That's fabulous. I was thinking of having an interior decorator come in to give me some ideas for a few improvements."

"You know Rob's not going to allow that," Monica interjected.

"That's not a bad idea," Marissa said leaning forward and nodding.

Monica's lips vibrated when she puffed a breath of air. Cupping her chin on her hand, she turned away to watch the people at the table next to theirs.

"Do you have any suggestions for companies? I could ask my Mom, but our taste differ."

"Of course. I'll email a few names to you and you can check them out. Pick the one that most closely represents your style." Marissa clasped her hands. "Speaking of Rob, what is he doing while you're here with your friend?"

"He's probably still at work." Jan looked down at her chair and fidgeted with the back spoke.

"Well, I better get going before I'm missed. Have a good night, ladies," Marissa said as she turned around and walked away.

"Missed by who, your parole officer?" Monica mumbled.

"Why are you so miffed?" Jan questioned her friend.

"I would be careful if I was you," Monica said in a stern voice. "From what you've told me she sounds like a stalker." She held her hands open in the air. "I mean, think about it. She shows up at your door and pushes her way in. She shows up wherever you are."

"Yeah," Jan said amused. "She's kind of my Mr. Daniels."

Monica glared at her.

"You know. Rob's Mr. Daniels. Remember, when he would track Rob down wherever he went and . . ."

Monica tilted her head and held her stare. "Besides, why does she care what Rob is doing tonight? She's always asking about Rob. You remember him, right? The guy that you married. Why should she care what he's doing?"

Jan huffed and fell back into her chair.

"All I'm saying is you don't know a thing about this woman, but she knows an awful lot about you." Monica picked up her soft drink and plucked off the napkin that stuck to the bottom. Despite the loud, blaring noise throughout the food court, the awkward silence hung in the air between the two of them.

Jan leaned forward placing her hands on the table. "I know you don't like her and you're not the only one. And, I'm a little suspicious too, but I really want my house in the magazine. It just seems like every time I talk about this woman people are warning me. Like the way Rob and Denise act when I mention the name 'Marissa.'"

"Denise? There's more?" Monica's eyes widened and she jumped forward to the edge of her seat.

"When Rob first met her, he looked like he saw a ghost." Jan sat back relieved to share the information. "Then every time they've encountered each other, to me it looks like they're having a heated conversation, like some kind of serious argument."

"Hmmm, interesting." Monica moved in closer.

"Well," Jan covered her mouth with her finger, "that was the interesting thing until the other day. When I told

Denise about Marissa, she acted the same way."

Jan started to eat her food again, cutting it into small bites. "Oooh, this stuff is cold." She spit the food into a napkin, crumpled it into her hand, and set it on the plate. She turned her attention back to her friend. "Do you think there could be some connection between her and the Nichols family?" Jan's eyes opened wide and she covered her mouth as she took a deep breath. "Do you think maybe Ed had an affair with her and now the whole family is ashamed?"

Monica busted out laughing and swiveled to the side of her chair. "Are you kidding? Ed? An affair?" She wiped the tears from the corners of her eyes. "I love Ed, but he's too fat and lazy to have an affair. Affairs are too much work." Monica flashed a grin. "I know."

"Well, I'm still excited about being interviewed by *Michigan Homes*."

"Oh, you are so clueless." Monica shook her head.

"Who are you shopping for tonight, yourself or others?" Jan placed her last napkin over the plate.

"Both. I need to get some heels to go with that new black dress I bought at that boutique when we were in Traverse City for the medical convention. Remember? Open back, halter top, mid-thigh."

"Yeah, yeah, yeah, I remember." Jan gave her a curious look. "But I thought you bought shoes to go with the dress when you were there?"

"I did. But you can never have too many. Monica shrugged. "Besides, no matter how big my ass gets, the purse and shoes always fit." She grinned.

Jan laughed heartily, amused by her friend's insight. "Okay. So, anyone else that you're shopping for tonight?"

"If you find something you like, let me know. I'll buy it, wrap it up, and give it to you for Christmas."

"Oh, come on." Jan moaned. "But it won't be a surprise then."

"Aren't you a little too old for that by now?"

Laughing, the two women picked up their trays and using what napkins were leftover, wiped off the table. Walking away from the court, they headed toward their favorite department store.

"So, who are you shopping for tonight?" Monica looked over at her friend as they walked through the crowded aisles.

"As many as I can get done and get—"

"Wait." Monica put her hand on Jan's arm to stop their pace.

Staggered by the abrupt halt, Jan stumbled a couple of steps.

Monica looked her in the eye. "Did Rob give you your allowance?" Quickly, she turned away as she laughed at the notion.

"Yeees." Jan sneered through her teeth and her shoulders slumped. "Yes, he gave me my allowance," Jan said enunciating every word. "But it doesn't matter." She shook her head. "Because, with my residuals from Michael's company I figured out a way to funnel some cash into my own fun fund." Jan pointed her finger at her friend, winked, and clicked her tongue.

"Okay, first, don't ever do that again."

Jan smirked and shrugged.

"Second, why would you use your cash fun fund for gifts for your family and friends? Why?" Monica threw her hands up and slapped her sides. "Have I taught you nothing? Why not go for a business trip, a.k.a., spa-get-away?"

Mall patrons walked by, brushing and bumping them as they stood in the middle of the aisle.

Jan took a deep breath. "Hmmm, I didn't think of that." She tapped her index finger on her cheek. "Well, it's not like I'm going to use all my cash. Just combine a little with my," Jan cleared her throat, "my allowance to give gifts that meet my standards and not Rob's."

"I'm ashamed of you," Monica said as she turned away

and started walking through the crowds.

Jan smiled as she walked alongside her friend, feeling proud of herself for standing her ground.

Monica stopped abruptly and pointed down the concourse. "Is that who I think it is?"

7 DOPPELGANGER

"Again? I said, yes. I have my allowance." Jan stopped and stared ahead. "Oh my gosh, it's Harold." She put her hands on her chest. "The last time we met was here in the food court. He was heartbroken when he found out I was married." Jan sighed.

People brushed by Jan and Monica as they stood quietly, watching Harold from the middle of the aisle.

"He doesn't look heartbroken now," Monica chuckled.

"What do you mean?" Jan's arms dropped to her sides. "He looks miserable."

"It looks to me like he's pretty happy. He's got a silly grin on his face and he's sending thumbs up to somebody in the lingerie store."

"Probably his niece," Jan said warmly, recalling their encounter and tender embrace. "He was here for her birthday party last summer at some kid's build something store and that's when we ran into each other."

"His niece? Kid's party? Now they're at a lingerie store?" Monica laughed. "Unless he's a dirty uncle, I don't think that's his niece."

Jan gave her friend a disgusted look as they proceeded to walk toward him.

"Harold? Is that you?" Jan reached out and gently touched his arm.

"Jan," he said as he turned a surprised look her way. He held out his hand to shake, but Jan came in for a warm, embracing hug.

Harold awkwardly put his arms around her and patted her on the shoulder several times. He took a quick step back. "I'm so glad you're here. There's someone I want you to meet."

Jan's sympathetic smile for her ex-beau turned to concern.

Harold turned his attention to Monica. "It's been awhile. Good to see you again, Monica."

"Harold, it's good to see you again too." She happily watched, entertained with the awkward interaction between the two of them.

"Stick around," he said, "I'd love for you both to meet her." He smiled at them, then clumsily looked back at the store. He took a few cautious steps toward the entrance and peered in, then sprang forward.

Harold waved to someone in the store. "Here she comes," he said to Jan and Monica as he raced back to them.

The woman walking out of the store took long, smooth strides in her three-inch heels. Her hair gently flowing from the slight breeze created from her pace. She was carrying a half dozen pink shopping bags with pink ribbon handles straddled across her arms and a couple in her hands.

Jan's jaw dropped as the corners of Monica's mouth turned up.

Harold held out his arm to her and pulled the woman close, giving her a squeeze around her waist. He took the many bags from her and handed them to his driver who was standing about twenty feet away.

Jan recognized the gentleman from her days of dating Harold. He always dressed in a suit and knew his cue from his many years of experience working for Harold.

Jan and Monica hadn't noticed him standing off to the side until then. They watched in awe as the man gathered the many shopping bags adding them to the dozen or so he already had from other stores.

"Thank you, Fred," she said politely.

"You're welcome, miss Carrie."

"Carrie, this is Jan. My friend I was telling you about and she handles my marketing account at Hedge," Harold said then turned to Jan. "Jan, this is Carrie Edgeworth. We've been seeing each other for about . . ."

"I think about three months now," Carrie said.

"Ha, ha," Jan lightly laughed trying not to sound jealous. "How nice for the both of you."

Harold looked down and sighed. "After we saw each other last summer and you were married, I realized I needed to move on."

Jan's heart sank when she realized she'd been replaced. She stood face to face with a woman who could have been her twin. Jan thoughts raced. *No, no you don't need to move on, Harold. I can always be your one true love, can't I?*

Both women continued to smile at each other. Their eyes inconspicuously checking out the other.

Harold cleared his throat to end the awkward silence. "Well perhaps we should get going, Carrie. We don't want to be late for our dinner reservations."

After a deep breath, Carrie broke the stare down and turned to him. "You're right, Harold. Nice meeting you, Jan."

Harold patted Jan on the back. He turned away and slipped his arm around Carrie's waist guiding her through the crowd.

Jan stood there with her mouth open, feeling disbelief at the cold gesture instead of the warm embrace he used to give her. She watched until they disappeared among the shoppers. "I don't believe it. I've been replaced by another woman. Who looks exactly like me."

Jan broke out of her trance and turned to Monica. "What are you grinning at?" She snarled.

"Maybe you have a twin you never knew about? Or, someone stole your DNA and cloned you." Monica was laughing harder. "Oh, oh, wait, I got it. Harold stole your DNA and he paid somebody to clone you." Monica walked away as she shook from her amusement. Holding her side, she leaned back against a store wall, laughing so hard that tears were streaming down her cheeks.

A stranger walked up to Jan. "Is your friend okay? It looks like she's going to be sick," he said with concern.

"She's more than fine." Jan huffed. "But just in case I'll be sure to take good care of her when we get back to my place," she replied dryly.

Jan looked at her phone then walked over to where Monica was outside the lingerie store. "If you're done having laughs at my expense, then we should go. Rob sent me a text saying he and Pete just got home."

Monica wiped the tears from her eyes as her laughter slowly came to a stop. "But we didn't get to do any shopping yet. I need shoes," she said still chuckling.

Jan walked away from her friend leaving her to catch up.

"Hey, what's the matter with you? I just found it funny that Harold found someone who looks exactly like you. And, he was so excited about introducing you to her. Don't you think that's strange?" Monica lowered her voice. *"Jan, I want to introduce you to yourself. Yourself, this is you."*

"I guess. Kind of." Jan moped. "Her name sounds familiar. Edgeworth. I know that name from somewhere."

Monica gave her a strange look, then shook her head.

Jan walked to their exit not saying anything. Mostly, I can't believe how deeply it hurts me that he found someone else, Jan pondered. *But I wasn't in love with him. Why do I even care?*

"Those guys are going at it again," Jan said exasperated. She closed her car door and maneuvered herself between the roadster and Rob's truck toward the entrance that leads into the house.

"They're guys. That's what they do." Monica followed her. "You're just not used to it because you didn't have any brothers."

"But it's like they're always fighting with each other."

"Guys are very competitive. Can you imagine if they acted like us?" Monica switched up the tone of her voice. "Oh, Rob, I love your flannel shirt. Where did you get it? I bought it at big-and-strapping. I'll give you my friends and family discount."

Jan cringed at the thought. "I'm just saying, wouldn't it be better if they cooperated. At least be allowed to finish their sentences?"

"You were supposed to talk with Mr. Daniels today. The DEQ issue isn't going away on its own," Pete said waving his hand in the air before taking a swig of beer.

"I know that, but we need to—"

"We need to get Daniels to do his part and—"

"That's what I'm trying to say. So, you and the—"

"But you need to make it happen now so that—"

"See what I mean," Jan said as she turned to Monica.

"Now I won't be able to not notice it. Thanks a lot."

"Notice what? What do you mean?" Rob quizzed them as they entered the kitchen.

"They noticed that you're not taking me seriously," Pete said as he walked over to Monica for a kiss. "I did my part today. I've got the name of a company to do our own soil testing."

"Why didn't we realize this sooner?" Rob lamented. "We should have done soil tests ourselves before we even broke ground."

"Listen, I'm sorry, but this isn't my fault." Pete turned and walked back to the counter where he was standing. His hands in his pockets. He took a deep breath and glanced at Rob making brief eye contact.

"Damn it, Pete. I count on you and you let me down again."

"I let you down?" He walked quickly toward his brother. "I let you down? You're letting me down and this company." Pete looked down at the floor as he shook his head. "Listen, I told you." Pete stopped talking and looked Rob square in the eye when he heard his words. "I told you it's not going away. So, deal with it."

Rob huffed and took a drink from his long neck. "Yeah, Mr. Daniels is supposed to be at the site tomorrow. I'll talk to him then."

"Is some of that beer for us?" Monica asked walking over to the refrigerator. She removed two bottles and handed one to Jan.

Jan sat the beer down on the island before seating herself. Struggling, she gripped and twisted at the bottle cap. "Can I have an opener?"

Her husband came over and easily twisted off the cap.

"That's why I married you," she said trying to lighten the mood but no one acknowledged her humor. "Okay, first, let's stop bickering amongst ourselves. It's not helping. Second, how serious is this? Like shutting down the project serious or shutting down Nichols Construction Company serious?"

"They won't shut us down, but they can shut down the project. And, that's our meal ticket for a couple of years. Not to mention the opportunities for other projects of this magnitude that will come our way. But if we can't succeed, then none of it will matter," Rob lamented.

"Okay, so the facts are that the DEQ is taking soil samples and testing them. Are they going to share the results with us?" Jan turned a inquisitive expression to each of them.

"They said they would. But it'll probably take a couple of weeks before we get them," Rob said nodding his head.

"We've got cameras on the site so we can see what

areas the DEQ is taking their samples from and do the same ones. I'll get with the testers first thing in the morning to start work," Pete said looking at Rob.

"Do we need to call Christie and Manny?" Jan asked.

"Nah, it's too late for more company tonight," Rob said as he yawned.

"I meant for their legal advice dealing with the DEQ," Jan said.

"Oh yeah, I knew that." Rob nodded. "I was just messing with you." He looked at Pete. "What do you think?"

"I agree with Rob. It's almost midnight. Too late for more company tonight."

Jan rolled her eyes and smirked at Monica. "Okay then, what about dinner tomorrow? Are you ready for a tailgate party?"

Monica snickered and put her head on the crook of her arm, closing her eyes.

"What?" Pete jolted back. "What tailgate party? I thought we're all coming over her for Thanksgiving dinner. Now you're telling me that you're going to the Detroit game and a tailgate party? Where'd you get the money for those tickets? Huh, Rob?"

Rob threw his hand in the air and it came back to hit his thigh. "We're not going to the game. We're having a tailgating party *theme*, he emphasized, for Thanksgiving dinner to go along with the game."

"And, start a new family tradition," Jan added.

"Oh," Pete shrugged. "That sounds good. I like it. But then, there's not a whole lot that I don't like."

"It was my idea, honey," Monica said not lifting her head and eyes still closed.

"You're a genius, baby."

Monica grinned. "I'm a tired genius. I've been up for over eighteen hours doing rounds."

Jan squinted at her friend. "Rounds?"

"Rounds of shots. The interns wanted me to go out

with them after their shift," Monica shrugged. "So, I did."

Pete squirmed, then raised his finger and opened his mouth.

"What?" Monica sat up.

"Nothing." Pete stepped back. "I wasn't going to say anything."

Jan made eye contact with Rob and they smiled at each other.

"I've got a lot of food for tomorrow's dinner, but—"

"Tailgating party," Monica laid her head back down on her arm.

"Tailgating party. But I'm not sure it's going to be enough," Jan said with her arms opened wide.

"Listen, I told you I'll bring some food," Monica said.

"Does Ed and Denise know about this?" Pete asked.

"Don't ask?" The other three shouted at the same time.

"I'll bring the baked beans, potato salad, and a pasta casserole," Monica said yawning as she checked her watch.

"How are you going to get all that done between now and noon tomorrow? Jan questioned staring at her friend with disbelief.

"I promise you. I will deliver." She stood up and started to walk to the door that led to the garage. "We need to get going. I can't keep my eyes open any longer. You ready?"

Pete finished off his beer. "Yup."

The four of them walked to the mudroom where Monica and Pete put on their coats.

"See you tomorrow," Pete said as he walked out the door with his hand on Monica's lower back.

"See you tomorrow," Jan and Rob replied in unison closing the door to the garage.

8 THANKSGIVING DAY

Jan looked out standing in the archway from the kitchen and sighed with happiness. Her eyes scanned around her great room. She observed Rob's family watching the Detroit football game, having a few beers, and enjoying the snacks she had prepared.

"What's the score?" She asked openly. No one replied or even acknowledged her question.

Fine, she thought. So, the game wasn't going well. She knew there would be better days ahead for Detroit football. No need to be a fair-weather fan. But she didn't dare tell the rest of them because they would just want to argue about it.

"Oh, God damn it. Not again."

Jan brushed back, not sure which one said that. She watched as if in slow motion everyone in the room jerked, feeling the blow that the Detroit football player just received.

"Are you sure I can't help?" Denise was sitting between Ed and Pete on the couch. She scooched to the edge of the cushion, then lifted herself off.

The two guys looked at each other and split the difference between them so no one else could sit there.

"I saw what you did," Denise scolded. "I'm coming back after I help Jan."

"Okay. We'll make room for you," Ed said then winked at his son and elbowed him in the side.

Pete emitted a sinister laugh and nodded.

Denise followed Jan into the kitchen, pausing to look around, she seemed slightly shocked from the lack of food preparation activities.

"I appreciate the offer, Denise. But Rob and I are going with a tailgate theme for this Thanksgiving dinner. Goes with the football game," Jan said as she checked the refrigerator for more dip. "Don't you agree?"

"A tailgate theme? Huh," Denise said as she made eye contact with Rob. "So, not the traditional Thanksgiving dinner with turkey and sides?"

"Oh, they'll be turkey. Rob's deep frying it," Jan closed the appliance door and paused as she watched their reflections in the stainless steel door.

Rob frowned and shrugged.

Denise opened her arms and shook her head.

He pointed at Jan with a questioning look and mouthed the words *what was I supposed to do*.

Jan turned slowly to give them a warning, then walked over to the island with a container of dip and a clean dish.

"Yup, all my wife's idea," Rob said loudly.

Jan rolled her eyes as she spooned the salsa into the serving dish. "What do you think, Denise? Do you like it?"

She cleared her throat, pursed her lips, and nodded. "Uh huh," her voice was squeaky.

"Great," Jan said and smiled. "Then we'll do it again next year." In her peripheral vision she caught Rob and Denise in an angry stare down. As she walked out of the kitchen leaving the two to argue, she heard her husband and his stepmom mumbling to each other.

Through the window, Jan saw a car park on the road in front of their house. "Monica's here," she announced.

Pete didn't budge. His eyes were on the TV and a beer

in his hand.

"Pete, Monica's here. Aren't you going to greet her at her car?" Jan looked at him curiously.

"She's been here before. She knows her way around," he replied still not moving.

"Oookaaay," Jan said as she went out the front door. She waved to her friend as she skipped down the steps to the sidewalk.

"So, how's the Nichols family adjusting to the new idea for Thanksgiving dinner?" Monica gave a mischievous look as Jan approached her.

"So far, not well. Denise is beating up on Rob in the kitchen for letting me do this. And, besides Pete the others including Ed don't know yet." Jan swallowed back the pain of a bad idea. She turned to look around the neighborhood. Already feeling like an outcast, as she stood there. She couldn't shake the feeling that someone was watching her.

Monica gestured to the other side of the street. "I think I'll stand over there. So, then when Ed realizes there's no mashed potatoes and the house explodes, I won't get hurt." She handed one of the three casserole dishes to Jan.

Jan's face turned worrisome and she took a deep breath. "If that's Mr. Daniels here to ruin my holiday, I swear that I'll just . . ."

They both turned to watch a dark sedan with heavily tinted windows drive slowly up the street. The car sped up as it approached, then quickly passed by them.

"That's right, Mr. Daniels. You better get out of here," Jan said as she shook her fist at the car.

"Is he really still doing that?" Monica questioned as they started up the steps to the front door.

"Rob swears he's not. But it seems like I still see those dark cars wherever we go?"

Monica slipped off her shoes once inside and set her things on the foyer table.

"Baby, I missed you," Pete shouted as he came running

over to her. He opened his arms for an embrace.

"Shut up and get off me," she said as she pushed him away. "What's the score?"

"Thirty-five to ten." He shook his head. "Not us. Coming up to half time," he obediently replied.

They won't tell me the score when I ask, Jan thought as she carried the two dishes to the kitchen. But they tell Monica? Jerks.

"Hellooo."

Jan heard her mother's voice, spun around, and started toward the foyer with the dishes in her hands. She stopped, looked at them, and turned back toward the kitchen.

"Here let me help you with that," Brian said as he took the dishes from her.

"Thank you." Surprised by the gallantry, Jan appreciated the help and went to greet her parents.

"Mom, Dad," Jan said as she stepped into the foyer. "Happy Thanksgiving." She hugged each of her parents helping them remove their coats and hang them in the closet.

"What's the score?" Charles demanded as he marched into the great room.

"You don't want to know," Ed replied standing up and extending his hand.

Charles gave a hard handshake as he shook his head in disgust.

"Dad," Jan said with a nervous laugh in her voice. "Don't be a fair-weather fan." She held out her arms. "Don't worry. They're gonna win. They have to," she choked it out.

"Princess, I hate to spoil the ending for you, but there's not a snowballs chance in hell they're going to win this one. What makes you think they have to?"

"Because Jan and I have a bet on the game," Rob chimed in. "Detroit loses we spend Christmas day at the Nichols family cottage in Caseville. They win, we're spending Christmas day at Busha and Jaja's."

Jan looked from left to right as the snickers and moans echoed in her ears. I shouldn't have said anything, she thought. Oh no, what did I do.

Beth sat on the arm of the sofa next to her husband. She looked at Jan with disappointment.

"It's not definite yet, Mom" Jan said as she tilted her head seductively at her husband. "I think Rob will let me off the hook for this one. Won't you, honey?"

"Nope. A bet's a bet." He grinned at Jan.

"Well, then I'll wish you a Merry Christmas now because I won't see you at your grandparents' farm," Beth complained.

"Rob, come on. You can't be serious about holding me to this bet. You picked Tennessee before I had a chance to open my mouth."

"Are you trying to weasel out of this? I should have known better than to marry a spoiled brat." He looked at her parents. "No offense."

"None taken," they replied.

Jan's mouth dropped open.

"Next time don't make a bet you can't keep," Rob said.

"I'll have you know that I can keep your stupid bet," she said shaking her finger at her husband as she placed her other hand on her hip.

"The bet stands." Rob mocked his wife by placing his hands on his hips, doing a head toss, and stomping his foot. Dropping his hands to his sides he laughed with the others, then sat down on a straight chair he brought in from the kitchen.

"Robert Joseph," Ed barked causing everyone to jump. "Out to the garage."

"Oh shit," Rob mumbled.

Pete and Brian busted out laughing.

"Should we go watch?" Brian looked at Pete. "We haven't seen this in a long time."

"Rob's gonna get a beatin'. Rob's gonna get a beatin,'" Pete chanted.

Brian joined in while looking at his phone.

"What does that mean?" Jan asked with concern.

"When we were kids we got spankings once in a while," Pete explained.

"Not me," Brian said looking up from his phone.

"That's archaic." Monica said dryly. "Spankings? Did you like them?"

"That depends on who's giving the spanking." Pete continued following his girlfriend's lead.

"That depends, are you the sub or the dom?" Monica grinned.

Everyone moaned.

"I'm not sure," Pete smiled. "Which one do you want to be?"

"Just pick one," Monica ordered.

"I'm gonna guess that Pete is the sub and Monica is the dom," Brian said expressing his amusement at the notion.

Denise walked away shaking her head. "I'm going to make some coffee."

"I'll help you," Beth said following closely behind her.

"Me too," Charles joined them.

Jan sat down next to Brian and whispered, "Don't end up like them."

"Not a chance in hell."

They both laughed.

"Do you mind if I ask what's keeping you so busy on your phone? A girlfriend?" Jan inquired.

"No girlfriend. Just friends," Brian explained "After high school a lot of my friends went off to college. But not me. And, I'm starting to regret it."

"It's not too late. You can still go," Jan encouraged.

"I'm thinking the same thing," he said, then turned a concerned look to her. "But I'm also thinking about what will Rob say."

Jan shot a surprised look at him. "He's you brother. I

would think he'd be happy for you."

"I'm not so sure. But I think I want to find out sooner than later."

"Brian, that's great." Jan grabbed his hand and gave it a squeeze. "I want to be the first to congratulate you."

"Thanks, sis."

"Well, I for one am really looking forward to Christmas at the cottage this year," Pete said openly. "With the cold weather we've been having it's going to be a great time for us."

"You're hoping for a white Christmas?" Jan asked.

"I don't care if it's white or blue. But it has to be freezing cold," Pete replied.

Jan and Monica gave him a strange look.

"Hey, look at that," Pete pointed at the TV. "That player's number is zero. Zero equals nothing. Why would you want that for your number?"

"There's been a few players in different sports that have had the number zero. But I don't think it's allowed in football anymore." Brian said. "I don't think I would like having zero for a number," Brian said.

"I couldn't give a shit less if I'm getting paid millions of dollars a year. They can put a question mark on my back for all I care," Charles said coming back into the room holding a cup of coffee followed by Beth and Denise. "What's the score now?"

"Worse," Pete replied.

Jan stood up and whispered to Brian. "I'm going to see if Rob is okay."

"Be careful," he said with a teasing grin.

Jan cracked the door to the garage and peeked out on her husband and father-in-law.

"I'm not smelling turkey. Where the hell's the turkey?" Ed asked Rob.

"I thought you called me out here to yell at me."

"Yeah, sure, I'll do that too. But where the hell is the turkey and all the fixings?" Ed threw his hands in the air.

"I know. I know. This is Jan's first time cooking for Thanksgiving."

"What's that got to do with anything. It's Thanksgiving Day and I want a goddamn meal. Denise would have sent you all home by now with your bellies full and a doggie bag to boot."

"Well, Jan wanted to have a tailgate theme. So, I'm gonna deep fry the turkey."

"Deep fry it. What the hell!"

"Yeah,' Rob continued cautiously. "Remember when Johnny did that at his cottage. I thought you liked it. And it goes with the tailgate theme for the football game."

"Tailgate theme! *What the hell!*" Ed hollered.

"Keep your voice down," Rob warned. "It was Jan's idea. Denise is already upset about it."

"It's Thanksgiving. Isn't there a law that the turkey has to be cooked in the oven with stuffing and giblets and all that shit."

Jan rolled her eyes, closed the door, and walked over to the kitchen sink rinsing dishes and placing them into the dishwasher.

"I think I better start doing the turkey now," Rob said coming in from the garage.

"Yes, we better get the food out. Everyone looks hungry," she said working hard to keep her discouragement from showing.

Jan leaned against the wall, thankful that the meal was finally over. The pain of feeling the rejection from everyone's shock and disappointment at not having a traditional dinner was devastating to her.

She watched the others as they hissed and booed at the game. Her arms folded across her chest, she gritted her teeth anticipating her husband's in-your-face behavior she was about to receive.

"Oh," Rob slapped the arm of the sofa and jumped up.

"That's it. Game over. Final score ten to forty-seven. Jan, did you hear that?" He looked around the room until he saw his wife's piercing stare. "Guess what, honey. Guess where we're going to celebrate our first Christmas together?" He came over and tried to put his arms around her.

Jan coldly brushed him away and walked to the other side of the room.

"Kitten, this was an interesting, albeit delicious, twist on Thanksgiving dinner," Beth said as she walked up to her daughter with her coat over her arm and purse in hand.

"Are you and dad leaving already?"

"Yes, we need to go to, you know, your dad's side of the family and visit with them for a while." She gave her daughter a quick hug. "Charles, are you going to say goodbye to your daughter?"

Jan squinted. "Dad's side? Who's that?"

Beth cleared her throat. "You probably wouldn't remember them. You were pretty young when we used to visit with them regularly. But we're getting reacquainted now. Isn't that right, Charles?"

"What are you talking about?" Charles gave his daughter a hug. "Thank you for a delicious dinner, Princess."

Beth rolled her eyes and shook her head as she walked toward the front door. "He never keeps up with the conversation."

"Happy Thanksgiving," Charles shouted out to everyone. He waved as he closed the door behind him.

"We should be going as well," Monica went to get her coat.

"I'll get your dishes to take home," Jan said as she swiftly walked into the kitchen.

"Me too," Brian said. "Thank you, sis, for—"

"Oh no you don't," Denise stepped in front of them. "The three of you aren't going anywhere until I say so." She pointed at the sofa. "Now sit back down."

The three sulked back into the great room. Pete pounced down onto the cushions while Monica laid her head back.

Brian slouched down and cupped his chin in his hand resting his elbow on the arm of the sofa.

Jan returned from the kitchen and looked around. "What's going on? Why aren't you getting your coats on?"

9 GIFT LISTS

My parents left, but all the others look like they're settling in for a while, Jan pondered as she surveyed the great room walking over to an empty chair to sit down. The game was over. They ate. They drank. She wondered what was left to do? Feeling exhausted, she desperately wanted them to go home so she could go to bed.

"Okay, everyone pay attention. I'm giving you a piece of paper and a pen and you're going to write down three to five things that you want Secret Santa to bring you," Denise excitedly announced. She smiled at everyone in the room until her eyes meet Jan's. "Unless someone wants to take this away from me too." Her eyes narrowed.

Jan fell back in her seat shaking her head with a fearful expression.

"Good," Denise said taking a deep breath. "Then let's get on with it."

"Oh no, not Secret Santa," Pete moaned.

"Why do we have to do this?" Rob complained. "We tried it in the past and it didn't work."

"It didn't work because it was the four of you guys and me. But this year we have two more women. So, it should make things interesting." She grinned and continued to dispense the paper and pens.

"Jan and Monica didn't say they want to do Secret Santa," Brian protested.

"Yes, they want to," Denise replied as she looked at them nodding her head.

"Actually, I'd prefer not to. But—"

"See," Pete shouted out. "See, they don't want to."

"But" Monica glared at Pete, then continued. "If it makes you happy, Denise, then I'm willing to participate in this splendid holiday tradition." She turned a smug expression to Pete.

"Jan?" Denise looked her way.

Jan turned a surprised look to Denise, then feigned a smile. "Yes, I want to as well. Secret Santa can be a lot of fun." She turned to Monica and glared.

"See? Told ya. Now start writing everyone. You have fifteen minutes."

"I'll sit this year out." Pete said as he set his materials on the end table and relaxed back on the sofa.

"Just write your damn list already," Ed roared at him.

Pete jumped up, grabbed the pen and paper, and started scribbling. Pausing, he peered over to look at Monica's list.

She smiled widely and gave him a gentle push away from her.

He leaned over and whispered in her ear, then started writing furiously. He folded up the paper, sat back, and cleared his throat. "Okay. I'm ready."

Monica was snickering and leaned into Pete giving him a little shove.

Denise looked up from her lap where she was writing her list using a magazine for support. "What's so funny, you two?" She gave them a curious stare. "I'm warning you. Don't try any funny business or your Secret Santa will bring you a piece of coal," she teased.

Monica snort laughed as Pete tried to quiet her down.

Denise folded her paper, sighed, and looked around the

room. "Okay, everybody. Time to turn in your lists." She carried a small wicker basket around the room. "Drop 'em in." She tossed the container a couple of times. "Anyone one to pick first?"

"I do." Ed held his hand out, flexed, ready to dig into the stash of papers.

"Okay, we have our first Secret Santa."

Ed squinted, then held the slip of paper further away. He looked at Jan, then quickly turned away. Nodding he then folded up the paper and place it in his shirt pocket.

"Who's next?

"Me." Wearing a big grin, Pete stood up and walked over to Denise. He took his time, then removed a very small square. He looked at Monica, pointed at it while nodding and started laughing. "Okay, let's see what this naughty girl wants for Christmas."

"How do you know it's a girl?" Brian boringly questioned him. "I think Pete and Monica are cheating, Denise."

"Well. I hope not. I don't want to have to kick anybody out of the tradition, but we all have to play by the rules," she cautioned.

"Denise, why don't you pick next. You worked so hard coordinating this lovely game. You shouldn't be stuck with the last one." Monica tossed her hand at her.

"That's so nice of you, Monica."

Jan rolled her eyes and crossed her legs and her arms.

"Okay, let's see who I get."

Pete pointed at the list he selected and whispered to Monica.

The smile from Denise's face dropped. "What the hell is this? Is this some sort of sick joke?"

Ed jumped up and looked at the slip of paper.

Everyone started moving to the edge of their seat, curious about what they were reading.

"Pete, what the hell is this supposed to be. Take this back and write something decent," Ed ordered.

Pete jumped up. "But it was supposed to be for . . . Monica was supposed to . . . Denise, I'm really sorry. I didn't mean for you to read that."

"Just fix it," Ed demanded.

Pete found a pen and tore a sheet out of a magazine and started scribbling.

Monica laughed and fell over sideways onto the sofa.

"Here you go." Pete held his hand out toward Denise with the crumpled paper.

"No, I don't want it. Give it to her." She pointed to Monica.

"No, no. It's okay now." Pete grabbed Denise's hands trying to force her to take the crumpled paper.

"I don't want it," she argued and struggled to keep his hands away. "Just drop it in the basket."

She pushed the basket at him and he shoved it away.

"Please, for the love of God." He pushed his note into her clenched hands.

"Yuck. Why is it wet?" She held the note out and shook it several times to straighten it.

"Oh, sorry." Pete squirmed. "My hands are sweaty."

Denise rolled her eyes in disgust. She peered at the slip of paper for several seconds before the repulsed look on her face relaxed. "Fine. I'll accept it."

"Not really a Secret Santa anymore now, is it?" Brian amusingly commented.

"Oh, just pretend like it didn't happen," Denise remonstrated. "I've had to do it plenty of times since I've known you boys. Okay? Who's next?" Denise's irritation with the group's behavior was showing in the tone of her voice.

"Brian," Monica said and slid down to the end of the couch to be closer to Jan. She leaned over to her and lowered her voice. "I was surprised that Ed didn't blow up about dinner. What happened?"

Jan set her phone down in her lap, took a deep breath, and rolled her eyes. "Rob told Ed about it when they were in the garage. He blew up then," Jan mumbled and turned her attention back to her phone.

Monica snickered and peered over at Jan's screen. "What are you looking at? Isn't that the woman we saw the other night with Harold?"

"I've been checking her out and she does seem like a really nice person. She's actually a little older than me, thirty-two." Jan looked at her friend for her reaction.

"Why does this guy have such a hold on you?" Monica turned a curious stare her way.

"He doesn't," Jan said knowing she wasn't being truthful. She took a deep breath. "I'm just curious about his new girlfriend. Her family owns the Top of the Hour Marketing firm that her grandfather founded. I bet she just wants to take Harold's business from Hedge and then she'll dump him."

"Whatever you have to tell yourself to sleep at night." Monica sat back shaking her head.

"Denise, let's go," Ed said standing up and going to the closet for his coat.

Jan and Denise walked out of the kitchen to the foyer where Ed was holding her coat for her. She turned her back to him as he let the coat slide up over her arms.

"We'll walk you out," Rob said jumping up from the couch.

Denise was acting aloof, but cordial as she stepped outside to leave.

Jan could feel an awkwardness as the four of them stood on the front porch saying their good-byes.

"The food was delicious, Jan," Ed said. "Very, uh, unique idea for a Thanksgiving Dinner."

Denise quickly turned a surprised expression at him. Giving him a dirty look, she huffed and turned away.

"Thank you, Ed," Jan pressed her lips and nodded.

Ed elbowed Denise.

She turned to Jan. "Yes, uh, thank you I guess, for dinner," she said shrugging.

"Yup, you're welcome. Well, I'll just go back inside and continue tidying up," she said as she slipped past them back into the house.

"It's a lot of work to throw a party, you know," Denise shouted back while walking to Ed's truck.

Jan stopped in her tracks. She wanted to turn around and yell something back. But decided to save her energy, what little she had left and avoid a family argument, another family argument.

She went back into the kitchen looked around the complicated mess, then grabbed two beers from the refrigerator. She went to sit down next to her husband on the couch. Sitting silently, she stared straight ahead, decompressing as her thoughts replayed the day's events.

"So, how do you think things went today?" She turned her head to look at her husband. "Good? Bad? Improvement opportunities?"

Rob took a deep breath with pressed lips. He turned to Jan. "Bad. Improvement opportunity? Give it back to Denise and let's never try this again."

Jan turned a hurt look to her husband. Her mouth dropped and bottom lip quivered.

"Honey, I'm just saying–"

"Ha-ha, just messing with you," Jan said as she gave a gentle push on Rob's arm. "Deal. Denise can have all the parties she wants. I give up," she said while yawning.

Rob stared curiously at his wife.

"Speaking of what I'm good at," she grinned, "I'm going into the office for a couple of hours in the morning. But I was wondering if you wanted to start cleaning the garage after I get home?"

He turned quickly to look at her. "Clean? Tomorrow? It's Black Friday. I'm going shopping. I just figured you were too. You know, going with your girlfriends or something."

Jan leaned backwards. "What? You're going shopping on Black Friday? Why? It's crazy. I tried it once and I'll never do it again."

Rob pulled back and gaped in disbelief. "You take a day off from shopping? I never imagined it."

"I never imagined that you would go on the—" Jan slumped. "No, wait. I get it now. I know why you shop on Black Friday."

He smiled. "What's your reason for not—" He leaned his head to the side. "Okay, I get it now too. You don't think you need to save the money."

Jan clenched her jaw. "I haven't had to until this year." She smirked.

"Uh huh." He glared at her, then started chuckling. "You're welcome."

"I'm welcomed?"

"Actually, that was meant for your parents."

Jan huffed. "Well, even though today wasn't a traditional Thanksgiving dinner, I still thought the food was really good. Did you have some of that pasta casserole that Monica brought over? That was so delicious."

"Monica brought that? I never would have guessed that she could cook."

"She's half Italian on her mother's side. So yeah, she can cook. She once cooked an entire Italian meal for my parents and I. And, my parents had a little too much vino and started acting really goofy singing Sinatra songs and acting out these movies." Jan smiled recalling the memories.

"You think your parents are goofy only when they drink wine?" Rob said smugly as he stared at her.

"Okay, sorry I shared." She turned away.

"Just teasing. Your parents are great. And, very helpful to us." He turned to sit sideways and face her. "Besides they had you and I'm forever grateful."

Jan looked at him suspiciously. "Grateful for . . ."

"For you." He gave her a surprised look. Then pulled

her close. "I love you. And," he cleared his throat, "in all honesty, I thought today was great. I really liked the tailgate theme with the football game. But we're spanning generations here. So, we need to keep that in mind when having our parties."

"So, we can have another party?" Jan sat up to look at her husband.

He pulled her back into his arms. "Not anytime soon. But maybe someday."

Jan yawned again and settled into her husband's arms as her eyes started closing. "Maybe we should head upstairs."

"In a minute," he said laying his head back on the couch cushion. "I just want to savor this moment."

10 MEAT ME

Jan woke up and smiled when she saw her husband lying next to her. "You're still here. It's Sunday and you didn't run away from me."

"With all the help you've been giving me with my company this week, I can stay home today," he replied.

He propped himself up on his elbow, head on his hand. "You are so smart, and so beautiful. How did I get so lucky?" He gently stroked her cheek with the back of his fingers, then brushed her hair back. Leaning over, he kissed the top of her chest.

Closing her eyes and clutching the sides of her pillow, she breathed heavily as he continued the kisses down across her belly. Her body arched beneath him as he slid his hands over her hips. She relaxed back and relished in the morning's intimacy.

"So, what are we going to do with all this time on our hands," Jan said as she tied her robe. "A whole day," she said excitedly with a laugh.

"What do you mean? I thought you were going shopping with your girlfriends today?"

"Monica can't make it. So, we decided to reschedule." She smiled with a tilt of her head. "Sooo, what are we going to do?"

Rob looked away without answering. He zipped-up his blue jeans and headed for the door.

"Rob? Wait for me," she said following behind him. "Do you have plans for today? It's not work, is it? And, you're just not telling me?"

"Nooo. No, not work," he said as he gamboled down the stairs.

"Want to go shopping? I know." Jan rolled her eyes. "But I promise I won't spend any money." She raised her pinched fingers in front of her face. "Well, maybe just a smidge."

"Jan, honey," Rob took a deep breath, "I already made plans for us." He stopped and turned around to face her.

"Oh yeah. What did you have in mind?" She snuggled closer to her husband and placed her hands on his bare, muscular chest. "Back upstairs? Couples spa? Wine tour?"

"Actually, Ed and Denise invited us over for an early dinner."

Jan's hands dropped to her sides and she stared at her husband momentarily. "When was this? Because, as you know, we just saw them three days ago on Thanksgiving Day and they didn't say anything to me."

Rob squinted as he looked up in the air. "It waaas . . . oooh . . . probably Friday." He looked back at her.

"Friday? The next day?" Jan huffed. "Why didn't you tell me sooner?"

"Mostly, because I knew you'd react like this."

Jan scowled and started back up the stairs.

"You're going to shower and get ready, right?" Rob shouted to her. "Can I bring you some coffee? Is that a no?"

"Promise me you'll be nice?" Rob pleaded.

"Just ring the damn doorbell," Jan snarled. "I'm always nice." She heard other voices from inside the house. She looked at her husband questionably. "Who else is here?"

"Oh, I don't know—"

Monica opened the door. "Ha, so all of you didn't go shopping without me. I thought for sure you would." She stepped back and opened her arm to the inside of the house. "Come on in."

Jan's brows furrowed. "Why are you here?" she asked as she stepped inside. In her peripheral vision she saw her friend look at her husband, then grit her teeth. You're all here, she thought as she looked around the room at Pete, Brian, and Ed. Everyone knew about this but me. The smell of roasted turkey, stuffing, potatoes, and gravy filled the air arousing her appetite. Damn that smells good, she thought. But first, she had a score to settle.

"Is that Rob?" Denise shouted from the kitchen.

Jan turned and mouthed "Rob? Not Jan and Rob?" to her husband as she glared at him.

"Yes, Denise. Rob *and Jan* are here," Ed shouted.

Denise ran into the living room and stopped abruptly. "Oh, Jan," she said as she wiped her hands on her apron. She smiled nervously. "I thought you were going shopping with your girlfriends today?"

"That seems to be the consensus," she replied dryly.

"This is good," Denise blathered. "I can use some more help in the kitchen."

Jan took a deep breath and glared at her, holding back what she was thinking. *Well, I just got through with having a Thanksgiving dinner, whether anybody liked it or not. And, I sure as hell am not going to contribute to another one.* Jan walked over to Denise's recliner and settled into it. *Wow, these are comfortable. Now I understand why everyone wants one. I want one too.* She brushed her hands over the taupe microfiber padded arms. Leaning back, she gave it a push and the foot bench popped out. Laughing, she crossed her ankles and stretched her arms behind her head.

"Rob, you heard Denise. Get in there and help her in the kitchen," she said with a disparaging tone. "But bring me a beer first."

Monica, Pete, Brian, and Ed were trying hard to hide their amusement.

"Those looks on your faces are priceless," Jan said as she wagged her finger back and forth from her husband to her step-mother-in-law.

Denise huffed and scrambled off to the kitchen.

Jan tensed up, but tried not to show it when Rob walked over and knelt on one knee beside the chair.

"I thought you promised you were going to be nice," he whispered firmly.

"I said I'm always nice. And, I am. What did I do that's not nice? I'm friendly. I smiled at everyone." Jan glared back at her husband.

Rob sneered some profanities and lifted himself off the floor while leaning on the arm of the chair. "I'll be in the kitchen helping Denise, like a proper guest would."

"Great. And, don't forget that beer."

"So, sis, are you excited about spending Christmas day at the cottage this—" Pete grunted from Monica's elbow going into his side.

Ed and Brian leaned forward and glared at him.

"I sure am, Pete," Jan said enthusiastically. "I've never been there before, but I'm willing to check it out." She leaned forward and spoke to Pete in a soft voice. "I heard it's going to be a really great time."

Ed, Brian, and Pete simultaneously turned their heads to stare, mouths opened, at Jan.

She reached up to take the glass of beer from Rob. "Isn't that right, honey?"

He rolled his eyes as he returned to the kitchen.

"I'm gonna see what the hell is taking so long in the kitchen," Ed said as he darted across the room.

"I'm gonna get another beer," Brian said as he left the couch sounding bored with the family drama.

Pete looked at the two women left in the room with him. "I'mmm . . . getting the hell out of here," he said as he raced walked toward the kitchen door. Stopping abruptly, he turned and looked at Monica. "Nothing personal, baby. I just—"

"Go!" Monica pointed to the kitchen.

Jan looked at Monica and the two snorted as they tried to cover up their laughter.

"I'm impressed at how well you're taking this," Monica said.

Jan pushed her head back into the cushion. "I'm mad as hell, but I'm also so tired of fighting about shit like this." She took a sip of her beer.

"Oh, you are mad. You're still swearing and I'm the only one in the room to hear it."

"I give up. As Rob says," Jan lowered her voice, 'You're a part of the Nichols family now. You must succumb to our ways.'"

"He said succumb?"

"Okay, he didn't say succumb." She shook her head at her friend. "But what's the difference? Succumb? Cult?"

"Families are all different. I know, because I went through enough of them growing up."

"Yeah, I know. Sorry." Jan's eyes looked downward. "I only had Mom and Dad." Jan sharply turned her attention to her friend. "As you, Gina, and Christie like to point out may I remind you."

Monica snickered at her frankness.

"I just didn't realize that his family would behave so differently from mine."

"You say that, but did you ever stop to think about how weird your family is to Rob?"

"What? We're weird?" Jan pondered the idea momentarily as Monica watched the revelation on her face.

"But not as weird as . . ." She pointed at the kitchen.

Monica nodded.

"Me too?" Jan grimaced as she pointed her finger into

her chest.

Monica grinned as she nodded.

Jan gave her friend a shocked stare, then reclined back into the chair. "Oh well, I'm still never getting out of this chair."

"See? Weird," Monica said as she sat back on the couch.

Denise bounced into the doorway from the kitchen. She slapped and battled several arms as they pushed her into the archway leading into the living room. She stopped swatting when she saw Jan and Monica watching.

Jan flung the recliner to its upright position and Monica jumped to the edge of her seat.

Denise stopped fighting. One last hand stripped off her apron. She froze, starring at the other two women. She stood there smiling, then a hand reached out holding a drink. "Thanks a lot," she screamed back at them as she grabbed it, then walked over to the couch and sat down.

Jan and Monica couldn't help from snickering at the demonstration.

"What happened to your apron, Denise?" Monica looked at her curiously. "Did you trade it in for a glass of scotch?"

All the women laughed and Jan reclined back to her prostrate position.

"They kicked me out," Denise said with indignation. "All these years I've been making Thanksgiving dinner for them, and now they put a drink in my hand and kicked me out of my own kitchen." She looked at Jan and Monica and shrugged.

"Is dinner ready?" Monica gave her a sly look. "Everything smells delicious."

"Yes."

"*Saweet*," Jan squealed, collapsing the recliner to its upright position with a loud clang. "Wow, you couldn't sneak out of these things if you wanted to." She rubbed the arms as she leaned forward to lift herself out. "Still love this chair though."

"Jan, wait." Denise ran to get in front of her. "The guys are setting the table and," she rolled her eyes, "trying to be helpful. Why don't we give them a few minutes and let them call us in when they're ready?"

"Because I don't give a shit when they'll be ready. And, they're probably in there drinking and not doing a God damn thing," Jan said as she kept walking toward the kitchen.

Monica caught up with Jan and Denise and the three women walked into the kitchen one following the other.

"Looks great." Jan turned to look at the other two women with a drawn out, approving nod.

Rob pulled out a chair and signaled for Jan to come over and sit down.

She smiled and chose a seat between Ed and Brian.

"Oh, sorry. I can move," Brian said as he started to get up.

"No, no. That won't be necessary." Rob glared at Jan and sat at the opposite end of the table.

Ed reached for the turkey and pulled it closer to himself.

"So, is it just me or is there some tension in the air," Pete said as he looked around table at everyone.

Monica kicked him under the table and he made a muffled whimper.

"So, Denise, how much work is it to decorate for the holidays?" Monica tried changing the subject.

"Well, I don't decorate here. I decorate the cottage." She pressed her lips and paused. "It's a lot of work to decorate the cottage, but wait 'til you see it." She beamed. "It's like a Christmas fantasy."

Jan tucked her chin as she stared at Denise. She let this one go but felt there is no way you can turn a cottage into a Christmas fantasy. Not unless you have a magic wand, she shook her head.

"Well, with as cold as it's been, I'm excited about

Christmas at the cottage because—Oooh!" Pete leaned down and grabbed his shin. He turned a frustrated look at Monica.

"Whatever you do, don't mention football," Rob teased.

Why am I even here? They obviously weren't expecting me, Jan sulked. Shifting in her seat, she played with her food, moving it around on her plate with her fork. If it were possible, she would have simply disappeared.

"Everyone can help themselves to desert whenever they're ready." Denise sat back and placed her napkin alongside her plate. "I know I'm gonna need a couple of hours."

"Excellent meal, Denise," Ed said as he patted her back. "Another Thanksgiving feast."

Jan abruptly turned to Ed. "Is that another as in this year? Or, another as in she's added another year to her score?"

"Jan." Rob stood up making a screeching sound when his chair slid back. "Let's talk in the other room."

Rob led the way into the living room followed by Jan going to the area that was furthest from the kitchen.

"Boy, that was one delicious meal," Jan said as she rubbed her tummy.

"Yes, it was. But" Rob stopped walking and spoke in a hushed tone. "I thought you said you were going to be—"

Jan opened her mouth to speak, raising her finger to make her point. But she stopped when she saw that her husband realized the error in his statement.

He paused as he looked upward and took a deep breath. "I asked you to be nice."

"Yes, you did ask me to be nice. But was it nice of my husband and his family to conspire behind my back to have a second Thanksgiving dinner without me?" Her voice squeaked as she quietly emphasized her point. "You tricked me into thinking it was just another meal with Ed and Denise."

"I would think you'd get the message from today's events," he said shaking his finger at her.

"Get that thing out of my face," Jan said clenching her teeth. "And, I got the message a long time ago. That it's okay for me to be your wife, but not a part of the Nichols' family."

Rob gasped. "That's not true. Besides, what about you and your parents. You guys are all stuffy and act like your better than everybody else."

Jan's jaw dropped. "We are not stuffy." The corners of her mouth turned down. "The Nichols are so laid back, they're nothing but a lackadaisical bunch. It'd be nice to see a spine once in a while.

"Wow, I can't believe you just said that." Rob shook his head slowly. "The Nichols family are hard workers. And, I thought you were one too. But you're just nothing but a spoiled brat."

"You say that like it's a bad thing. But when I see something I want, I just go for it. If that makes me a spoiled brat, then so be it."

"You're too competitive. And, this time it's creating a family fight of astronomical proportions." His voiced screeched.

Jan stared at him with pressed lips and arms crossed in front of her chest.

Rob turned and looked back at the kitchen. "What are they doing now?"

Together they walked back into the kitchen and saw the others exchanging money across the table.

"So, who won the bet?" Rob asked as he glared at them.

"And, you call me competitive?" Jan shot back.

"Here's your doggie bags," Denise handed each one of her stepsons a large, brown paper sack.

Rob put one arm around Denise's shoulders for a quick hug. "Thanks, Denise. Everything was delicious." He paused and turned a serious look to her. "Listen, I'm really sorry—"

"No need to apologize," Denise said throwing her hand at him. "You're just going through some growing pains together as husband and wife. It'll get better over time."

Jan looked around the room as the others were getting their coats.

"You ready?" Rob looked at Jan.

"Would you mind warming up the truck and I'll be right there." After her husband was out the door Jan lingered behind. She cleared her throat. "Denise, dinner was great. And, I want you to know that I concede to you being the better of us at cooking and throwing parties. From now on all family parties are yours for the throwing," Jan said smiling at her play on words.

Denise laughed out loud at her. "Is that what this was all about." Denise patted Jan on the shoulder. "Sweetie, you are so far out of your league that you didn't even know it.

Jan's eyes widened and she felt belittled by her step mother-in-law's reaction to her attempt to make amends. "Okay then. Thank you for dinner," she said in a surly manner. She slipped her coat on while Ed and Denise stood by, waiting for her to go out the door.

11 ROB BASHING

Jan and Gina closed the roadster's car doors and headed into the restaurant to meet Monica and Christie.

"Boy, am I ready for this lunch," Jan said as she pulled out a chair and sat down.

"That hungry, huh?" Christie remarked.

"No, I need to tell you guys about Sunday." Jan leaned forward. "After everything I went through to prepare a fabulous Thanksgiving Day meal for his family, you are not going to believe what happened."

"I was there. You don't need to tell me," Monica said glibly.

"Yeah, and I just heard it in the car." Gina rolled her eyes.

"Monica already told me," Christie added as she checked her phone.

"Well, how am I supposed to feel better if no one wants to listen to me." Jan opened her hands palms up. "You're my friends. You're supposed to be supportive."

"What now?" Monica chided.

Jan dropped her arms as a shocked look came over her face. "What do you mean 'what now?'" She said with a squeaky voice. "Like I do this all the time?" Jan frowned.

"Weeell, you kinda do," Gina commented.

"Yeah. It's become chronic with you since you got married," Christie added to the argument.

"You're doing it all the time now." Monica sighed. "You're becoming boring to be with."

Jan's mouth fell open.

"You're always complaining about your husband and his family," Christie said while looking at her phone as she swiped it sideways.

"Well, you guys complain about your," Jan paused and looked at each one of them. "boyfriend, husband, boyfriend too," Jan said as she pointed at Gina, then Christie, then Monica.

"Yes, but not as much as you," Monica said while chewing and pointing at Jan with a piece of bread in her hand. "You're chronic about it." She set her bread down and wiped off the tips of her fingers with her napkin.

"I think it has to do with her needing attention," Gina said as she looked at the other two women as if Jan wasn't there. "Since Jan is an only child, she probably never got to experience sharing like the rest of us."

"I'm right here." Jan shook her head with a scowl. "Besides, Monica's an only child too."

"I had steps."

"Not all the time. They mostly lived with their fathers."

"Enough to keep me balanced and not self-absorbed." She flashed a wide grin.

"Fine. Then I won't talk anymore." She crossed her arms, pressed her lips, and looked out across the room.

"Yes you will," Monica said confidently.

"It's unavoidable," Gina added.

"Since Jan isn't talking, can I take my turn now?" Christie asked enthusiastically.

No one answered as Monica and Gina ate their bread and Jan held still.

"Great. So, Manny and I—"

"Okay you're right," Jan blurted out.

"Hey!" Christie slammed her palms on the table. The nearby patrons jumped. "I was talking."

"Okay." Jan fearfully sat back in her chair.

"So," Christie cleared her throat and looked at Jan with narrowed eyes. "Manny and I had Thanksgiving dinner with his abuela. She is such a sweet lady. She made these traditional mantinadas and they were so delicious."

After an awkward pause the others looked at each other.

"That's it?" Gina cringed, shaking her head. "No fighting, swearing, crying? Nothing juicy?"

Jan tucked her chin and her eyes widened.

"What do you mean juicy? That's a sweet story about a sweet lady. You have no idea what this woman's been through all her life."

"Well then, tell us all about that," Monica said using her straw to mix the ice around in her glass.

"I can't share her life story. It's private. Would you like the recipe?"

"Yes," Monica said. "Jan, you're up."

Jan sat quietly, wide-eyed.

"Jan," Monica snapped her fingers in front of her face. "Go."

Christie sat back with her arms crossed and pouted.

"I, uh, forgot what I was going to say," Jan stammered.

The three women shook their heads and grumbled.

Frank set a plate of food in front of each of them. "Is there a problem, ladies?"

"Not with you, Frank. It's Jan." Gina coldly pointed at her.

"Yeah, she got us all excited about some juicy talk, then forgot what it was," Monica added with a grin.

"What? Are you kidding me? All of you said that—" Jan let out a loud groan as she slouched in her chair.

"Uh huh, I see." Frank stroked his chin as he looked at Jan. "So, it seems it's becoming a continuous problem with her." He looked at the others. "Am I right, ladies?"

Jan gasped, sat up straight, and pointed an accusatory finger at him. "Are you just trying to impress Rosie?"

"Shhh," Frank put his finger to his pursed lips. "She might hear you."

"She will hear me if I don't get some respect around here," Jan demanded.

"How about free cannoli for everyone?" Frank offered.

"Now that's the kind of respect I'm talking about." Jan grinned at her friends.

"Speaking of respect. What is everyone asking for from Santa this year?" Christie pointed at each them with her fork.

"Well, I'm not going to count on it, but when Michael and I were out shopping he wanted to stop at a couple of jewelry stores. He told me he wanted my help picking out a necklace for his mother. But he also was asking me what type of settings I like the best and other things about jewelry." Gina looked excitedly at her friends' faces.

"Gina, that's wonderful," Christie said patting the back of her hand.

"But like I said, I don't want to get my hopes up."

Monica picked up her glass of water and sipped. She held her focus on Gina. She set the glass back down and after a long deep breath she smiled at her. "I'm very happy for you. I didn't think I would be the last one to get engaged, but it is what it is." She shrugged.

"Oh," Gina cringed. "I'm sorry. I didn't think about it that way. I thought all of you would be happy for me."

"We are, Gina. Don't you worry about anyone else. You need to enjoy this moment for yourself," Christie comforted.

"I am happy for you. It's just that surprisingly, it's stirring up some emotions in me that I didn't know I had," Monica looked away thoughtfully staring out across the room.

"As you know, Manny and I are going to Mexico for the holidays. So, instead of buying something for each other and having to carry it on the plane, we're going to shop for each other while we are there."

"I'm getting a new car," Jan blurted out, crossed her arms, and held her chin high as she looked around at the others.

"I told you to get help for that perpetual lying," Monica scolded.

"It's not lying. A car is on my list to Santa. I'm telling my version of the truth. It's easy for you to be so blunt always. Everyone is afraid of you."

"Everyone is afraid of me?" Monica's lip quivered.

"Uh oh." Jan feared she pushed her friend's button too soon after hearing Gina's news.

"Are you?" Monica whimpered.

"I wasn't until now."

"Ha-ha. That's okay. I know everyone is afraid of me. As well they should be."

"I'm not afraid of you," Christie spoke up

"Me neither," Gina added glaring at Monica.

"Speaking of afraid, have any of you noticed how the headlines are always about Detroit and some investigation lately?" Jan scanned her friends' expressions to her question.

"It's one of the largest cities in the Midwest. Cities are always having issues of one type or another. That's what keeps us attorneys in business," Christie joked.

"Besides, you don't know if there's any substance to it or if the media is just trying to sell papers," Gina explained.

"Why are you bringing that up anyway?" Christie gave her a concerned look.

"No reason other than it's annoying. Isn't there anything else to report to the public that has substance?" Jan looked down and fiddled with the edges of her napkin. "Well, there is one more thing. I've been helping Rob with his company's books."

"You mean the Nichols Construction Company's

books?" Monica gave Jan a stern look.

"Okay, okay. I get it." Jan took a deep breath. "I'm slowly but surely getting his, er, I mean the company books in order. But what's strange is that there seems to be some money missing."

"Why are you doing the work? What happened to his office manager?" Christie looked curiously at her.

"She left, long story. But Rob's been trying to do it all himself—"

Monica took a deep breath, leaned forward on her elbows, and opened her mouth to speak.

"The bookkeeping. Stop trying to turn everything into an argument." Jan tilted her head displaying her annoyance.

"I guess she's not afraid of you either," Gina said expressing her amusement.

After lunch with her friends Jan returned to work and prepared for a busy afternoon of calling clients and several meetings. She noticed Marjorie's son, Howard, strolling by her office several times. Marjorie, Jan's former boss, held the director's position that Jan now filled. She was a tyrant of a boss and the company, owned by Marjorie's uncle, had her removed.

"Hello?" Jan said as she stepped outside her office door.

"Oh, hello," he said trying to act surprised. "I was wondering if I could walk with you to our directors' meeting?"

"Sure, why not. Let me grab my things."

They walked together and as he talked Jan started thinking about who in the world would possibly have sex with Marjorie to produce Howard. He's not too bad-looking, not at all like his mother. The father must have been the better looking of the two. Or, maybe he was adopted. Nah, she wouldn't go looking for—

"So, what do you think?" He asked.

Jan shook her head. "Think? About what?" She stared blankly at him.

"Is my voice impervious to you?" He huffed. "You never listen to what I'm telling you."

"Oh, but I did. I just thought you had more to say. For instance, what about primetime ads, focus groups, and customer surveys?"

They stopped in the middle of the hallway.

"I was talking to you about my mother. How are all those things you just mentioned going to help with that?"

"Oh." Jan didn't move. "Well, in that case, I'm not sure. What options have you considered?"

He sighed. "Consider yourself warned." He turned and walked away.

"Warned? Howard?" She started running after him in her heels. "What does that mean?"

Howard went into a meeting room and closed the door just before Jan ran up to it.

She stood silently thinking about what he had said. "*Warned.*" She grimly opened the door and walked into the conference room contemplating his message. She saw him seated between two directors at the large, oblong table. She sat across from him, but he refused to make eye contact. The meeting began, but all Jan could think about now was *Marjorie.*

After dinner Rob turned a concerned look to his wife. "Honey, I'm worried about you," he said putting away the last dish from the dishwasher. "You look like you have a lot of stress. Did something happen at work today?"

Jan wasn't sure she wanted to share with Rob about the conversation she had with Marjorie's son. She wasn't sure what was said to tell him anyway. "I had a strange conversation today with another coworker. But it's work related and I don't want to bore you with the details."

"You sure? I'm a good listener, you know."

Jan grinned at the irony of his statement. "I'm sure. It'll work itself out." The creases in Jan's forehead started to disappear when she sifted through the mail. "Several more Christmas cards, how nice," she said softly. She went to a drawer and removed a letter opener.

"More cards?" Rob picked up the stack and looked at the return addresses.

"Honey, that's what people do this time of year. Send good wishes to family and friends. Haven't you sent any cards before?"

"No. I don't think my dad ever did either."

"What about your mom or Denise?"

"Mmm, not sure, but I don't think so."

"Hey, I've got a great idea."

"No."

"You don't even know what I was going to say," Jan protested.

"Yes, I do. You were going to say that I should send some Christmas cards."

"See, you're wrong. I was going to say that Nichols Construction Company should send some Christmas cards, to its customers." Jan smiled and opened her arms wide.

"Same thing. No."

"A lot of companies do."

"Still no."

Jan smiled at him and continued cleaning off the counter. Since I'm head of marketing for Nichols Construction Company, I think I'll take matters into my own hands, she thought.

12 HEDGE CORP CHRISTMAS PARTY

Jan walked swiftly through the Troy Mall to her salon appointment, frequently looking back over her shoulder. She had the strange feeling that someone was following her and it wasn't for good reasons.

"Hey Jan. Your hair still looks great. What brings you in today?" Becky was standing at the counter leaning on her elbows for support. She raised one hand to push up the bridge of her glasses.

"I have my company Christmas party tonight and I want to look fabulous."

"Well then," Becky waived her jazz hands, "that will be easy for Gary, because you already do look fabulous," she said as she led Jan to her stylist.

"You are so kind," Jan acknowledged.

"So, the big party is tonight. How are we going to show everyone who's the boss?" Gary asked standing behind her while she sat in the salon chair. He gathered all of Jan's strands of hair together. He fastened her hair with a clip as they looked into the mirror together. "What do you think? Curl cluster, French twist, blowout? Or, chignon?" He aligned his face next to hers and they seductively stared at their reflections in the mirror.

"Mmm," Jan turned her head slightly left, then to the right. "I'm thinking . . . chignon." She turned to face Gary, nose to nose. "What do you think?"

"I think you're right. A mature, classy look. Not too many women can pull it off like you can." He pulled her hair up and knotted it near the nape of her neck. "Such superb décolletage," he said admiring Jan's structure through the transparent wrap.

"And what color of polish are we going with? What is the color of the dress you're wearing?" Connie, the manicurist, asked as she examined Jan's hands.

"What other color is there for Christmas? Red." She expected everyone to agree with her.

The styling team returned moans and flashed disappointed faces at her.

"What's the matter? I shouldn't wear red?"

"Red is okaaay," Connie droned. "But you'll see everyone will be wearing red. Beautiful color, but a woman as stunning as you should stand out in the crowd."

"Connie's right, Jan." Gary rested his elbow on the back of his hand as he pointed at her. "Do you still have time to shop before the party? I saw the most fabulous black sequin gown at that . . . that . . . Connie, what's the name of that store?"

"Which one? We're located in a mall," she retorted.

"The one you and I passed when we were speed walking at lunchtime the other day."

"Oooh, that one." Connie started removing Jan's old polish. "I don't remember."

"Anyway, stay on this level and go into the mall. It'll be on your right about four stores down."

"That sounds wonderful. Thank you. I'll check it out." I know what store they're talking about, Jan thought. *But the price tags on those gowns, well, they even make my eyes pop out.*

"Stick with your red dress this time. But you have to get that dress for the next occasion. And, you'll have to let me see it on you," he sang his finish. "So, are you excited about tonight?"

"I was, but then I got this creepy feeling that someone was—" Jan couldn't believe who she saw walk into the salon. "Marissa."

"You got a creepy feeling that someone was Marissa?" Gary repeated chuckling. "That's odd."

"No, I mean there's Marissa. We just met a few weeks ago." Jan pointed a limp finger at the other woman.

"I never saw her before, but she looks like she has a pretty decent head of hair," Gary commented as he walked to the customer counter.

"Sorry about the wait. Our receptionist went to lunch," Gary said as he looked around for Becky. "Or somewhere," he mumbled. "Anyway, who are you here to see today?"

"Oh, I don't have an appointment today. I'm just here to buy some products." Marissa grabbed a lock of her hair. "I have such problem hair and I was just looking around to see . . . Is that Jan?" Marissa walked toward her.

"Marissa, I'm surprised to see you here. Do you come here often?" Jan braced herself in the chair with a white-knuckle grip.

Connie tugged on Jan's fingers to loosen them from the clasp she had on the arms of the salon chair. She mumbled complaints from the interruption as she worked on her nails.

"Once in a while. I just happen to be in the area today."

Gary and Connie exchanged glances expressing their skepticism while they attended to Jan.

"So, this is where you go to maintain your beautiful looks? Great place." Marissa panned the salon from where she stood.

"Yes, it is. I've been coming here for a long time and we're like family now." Jan smiled at Connie.

"You bet." Gary patted her shoulder.

"Uh huh." Marissa looked at her phone, then turned to

Jan. "What's Rob doing today? Did you leave him with a honey do list?" She chuckled.

Jan pulled back her head in surprise. "He's probably at work." She remembered what Monica said about how she's always asking about Rob. And now, it seemed very obvious.

Marissa nodded. "Hmmm. Well, don't forget our interview this Wednesday. I have to run." Swiftly she walked out of the salon turning back to give a brief wave.

"That was weird." Jan stared at the door.

"She didn't buy any products," Connie said suspiciously.

"What interview?" Gary asked curiously.

"She's supposedly, I mean she's with *Michigan Homes* and—"

"What do you mean 'supposedly?'" Gary teased. "Spill, please."

Jan sighed. "I'm not sure. I was excited when I first met her and she said they were going to interview Rob and I about our home. But she keeps promising an interview and it doesn't seem like it's going to materialize."

"Have you checked out the magazine online? They probably list the editors so you can find out what level she is," Connie suggested. "You don't want just anybody coming into your home."

"Yes, you're right. I don't want just anybody in my home." Jan thought about how Marissa pushed her way into the house the first time she was there. But didn't dare say anything to Gary and Connie about it. They would think she was insane for not having called the police.

As Jan walked away from the salon, she reached to feel the back of her hair. *I love how Gary works his magic every time.* She carried her purse in one hand and a small bag from the salon in the other. I have no reason to go into the mall area today, she thought. But it wouldn't hurt to checkout that dress Gary was talking about, she rationalized. Black sequins are . . . *oh my.* Jan stood outside the store window looking up at a mannequin in a black sequin, floor length gown with a side slit up the thigh. "Sleeveless, fitted through the torso, and a plunging neckline." Jan closed her mouth to swallow. "It's perfect," she mumbled.

"Hello," a man stuck his head out of the store entrance. "Would you like to come in and try it on? I think it would be perfect for you."

Jan forced herself to take her eyes off the dress and acknowledge the man's question. For an awkward moment she could only stare at him as she contemplated what will happen if she put that dress on. "Yes, I'd love to," she said as she followed him into the store.

"My name is Robert, by the way. I'll be right back," he said as he headed to a door, then stopped and turned back to Jan. "You look like about a size eight. Am I right?"

"Yes, you're good." Jan looked over the store displays and realized this was a dangerous move, because there was nothing she didn't like. "I wish this was my closet," she commented.

"A lot of women feel that way," the salesman said as he returned with a long garment bag. "And surprisingly, a few of them do have a closets just like this."

He carried the gown into a large dressing room. In it was a cushioned chair and ottoman for the customers comfort while changing. He carefully unzipped the bag and removed the gown. Flowing, he hung it from a clothes bracket on the wall. "Would you like assistance putting it on?"

"I don't think so, but I'll call you if I do," Jan politely replied.

The man left the large fitting room and closed the door.

Removing her clothes, she never once took her eyes off the dress. Despite the black sequins, the inside of the dress was soft and silky, and felt luxurious on her skin. I've had a lot of gowns in my time, but never one as fabulous as this, she thought.

"Robert, I could use some help zipping the back of the dress," Jan called out.

"At your service, Miss . . ."

"Jan." She placed her hands on her hips and stood straight and tall. She tingled at the feeling of Robert gently pulling the zipper up to her lower back where the dress stopped.

"Miss Jan." He placed his hands on her shoulders. "So, what do you think?"

Neither of them could take their eyes off the image in the mirror.

"Believe it or not, you're the first woman to try this dress on. So, you may be the only woman who ever wears this beautiful creation."

Jan smiled wide, then stood on her tip toes and slipped her bent knee out the side slit.

"Your hair is perfect. With three-inch heels, your look will be flawless," Robert complimented.

"I'm not seeing a tag," Jan spoke softly as she looked over her shoulder at him.

He smiled. "I think we can work something out."

"You've been gone a long time," Rob said with his head down as he continued to check his phone messages. Pressing the lock button and slipping it into his shirt pocket, he looked up at his wife. "Wow! You look fabulous." He paused, then looked from side to side around Jan. "Where's all the shopping bags?"

"This is it." Jan held up the little salon bag that held some trial size products to show him.

He looked inquisitively at her and tucked his chin. "That doesn't seem like you. Are you feeling okay?"

"Uh huh." She looked at the clock on the oven display. "We better get ready if we're going to arrive on time," she said as she headed toward the stairs.

Rob followed Jan into their spacious bedroom. She

peeled off her white t-shirt and skinny blue jeans, dropped her bra and panties on the floor, and tip toed to the dresser.

Her husband watched her as he removed his clothes, dropping them in the spot where he as standing. He came over to where she was selecting accessories to go with her dress for the evening. Sliding his arms around her bare waist he nuzzled next to her ear. "What time does the party start?"

Jan brushed up against Rob and smiled. "I think it starts when we get there."

Rob pulled her close and with their arms around each other they took several steps toward the bed.

"Oh no," Jan blurted out. "I forgot to stop at the pharmacy to . . . you know.

"No, I don't know. Don't care." Rob slowly ran his hand up and down her thigh.

"To buy some of those inserts." She leaned back as he kissed her chest. "We should stop," she whispered.

Rob slowed down. "Do we need it? Is it gonna hurt one time without it?"

Jan giggled. "It's not gonna hurt," she whispered into his ear. "But are you willing to take the risk?"

"Try and stop me." He lifted her up and wrapping her legs around his waist he carried her to the bed.

Jan took Rob's arm as they entered the lobby of the large banquet hall. "We're in the State Room, straight ahead."

They stood together in the arched doorway looking for familiar faces.

"I'll see you later." Rob dropped Jan's hand and headed toward a prospective client he spotted across the ballroom.

"No." Jan grasped his arm with both her hands. "Don't go. Don't leave me alone. I've got a bad feeling about this party."

"Honey, what are you talking about?" Rob chuckled and shook his head, appearing astonished by her reaction. "This is your office party. Don't you know everyone here?"

"Yes, but I . . ."

"And, you're a director so people will be falling all over themselves to get a chance to talk with you."

"Yes, but . . ."

"You're gonna be busy and if I stay with you I'll be bored." Rob held his arms out. "So, I'm gonna go drum up some business for Nichols Construction Company. And, you go show those people who's the boss." He gave her a quick peck on the side of her cheek and tried to pull away.

"But Rob," Jan said as she clutched his arm tightly wrinkling the fabric where her fingers were pressing in.

Rob looked at her with pain on his face as he tried to wriggle his arm loose from her grip.

"I've got a sinking feeling like something bad is going to happen," she whispered as she moved closer to her husband looking into his eyes, pleading.

"Honey, that's ridiculous."

"Jan, great to see you." Bob Watts, a manager at Hedge, walked swiftly with his wife toward her.

Jan dropped her husband's arm and turned to greet them. She didn't want anyone at the company to see the stress she was feeling. The uncertainty from Howard's *warning* to her, but what was it?

Rob took several steps away from his wife. "Hi folks." He waved. "I've got some business to take care of, but we'll catch up later. Okay?"

"Sounds good," Bob shouted at him as he scurried away.

"You look fabulous," Myra said.

"And you two make a smashing couple. You're the best looking ones here." Jan smiled at them before her eyes drifted to keep watch on her husband.

"Wow, that music is loud." Bob winced as he looked around the ballroom.

"Nothing like a live band for party music," Jan said loudly as she leaned toward the couple.

Myra started swaying her hips to the sound. "I kind of like it."

Bob slipped his arm around his wife. "Myra, may I have this dance?" He grinned.

"I thought you'd never ask," she replied as the two walked toward the hardwood floor.

"Wait," Jan shouted and reached out for them. "Don't you want to talk some more." Her arms dropped to her sides. She stared at the dance floor full of happy couples.

"Where's Rob?" She mumbled as her sinking feelings came rushing back. She raised herself up on her tip toes, giving her a little more height than what her heels already provided. She scanned the vastness of the crowd but the dim lights made it difficult to recognize the faces. "Where is he?" She huffed and dropped back on her feet.

"Jan, looks like a great turn out for the party."

Jan spun around on her heels. "Harold, my favorite client." She leaned in cheek to cheek and a gentle hug. "I'm so glad you're here." She held out her hand to his girlfriend. "Nice to see you again, Carrie."

"You too." She grabbed Jan's hand in both of hers and held it tight. "Your dress looks fabulous. Red is the perfect color on you. You'll have to tell me where you shop."

Jan laughed lightly. "Yes, of course."

"Harold, I'm going to the women's room," she said as she started to walk away. "Save a seat for me?" She blew him a kiss.

"You bet." He watched as she disappeared into the party.

"Harold, you look great," Jan exclaimed trying to get his attention. "Different foods? Exercise?"

"Carrie. Jan, it's Carrie that has me looking great." He took a step closer to Jan. "She's great. I never thought I could meet someone who can make me feel so alive."

"Harold, I'm going to say this just because I care so much about you. ,do you think things are moving a bit too fast?"

"What?"

"Are you sure she has your best interest at heart. After all she—"

"Of course." His forehead wrinkled. "Of course, Carrie has my best interest at heart. And, I have her best interest at heart." Harold took Jan's hands into his. "Jan, I know we were together for a while, but it didn't work out. Believe me, Carrie and I, we're good for each other."

"But Harold, she works for her father's company, that is also a marketing company." Jan shrugged as she held her arms open. "Like Hedge." She stepped closer to him. "Harold, are you sure she's not just using you to get your company's account?"

"Jan," Harold said as he shook his head. "I don't know where you got your information from, but Carrie has never brought up the subject of my company's marketing account."

"Not yet, but she—"

"You don't have to worry. My account is safe with you at Hedge."

"But . . ."

"Jan, I know you mean well. But Carrie and I, well, we're in love. I appreciate your concern. I know you care about me and I still and always will care about you. But you're going to have to trust me about this."

Jan couldn't believe what she was hearing. Harold wasn't going to listen to her and she didn't know what else to say.

"I'm going to my table now." He smiled at her. "We'll talk more later?"

"Yes, of course," she said softly as she watched him walk away. Her heart ached, but she couldn't understand where those feelings of loss were coming from.

"Well, Hellooo Jaaan."

White ran across Jan's face. She'd recognize that voice anywhere. Making a slow, pivotal turn on one heal, she came face to face with the other woman.

"Marjorie Hardcastle." Jan took in a deep breath as she stepped back, feeling lightheaded. "What are you doing here? Uh, I mean, how are you?"

"Well to answer your first question, Jaaan. As you now know since taking over my position as Director at Hedge Corporation, that my Uncle and Aunt own the company. Aaand, since the party was open to all family members, I thought 'wouldn't it be nice to chat with Jaaan and wish her a Merry Christmas.'"

"You came here," Jan swallowed hard, "for me?" The tone of her voice rose higher.

Marjorie furrowed her brows. "I came here because it's my family's party and I thought—"

"You came here for me?"

"I came over to you to wish you—"

"Good luck in my new position?"

"A Merry Christmas," Marjorie's tone was wrought with frustration.

"Oh, right, Merry Christmas. Yes, thank you." Jan nervously laughed.

Marjorie continued to curiously stare at her.

"And," Jan nodded, shrugged, and held her arms open by her sides, "Merry Christmas to you too."

Marjorie came in, full frontal force for a hug.

Jan was immobilized, arms sticking out by her sides, constrained from the grip. Stretching her hand, she gently patted Marjorie on the back.

After several seconds, Marjorie let go, stepped back, and straightened her dress. She smiled at Jan. "Just one more thing. I'm not supposed to tell you this, but there's going to be a surprise at work on Mondaaay and I think you're going to liiike it," she said as she walked away waving her hand in the air.

Jan's heart raced and her skin crawled as she watched her former boss, the woman she feared the most, enter the crowd and disappear. Someone touched her arm and she jumped with a gasp.

"Are you okay? Who was that?" Rob asked as he stood next to his wife.

"The grim reaper of careers." Jan slumped.

13 SHE'S BAAACK!

"Hey, that's not garbage, that's my lunch. Don't throw it away," Rob said as he took the contents from Jan's hands just as she was about to put it down the garbage disposal. "Food combinations you wouldn't imagine taste great together. Do you want some?" He displayed a big smile in her direction. "What's wrong, honey?"

She rolled her eyes as she tried to find the words. "When I saw Marjorie Saturday night at the party, she said there was going to be a big surprise today at work." Jan swallowed and raised her brows. "When she said it, I didn't think much of it. I was just so shocked to see her there. I thought she was," she cleared her throat, "kicked out of the company and the family."

"Hopefully it's not that she's coming back to work at Hedge. Do you think that's it?" Rob's expression reflected his wife's.

"I . . . I don't know. I don't know what to think. We weren't given any indication that things were going to change before we left work on Friday." Jan slowly shook her head. "My staff is going to be surprised and upset if she comes back. They may even quit."

Before exiting the elevator on the fourth floor at the Troy Professional Center, Jan stood tall, tugged at the hem of her suit jacket, and took a deep breath. Hedge Corporation, a marketing firm where she was a director, encompassed the entire fourth floor of one of the twin towers. The structures rose up over the surrounding landscape and neighboring office complexes on Big Beaver Road. She loved the luxurious professional complex, feeling right at home. She was thriving at her career having been at the corporation for eight years, right out of college.

"Good morning, Jan," Tracey met her with an arm full of files. "Did you have a good weekend? Yes, me too. Great. Now that we're over the pleasantries we need to—"

"Notify all of my team that we're having an emergency meeting right now in the conference room." Jan removed the stack of papers from her administrative assistant's arms.

"Wow, Jan, you look terrible. We can go through the pleasantries if you want to. Is everything okay?" Tracey tried to smile.

"I'm afraid we're about to find out. I'll set these in my office while you round-up the others," Jan instructed as she took long, swift steps to her office. As she went down the hallway nicknamed executive row, Jan could see the light coming out from under Mr. Albright's office door. She hesitantly stood still with her hand on her office door contemplating to go in to talk with him. It's probably too late anyway, she thought. She knew that if Marjorie said something was going to happen, then forces were already in motion and there's nothing anybody can do about it now.

"Jan, you made it in today too," Bob said as he approached her office. "That party Saturday night was so great, I thought the entire office would be nursing hangovers for a week." His cheerfulness stopped abruptly. "What's going on?"

"You didn't see her at the party?"

"Who? Who are you talking about?"

"Marjorie," Jan whispered.

"Nooo. She was at the party? You saw her? What happened?"

"She said there's going to be a surprise today at work."

"Oh no." Bob covered his face with his hands, then brought them down and looked closely at Jan. "I thought she was fired. Kicked out of the office and the family business," he said softly looking up then down the hallway.

"I did too. Maybe something changed. We're about to find out. I asked Tracey to get everyone into the conference room."

"I'll see you in there."

Jan set her things down, then closed her eyes fearing the worst. *If she's back, then what happens to me?* After a deep breath, she picked up her notebook and pen and headed down the hall to meet with her team.

The staff shifted and fidgeted in their chairs around the long, oval-shaped conference table. Jan paced up and down between the seated staff and wall furthest from the door.

"Maybe I should be closer to door?" She mumbled.

"What?" Tim asked.

"Oh, nothing." She forced a weak laugh.

"Why are you so nervous?" Tracey asked.

"Who? Me, nervous?" Jan threw her hand at her. "No. I'm not nervous. I'm sure Mr. Albright only has good news to tell us. He is after all the president and will probably—"

"I don't neeed you to announce my return. I will do it myself."

The staff's mouths dropped open and gasp of horror were heard throughout the room.

"They need their leader to let them know nothing is going to change," Mr. Albright argued.

"Weeell, maybe things will change. We'll have to wait and see won't we." Marjorie stepped into the conference room. "I'm baaack," she said with a smile.

Mr. Albright stood in the doorway. "Everyone, I want you to know that—"

Marjorie slammed the door shut and started wringing her hands as she walked around the table looking out into space. "Sooo, let's see now. Where were we? I believe I was the director and Jaaan was the manager. During my sabbatical it seems she did a great job, so Mr. Albright told me. Company revenues are up. Employee satisfaction is up. Everything is up, up, up." She stood still and looked at Jan. "And, it's going to stay up, because Jan will continue to be the director."

Sighs of relief were heard and mumblings of "oh thank God."

Marjorie smiled before continuing. "Nooow this may come as a bit of a shock to some of you, but Mr. Albright is retiring at the end of this year."

Jan gasped and grabbed the nearest chair for support. The others looked at her with sympathetic faces. "Who will replace him?" She fearfully asked.

Marjorie smiled wide. "I'll be replacing Mr. Albright as president. Yours truly."

Feeling weak, Jan slid down into a chair.

"We'll be spending lots of time together, too, as Mr. Albright says, keep everything up." Marjorie walked over to the door. "Now I'll get out of your way, so you can continue your staff meeting." She paused with her back to the room. "Oh, and Jaaan, I have a smidge of a to do list for you. I'll just email it to you." She left closing the door behind her.

"Are you going to be okay?" Bob asked looking at Jan.

Jan stared at the wall across the room. "I'm not sure."

"Jan, pssst," Tracey tried signaling her boss.

Jan turned a dazed face to her.

"The staff? What do you want them to do?"

Everyone was looking at her waiting for her to say something.

Jan looked around the room at all the worried faces.

"Oh yeah, the staff." She took in a breath and stood up. "Okay, so that's the surprise news. Unexpected, surprise news," Jan's voice trailed off. She drew in her lips for a moment. "Let's continue on just as we were doing." She shrugged with her arms out, shaking her head.

The serious look on the employees faces as they left the room quietly indicated to Jan that she needed to give them more answers.

"Jan?"

"Yes, Tracey."

"Regardless of whatever happens from here on out, I just want you to know that I appreciate you giving me the chance to be your administrative assistant after the other girl was promoted."

"There was no doubt in my mind that you were the right person for me," Jan said. "And, I'm going to do everything I can to make sure we are all okay and secure with our jobs." She turned her attention when she saw Bob walking toward her as Tracey left the room.

"It was bad enough when she was director, firing people at will. What's going to become of this company now with Marjorie as president?" Bob asked as he joined Jan walking out of the conference room.

"I have no idea what to expect from her this time." She stopped in the hallway to look at her co-worker and friend. "I'm going to see Mr. Albright to get more answers. I'll let you know what I find out."

Bob turned down the aisle of office cubicles and Jan proceeded to executive row.

She paused outside his office before entering to organize her thoughts. "Mr. Albright, I was wondering if we could talk for a moment?"

"Jan, it's great to see you," he said as he pointed to the left. His mouth moved. *She's next door.*

Jan nodded. "Sir, I just wanted to say what a privilege it's been to work with you. I've learned," Jan watched his curious behavior, "so much from you."

Mr. Albright typed away on his phone, then set it down. "Oh, believe me, Jan, the pleasure has been all mine. You are a brilliant, creative, person and you'll continue to do well in your field."

Jan's phone notified her that she had a message. After a few seconds she replied to it.

"Thank you, I appreciate those words. Well, back to work."

With her chin resting in the palm of one hand, Jan drummed her fingers on the table with the other, looking around as she waited in the restaurant. She stood up when she saw Mr. Albright arrive.

"Please, Jan, sit down," he said walking over to the booth.

A waiter came over to them. "May I get you something to drink? And, maybe some appetizers to start? I can tell you about our lunch specials if you would like?"

"I'll have water," Jan replied.

"I'll have a double Cognac, neat."

Jan widened her eyes and her hands slipped off the table as she leaned back in her seat.

"I'm done with the company anyway. What'da they gonna do to me if I show up with a little alcohol on my breath? Fire me?" Mr. Albright laughed. "Don't answer that." He pointed a finger at Jan while holding his drink.

She laughed and empathetically smiled.

"I'm ready to retire, but I didn't want it to be this way. I wanted it to be on my terms." He waved his drink through the air. "Oh, well."

"Mr. Albright, what happened? Why did she come back? Who let her—" Jan looked down at the floor, shaking her head. "I'm sorry. I just have so may questions. I need to explain something to my staff. I think they're updating their resumes as we speak." She looked gravely at him.

Mr. Albright nodded, then let out a long sigh as he sat back in the cushioned bench. "I'm in the same boat as you, Jan. I just got my notice at the party as well from her uncle that owns Hedge." He took a sip of his drink. "I left after that. There wasn't going to be a good time for me that night."

The waiter returned. "Are you ready to order?"

"I'm not hungry, thank you," Jan solemnly replied.

"I've already got my lunch," he said raising his glass.

The waiter turned and started to walk away.

"On second thought. I'll have desert. Bring me another one of these."

"Very good, sir."

"I'm going to miss working with you, Mr. Albright. You are the brains of the company. You raised it from fledgling to the multimillion-dollar corporation it is today."

"Thank you. It's good to know someone understands the blood, sweat, and tears I put into Hedge."

"Are you going to be okay?"

"Yeah, sure. Leaving on a sour note. But once I put my boat in the drink, I'll probably forget all about that place and think why didn't I leave sooner."

Jan smiled. "Is there anything I can ensure continues after your retirement? Your legacy?"

"There is. Hedge is the number three marketing company in Michigan." He sat back and looked off. "My goal was to take it to first place." He turned back to Jan. "We were on track to do that until the economy plunged early this year." He solemnly nodded. "So close." He smiled and looked Jan in the eyes. "But it can still be done. The same hits we took, well so did all the other companies. With the aggressive approach you've taken, you can make Hedge number one in marketing in a few years tops."

"Consider it done." Jan sighed and looked at her watch. "Well, I should be getting back. Will you promise me you'll take a cab home?"

"I will. I promise." He stood up to hug Jan before she

left.

I hope I can deliver on Mr. Albright's vision for the company, Jan thought as she walked to her car. With Marjorie back and Harold's girlfriend in the picture, the stakes have never been higher.

14 WORK, WORK, WORK

"Why is your laptop on the table? I thought we agreed we wouldn't bring our work to dinner." Rob complained as he walked into the kitchen.

"I know. I know, Rob." Jan looked at him with pleading eyes. "But Marjorie came back today. And, she's making a lot of unreasonable demands."

"Well, okay." He sighed deeply. "Then I'll bring my paperwork to the table too. If that's okay with you?"

Her eyes opened wide and she sat back in her chair. "Yes." She nodded quickly. "Yes. Of course."

"Just this one time though. Right?"

"Yes, absolutely." Jan smiled. "One time. Promise," she said loudly as her husband walked back to the mudroom to get his briefcase.

He took another breath as he stepped back to the island, withdrew a stack of papers, and slapped them down on the surface.

Jan jumped, then eyed the stack of documents.

Leaning on the island, Rob looked down at his work. He started to spread the papers out across the granite top.

Jan moved her chair over slightly along with her laptop to make more room for him and returned to typing furiously, all the while looking at the screen, trying to ignore her husband's actions.

"Remember when we talked about replacing my bookkeeper a couple of weeks ago? And, you said you could help me manage my company? Can you help me with this too?" Propping himself up with one hand on the island and one on his hip, he looked at Jan with desperate eyes.

Jan stopped working and slowly sat back, stunned by her husband's request. "Rob, of course I can help. I think." Jan pursed her lips with a curious expression.

"You can?"

"Yes, I think," she said with a cautionary tone. "It depends on the issue." Jan wanted to make this work with her husband. But now was about as bad of a time as it could get given her situation at Hedge. Jan had always thought about how nice it would be to work with her husband at the same company. She saw other couples coming into Hedge together and it seemed very supportive to be able to share discussions about the boss, new ideas, projects, and problem solving together. She knew the possibilities of it ever happening were slim to none because they worked in such different worlds. She had a career in marketing climbing the corporate ladder in a professional office environment. And, her husband's company was commercial construction and he worked mostly out on the work sites. Although Nichols Construction Company maintained a small office, it was not the environment she pictured herself in.

"Where do we start?" Jan was eager to help her husband's company and be a part of his team for a change. But she knew she still had to address Marjorie's demands before nine o'clock tomorrow morning. No matter, that wasn't what interested her most right now.

"Thank you." Rob put his hand around Jan's neck and leaned in for a kiss. "Can we start with putting the company finances in the computer and," Rob pressed his lips together as he sighed, "automate everything."

Jan was momentarily catatonic. *He's asking you for help, with his company. Don't make fun of him or question his reasons for not being automated already.*

"Yes, we'll start with a spreadsheet and if we need to, then we'll change to a database later on down the road. Show me one of your forms so I can set up the column headings." Jan's phone lit up and she leaned over to look at it. "Oh, that's Christie. This shouldn't take long. She's probably calling about lunch tomorrow.

"Yes, I still have that fluted, blue glass bowl." Jan smiled at Rob as she listened to her friend. "Okay, sure. Rob and I are in for the night. Come on over."

She set her phone down. "Well, you heard that right. Christie and Manny will be over in a few minutes to pick up a serving dish that she wants to use for a family party next weekend."

"Fine, but I hope they won't stay long because we've got a lot to do." He shuffled through the papers. "Here, this form is a good example."

"Hmm, okay, not bad. About thirty-two different fields."

He turned the form over.

"Huh, more fields." Jan turned to look up at Rob as he leaned over her shoulder propping himself up by his arms on the island.

"No problem. Spreadsheets are dynamic. We can do this." Jan studied the multi-sheet carbonless form. "Why does it say 'DBA' after your company name?"

"We're registered with the county, Doing Business As. I thought you would have known that."

"I do. But it surprises me. Nichols Construction Company isn't incorporated?" Jan asked fearfully.

"No, I just never got around to it," Rob said walking away into the pantry and coming back with a box of crackers. "What are we having for dinner?"

"Okay, not to worry, but we need to get the company

incorporated." Jan tapped her fingers on the granite while supporting her chin with her other hand mulling over the details on the paper. "Can you get the Colby cheese out of the fridge and make a plate for us to snack on?"

"So, I'm making dinner tonight?" Rob teased, but gladly set out the food.

"Do you need all of these fields? Could some of them go away?"

"Hmm," Rob chewed his food as he looked over Jan's shoulder.

She turned to face him.

"What?" He said after swallowing.

"You were chewing in my ear."

"I thought you liked that," he said teasingly with a smile.

Jan smirked and shook her head.

"I don't need—"

"Hold up," she said getting up to dig through her work portfolio. She pulled out a red, felt-tipped pen and sat back down. "Okay, go ahead."

"This one. This one." Rob pointed. "Hmmm, if we remove some and I need them later, can we bring them back?"

"Sure. That's the nice thing about automation."

"Okay, then, you can remove those two also."

Jan waited, hoping for more. "That's it?"

"Thaaat's pretty much it," Rob said picking up the form, looking it over. "Commercial construction is very complex," he said sternly and handed it back to Jan.

"I know. I was just hoping to simplify a little more." She smiled at him. "But this is a great start," she said pulling her laptop over and starting to type again. "There." She called Rob over. "See how I entered the field titles into this spreadsheet across the top?"

"Yeah, but—"

"I'll also create a form that you can use and it will automatically store your data here. You'll be able to calculate some metrics and do a lot of other cool stuff with your data."

"Hmm." Rob nodded.

Jan could tell he wasn't getting the full grasp of what it meant to have all his information in one place. "I'll work on this a little more and show you an example." She continued pounding away on the keyboard.

The front doorbell rang and neither Jan nor Rob moved.

"Honey, can you get that?" She asked without stopping what she was working on.

"She's your friend."

Jan stopped, sat back, and looked at her husband.

The doorbell rang twice.

"Coming," she shouted in the direction of the door. She tilted her head at her husband. "They're our friends." Jan slid off her high chair. "But I'll get the door and you can set out more cheese and crackers."

"Great. I knew there was going to be some work in this for me."

Jan sprinted to the front door and peeked out the side light before opening the large, heavy wood entry.

"Thank you so much, Jan, for letting me borrow your serving dish."

"No problem. I'm not using it." She put her finger on her cheek and looked up. "In fact, I'm not sure I ever have." She laughed. Holding the door open, she stepped back and held her arm out. "Come on in. Rob and I were just in the kitchen going over some paperwork."

"Are you sure we're not interrupting your dinner or something," Manny said as he followed behind his wife and Jan.

"Not at all. As a matter of fact, you may be able to help us."

"I assume everyone's drinking," Rob said as he brought out four longnecks.

"I don't want to be too much of a bother," Christie

cringed, "but do you have wine?"

"Yes, we do. Or, as we like to say—"

"Rob, don't say it," Jan interrupted.

"We have wine for the whiners."

"Oh please, I can't believe he just said that." Jan put her head in her hands.

"No problem for me, as long as I get what I want. *Wine*," Christie squealed.

Rob brought over a stemmed glass half filled with Cabernet Sauvignon.

"So, Jan you said at the door that there's something we can help you guys with?" Manny looked first at Jan, then at Rob.

Rob took a deep breath and crossed his arms still holding his bottle of beer. His mouth pressed and he leaned against the counter away from everyone else sitting at the island.

Jan saw that he was distancing himself, uncomfortable with the subject. She knew it had to be addressed and turned to face Manny. "How quickly, effortlessly, and low cost, can we turn Nichols Construction Company into a Limited Liability Corporation?" Jan asked.

"NCC's not an LLC? Wow, I would have thought it was," Manny commented with his eyes wide in disbelief.

Rob shifted his weight to his other foot and tightened his crossed arms.

"So, what is the company right now? A partnership?" Christie asked sitting at the other end of the island with her legs crossed leaning forward and clutching her glass.

"DBA." Rob replied dryly.

Jan could tell that all this talk about incorporating was offensive to his ability to run his business. And, this talk versus getting his books automated was frustrating him even further.

"I just never got around to incorporating my company. I was too busy running it." He sighed.

No one said anything for an awkward moment.

"Okay, well, I suggest you get your ass incorporated as quickly as possible before something happens and you lose everything. Including your home, truck, yup pretty much everything." Manny said firmly while nodding his head directing it at Rob. He drank from his beer and Christie took a sip of her wine waiting for Rob, or Jan, to say something.

"Can you help us?" Jan asked. "We'll pay for your services of course."

Christie and Manny looked at Rob.

He was staring down at the floor with his arms still crossed.

"Rob, are you okay with them helping us? They're our friends. So, if there's any attorneys we can trust, it's them," Jan asked her husband.

"Whoa, nobody said anything about trust," Manny laughed. "Just kidding, man. Christie and I can get the job done quick. We can always change things as needed. But whether it's us or some other attorneys, you really need to incorporate—now."

"What do I need to do?" Rob asked, then took a swig of beer.

"Can you come to my office tomorrow morning?" Manny asked. "I'll ask you a few questions like who's CEO, and other positions, if there's a board who's on it." Manny waved his hand in the air. "You know, stuff like that. It'll be easy."

Rob looked at Jan. "I'll be there," he said nodding his head.

Jan sighed a deep breath of relief as she smiled back at her husband. "Oh, before I forget here's the dish." She picked up a box from the counter and handed it to Christie.

"Hmm, I was expecting just a dish. But this nice, sturdy box with all the bubble wrap will certainly hold some food." She tugged at the plastic. "Is the dish even in there?" She teased.

"Won't you be surprised on Saturday when it comes time to serve dinner," Jan teased. "That reminds me, since you're our attorneys now you should be invited to the Nichols Company Christmas party this Saturday. If you can take a break from your family party, come join us for drinks at least."

"We'll try," Christie said as she and Manny started back for the door. "But no promises."

"That's all we can ask for on such short notice," Jan said appreciating the gesture.

"Oh, I can't get used to this cold weather again," Manny moaned as they stepped outside.

"Better try. I read that this December is supposed to have some record low temperatures," Jan warned.

"Thanks again, you two. I'll see you at your office tomorrow around nine o'clock," Rob said as he waved then closed the front door.

"Are you okay?" Jan asked when they were alone. She walked up to him and placed her hands on his chest, looking up at him.

"Yeah, of course. I probably should have incorporated years ago. But well, I heard it cost a lot of money."

"It might be several thousand dollars."

"Several thousand dollars?" Rob raised his voice as he threw his hands in the air. "I should be an attorney and forget this construction business."

"It's not like that, Rob. They don't pocket the money." She took his hand and led him back to the kitchen. "They have overhead costs to pay. Just like you do."

"Still, that's a lot of money for some paper."

"Paper that's going to protect your ass," Jan said as she shook her finger at him.

"Well, regardless. It's back to work for us right now," Rob said as he and Jan sat back down at the island.

"Why don't we take a look at the finances. There's something I wanted to show you," Jan said opening up her laptop, moving her mouse around, then clicked open the file. "See this. At first glance of the company books it looks like the money is only dribbling in." She turned to him. "I didn't realize how much my money contributes to our household budget. I'm not sure what we'd do without my paycheck." Jan boasted as she used both hands to push her hair back gathering it all into one hand and letting it fall gracefully on her shoulders. Her chest rose and fell with a deep breath as she looked confidently at her husband.

Rob looked astonished. "Nichols Construction Company is a profitable and successful company. I know we've got to be making a good amount of money. When I make these deals with my customers, I add a sizeable amount of overhead for contingencies," he snarled back at her.

"Well, where is it? Because, this isn't getting us into the billionaires club."

"That's what I'm trying to tell you," Rob said slapping his hand on the island. "I don't know where it is. I don't know what the office manager did with our finances before she left."

Jan's expression changed from curiosity to concern. "Do you think she was funneling the money out of the company? Possibly even out of the country?"

"Glenda?" Rob wrinkled his forehead. "Naaah."

"I've been studying the books for two weeks now. And, I haven't been able to find where all the profit is going." She leaned over and squeezed his hand. "Honey, I think you need to consider the possibility that your bookkeeper was stealing from you."

His chest heaved with a deep breath. "But how?. And how am I going to explain this to my dad and brothers?"

"We'll figure something out. I need to finish analyzing the numbers before we say anything to anybody."

Jan could sense the stress her husband was feeling with all the evening's business issues thrown at him. Wanting to change the subject, she set the company paper next to her laptop and started to enter the field titles into the automated form. She paused and laid her hands in her lap. "You know what? I like this. Me and you, working together." She smiled at her husband.

"I do too. But I feel like this is going to be too much work for you to keep up with and do your own job at Hedge."

Jan stared wide-eyed at him. "How is the search for a new bookkeeper going? Do you have any leads yet?"

"A few people told me they have a cousin or a brother or some relative that could do the job. But when I ask for their credentials they never come through." He held his hand up in the air. "If this is too much work for you, then maybe I should consider calling a temp company."

Jan huffed and turned back to her computer to proceed with the spreadsheet. "A temp isn't the answer."

"I know a temp is not what you want, but how else am I going to find somebody?"

Jan's shoulders dropped and she looked at her husband. "This actually is what I want." She held her hands open. "I really enjoy managing Nichols Construction Company. But I don't feel like I can quit Hedge Corporation just yet. Until I can figure out just how profitable your company is, we need my paycheck." Jan picked up the laptop in one hand and her beer in the other and walked into the great room. Getting comfortable on the couch and her feet up on the coffee table, she proceeded to work.

"I'm surprised you would even consider leaving Hedge." Rob set his beer down, grabbed the remote, and turned the TV to the Detroit basketball game. He sat back with his feet up on the table, and laid his head on the back of the sofa.

"I wasn't going to until Marjorie came back," Jan talked while focusing on the work she was doing. "Now, it's painful to think of going into the office. It feels like it's sucking the life out of me. I'm overworked. The staff is scared for their jobs." She shook her head while keeping her eyes on the laptop display. "Oops. Backspace, backspace. There. And, you know what else, Rob? My friends don't even understand me anymore. You know what I mean? Rob?" She looked over at her husband.

With his head comfortably nestled on the back of the sofa, Rob's snoring was getting louder.

"Great." Jan's chest heaved with a deep breath. "Now that I've finished his work, I can get back to mine. But first I need to tuck my husband into bed."

Jan went back downstairs after tossing and turning for over half an hour. She grabbed a bottle of water from the kitchen pantry and went to sit on the couch. Staring out into the dimly light room, her anxiousness about not sleeping just made it worse. She fished between the cushions and withdrew the book. Maybe reading will help me relax and fall asleep, she thought.

He moved his arm around her and pulled her close.

Jan slid down on the couch making herself comfortable and continued reading.

"We shouldn't be together," she moaned. But she knew their chemistry was too powerful to keep them apart.

Jan looked over at her phone and sighed. She placed the open book face down on the cushion beside her. "Hello?" She paused from reading but not taking her eyes off the book.

"Hello? What's the matter? Isn't your caller ID working?"

"Oh, Monica. I was just busy," she squinted as she continued with her version of an explanation, "working on Rob's books. Why are you calling so late?"

"Okay again, it's not Rob's books. It's the family's company's books. And, oh by the way, Christie called me and she wants to switch girls' lunch to dinner tomorrow night at her place. Can you make it?"

"Yeah, sure. But she was just here tonight. Why didn't she mention it then?" Jan said combining it with a yawn as she stretched.

"You just yawned in my ear. I don't know. Why don' you ask her tomorrow night yourself?"

"Sorry," she said with another yawn.

"Okay, I'm going to hang up now and you need to go to bed," Monica advised.

Jan locked her phone and set it down beside her. "I need to go to bed? You need to go to bed," she muttered. Picking the book up she smoothed the wrinkled page and continued reading.

"I have to have you now and forever." He kissed her passionately and . . .

15 INTERVENTION

"Do you believe it? Only sixteen more days until Christmas. I still have so much to do and I don't know how I'm going to get it all done." Jan glanced at her husband before taking a sip of her coffee. She turned back to her laptop to make some more changes on her presentation for her nine o'clock meeting.

"What is it that you have to do yet? Aren't you done shopping?" Her husband looked at her with furrowed brows.

"Yes. No. I mean there's more to it than shopping. There's wrapping, decorating, baking, sending out greetings." Jan threw her hands in the air. "The list goes on."

"Denise can probably help you with all of that," Rob said, then he cringed.

Jan turned an icy stare at him as she started to pack up to leave for the office.

"Have a nice lunch with you friends today." Rob kissed his wife on the cheek as she turned to go out the door.

"Oh, I forgot to tell you. We're not having lunch because we're meeting at Christie's after work." Jan flashed an '*oops*' look at her husband. "So, I guess you'll be on your own for dinner tonight."

"Okay. Have fun and I'll see you when you get home after your girls' night. Don't stay out too late." He flashed a smile at her before closing the door.

"Uh huh." Jan mumbled to herself as she sat down in her car. "He's planning to go to Ed and Denise's for dinner. And, from the drool already showing up on his lips, I would say he's looking forward to that more than if he were coming home to me."

More work and longer days. They don't teach you that in college, Jan pondered leaning back in her executive chair. She looked at her phone for the time. Dropping it in her purse she felt she gave enough of herself to Hedge for the day. She cautiously left her office and made her way to the elevator, keeping a lookout for Marjorie the entire time. She went to meet Gina in the other tower hoping they could ride together to Christie's house.

"Michael, what's wrong? Where's Gina?" Jan asked when she entered the Michael Goodson & Associates Investment Company office. Prior to Marjorie's return, Jan would occasionally stop by her friend's office for a quick chat. But when Gina's desk was deserted, Jan became concerned.

"I, uh," he stammered as he avoided eye contact. "Jan, she left and . . ." Michael Goodson was the owner and CEO of his own financial company. A legendary playboy until he and Gina started dating. Now he was off the market.

"She left?" Jan asked confused by his emotional behavior. "She didn't leave you, did she?"

Michael covered his eyes with one hand and propped his elbow with the other.

Jan gently touched his arm. "Michael, I'm so sorry. I'll leave you alone. But when I see Gina I'll let her know how much you're hurting."

Michael nodded while still covering his eyes.

During the ride down in the elevator Jan contemplated how she would tell Gina how badly Michael is heartbroken. How she could do this to him when he's all she ever wanted since she met him. And, now she's dumping him? Jan thought about how peculiar this situation was. She considered that there could be something wrong with him that she wasn't aware of. Cringing at the idea, she walked out of the elevator feeling more confused than ever. While slipping on her red leather gloves and tightening her scarf around her neck, she pondered, why wouldn't Gina have said something to me or the others? Even though, none of us are very good at keeping secrets. Jan pulled the car door closed.

As she drove down M-53 to the small town of Romeo. Jan's mind continued to race with questions. Something doesn't seem right, she thought and she wondered why her friend would exclude her from something this important. Maybe I should just turn around and go home. I'm getting the sneaky suspicion that this isn't about Gina at all. Jan parked her car close to Christie's house. The only available space on either side of the street leading to the cul-de-sac. Jan sat in her car and watched the front door. Fine, she thought, let's get whatever is going to happen over with.

Jan stood outside the front door ready to knock when she heard the voices from inside. Laughter and lots of chatting going on and some of them sounded familiar. But it was obvious that there was more than just Christie, Gina, and Monica in the house. Why were there so many here tonight? She looked back at the street and reviewed the cars. That's Denise's, I think. And, that one belongs to . . . *my mom!*

Rather than announce herself Jan slipped inside quietly. Quickly removing her coat, she placed it on a chair near the foyer table with her handbag. From a corner view she watched the women mingle in the family room. Who are all these other women anyway, she wondered?

Christie's powder room was down the opposite hallway. She snuck over and walked toward the group of women from that direction giving the impression she was here the entire time.

Gina was closest to the archway and Jan started with her. "Well, I hope you're happy," Jan lambasted. "Michael had me believing you left him."

"He did? He covered for me? Oh, he is such a great guy," Gina said affectionately.

"Well, you need to be nicer to him, because he's a great catch."

"Hah! I need to be nicer to him?" Gina pointed her finger at Jan. "You need to be nicer to your husband, Jan." She walked to the center of the room. "Hey everyone? Ladies, can I have your attention?"

After a few seconds of conversations wrapping up, the room was silent.

"Jan's here. Christie and Monica, can you help me?"

"Jan, this is an intervention," Christie said as she walked toward her. "We all believe that you need to be nicer to your husband. A kinder, more loving wife."

"Who doesn't always talk shit about him behind his back," Gina added.

"*Whaaat?*" Jan stood on the side with her mouth open not believing what she was hearing. "You are accusing me of being a bad wife?" She looked around the room at the other women.

"Not me. I'm just here for the drinks," Monica said as she sat coolly on the sofa holding a beverage. "Besides, I don't like your husband."

"Is that what this is about?" Denise interjected. "I thought this was going to be about a few women getting together to share stories and ideas. Kind of an entrepreneurial building session for each other. Why would you accuse Jan of something like that?" She looked at the two women with disappointment. "She's a saint. You don't know what it's like to live with Rob. I can tell you, he's not an easy guy to get along with."

Jan's felt her stomach unclench as she appreciated Denise sticking up for her. "Besides, I am nice to Rob," Jan defended herself. "Just last night I helped him with his company paperwork and made plans to go from DBA to LLC," Jan proudly spoke. "Hah, so how many women can help their husbands do that." She glared back at them.

"If you're so smart," Christie walked up to her face to face, "then why did you allow your husband to run his company as a DBA all this time instead of telling him to incorporate?"

Some of the women gasped and looked suspiciously at Jan. Groups started to whisper and point.

"I . . . I didn't know his company wasn't incorporated. He never said anything about his work. I just assumed," Jan said as she backed up to the wall as Christie continued to approach her.

Beth walked over to Christie and placed her hand firmly on her shoulder. "Christie, from one powerful woman to another, I strongly recommend that you call off this intervention nonsense."

"Yes, Beth," Christie softened her tone. "I probably shouldn't have invited you anyway since she's your daughter."

"You probably shouldn't have invited any of us since Rob is the one who needs intervening.

"Wait a minute," Denise walked over to them. "Rob's a little rough on the edges, but he's still a good man and husband to Jan." She turned to face her. "Right, Jan?"

"Well, the good man is keeping my daughter from being with her family on Christmas day," Beth said angrily.

"Oh, she'll be with her family all right. The Nichols family," Denise retorted.

"Ladies, ladies, do you realize what's going on here?" Monica shouted from her seat.

"Yes, this was a stupid idea," Beth said as she picked up her coat and walked to the door. "Christie, you're on my shit list until you apologize to my daughter." Slamming the door behind her as she left.

"I'm going home too. This was the most ridiculous excuse for a get together I've ever heard of," Denise added as she left the house.

The remaining women stared momentarily at Jan, Christie, and Gina, then started to have their own conversations again.

"Who are all these other people?" Jan asked Christie.

"These are members of my family's firm. My dad wanted me to start some sort of women's mentoring program. So, I thought I'd invite them over and kill two birds with one stone."

Jan sighed as she looked up to the ceiling.

"I wasn't a part of this by the way," Monica said as she joined them.

"Yes, you were," Gina countered. "You said you thought Jan talked badly about Rob."

"Yes, I said that. But I didn't say I didn't like it." Monica snickered.

"Okay, I get it," Jan said. "I talk too much about myself. I promise you, I'll never talk to any of you ever again."

"Jan, that's not what we meant," Christie turned an annoyed glare to her.

"I'll talk to her," Monica shoved the others away as she took Jan by the arm into the kitchen.

"Why did you just drag me in here?" Jan suspiciously eyed her friend.

"So, Nichols Construction Company is incorporating?" Monica gleefully asked.

"Yeees. Whyyy?"

"Tell you what, you help me and I'll help you." Monica directed her to sit down at the table as she sat across from her, leaning in.

"What do you man?" Concern ran across Jan's face as she briefly glanced at Monica while looking past her to signal for help.

"You help me get Rob to make Pete second in command and I'll help you get out of their family's Christmas plans. Although I'm going to be there too, so I don't know why you wouldn't want to be there. It would be fun." Monica winked with a devilish grin. She sat back and drummed her fingers on the table.

"How can you help though? What am I going to say? Uh, hey Rob, I'm sorry but I broke my foot and I can't go to your family's cottage for Christmas." Jan frowned while getting a beer out of the refrigerator for herself. "Because, that'll never work. He'd just carry me." Jan thought some more. "Rob, I'm sorry I can't be at your family cottage for Christmas, but I only have six months to live and I really want to be at Busha and Jaja's one last time for Christmas," Jan dramatically emphasized. She sighed as she hit the counter with the palm of her hand. "That won't work either. Why does he have to be so good at observing all the details all the time?"

"May I remind you that you had the guy believing you were working overtime at Hedge and going to the gym to workout. But instead you were really moonlighting at Michael's company?" Monica said with admiration.

Together they busted out laughing, cold sinister laughter.

"Seriously though, I want Pete to be Rob's equal or at the least second in command," Monica explained. She rested her chin on her hand and studied her friend's reaction to her request.

"Sure, okay, I guess. I have no idea how Rob's going to structure the corporation and he never asked me for my opinion."

"You need to talk to him before the paperwork is final. He knows how to provide the business, but you're the one who knows how to run the business."

"Monica, it's not my company. It's Rob's. And, no more would I want him telling me how to run my career, would he want me telling him how to structure his company."

"It's not Rob's, okay? Let's get that straight. Pete and Brian put in just as much time, if not more than Rob," she emphasized.

"Jan get over here. We're not done teaching you your lesson yet," Christie laughed as she signaled Jan.

"Well, it's obvious the alcohol is taking over. Are we sure this was supposed to be about me and not just an excuse to have a girl's party?" She looked at Monica cleverly.

"Any reason is a good reason for a drink. Join me?"

Jan followed her friend into the family room carrying her beer.

"Sit down on this chair, Jan," Christie instructed. "Then the junior assistants are going to take turns questioning you."

"Okay, I've had enough of this crap," Jan mumbled. She reached into her pocket and pulled out her phone. "Hello Marjorie. What can I help you with? But it's late."

Jan paused, then rolled her eyes. "Okay, yes I'll have it on your desk first thing tomorrow."

Jan frowned. "You heard that. I have to go."

"Oh no, not already," Christie protested. "Who are the junior assistants going to question?"

"Why don't you tell your boss where to go?" Monica complained.

Actually, I'd like to tell all of you where to go, Jan considered while smiling at her friends as she put on her coat and gloves. Throwing the scarf around her neck as she went out the door shaking her head as she walked to her car.

Entering her house from the garage, she gave the door a hard shove behind her creating a thunderous slam. Struggling with her coat, she stripped it off and threw it on the floor. *Who cares what they think? They have no idea what I'm going through, with my marriage, my career, and now, Jan's eyes teared up. I won't be going to Busha and Jaja's for Christmas.* The sting of her friends accusing her was excruciating. Shrieking, she picked up her coat and threw it onto the mudroom bench.

"Hon, is that you? You're home early."

She gritted her teeth. That was the last sound in the world she wanted to hear.

She took a deep breath to calm herself. "Yeah, with work tomorrow I thought I'd get home early and get some rest."

Rob walked into the kitchen where the lights were on.

She hoped he wouldn't see her tear stained face in the shadows where she stood. Quickly getting a tissue, she dabbed her nose and cheeks. "Boy, it's cold outside," she said as she walked calmly into the room.

"How about I help you warm up," he came over to her and wrapped his arms around her, placing his head on hers.

This feels so right, she thought. My husband's strong arms around me to protect me.

Scooore Deeetroit! That's the second hat trick this evening! What a hot streak this team is on, the television blared.

Rob ran back into the great room.

Pausing, Jan scowled as her arms dropped to her sides. She grabbed a bottle of water from the pantry and stomped up the stairs.

"Everything all right, hon?"

She looked back at her husband on the coach. "Yup, I'm just tired. Going to bed now."

"Okay, I'll be there soon," he replied not taking his eyes off of the TV. "Man, Detroit's hot tonight. What a game."

Jan's muscles tensed even more as she went into her bedroom and changed into pajamas. She scrubbed her face exceptionally hard and brushed her teeth vigorously.

As she pulled back the comforter and laid down, she pulled her pillow under her head.

So, I'm an abusive spouse, my best friend is blackmailing me, my parents have expectations that I can't meet, my boss is overloading me at work, and my husband is using me to manage his company. My life now? Yeeuup, sounds about right. Jan pressed her eyes closed as she punched her pillow, then flung her head into the down feathers.

16 POWER STRUGGLE

Only two days after this woman's been back, and already I'm going crazy, Jan sneered. Now I'm struggling again to set boundaries at the office, intervene when she creates scenes in front of the staff, and . . . *errr!* Raising a fist, she stomped into her closet and furiously pulled at the hangers one-by-one.

"A power suit isn't going to do it today," Jan said as she pushed one suit jacket after another in her spacious walk-in closet. "I need a suit of armor." Standing in her undies, she finally selected a charcoal gray tweed jacket with solid black ankle pants and matte black heels. She removed the jacket and pants from the racks and held them up to herself while looking at the full-length mirror.

"I think you look good just the way you are." Rob grinned. "I know you're making me feel powerless right now. You could have your way with me," he offered as he walked toward her. He slipped his arms around her from behind and held her tight, the sides of their faces touching as they looked into the mirror together.

"I wish I could." She held onto her husband's arms.

He kissed her hair, holding her tighter.

Jan started to melt in his arms. "Can you be my suit of

armor?" She whispered as she relaxed in his arms.

"I'll be anything you want me to be," he said softly removing the clothes from her hands and throwing them aside. "Nothing says 'I'm powerful' more than a woman who's satisfied," he whispered as he kissed her neck and shoulders.

Jan rolled off her husband and laid next to him on the closet floor breathing heavily. "I think you're right about the power thing," she said breathlessly.

Looking over at her husband, they laughed together.

"I think I'm getting my power back again," he said and leaned over, stroking her naked body.

"Oh, that sounds wonderful," she said sitting up and lifting herself off the floor. "But I'm going to be late for work now as it is." She walked over to her pile of clothes she intended to wear that day and gathered them together. She shook the wrinkles out before putting them on to wear.

Rob reluctantly let her go and sat down on the leather padded bench in the middle of the closet room to watch her.

"Don't you want to put on some underwear or something before sitting on that nice leather furniture? It has to last us a long time," she teased.

"I've taught you well,' he laughed.

Jan sighed. "I want to stay and have more fun with you. But you know how much pressure I'm under at work right now. I still can't believe she came back. And worse, Mr. Albright is retiring. Who's going to have my back?" She held her arms open and the stress returned to her face. "Oh, Rob, what am I going to do? This is my dream job with the perfect, or what I thought was the perfect company," her voice dropped.

"Keep talking. I'm listening." He smiled.

"Now you're just being silly." She met his smile with

one of her own. "Wow, that felt good to laugh. I feel like I haven't done that in days. Thanks, honey." She quickly kissed him on the lips and stepped away before he could take control of her again. After picking up her heels she headed down the stairs as he followed behind her. She stopped abruptly and turned around to face him. "By the way, why are you still here and not at work?"

He gave her a blank stare before answering. "I thought you could use some moral support, so I stayed behind for you today."

She gave him a suspicious look, then turned to continue down the stairs. "Liar."

"Okay, Pete and Brian are going to be at the work site this morning and since you've been helping me with the books, I figured I'd just take it easy for one day."

Jan gave him a wide-eyed nod, but still suspected some other reason. "I'm glad to hear you're finally thinking of yourself for a change." She stood on her tiptoes and gently kissed his lips. "I'll see you after work, okay?"

Jan peeked around the door into her office, feeling thankful that her boss wasn't waiting for her, she took a step inside.

"Good morning, Jaaan."

The hairs on the back of her neck stood up. "Shit! I can't even get to my desk," she slurred.

"I saw you park and get out of your car, so I thought I'd greet you at your office. I hope you don't mind?"

"So, we're watching the parking lot now too? That's intrusive." Jan pressed her eyes shut and shook her head. "I mean intuitive. I mean . . ."

Marjorie laughed. "That's okay. I know what you meaaan. But the truth is I was just admiring this beautiful morning sunshine out the window," she shrugged, "and then you showed up. No biggie."

"Oh, really? I have to say, Marjorie, you seem so

relaxed. Are you okay?"

Marjorie narrowed her eyes. "Why don't we get to work and we'll both feel better."

"Yes, of course."

"Jan, you don't have to be afraid of me. I don't blame you for what happened."

"No. I mean right. I mean I didn't have anything to do with your getting *fi-eeer, dischaaar* . . ." Jan gave Marjorie a helpless look and shook her head.

"I know that." Marjorie breathed. "Mr. Albright did what he thought he had to do. But now he's retiring so it doesn't matter, does it?"

Jan didn't have an answer for her boss and just stood there, staring at her.

"And, by the way, I was on a sabbatical." Marjorie paused. "This is good we talked. Cleared the air. So, we good?"

Jan was frozen.

"Jaaan?"

"Yes, yes, we're good. So good." She nodded. "I didn't get much sleep last night," Jan puffed through pursed lips, "delayed responses." She pointed her finger to her temple and made a circular motion.

"Uh huh," Marjorie displayed annoyance at her behavior. "Well, your admin assistant—"

"No, not Tracey. She didn't do anything wrong. Fire me instead." She pressed her eyes shut tightly and waited for it to happen.

Marjorie cleared her throat and crossed her arms. "Your admin assistant, Tracey has some files I wanted you to look at and prepare presentations for the clients." She stopped talking and glared at Jan.

"Oh." Jan slowly opened her eyes, then looked at the floor as she nodded. "Okay. I'll have them next week."

"Tomorrow."

"Tomorrow?" Jan panted. "Tomorrow. Yes. Okay."

Two o'clock and I'm only done with half of these projects, Jan lamented. I'll probably end up taking this crap home with me again tonight. That never happened when Mr. Albright was my boss. He was a reasonable man.

"Jan," Tracey poked her head in the door. "I've got some bad news. Marjorie dropped off more files."

"What? Is she crazy?" Jan threw her hands in the air. Why me? I've got more than enough work to do. Why can't Howard have some more responsibility." Jan jumped out of her chair. "I can't continue this way. I need to talk to her."

Tracey dodged out of her way but followed closely behind. "Jan, don't do anything you'll regret. I love having you for a boss. If you go, I'll go."

"I'm not going to regret this. I need to do this."

Jan pounded on the door jamb as she continued walking into Marjorie's office and up to her desk. "Marjorie, we need to talk."

"Yes, Jaaan." She set her pen down and folded her hands on her desk. "Is there a problem?"

"Marjorie, your piling too many projects on me. I'm overworked and I know that the other directors aren't getting enough work to do. They're standing around talking about their golf games."

"Are they as good as you at doing their jobs?"

"Uh, well, I don't know. Aren't they?"

"Why do you think they stand around talking about their golf games?"

"Because they're not that good?"

"You're the best, Jan. The work you do is incomparable to any other director."

"Oh, I didn't know that. I felt like I was being picked on."

"Picked out is more like it. Picked out as the best of the company."

Jan pressed her lips together. "Well, that's nice to hear. I feel like I've been working way to hard lately. Good to know my work is appreciated."

"So, will there be a problem getting those presentations done for tomorrow?"

"Well, I . . ."

"Tell you what. You have been working hard. Why don't you just finish that first set for tomorrow and the second set that I sent over in the afternoon can be done for next Monday. You can have over the weekend to work on them." Marjorie smiled.

"But"

"But what?"

"This weekend is my husband's company Christmas party and I need to be there."

"Well, what is that? A couple of hours at night? That shouldn't stop a bright, young person like yourself from completing your goal. Should it?"

"No, it shouldn't," Jan said through her teeth, wearing a smile. She left her boss's office stomping down the hall with her assistant following behind her.

"Jan, I'm so sorry you've got all this work piled on you. Is there anything, anything, that I can do to help?" Tracey looked at Jan as she speedily walked behind her to keep up as they dodged co-workers and office equipment.

"Thank you, Tracey. I appreciate the support," Jan glanced at her as she moved through the aisle. "I'll put together a list of graphics that you can find and if you can come up with some bullet points on some of the products that would be very helpful."

"You got it." Tracey smiled as she took a deep breath.

"But" Jan stopped and looked at her, "only work your core hours, okay?" She started walking again. "I don't want you wasting your life away like I am."

As they arrived at Jan's office, Tracey looked curiously at the stranger standing at her desk. "Can I help you?"

"That's okay, Tracey. I got this."

"Carrie, nice to see you again. But aren't you in enemy territory?" Jan teased.

"Yes, but that's not what I'm here about, Jan. Can we talk privately?"

"Of course. Come into my office." Jan stepped inside and closed the door after Carrie entered.

"Jan, I know your suspicious of my motives for seeing Harold. But I can assure you they're real. I didn't start dating him because I wanted his account." She sat back and laughed. "There's plenty of easier ways for me to get accounts other than dating someone," she said, then leaned forward and looked seriously at Jan, "or, even marrying someone."

Jan's jaw slackened and she rested back in her chair. "That's pretty serious. You and Harold have talked about marriage?"

"Yes, the subject comes up more and more we're together," Carrie said pulling at the edge of her skirt and crossing her legs.

"Harold is a wonderful man and I don't want to see him hurt," Jan warned.

"You should have thought of that before you let him go."

Jan took in a deep breath from the sting of her comment. "Yes." She nodded looking down. "I should have. You're right."

"Listen, Harold told me in no uncertain terms is he going to take his marketing account from you." She shrugged. "And, I'm okay with that. Like I said I'm not seeing him for that. I'm seeing him because *he's* what I want."

"I understand."

"So?" Carrie held her hands open and looked curiously at Jan. "Do we have your blessing?"

"My blessing?" Jan laughed slightly, then stood up and walked around the other side of her desk. "Yes, of course. You and Harold have my blessing. You're a lucky woman to get such a wonderful man. I know he'll be good to you."

"Well then, I better get out of here before the enemy holds me hostage," Carrie teased. "I'll see you around, Jan."

At home in her library, Jan took a drink of her coffee. She squirmed in her chair as she continued working on the presentations. "Okay, what product do we have next?" She set her work laptop on the desk, opened it, and clicked-on her company's presentation template. She reviewed the paperwork that was provided as part of the package. "Huh, no wonder they're looking for a new marketing firm. This doesn't do anything for the product." She observed how the fonts were blending in with the background making it hard to read. There were no interesting features about the product itself, just some glitzy pictures of models. "Everybody knows if you're going to use a picture then make it a puppy or a kitten. Well, we're going to fix all that and make you number one in your field." She started typing furiously, then paused to position the mouse in another text box, and started again.

"Jan, what are you doing? It's after eight already. Did you eat anything?" Rob came over and kissed his wife on the cheek.

"Rob, I can't stop right now. I have to have three more presentations done for tomorrow morning for Marjorie."

"You need to talk to her."

"I did. It didn't get me anywhere." She paused and looked up at him. "Don't tell me you brought home more Nichols Construction Company work for me to do?"

"I did."

"Rob, I can't help tonight. It'll be midnight by the time I get all this done."

"Don't worry about this. It can wait." He stood there smiling. "So, you've been hinting about taking some time off from work. Do you think you could take tomorrow afternoon off?"

Her face lit up. "Really? What did you have in mind?"

"You could help me with these forms?"

Jan sulked. "I'll see what I can do," she moaned.

"Thanks, hon. I'll bring you a sandwich."

She waited until he left the room. "A sandwich for my troubles. Great." She lowered her eyes to the monitor and pondered the next bulleted item to add. Looking back at the door, she wondered what sports teams were fighting about now. "Rob, the TV is awfully loud. Can you turn it down? It's difficult to concentrate," she shouted. He must be in the kitchen, she thought.

She left her desk and went to the great room where the TV was off. She followed the arguing to the kitchen and stood in the doorway. "What's going on?" She gave Rob and Pete a concerned look.

"I was telling Rob that the DEQ is willing to work out a deal with us. But he doesn't like it," Pete explained.

"I'll let my wife know what's going on, Pete, that's okay," Rob shot back.

"Rob," Jan huffed.

"It's too much money. There's got to be another way. Maybe we can make the DEQ pay for some of it." Rob added.

"Taxpayers' money for a commercial business? Probably not." Jan commented. "How much are we talking about?"

"More than a hundred K," Pete said.

"Wow." Jan sat down.

"We could ask the Daniels Corporation to kick in half of it or more. It's their center." Jan held her hands open. "What other options do we have?"

"Fines and fees. And, ultimately shut down the project." Pete grumbled.

"I'll talk to Mr. Daniels in the morning," Rob said.

"You better give him a call now. Give him a heads up so he can sleep on it and come in with the money tomorrow," Pete advised.

"Pete's right, Rob. This is too important and too urgent to let it go another minute much less another day."

Rob wrinkled his face. "Who's in charge here? Who's running this company anyway?"

Jan slipped off her chair to stand up. Her disbelief at her husband's reactions to her comments were frighteningly aggressive. "Rob, I'm not trying to run the company for you, but Pete is right. You should listen to him."

"You tell him, sis. But be careful." Pete started heading toward the door. "He's already got you working for free on the company books, what's next?"

"You're telling people about helping me?" Rob glared at her.

"No. Well, yes, but . . ."

"That was supposed to be between you and me."

"You never said that when we talked about it. How was I supposed to know you wanted it kept secret? With your office manager gone, who did people think was taking care of the bookkeeping?"

"Me. That's who. And that's all they need to know. It's nobody else's business how I run my company."

"Rob, it's not your company," Pete shouted back. "But you do what the hell you want. And, if Nichols Construction doesn't exist next week, I won't be surprised." He stormed out the door leading to the garage.

Jan sat down feeling momentarily light headed from the argument. "So, you're taking credit for my work?"

Rob turned and walked away from his wife running his hand through his hair, his other hand on his hip. He took a deep breath before turning back to look at her. "I'm not taking credit for your work. I'm just not telling anyone how the work is getting done." He stepped toward her and shrugged. "Nobody ever asked me. Not my brothers or my dad. And, I didn't see any harm in not volunteering the information. I screwed up. I'm sorry."

Jan listened to his explanation, sitting quietly on the

café stool, her expression unreadable.

"Please say something." He took another step toward her. "I love you and I didn't mean to hurt you." His words hung in the air.

"I see. You know I take my work seriously. I'm proud of everything I do and that includes managing the books for Nichols Construction Company. Are you taking me seriously? Or, are you using me for your own gain?"

He gently placed his hands on her shoulders. "You have no idea how serious I take you. How much I love you." Pulling her off her chair and close to him, he hesitantly met her lips.

"Will you be sharing this information with others now?" Jan's lips brushed his as she spoke and she pressed herself against him.

"I'll announce it at the party this weekend."

17 NCC CHRISTMAS PARTY

"Wow!" Rob's attention turned to his wife as she strutted down the stairs. Her hair in a French twist, wearing the black sequined gown, in three-inch heels with faux diamond studded black straps. "You look like a million bucks."

"Well, thank you, mister CEO slash owner of Nichols Construction Company." Jan gave her husband a suggestive look. "Incorporated."

Rob feigned surprise and placed his hand over his mouth as he offered his other hand to assist his wife. "Uh, But it didn't really cost you a million bucks, did it?" He gazed curiously at her while drawing her closer to him.

Jan tossed her head back and laughed. "Of course not, you silly. Just $999,999." She grinned and waited to see what his reaction would be.

He smiled and brushed her lips with a kiss. "Ok then, as long as it wasn't a million."

Jan leaned back slightly, trying to cool off the moment before it became too heated. But she had a hard time convincing herself it wasn't the right thing to do.

"How long would it take to completely redo this look all over again?" Rob asked as he continued trailing kisses down her chest.

"Oh, probably," Jan wanted to give into the feelings coming over her, "about eight hours or so," she said amused. "And, another $999,999."

"Hmm," Rob moaned as he slowed down. "Maybe we'll do this after the party. Make up some lame excuse and leave early."

"Sounds good, but it's your party." Jan was still laughing. "And our car is waiting."

"Tell me again why I'm having a company Christmas party?" Rob asked as he helped Jan drape the stole around her shoulders.

She held his arm as they walked outside to the limousine. "Is that Mr. Daniels?" Jan asked as she pointed to a dark sedan parked down the street. "You weren't going to go to the party with him and leave me home alone, were you?" She teased.

Rob paused before getting inside their car and stared at the other vehicle. "No. No, in fact, Mr. Daniels said he might be a little late tonight because he was stacked up with meetings all day."

"On Saturday? That's awful." Jan scrunched her face. "When does he make time for his family and friends?"

Rob took his eyes off the strange car and entered the limo. "Well, with the way Mr. Daniels mixes business with pleasure, it's hard to tell if he's working or playing anyway." Rob smiled and looked at Jan moving closer to her in the seat and taking her hand.

"Oh, I know all too well," Jan sighed.

"Well, I'm not sure who's in that other car. Maybe I should go check."

"No, Rob, please don't. Let's just go and have a nice time at *our* party. That car is parked in front of the neighbors so it's probably for them."

Rob and Jan looked around at the parking lot when

they arrived at the Wildwoods Banquet hall.

"Oh my gosh, there's a lot of people here already. We should have been in there by now to greet them." Jan grabbed her husband's arm. "I'm starting to feel a little nervous."

"You? What about me?"

"Okay, okay. We can do this." She smiled at him. "Deep breathes, one . . . two . . ."

They jumped suddenly at the pounding on the window.

"Get in here," Pete shouted through the glass. "Brian and I can't do this ourselves and it was your idea."

Jan and Rob looked at each other overcome with surprise, and after another deep breath exited the vehicle.

"Tall, smile, confident," Jan mumbled through her smile to her husband as they walked in together.

"Mr. and Mrs. Nichols, you look wonderful," the maître d said as he ushered them out of the lobby and into the coat room. "A few last minute instructions," he whispered. "At eight o'clock I'll announce it's time to sit for dinner. At nine-thirty I'll come get you to go on stage and make your big announcement. And, after the big announcement," he shrugged, "people can drink their asses off." With both his hands he gave them each a solid pat on their upper arms. "Sound good? Any questions?"

"Uh, no. I don't think so." Rob mumbled as he stood catatonic.

"Great, then it's showtime." He turned the two of them around to walk into the crowd as he went in the other direction.

"Wait. Where are you going?" Rob asked dreadfully.

"To check on the food." He vanished.

Jan and Rob stood there, facing each other, holding hands.

"I'm selling all the time. Why do I feel scared now?"

"We should greet our guest," she whispered.

They stepped into the vast room set with round tables covered in red linens and lined with chairs displaying bowties on the back. White tulle with miniature clear lights tucked inside streamed across the ceiling. Christmas décor draped the windows and a fifteen-foot tree towered near the stage. A large fieldstone fireplace midway down the wall between the lobby and the stage was the majestic focal point. The Wildwoods rustic charm felt comfortably warm, relaxing, and the guests appeared to be enjoying the ambiance.

"It's beautiful," Jan exclaimed.

"There you are. Finally," Brian said as he walked up to them. "Come on you need to meet the county commissioner. I saw in the paper the other day the county's thinking about building a new library after the community college took over the one they had."

Brian and Pete rushed him away leaving Jan by herself.

"How are you?"

Jan shrieked as she spun around. "Oh, Monica." She took several short breathes with her hands on her chest.

"Who did you think it was?"

"At the Hedge party she, my boss, . . . she. Never mind. It doesn't matter."

Monica rolled her eyes, then started to smile. "You're a nervous mess, aren't you? You thought this would be a great idea and look at the two of you. You're both a wreck."

"Does it show that badly?"

"Come on," Monica said as she pulled Jan by her arm toward the open bar. "We better get some drinks in you. By the way, where did you get that dress?"

"You will not believe it. Have you ever shopped at that little boutique outside of our favorite department store?"

"The one that's off limits to working class stiffs like you and me?"

"Yeah. Gary told me about this fabulous dress when I was getting myself all dolled-up last weekend for the Hedge party. So, I figured what the heck, I'll check it out. That doesn't cost anything, right? As I'm standing there, drooling, a man asked me if I wanted to try it on.

"You fell for the the ol' 'do you want to try it on' trick?" Monica snickered.

"You're laughing, but look at me." Jan sneered.

"You're right. Continue."

"It was magical. So now, here I am, gorgeous, for only six easy payments."

"Only six easy payments?"

"Only six." Jan grinned and nodded amusingly at her friend as she accepted the wine glass from the bartender.

"I'll make one of those payments if you let me wear it one time."

"Where are you going to wear it?" Jan shirked.

"In the bathroom right now to have sex with Pete." Monica voice was loud. "Come on, get real."

"Well, this dress—"

"I'm going to a medical convention in March and this would show everyone how successful I am," Monica accented her words as she ran a light touch of her finger down Jan's arms while raising and lowering her eyebrows.

"Okay, don't do that in front of everyone," Jan said smiling and looking around to see if anyone saw. "So, you'll make one of the payments to wear one time."

"Yes."

"How would you like to make six payments and wear it six times? Not that bad. Okay," Jan squeaked. "One payment. One wear. Deal." She stuck out her hand.

"Deal," Monica said suspiciously as she squinted at Jan. "I expect it to be dry cleaned and ready to go before March."

"Yeah, sure, whatever" Jan waved her hand and shrugged as her attention turned.

"Hi girls," Beth hugged her daughter then Monica. "You look absolutely stunning. I need to go shopping with you two again like we used to."

"Beth, you've taught us well," Monica said.

"Mom you look fabulous. Is somebody else doing your

hair? It's different."

"Hello ladies," Denise said as she walked up to them.

"Denise, you're a knockout," Monica complimented.

"Oh, thanks." Denise brushed her hair back. "I guess I'll have to get used to looking like this all the time now with all the success Nichols Construction Company is having." She quietly squealed.

"Yes, you will," Monica nodded.

"Where's Dad?" Jan asked her mother.

"He's talking to the township committee. Most of them are here tonight. So, that makes a quorum." Beth smiled with a shrug.

"It looks like the guys are standing off by themselves," Monica said to Jan. "Why don't we go check if there's anything we can do to help them?"

"I'll talk to you later, Mom." Jan followed her friend and looked back at her step mother-in-law. "Denise have a drink. You're too excited." She teased.

"What's the matter with you wall flowers? Are your dance cards full?" Monica said dryly.

Rob rolled his eyes as he huffed. "Does everything have to be a joke with you?"

"Yes, but that question wasn't necessary because you, the biggest joke of all, is here."

"Why don't you—"

"Rob, knock it off," Pete firmly directed his brother. "There's more important things to do than bicker with one another."

Pete's right," Brian added as he pointed at Rob. "Don't look now, but see that guy over there in the blue sport coat?"

Jan and Monica both turned their heads.

"I said don't look now," Brian exclaimed.

"Well, what did you expect? That's like saying don't think of the Statue of Liberty," Monica chided. "So, what are you thinking about now?"

"Again," Pete slowly patted the air indicating to calm

down, "let's not bicker."

"It looks like that guy might be a corporate spy here to steal customers, ideas, or who knows, could be worse." Rob grimaced.

"So, why don't you ask him to leave?" Jan questioned her husband.

"Gentlemen," Charles said as he and his wife approached the group. "Great party. For first-timers at this, you did pretty damn good. Do you have a minute? I want to introduce you to someone who could be a potential customer."

"Of course. But your daughter is the one who pulled this whole thing together," Rob said as he walked away from the others with his in-laws.

"I need a drink," Pete said as he placed his arm around Monica's waist and led her to the bar.

"Hey, isn't that the Mayor's daughter? I heard she goes to U of M." Brian stared, twisting his head as people moved around. "I'm gonna go introduce myself to her."

"And, then there was one." Jan's smile turned slanted. I'm the wife of the owner slash CEO of the company, she thought. This is a great company that— She pondered the ideas she had for the company and her eyes tapered in excitement. *And, I'm going to take this company far into the realms of a billion-dollar corporation.* She gasped placing her hand on her mouth. *I'm going to have a position in the company too.*

She swiftly strolled to the bar. Maneuvering herself through the crowd, she reached the end where the drink supplies were stationed. She grabbed a stack of cocktail napkins, jogged them, and started to walk away.

"Miss, if you spilled your drink, I can have someone assist to clean it up for you," the bartender offered.

"No, no. I didn't spill anything," Jan retorted as she continued walking away waving the napkins in the air. "I just want to start writing down some ideas."

She seated herself at an out of the way table where no

one else was seated yet. "Page 1," she wrote at the top right corner of the first napkin and circled it. Writing furiously, she filled the six-inch by six-inch square, set it face down to her left, and picked up the next one. "Two." She continued her writing. After the twenty-seventh cocktail napkin the stack measured one inch thick. Jan set her pen down, rubbed her hands as she looked around the ballroom for anyone she could recognize. "Wow, if these are all our customers or potential customers, then I'm in unfamiliar territory."

"What are you doing sitting there?" Monica asked as she walked over. "You're a hostess. A company representative. And, you're supposed to be working your ass off greeting people. You're supposed to be telling them how wonderful Nichols Construction Company is and what this company can do for them."

"In my defense, I am working my ass off," Jan retorted as she held up a filled napkin.

Monica grabbed it and placed it under her glass immediately soaking it from the drink's condensation. "Thanks."

"Hey, that's not what that's for. Those are my notes," she screeched as she lifted the drink and grabbed the napkin, carefully shaking it out to avoid smudging the ink.

"What is that? The next best-selling novel?" Monica sat down in the chair next to her and started reading. "Wow, this really is the next best-selling novel."

"It's not a novel. It's real."

Monica nodded. "I see that." She grimaced and tucked her chin. "Where am I in all this?"

Jan looked puzzled. "Oh. I didn't know you wanted to be a part of the Nichols company. You're a doctor. How will you fit in with the corporation?"

"I'm adaptable." Monica stood up. "You're not the only one who knows how to run a business."

"I didn't say that."

Monica turned searching the crowd, then walked away.

"Oh, by the way, I'm working harder than you are tonight."

"I didn't say you weren't." Jan's shoulders dropped as she sighed. "Oh well." She picked up her pen and grabbed the next blank napkin.

"The meal was wonderful," Jan said as she took her husband's arm and walked away from the table. "Rob? You didn't like it?"

"No, it was great, honey," he said as he watched a strange man talk to the invited guests.

Pete, Monica, and Brian came over to Rob.

"That clown is at it again." Pete pointed at the other person.

"I see that. Who the hell is he?" Rob muttered impatiently.

"He's been questioning the guests all night," Brian added. "They were telling me that he's asking things like how do we live, vacation, do for fun. That sounds strange to me."

"What the hell does it have to do with construction? Most customers want to know the materials, quality, engineering. Things like that." Pete said as the three brothers continued watching the unfamiliar guest.

"Well, this is the Nichols Construction Company family party. So, let's go find out just how he fits in," Rob said as he started walking toward the stranger.

"Great party," he said as the brothers approached. He excused himself from the other guest and stepped toward the brothers.

"Glad you're enjoying yourself. Misterrr?" Rob held his hand out to greet him.

"So, Nichols Construction Company throws a big ol' party right after getting a huge contract with Daniels and the City of Detroit. The man nodded. "Must be nice to have come into *sooo muuuch* money."

"Are you with the DEQ?" Pete stepped forward. "Because if you are, you should know that we have an agreement in place with them. We settled all are issues with them."

The suspicious visitor made a pathetic little laugh, turned away from them, and started to walk swiftly toward the exit.

"Wait." Rob ran after him. "Who are you? Why are you here?"

"Buddy, you'll find out soon enough. And, you're not going to like it." The stranger rapidly left the banquet hall and jumped into a waiting car as the others watched.

Jan and Rob exchanged concerned looks.

"Everyone, please take your seats. Our host of the evening, Rob Nichols, has a very important message he would like to share with you tonight," the maître d announced.

The five of them turned back to the ballroom.

The maître d ran through the crowded tables to meet up with them. "Not trying to sneak away, were you?" He teased. "Rob you're up, man. It's show time." He patted him on the back with a slight shove toward the stage.

Jan took her husband's hands and looked him in the eye. "Honey, you're going to be fine. Just say it from your heart."

Rob swallowed hard, then took the microphone from the maître d. He walked with a purposeful gate, nodding at friends and family, and waving to others seated further away before he reached the stage.

He jumped up onto the two foot elevated stage rather than using the side steps. Taking a deep breath, he looked over the audience. "Good evening, everyone. I hope you're having a great time tonight. You're all a part of my family. The Nichols Construction Company family."

The audience applauded.

From the back of the ballroom, Jan, Pete, Monica, and Brian watched, smiling.

DEBORAH KULISH

"What the hell," Pete said. "He's doing a pretty good job so far."

Jan grinned and nodded, clasping her hands in front of her chest, anxious for her husband's success.

"This is the time of year for celebrating with family and friends. And, I wanted you all to know that Nichols Construction Company has a new chief executive officer." He nodded. "That's me of course."

The audience laughed and lightly clapped.

Rob stepped around the stage and acknowledged their approval. "And . . ."

Monica nudged Pete's side. "Get ready, honey."

"Brian, my youngest brother, you probably all know him, is the new chief operating officer."

The audience applauded as Rob continued to talk.

"What the hell?" Monica turned coldly to Jan. "What did you do?"

"What? I didn't do anything. I didn't know who or how he was structuring his company," Jan said in defense.

"It's not *his* company," Brian stated. "And, I don't even want to be a part of this stupid company."

Pete turned and walked away, forcefully shoving the double glass doors as he walked out.

"Pete, wait." Monica ran after him.

"Oh great," Jan said as her head started to spin. "What the hell just happened?"

"Also," Rob continued. "I would like to introduce you to the person who made tonight's event possible." Rob shaded his eyes and peered into the crowd. "There she is. Jan, would you come up here, please?"

The faces all turned her way, waiting to see what she would do.

Jan looked back at the doors, then she looked at Brian.

"Well, what are you waiting for? His majesty is calling for you," Brian said as he swung his arm in the direction of the stage.

Jan walked gracefully, smiling, hiding the stress from

what she just witnessed.

"Everyone, this is my beautiful wife, Jan. Have a merry Christmas, happy holidays, and a great new year." Rob escorted his wife off the stage and they greeted the tables one by one.

Jan looked at her watch. It was after midnight and she felt the strain of the evening's event weighing on her. She spotted Monica at the table by herself nursing another drink. Walking over to her, she stopped in the middle of the dance floor to unbuckle the straps of her shoes and slipped them off. She wiggled her toes, lifted her dress off the floor, and tiptoed over carrying the heels with her. "Are you okay?"

"Did you know he was going to do this to Pete?"

"No, I had no idea. When we talked about it he made it sound—"

"Sound? What does that mean? Sound? You didn't make it clear to him that in no uncertain terms that Pete should be second in command? Or," Monica tried to hide her voice as it broke, "you're the boss, Rob. Take control of me," she said in a shrieky voice.

Jan sat quietly. Her friend was bitter that her boyfriend was disparaged by his own brother. And, she didn't complete the terms of their agreement. She felt that Monica deserved to be angry with her. "You're right, Monica. I didn't clarify the terms. I guess I'm not a very good friend and I let you down."

She studied her face. She had never saw her friend this upset about anything before. Her eyes were red from crying and blackened from the smeared makeup. She just looked, beat up, emotionally that is. Jan knew Monica was strong willed and when things didn't go her way, well, it wasn't good for anyone. "Do you know where Pete is?"

"Where do you think? He and Brian are at the pub. The other corporate headquarters," Monica said with a soft laugh.

"I like that." Jan was relieved to see her friend smile again. "How come you didn't go with them?"

"I can't tell you. You're the enemy." Monica sat back in her chair looking astonished.

"I'm not the enemy. I assure you." Jan leaned forward and opened her hands resting her arms on the table. "I see how hard Pete works. Rob's the one who doesn't. Or, he sees it but won't acknowledge it." Jan sat back in her chair. "Come to think of it, I don't know why Rob treats Pete that way. Jealous? Fear?" Jan shrugged and shook her head. "I don't know."

Monica stood up, threw back her drink, and stepped away. "Well then we're going to have to figure a way out of this mess that your husband created. Because otherwise, there's going to be two Nichols Construction Companies," she said decisively.

18 CHRISTMAS SHOPPING

Jan looked at the clock and moaned. She couldn't understand how she could be wide awake at 6:15 AM after only getting four hours of sleep. She looked over at her husband. He wasn't moving, other than his breathing. She thought about last night, how the Nichols Construction Company Christmas party didn't go as Rob had planned. How his brothers rejected his corporate structure for the family business. She was thankful that she had plans to go Christmas shopping with her friends today. She didn't want to even think about what it would be like alone with him all day listening to him mope about how they don't appreciate what he does for the company.

Slowly Jan slipped out of bed and tiptoed to the settee at the end. She picked up her robe and threw it on as she left the room and closed the door behind her.

At the breakfast nook table Jan opened her laptop and clicked on the file called Nichols Construction Company Books. After taking a sip of coffee, she reviewed another old form and entered the data in the spreadsheet. She noticed the totals were much more than what was written down by his former bookkeeper. Rob always said how he added-in some management reserve for each contract to handle unexpected issues. But he complained that his company made little profit due to overhead costs.

She continued to go through the forms, one after another, getting the bulk of the entries completed. Each time the results were the same. Jan knew she had to share this information with the others, but not today. After yesterday's event, she didn't feel up to it.

She stepped away from the table feeling good to be focused like a machine in the morning. These are my best hours, she thought.

She drank the last sip of her coffee, then stood up and stretched her arms over her head yawning as she looked out at the backyard through the patio doors.

"You're up early."

"Oh, you startled me," she said turning around to see her husband as he walked into the room. "I couldn't sleep so I thought I would get some work done on your forms."

Rob went to the counter and poured himself a cup of coffee. "How are the numbers looking? Is it worse than the bookkeeper said it was? She always gave me the impression that the company wasn't doing that well."

"Did you ever sit down together and go over the numbers with her?"

"I wanted to, but she always had an excuse why she couldn't. That always pissed me off, but what was I supposed to do?"

"You act like her boss. Tell her to show you the books."

"You weren't there with her. You don't understand how difficult it was to work with her. She was all motherly until you try to talk about business. It seemed like she was hiding something. But I thought it was some office supplies or food in her desk or something like that."

"I think she was hiding your money. Why did you hire her in the first place?"

"She was some friend of a friend of Dad's," Rob said as he shrugged.

"Huh, okay," Jan said as she stacked up the papers and closed her laptop. "Well, the numbers are looking pretty good so far. That's why I was curious why she always gave you a doom and gloom story. But I'm not completely done yet. So, we'll postpone the celebrating for now." She smiled at him as she maneuvered her way to sit on his lap as he tried to read the paper. "Don't we have some unfinished business from last night?" She nibbled at his ear.

"We do." Rob grinned. "But the bathrobe's not quite doing it for me the way that dress did."

They laughed as Jan moved to another chair. "How about if I make us some breakfast before I get ready to go Christmas shopping with my friends?"

"No, I forgot you were gonna be gone today," Rob moaned out the words leaning his head back. "I was hoping we could spend some time together researching a tech company to build the company website."

Dodged that bullet, she thought. "Oh honey, I'm sorry but I promised the girls a long time ago. It's kind of a tradition we have."

"Another tradition," Rob snickered.

Jan pressed her lips and tilted her head.

"I know. You go ahead and have fun. I'll ask Brian if he can—"

With a disapproving look, Jan shook her head.

"On second thought, I'll just putz around the house today. Maybe I'll go shopping too. You know, for a new tool or something." He smirked.

"That's my man. Making his own traditions," Jan said with a big grin.

The mall parking ramps were nearly full to capacity, but Jan managed to get her roadster squeezed in to a tight spot on the first level. She removed her phone from her purse as she strolled into the Troy Mall north entrance. *I just entered the department store on the first level. Where are you?* She sent the text message to all three of her friends.

Two alerts immediately sounded on Jan's phone letting her know that Christie and Gina replied. *Coffee shop center court.*

Uh oh, nothing from Monica, Jan thought, then a third tone sounded. *Just leaving the house. Don't start without me. Consider yourselves warned.* The text was followed by a winking face emoji.

"Whew! I was afraid last night might have ruined our friendship forever." Jan headed down the main aisle.

Gina saw Jan enter the shop and waved her over. "So how was the party last night?"

Jan made a face that stunned her friends.

"What happened?" Christie asked.

"I'm not sure I can talk about this until Monica gets here. She might get pissed if she thinks I'm talking about her behind her back."

"But I thought we always do that?" Gina quipped.

"This is different," Jan said as she leaned in to talk with her friends. "Monica wants Pete to be equal share in the company." She leaned back in her chair, slowly nodding her head, and waiting for her friends' favorable response.

"So, what's wrong with that?" Gina asked. "They're brothers. They all do the same amount of work for the family company."

Jan threw her hands in the air. "I'll be honest with you. I don't care. But Rob and Monica are at war about this. He's my husband. She's my best friend. What am I supposed to do?"

"*Sheee* is your best friend?" The two said unanimously.

"Oh, come on. You know what I mean."

"All right. We'll let this one go." Christie sneered.

"Let what go?" Monica looked the three of them over carefully. "What are you talking about? Is Jan getting the first word in on last night's event?"

"No. No. I'm not. I told them to wait for you."

"Well, that was stupid. I would have been blabbing my mouth off telling my side of the story."

"There's no side, Monica. I told you that last night."

She turned her nose up. "Huh, we'll see."

"Maybe we should change the subject," Gina suggested. "Because all I know is that you can deck every hall and light up the night, but the best holiday memories are made in the heart with friends and family."

"Yeah, it's the holidays. We're supposed to be merrily spending our money," Christie added.

"So, what is everyone getting their significant others for Christmas?" Jan asked.

"Cuff links," Gina said.

"Wallet," Christie shared.

"Gift cards," Monica said.

"Gift cards?" Christie gave her a funny look.

"What can I say. He likes his gift cards."

"How about you, Jan? You haven't said anything yet," Gina prodded.

"Coupons," she said proudly.

"And, I thought gift cards was a strange idea," Christie wrinkled her nose.

"What can I say. He likes his coupons."

They all laughed.

"I'm not talking about manufacturer coupons that you clip out of a magazine. I'm talking about some juicy coupons that I make myself. Trust me. He's going to love them."

"Wow, how juicy are they?" Gina asked.

"Oh, you know. A backrub. Five minutes of necking. Lap dance. I just don't know if I can commit to clipping coupons. That's one of my coupons."

"Why don't you at least give him some cash to go with his coupons?" Gina implored. "The poor guy is going to feel terrible."

"Yeah, especially if he gets you something really nice," Christy shook her finger, "then you'll feel like crap."

"Give him a piece of coal." Monica snickered.

Jan busted out laughing. "That's the best suggestion yet." She continued to chuckle. "But I do like the idea of some cash. I could give him a stack of twenty dollar bills to use with the strip tease slash dance coupons."

"Eeew, gross," the others complained.

"That way I get my cash back to spend on myself." Jan patted herself on the back, then reached over to Gina. "Thank you for the great idea."

Gina squirmed in her chair trying to dodge her hand. "You're disgusting. Don't touch me."

The four of them continued their discussion about family gifts while sipping their favorite coffee shop beverages.

Monica checked her watch. "We've been here almost an hour and we haven't been to one store yet. What's going on with us?" She turned an annoyed look at them.

"You're right. I only have a few more hours, then I have to get home for dinner," Gina said as she looked at her watch.

"Yeah, and I need to stop at the grocery store or Pete and I won't make it through the week."

"I've got coupons, if you need them," Jan offered, grinning.

"What happened to us?" Christie shouted getting the attention of everyone in the shop. "Dinner, grocery store, coupons?" She slammed her hands flat on the table. "We used to be fun. What happened to our fun?"

"Shhh," the others all sounded together.

"Don't you have to get home to Manny?" Gina asked with a curious look.

"Of course, I do," she said starting to laugh. "But seriously, what happened to us?"

They shared in the laughter at the notion of not being fun anymore.

"So, usually we make a plan for what stores we're going to shop at together and in what order," Jan said. "I need to shop at Tall Men's Clothier, Crafter's Cove, and Next Gen Tech.

"Well, you know with Michael I can certainly do Tall Men's Clothier, but then I also need to get to Kid's Can Build, and Unique Boutique.

"Given my family, I need all those and probably every other store here," Monica added.

"How are we going to handle this?" Christie frowned. "We used to all stick together and shop at the same stores."

"Because we only shopped for ourselves," Monica said.

"I guess we'll have to split up, do our shopping, and meet back here at a certain time?" Jan proposed.

"That stinks," Christie moaned. "The whole purpose is to shop together and have fun. I can come here anytime and shop by myself."

"I don't know what choice we have," Gina said. "Christmas is only a week and a half away. And, I need to crank this stuff out. Between working and partying, I don't have any other time available."

"It's eleven o'clock now. Be back here at five?" Monica looked at the others for a consensus.

"Fine." Christie reluctantly stood up from her chair and followed the others as they left the coffee shop each heading in opposite directions.

Crossing off the last store on her list, Jan walked out feeling relieved she was able to get her shopping done. Great, she thought, just enough time left to drop these bags off at the department store for wrapping and still meet my friends as planned.

"Thought I might find you here," Harold said as he walked up to her.

"What are you doing here? Last minute shopping?" Jan asked. But secretly she hoped it was because he and his girlfriend broke up. He still wants me, she reassured herself.

"I'm here because I wanted to talk to you, but without it being too obvious that we met," he said as he put his arm around her and pulled her out of the way of the other shoppers. "Jan, you know I care deeply about you." He laughed softly and shook his head. "In fact, if you told me right now that you were leaving your husband and wanted to run away with me, I'd probably do it." He sighed. "But you're not going to leave your husband. And, I found someone who makes me very happy." He looked into her eyes. "Carrie and I are in love. And, I hope I have your blessing to get on with my life as you did with yours."

Jan's eyes swelled with tears and she sat down on the bench as he sat next to her. "Harold, of course you and Carrie should be together." Jan looked down and then back to him. "If things had been a little different. If I had been a little older. Maybe, we would have been—"

"I know." He gathered her hands into his. "The first time we met, you were very young. And, I mean this in a good way, but you still had some growing up to do. Right?"

Jan nodded.

"But you were just so beautiful and smart. And, the way you took control of the room when you spoke," he paused and sighed, "well, I thought to myself, I want someone like that to be with me. Someone who can command the presence of an audience, not only with her looks, but with her talent."

"Oh, Harold," Jan stared into his eyes. "I never knew that's what you saw in me. I can tell you that I saw you as a handsome gentleman who took control and went after what he wanted, and achieved it. Very successful and accomplished."

He smiled. "But not someone you wanted to be with."

"But I—"

"Shhh, it's okay. I understand." He gazed at her. "You know I think we're very much alike, you and me." He started grinning. "So, it probably wouldn't have worked out anyway because they say that opposites attract, not people who have the same qualities," he said slowly adding the last words. "After we saw each other during the summer and I found out you were married, I realized I needed to move on."

In her mind Jan didn't want to accept it. Her thoughts raced. *No, no you don't need to move on, Harold. I can always be your one true love—can't I?*

"I'll always be fond of you, Jan. And, I wish you and your husband all the best," he said as he stood up and lifted Jan's hands to help her.

"Harold, that's so sweet. Thank you. I will always care for you." Jan tilted her head and smiled. "And, probably be wondering what could have been. But I know you need to be with Carrie now and I wish the best for both of you."

Harold put his arms around her and held her tight for a brief moment before turning to walk away.

Why do I feel so bad, so empty? Is it possible to be married and love one person, but still have feelings for another? Losing someone who loves you, even if you're not together, is heartbreaking. Jan took a few small steps and stopped. *He doesn't need me anymore.*

Jan was nearly spun around when a group of young shoppers ran past disregarding her space and bumping into her shopping bags.

"Hey," she shouted, but they kept going. She lifted her wrist to get a better grip on the handles and noticed the time on her watch. *Oh my gosh, I better get these to the department store for wrapping so I can meet the others on time. But I'm not sure I can walk much faster with what I'm feeling.*

Jan set several of her packages on the counter and left the rest on the floor until she had the opportunity to clarify her instructions.

"Can I help you?"

"Yes, I would like these items gift wrapped. I have more down here too," Jan made a slight laugh. "How long do you think it will take?"

"May I have your department store card and I'll check on that for you."

Jan dug in her wallet for her favorite, shiny metallic gray card, but when she looked at the slot where it usually was, there was a dismal looking blue card. She cleared her throat. "Here it is."

The store associate took it and stared at it. "Okay, I'll check on the gift wrapping charges for you."

"What do you mean?"

"I'm sorry, Ma'am. But free gift wrapping is only for platinum card holders, and you're . . . well, blue," the young woman shrugged.

"But I've always had my gifts wrapped here. I've never had this problem."

"Were you a VIP customer?"

Jan frowned. "Yes, until a few short months ago when I got married." The corners of her mouth turned down and she looked pleadingly at the store associate. "Are you sure you can't help me? I was platinum last month."

"I'm sorry we can't be of more help, ma'am," the store associate said and left the counter.

"Son of a . . ." Jan pursed her lips. "I don't know how to wrap gifts. Now what am I going to do with all this stupid stuff?" She mumbled as she walked away with her bags.

Jan heard the muffled sound of her phone's ring tone and reached into her purse to remove it. *Denise? That's odd. She never calls me.* She placed the phone next to her ear and spoke cautiously. "Hello, Denise. Is everything okay?"

"Of course it is, sweetie" she replied happily. "How about with you? You sound a little stressed."

"I have all these gifts and the department store isn't going to wrap them for free anymore. Seems I've fallen from grace with all my credit cards. Yesterday in the mail I received a blue replacement card for my shiny platinum one. They said they missed me and included a twenty percent off coupon."

"Oh great, a coupon," Denise said delighted. "Don't worry about it. I'll help you with the wrapping. Actually, that's what I was calling about. Just be at my house next Sunday at 1 PM with all your gifts. Oh, and bring as many friends as you like."

Jan stared at her phone from arm's length away after her step-mother-in-law hung up. What is Denise up to now, she thought.

19 PARENTAL THERAPY

After removing her coat and gloves, Jan slid into the booth next to Gina. She removed her phone from her handbag and placed it in front of her. "Hey," she said softly as she scrolled through the pages on her phone.

"Okay. What's wrong with her now?" Monica gave a parental look toward Gina.

"I don't know. Don't look at me. She hardly said anything all the way here." Gina shook her head. She looked with concern at the other two women. "And, I really tried to get her to talk."

"This sounds serious." Monica studied her face for a moment. "Jan? Jan, honey? Are you there? Did an alien invade your body? A quiet alien?"

The three women laughed at their friend's expense.

"No aliens invaded me. I'm fine," she briefly took her eyes off her phone to look at the other women.

Monica, Gina, and Christie stared curiously at their friend.

Jan saw in her peripheral vision Christie signaling to the others that she had an idea.

"Yeah, Gina, so I was just telling Monica what Manny and I did this weekend."

"Oh, yeah. What was that?"

"It was great. Manny and I, well we had such a great time." Christie glared at Jan. "And then we blah, blah, blah."

All eyes were on Jan as she continued to scroll and read her phone.

Jan sighed, shut off her phone, and sat back. She looked around at her friends. "Are you guys okay? Why are you looking at me?"

In turn they each took a deep breath and relaxed in their seats.

"What the hell were you looking at?" Monica demanded.

"I was just checking the weather. The roads. You know the usual stuff." Jan shrugged.

Her friends scrunched their faces at her nonchalant answer.

"Hello, ladies. I assume it will be the usual for lunch today? Half salads with grilled chicken," Frank continued his speech while pointing at each one of them. "Green tea, coffee, seltzer, and a bloody Mary."

"Spot on, Frank. But we're afraid Jan isn't feeling well," Monica said.

The corners of Franks mouth turned down. "Not in our restaurant." He pleaded with Monica. "If Jan is not feeling well then she needs to go home."

Jan smirked at Frank. "I feel fine. In fact, I'm excited about visiting my parents tonight."

"Oooh," the group moaned.

"Why didn't you just tell us?" Gina asked.

"Tell you what? I'm fine." Jan nodded. "I'm looking forward to seeing . . . my parents . . . tonight."

She drove onto the long, curved driveway and parked in front of the house. Will this evening have my parents on the attack about me not going to Busha and Jaja's for

Christmas, Jan wondered. She had thought about canceling on her mom. But she couldn't do it. Not to her mom. Her console and wisdom were what Jan looked forward to. It helped her in so many situations throughout her life. Unsure about how her visit with her parents would go tonight, she lifted herself out of her roadster and slowly walked to the front door.

After one press on the doorbell button, Maria, the housekeeper for the Brooks family for many years, opened the door wide. "Miss Jan, come in please. It's so good to see you again." Maria looked over her shoulder then back at Jan as she started to whisper. "You don't come to visit your parents enough. They talk about that." She nodded earnestly at Jan.

"I know. And, I feel terrible about it. I've just been so busy." Jan removed her coat and started to walk to the foyer closet.

"No, no. I'll take that for you. You're a guest here now." She smiled at Jan. "Now go see your mama and papa. They're in the study. They miss you." She waved her arms shooing her away.

"Thanks, Maria. You've always been so good to me." Jan flexed her hands as she slowly walked down the hallway. She stepped into the doorway and gave a slight knock on the wood framing.

"Kitten, come here. I'm so glad you could come over tonight. Is Rob with you?" Beth asked as she hugged her daughter.

"Rob's not here," Jan said in a choking voice. "He was invited to play poker at Michael's house. Hi Dad," Jan called out, barely able to wave to him as her mother held her arms down.

"Princess, you have to see these pictures. These are from our family Christmases when you were little."

"Let's see." She walked around to the other side of the desk and her eyes made a quick scan of all the old photographs. "Oh my gosh. What memories." She pointed at one. "I think I was about ten in that picture. Look at how big my hair was." She laughed with her parents, then she sighed. "I hope they don't bring the eighties hairstyles back, ever." She looked at her mom and they chuckled.

"This is nice we get to visit with you alone. Rob's a nice man, but it seems wherever he goes the rest of the Nichols clan follows him." Beth threw her hand in the air. "So much drama with those people."

"Beth, they're Jan's family now. So, you better watch what you're saying," Charles scolded.

"I'm not saying they're not good people. And, I did say Rob's a good man. But he's very demanding and isn't very tolerant of other people."

"That's okay, Dad," Jan said. "I actually appreciate the opportunity to vent. These past few weeks have been very trying for me. But not just because of the Nichols family. It's work and friends too."

"Sounds like you have a lot going on, Jan. Is there anything your mother and I can do to help?" Her dad asked.

"Maybe you can give me some advice?"

"We'll try. What's the issue about?"

"You were at the Nichols Construction Company Christmas party and heard Rob announce the new corporation structure, right?"

"Yes, but I don't see that as a problem."

"Pete and Brian don't like the structure and they're threatening to quit the family business and start their own company." Jan looked at her parents bemused faces. "That's the first part of it. The second part is," Jan took a deep breath, "They, or I should say Monica, expects me to do something about it."

Beth and Charles looked at each other and shook their heads.

"Well, first of all, Monica shouldn't be involved in a family's business decisions that's not her family," Beth commented. "You're smarter than she is. You don't need to take orders from her."

Charles rolled his eyes.

Jan smiled at her dad letting him know she picked up on his signal. "I know. But she and Pete are serious. And, anything Rob does to Pete, she takes it personally."

"What?" Beth gave Jan a stern look.

Jan held her hands open and shrugged.

"It sounds like the root of the problem is that Rob thinks he's the company and he's not seeing his brothers as capable equals," Charles summarized.

"That's it. And, I don't know how to get through to him that he needs to work *with* his brothers."

"There may not be anything you can do but to let this play itself out. However it ends up, it's not your fault, Princess. Everyone you're talking about in this scenario is a grown person who can take responsibility for themselves," Charles cautioned.

"You may not like what Rob is doing, but he is your husband. What if this whole thing blows up? Where does that leave you?" Beth questioned.

"I know. If this whole thing blows up," Jan sighed, "then it could end my friendships. Or, worse, it could end my marriage."

Maria came to the door. "Oh my, such serious faces. Is there anything I can get you that might help, a beverage, or a snack?"

"You know what, Maria? I feel like the three of us should get in the kitchen and rustle up some snacks for ourselves. Why don't you take the rest of the night off and go home?"

The women started to chuckle.

"Thank you, Mr. Brooks. That is very generous of you. Well then, if everyone is content, then I will be on my way," she said still laughing as she went.

"What's so funny?" Charles looked at his wife and daughter.

"It's Maria's time to leave now anyway. You're not

giving her a night off." Beth continued to laugh along with Jan.

"Well, how am I supposed to know that. I don't know what scheduled times she arrives and leaves."

"She's your employee." Beth snickered.

"That's okay, Dad. Details were always Mom's thing," Jan said protectively.

"But I did have a good idea, right?" Charles stood up and walked to the door, holding his arms out. "Let's go to the kitchen and get something to eat and drink."

"I could eat," Jan said as she followed her father out of the study.

"I could drink," Beth added with consternation. In the kitchen she brought out a platter of deli meats and cheeses. Another serving dish held an assortment of pickles, peppers, and olives. "Charles, would you please open a bottle of wine?"

Jan knew her way around the kitchen and gathered plates and flatware and arranged a place setting for each of them.

The three family members sat at the cozy breakfast nook table just off of the kitchen. With the large windows encircling the room, Jan remembered how sunny it would be in the summer time. You could look out the into the backyard and see the pool and well-manicured gardens.

"Princess, there's something else I wanted to ask you about," Charles said as he set his sandwich down and leaned forward. "There's a lot of news reporting about the City of Detroit being involved in something the FBI is investigating."

"Oh, yeah," Jan said as she pointed her finger. "I've been reading about that in the newspaper. They just keep saying they can't reveal any names while it's under investigation. Who do you think they're after?"

Charles paused and looked at Beth. "Have you talked about this with Rob? What's his take on the story?"

"To be honest, Rob and I haven't had time to talk

about anything except his company's need for automation. His bookkeeper left, not that she was any good anyway," Jan criticized. "But I've been helping him manage his company finances and setup his contractual and financial data on my laptop." Jan's voice dropped off as she watched her mother's reaction.

Beth's hand that was supporting her chin suddenly fell to the table.

"It's just for a short time, until he can get someone else."

Her parents sat quietly and picked at their food.

"You need to give him a deadline to get a replacement," Charles recommended. "Taking advantage of his wife, just because she can do the work, is not right."

"I know," Jan said as she fumbled with her napkin edges. "It really was only going to be for a few days or at most a couple weeks. But it's going on four weeks now. And, with my old boss back at Hedge—"

"Marjorie is back?" Beth blared.

"Oh, yeah, I didn't tell you that part." Jan sighed. "She's not as mean as she used to be, but she's really piling-on the work for me."

Charles reached over and held his daughter's hand. "We can't do anything about Marjorie. But if you want me to have a talk with Rob, then I will. I can give him some names of people that will work for him."

"The problem, Charles, is that he'll have to pay them to do the work. Our daughter is free," Beth said as she gave an annoyed look back at the two of them.

Jan turned off the ignition on the roadster after parking in the garage. She pulled her phone out of her purse and opened the text app. *Mom Dad, home safe. Thank you for a wonderful evening. Love you.* She pressed the send button.

I feel so much better, she thought as she entered her home. It always felt good to have a talk with her parents.

To tell them about everything that's going on, and receive their sound advice. From now on, she decided she was going to focus on her own needs and not someone else's. No one was going to take advantage of her again.

Jan opened the refrigerator to grab a bottle of water before heading upstairs when she heard the garage door close.

"Hi, hon," Rob said as he hung up his jacket and removed his shoes.

"You're home early. I wasn't expecting you," Jan said as she walked over and wrapped her arms around her husband. She kissed him on the lips, pressing against him and slowly moving her arms down his back.

"You *weren't* expecting me." Rob smiled and pulled her tighter. "What's going on?" They kissed long and hard.

Jan pushed Rob against the wall and raised her knee level to his hips. "Do you want to go upstairs?" She whispered.

Rob pressed his lips hard against hers and tugged at her blouse freeing it at the waist.

Jan unbuckled his belt and pulled his shirt free from his jeans. "Let's go," she whispered breathlessly, sliding her hand into his and entwining their fingers.

They started to walk swiftly through the kitchen as Jan led Rob holding his hand.

He stopped and she jerked back to face him. "Wait. Can we come back downstairs after? I have a new contract I need you to look at."

"Sure," Jan said and hurriedly turned toward the stairway, going through the great room with Rob following.

"Wait," she said as she stopped at the bottom of the stairs. "Does it have to be tonight? Maybe we should take care of that first."

Rob pulled her close and kissed her hard. "It's okay. We can take care of it later," he said softly.

"Wait. Stop. I can't stop thinking about it now." She

pushed his hands away and walked back to the kitchen.

"Hon, we don't have to do that now. Come on."

Jan carried her husband's brief case to the island using two hands. "How do you carry this thing around with you?"

"Let me help," Rob said as he reluctantly followed Jan's lead. He picked up the case easily with one hand and set it down, opening it, and removing some papers. "This is a new customer and we're meeting tomorrow morning to go over the estimate for a health care facility." Trying to rekindle the moment, he nudged his nose in her hair and kissed her.

Jan pulled her head away to study the document, then opened her laptop, and started entering some numbers. "Did you talk about costs yet?"

Rob stepped back, took a deep breath and sulked. "No. I always wait until I have my numbers checked by the bookkeeper. Usually there's no issues, but I never want to take a chance. It would be difficult to go back to a customer and ask for more money after a contract is signed."

"This looks good. But I would increase it about fifteen percent. I noticed that historically your estimates are close or a little under a few of the items, and you end up eating some of the costs."

"Really? I never got that kind of information before." Rob stood behind Jan to look over her shoulders. "How do I revise the estimate to show that? Just fifteen across the board?"

"No, I would only increase the higher priced materials and the labor. Most likely that's where the increase will come from." She looked at him. "If there is an increase."

Rob stared at the paperwork, then looked at Jan. "Can you revise this and have a new copy by morning?"

"Rob, of course. I've been helping with, uh, the Nichols Company for several weeks now. Don't you trust me?"

"I do," he said jerking back. "But it'll take a good hour to do all this. I'll be honest with you, I don't feel like doing this now. It's been a long day and I'm ready to go to bed."

"With the forms automated it's only a couple of simple entries. You go ahead. I'll get this done and be up there soon."

"Really? You don't mind?"

Jan realized her natural instincts took over again. *What the hell did I just do to myself again?* She sighed and smiled at him. "Really. Go."

"Thank you, honey," he said kissing her forehead. "Sure you don't want to come upstairs first before tackling that?" Rob had a suggestive look on his face.

"I'll be fine." She smiled back. And, Mom was right again, she thought.

20 CONSPIRACY

He moved his hand slowly, softly up her thigh.

She moaned and placed her hand on his, hoping she would find the will to stop him. She didn't love him, but their physical chemistry was an overpowering force.

"Hi honey," Rob said as he walked into the great room. "You got my message that I ate dinner with Mr. Daniels, right?"

"Uh huh," Jan continued to gaze into her book, as she gently bit on her finger.

Rob walked over to her, bent down to see what she was reading, and then sat down beside her.

Jan didn't budge or acknowledge her husband's presence.

"That interesting, huh? Can you read some of that to me?"

"What? Oh," Jan squirmed when she realized she was completely absorbed with her reading. "You probably won't like it. It's kind of a book for women."

"Try me." Rob smiled at her and moved closer, putting his arm around her on the back of the couch.

Jan took a deep breath, feeling a little embarrassed. "Okay, then. Here we go."

She picked up the book and licked her lips, giving her husband a shy look. "He wanted her. He pulled her close." Jan paused and looked at Rob.

He nodded and smiled looking at the book. "Nice, keep reading."

"She looked into his eyes and saw a gentleness she never noticed about him before."

Rob moved his arm from the couch onto his wife's shoulder. Taking a deep breath, he placed his other hand on her thigh.

Jan looked into her husband's eyes. "He knew his bad boy reputation preceded him. He hoped she would look beyond his past and see him for the man he is today."

Rob started to slowly rub his hand on Jan's thigh. He nestled her ear and kissed her neck.

Jan's heart beat faster as she continued reading. She dropped the book when her phone rang.

"Let it go to voicemail," Rob muffled into her hair.

The phone stopped and Jan tried to read once more. "He grabbed her—"

The phone started up again. Jan pressed her lips and took a deep breath. "Maybe I should answer that," she said as she wriggled her way out of her husband's grasp.

Rob threw his arm down on the cushion with a thud and glared at her. "It better be important."

"What's up," Jan said cupping the phone to her mouth.

"Where are you? Why didn't you answer the first time?" Monica demanded.

"I'm home. What's going on? Why all the urgency?" Jan watched her husband as she stepped away.

"We're going to meet at the other Nichols Construction Company headquarters for a meeting. We need you there. That is, if you're one of us?"

"Yes, Marjorie. I am a team player. I will bring the presentation to you right now. Just give me a few minutes to gather my things and I'm on my way."

"Marjorie? Whatever. Just get there fast."

"I'm sorry, Rob, but—"

"I heard." His chest heaved. He stood up and walked over to where Jan was standing. He pulled her tight. "Don't be long."

Monica led the way for the others into the pub. "We'll take that table over there," she said to the maitre d' as she kept walking not waiting for his approval.

They circled around the table and each pulled out a chair to seat themselves. The waiter came over to take their drink order.

"I'll have a tall beer and keep 'em coming," Pete said as he cupped his chin with his elbow on the table.

"*No!*" Monica interjected. "Four waters, thank you. We all need to have clear heads as we work through this issue." She pulled out a credit card and handed it to the waiter. "We'll also take an appetizer sampler for starters. It's going to be a long night." She turned to Jan with a glare. "This is all your fault."

"Me?" Jan pointed her finger at herself. "What did I—"

"Monica, knock it off with that crap," Brian voiced. "You called this meeting because we all have an interest in this. But if you're going to play the blame game, then I'm out of here."

"Okay, you're right."

Pete sat back in his chair and stared at his brother with astonishment. "How'd you do that?"

"You just don't let her take control," Brian replied, puzzled by his question.

He closed one eye and slanted his mouth, then turned back to Brian. "But I kinda like it when she takes control," he said softly.

Monica and Jan grinned at his attempt at discretion.

"Not all the time. You need to be in control when it counts," Brian said firmly.

"Hmm, okay. I think I get it." Pete sat back and

crossed his arms over his chest. "Let's continue."

Brian looked the other way as he rolled his eyes.

"Okay, well, the way that I see it is that you two have to start your own Nichols Construction Company," Monica leaned in pointing at the two brothers. "That way Rob will start to appreciate what you both do for him."

"You mean what we do for the company," Brian said dryly.

"It's for him, because he thinks he's the company," Monica replied as she glared at him.

No one spoke momentarily.

Pete picked up his glass of water and drank thirstily. "Boy, I could sure use a beer right now."

"It's not a bad idea," Brian said cautiously.

"Great. Waiter," Pete held his hand up signaling for him to come over.

"No," Brian stopped him. "I mean what Monica said is not a bad idea. I'm not saying I agree with you about Pete and me starting a new company. But maybe we just go through the motions so he thinks we are. That ought to get him realizing that he can't do everything himself."

"Okay, so, let's say we start to," Pete made quote signs with his hands, "go through the motions. What if he doesn't give a shit and cuts us loose?"

"Well what's the worst that could happen?" Monica asked.

"I could lose my balls," Pete replied dryly.

"That's okay. I'll still have my balls and I'll them with you," Monica said.

"Knock it off," Brian commanded.

"It's true," Jan said somberly. "I for one could see Rob just saying the hell with those two guys. I'll do it all by myself. The problem is," Jan pointed at herself, "he's got me doing all the paperwork right now. I'm not about to start digging ditches too."

"I was wondering how he was getting everything done," Pete commented.

"Why are you doing it? Why didn't he—we hire a new bookkeeper?" Brian looked curiously at Jan.

No one said anything.

"Wow, I think I just answered my own question. And, maybe I'm not valuable to the company," Brian said as he leaned back and sighed. "I knew we had the issue of not having a bookkeeper, but it never occurred to me to discuss the issue with Rob."

"And, Rob didn't come to us either," Pete added. "Don't blame yourself."

"Listen, you guys can't leave the company or I'll go under. I can't keep up with my career and take care of Nichols Construction Company all at the same time."

"So, what do we need to do first?" Pete asked.

Jan placed her hands flat on the table as she looked at each of them while explaining. "The issue is—"

"Wait." Pete stopped her. "The issue is Rob needs to see me as capable so he can have confidence in me to run the company as well as he can." He paused and pressed his hands together. "And, that's on me to show him that I can handle it. So far, I haven't been doing the best job of that. I need to act like a boss instead of a goof-off."

The others sat back, opened their eyes wide, and smiled.

"Well, look at you, growing up so fast," Monica complimented. She held his hand and looked at him. "Seriously, I'm proud of you for recognizing your part in this."

"That's great, bro. And, that's definitely going in the right direction. But what are we going to do about those corporate papers?" Brian looked at Jan.

Monica and Pete looked at Jan.

"Why is everybody looking at me?"

"You're the one with the MBA," Monica acknowledged. "If it was something medical, I'd come up with the solution." She pointed in the air. "Hey, what if we give Rob a lobotomy and . . ."

The others displayed their disappointment with her and shook their heads.

"Wow, tough crowd."

"Sis, Monica's right though. You're the one with the business degree and background." Brian appealed. "Wish it was me, but it's not."

"What's that all about?" Monica asked.

"Brian wants to go to college in Ann Arbor and get his degree in architectural engineering. After that, the plan is he'd come back to the company, start a separate division and they could stop hiring other companies for their architectural services. It would be a perfect fit." Jan nodded as she smiled favorably at her brother-in-law.

"So, why don't you?" Monica turned to Brian.

"Why do you think?" Brian and Pete sounded together.

"The same reason we're all here right now," Brian finished.

"Well, he has to be stopped." Monica looked at Jan.

Jan sighed as she looked at the three hopeful faces. "All right. I'll see what I can do."

"Great," Brian smiled.

"Oh shit," Monica said as she focused on the door. "Look who just walked in."

"Rob?" Jan pressed her hands on the table, ready to get up and run. "What are we going to do? It's not like the four of us can hide here."

"Don't panic," Monica said as she watched him. "He didn't see us yet. Pete and Brian, you two get up to the bar without being seen and act like you've been here the whole time. I'll sneak over by the door and after you greet Rob, I'll act like I'm just walking in."

"What about me?"

"You sneak out the door and go home."

"But why do you get to stay?"

"Because, I haven't had my drink yet."

"Me either." Jan pouted.

"You need to go home and start your research.

Remember? We're counting on you."

"And I thought this was going to be fun," Jan said as she turned and stomped out of the pub.

"What a friend and brothers-in-laws they are? They suck," Jan mumbled as she walked into her kitchen. As she set her handbag on the counter, she heard the vibration from her phone. "Now what?" She dug it out and looked at the caller ID. "Marissa?" Jan groaned as she put it to her ear. "Hi Marissa. Now is not a good time."

"Oh, well, I'm sorry to hear that, Jan. But I just wanted you to know that we're getting close to having a time for the photographers to come over. Are you and your husband available on Saturday?"

"No."

"Sunday?"

"No. In fact we're booked solid through the rest of the year. It'll have to wait until after the holidays."

Jan heard a deep sigh from Marissa.

"Is it okay if I come over and gather a little more information—"

"No. I said we're booked solid. Happy holidays to you. And, if you ever were seriously going to bring a photographer from *Michigan Homes* to our house, you can call me next year." Jan punched the end call button on her phone and set it down. *That felt good. But I kind of miss the ol' flip phones at times like this. The added dramatic effect of snapping that thing closed after a heated phone conversation was therapeutic.* She leaned against the counter to take a moment and reflect on the day's events.

Jan checked the pantry for dinner possibilities. "Let's see, mac and cheese, wild rice, or baked beans?" She mumbled. "Boy, the man sure does love his baked beans." She laughed. Not liking her options, she walked back to the kitchen and opened the refrigerator. "I guess I have no choice but to make romaine salads with yesterday's leftover chicken on top."

She set all the ingredients, dishes, and kitchen gadgets that she would need on the island. "Time to get to work," she said as she sighed and picked up her phone. "Hi Christie. Do you have time to talk right now?"

Jan paused to listen. "No, not about what I'm giving everyone for Christmas because it's all a bunch of shit." She rolled her eyes. "I'm calling about Nichols Construction Company and the incorporation document. How much more would it cost to change it and who has the authority to do so?"

She listened as she chopped the lettuce and used her hands to scoop it into two bowls. "Okay, then can your law firm represent Rob as one entity and a second entity that consists of Pete and Brian?"

Jan took a deep breath. "Because none of the parties will agree that the Nichols company was properly structured."

She rolled her eyes. "You said 'get to the point'? Okay. Pete and Brian are pissed because Rob cut Pete out of having equal partnership in the family company. And, they want to fight it."

Jan set the phone down, placed it on speakerphone, and continued working on the salads. She listened to the distant sound of her friend's voice going on for several minutes.

The salads were complete and she set them in the refrigerator until Rob would get home. Picking up the phone she held it a several inches away from her ear. "So, it would require all new paperwork whether it's one company or two. Uh huh, you don't recommend having both entities represented by your firm. But you'd be willing to recommend another law firm for either of them to go to for legal advice."

Jan took the phone off speaker and pinched the phone between her shoulder and ear as she moved about the kitchen. "Uh huh. Uh huh. But let me ask you this, if your firm recommends the alternate, how is there still no conflict of interest? You're obviously friends with the other firm, right?"

She gasped when she realized that was questioning her friend's integrity and it was adding another fifteen minutes to the conversation. Forget about the details and just go along with what she says, Jan reminded herself.

"Okay, okay. I'm sorry. I didn't mean to imply anything. I know it goes on all the time." Jan nodded. "I'll let Pete and Brian know this information and have them call you to get a referral."

She removed two sets of flatware from a drawer and placed them on top of paper napkins at the table. "No, I'm not calling on Rob's behalf. It's for Pete and Brian."

Jan leaned against the counter at her hip. "Why would that have made a difference?"

She went back to the pantry to search for a quick snack. "Oh my gosh. This is getting so complicated. Okay, I will inform Rob, Pete, and Brian about what you have just told me. Thanks." Jan ended the call, but still had reservations about whether she should tell Rob anything.

How did she get caught in the middle of this, she wondered? Rob is her husband and she knew she shouldn't be keeping anything from him. But she didn't agree with what he's done. Jan leaned against the door frame and pressed her eyes closed. What was she supposed to do?

"Hey, Jan?"

Walking into the kitchen, she feigned surprise to see him. "Hi, honey," she said walking over to him and gave him a quick kiss on the lips. Did he see me as I was leaving the pub, she wondered? If he did, he's acting awfully cool about it. "I've got lettuce salads with chicken for dinner. You interested?"

"What's the entrée?" He teased.

Jan set the salad bowls and a bottle of dressing on the table. *I need more time to think about this. I'm not ready to tell him now.*

"Is everything okay? You seem a little preoccupied," Rob said as he washed his hands at the kitchen sink.

"Oh, you know, the usual, work is just getting so demanding. The idea of going to another company is starting to enter my mind." Jan said as she drizzled ranch on her salad. "Hah, I just thought of something funny. Maybe I could work for your company?" She watched for her husband's reaction.

"Not a bad idea." He went into the refrigerator and grabbed the loaf of bread. "With all the work you've been doing I should probably pay you something. Shouldn't I?" He sat down and removed a slice of bread, offered it to Jan. Shrugging he took a bite, set on the edge of his plate and removed two more slices before starting to eat his salad.

Jan sat and thought about it for a while. "Is that really such a bad idea?" She posed the question to her husband.

"No, it's not. I personally would love it. But you've always wanted the corporate life. You're a director now and could be president yourself in a few years. Would you be willing to give all that up?"

"But with Marjorie back I could be fired tomorrow too."

"They're not going to do that," Rob leaned back and smirked. "Even if Marjorie proposed it, nobody in their right mind would go along with it. Because, they know you're the brains of the entire operation."

"Thank you for that, but so was Mr. Albright." Jan smiled at her husband's compliment. She tossed her salad with her fork and tried to come up with the words to tell Rob about what his brothers have planned. *How do I get it across to him that he's tearing apart his family's company? And, how much it would hurt his family. It was his mother's wishes to continue this business. But I'm sure if she was here now she wouldn't be happy with him.*

"We didn't get to talk before I left earlier. You seem a

little more tense than usual yourself. Did everything go okay at the job site today?" Jan asked innocently.

"Yeah, but Pete and Brian took off a little early and then I found them at the pub with Monica just before coming home."

"Oh," Jan mumbled as she stared down at her food. "Did they say anything about what they were doing there?"

Rob set his fork down and turned to face Jan. "You know why as well as I do," he said looking at her suspiciously.

He did see me, she thought. How am I going to explain to him that I don't agree with his plans for the company? He's going to think I'm a traitor to him.

"They're all still pissed because I incorporated the family company without consulting them. Pete and Brian that is, not Monica. She's not a part of the family."

"Yet," Jan shot back, then cringed wishing she could take it back.

"Hey, don't say that. Just the idea makes me sick." Rob feigned shuddering.

"I know you don't like her, but she really is a nice person with good intentions. She's just a little rough around the edges."

"Well, I'm sick and tired of her sticking her nose in where it doesn't belong." If you could say something to her, that'd be great."

Jan sighed and pondered his request. *Oh, I'll say something all right. But you're not going to like it.* "Did they say anything about me?" She dared to ask, wanting to know if she still had to be worried about her meeting with them.

"Of course," Rob said with an annoyed tone.

Jan's face expressed concern. "They did? What did they say?"

Rob took a deep breath and smirked at her. "Monica wanted to know what you're doing tonight, because she might be around to pick you up to go out drinking and have a girl's night out."

"That's it?" Jan breathed a sigh of relief.

"That's it? Seriously? If you think you're going out drinking tonight with your friends and going to work tomorrow, then you need to get your head examined."

Jan pressed her lips to keep from smiling. "So, that's what all this frustration was about? Honey, I'm not going anywhere tonight," she said as she patted his hand. *Whew, coast is clear. But I still have the other issue to deal with.*

They sat quietly and continued to eat their dinners.

"Honey, if you didn't have Nichols Construction Company, then what do you think you would be doing right now?"

Rob stared out into space as he chewed. "I'm not sure. Construction is what I know. All I can say is if I didn't own the company, then I'd probably be working for one. Why do you ask?"

"You know, I was thinking about what you told me about your mom wanting to keep the company going and how proud of you and your brothers she would be right now."

Rob continued eating forcibly spearing the salad without reacting to her comments.

"Is there any work I need to do for the company tonight? If not, I was thinking I would just go to bed early. I'm feeling a little exhausted."

"There's always going to be work to do," Rob said as he carried his plate to the kitchen sink. "But you should take a break from it and get some extra rest."

"Thanks, hon," Jan said as she stood up. "Can you pick up the kitchen? I think I'll head upstairs right now." *This will give me the extra time to think about Nichols Construction Company and how to handle the divided parties.*

21 DINNER WITH FRIENDS

"Please don't bring up the corporation at dinner tonight." Jan gave her husband a warning look.

"I don't intend to," Rob said in a patronizing tone. "But if Manny brings it up, what am I supposed to do?"

"He won't. He shouldn't. It's attorney client information. You don't just go blabbing about legal business in a restaurant."

"If that's what you say."

Jan smirked at him.

"What? I'm just saying. In all those television shows attorneys are always talking business with their clients at restaurants."

"That's not reflective of real life. And besides, if Manny does bring it up, then change the subject," Jan instructed as she stepped out from her husband's truck.

She took his arm as they walked up to the restaurant. Rob held the door as she entered first.

"There's Michael and Gina." Jan waved to them as they walked over to the table.

"What's keeping the others?" Jan asked as she sat down when Rob pulled the chair out for her before seating himself.

"Christie and Manny are running late. But Monica isn't sure she can convince Pete to go."

Rob rolled his eyes.

Jan gave him a stern look.

"Uh oh. I saw that," Michael snickered. "What's that all about?"

"Pete and I are having a disagreement," Rob said with an annoyed tone. "He'll get over it."

Jan frowned as she made eye contact with Gina.

"So, who needs a drink? This should be fun. Right?" Gina grinned as she held her hands open.

The waiter walked over and placed cocktail napkins in front of each of them.

"You're not Frank," Gina accused, giving him a suspicious look.

"No, I am not. Frank works the day shift." He smiled with his hands clasped in front of his chest. "May I be of service?"

"Yes, of course," Michael said. "They're just used to Frank. We'd like to order some drinks." He turned a glaring look to Gina.

"Don't order drinks without us," Christie called out as she and her husband walked in.

"I'll come back in a few minutes, after the additional guests have arrived," the waiter said as he walked away.

"No, no. Don't go," Michael pleaded as he reached out to him.

"Sorry about being late, but I had to take a phone call just before we were ready to leave." Christie looked at the others around the table. "What's going on? Why is everybody so quiet?"

"Monica—" Gina started to talk.

"And Pete are here," Michael shouted out. "Hey, guys."

Jan and Gina shifted their chairs over slightly to accommodate them at the table.

Jan turned to Monica and smiled, but Monica wouldn't

make eye contact. She looked to get Rob's attention, but he wouldn't acknowledge her either. She looked around the table at the others and forced a smile.

"Does anybody have a knife? I'd like to cut this tension now, so we can start having some fun," Manny commented.

Most laughed, but Rob, Pete, and Monica didn't respond.

The waiter returned to their table. "Would anyone like a drink?"

"Oooh, you bet," Manny said. "A round of tequila shots for all of us. We need to loosen up a few stiffs here. And, I'll have a double scotch, neat."

"Gina and I'll have the same drink," Michael said.

"But I'd like mine on the rocks," she added.

"I'll have a margarita made with one-hundred percent agave tequila and curacao with a salted rim," Christie ordered.

"Oh, baby," Manny put his arm around her shoulders. "You're getting wild tonight. I like it."

There were some chuckles and the four of them started to talk about their work until the waiter completed getting their drink order.

"I'll have a beer," Rob said.

"Same here," Pete added. "Hey, Gina want to pass the bread this way?"

"I'll have the same drink as Michael and Manny," Monica said, then looked at her phone.

Jan cleared her throat. "I'll have water," she whispered.

"Okay, so I have a round of tequila shots. Four double scotches, three neat, one on the rocks. Two beers. One margarita with one-hundred percent agave tequila, curacao, and a salted rim. And, one water," the waiter announced.

"Who ordered the water?" Gina asked looking suspiciously at the others.

"I did," Jan said as she blushed and raised her hand slightly.

"What happened to you? You used to drink the rest of us under the table in college," Christie accused.

Rob turned sideways on his chair with a surprised expression, leaning back to get a good look at Jan.

"Well," she laughed slightly. "I don't think I drank that much." She shook her head.

"Oh yeah you did," Gina said. "And, remember that secret hangover recipe she would use so she wouldn't be sick the next day. She'd get up bright and early go off to class, while the rest of us were holding ice packs to our heads and taking turns holding each other's hair back."

"That's right. I've been meaning to ask you about that hangover recipe," Christie pointed at Jan. "Will you please share it with me?"

"Why do you need a hangover recipe? You going back to school?" Manny teased.

Jan looked down and fumbled with her napkin. "It doesn't always work for everyone."

"It worked great for you. But still, what's with the water?" Gina questioned.

"Oh, all right. I wasn't going to drink that much because I have Hedge presentations to prepare tomorrow. But what the heck."

The waiter returned with a large black tray and started setting filled shot glasses in front of each of them before setting down their individual drinks.

"Uh, sir?" Jan tried to get his attention. "I'll have a beer."

The others laughed.

"You're living on the edge, Jan," Christie commented.

When Jan's beer arrived, she placed it right alongside her husband's beverage.

Gina widened her eyes and took a deep breath as she pointed across the room. "Look," she whispered. "It's Rosie. And look at Frank. He's all dappered-up to take her out on a date."

"Good evening, everyone," Frank said as he stopped

by their table with Rosie. Her arm was in his and he held his hand on hers.

"Good evening, Frank, Rosie," Gina said.

"Tony is your waiter this evening. He's excellent and will provide service that exceeds your expectations," Frank explained. "Well, I'll be out of your way. Enjoy your evening."

"You too, Frank, Rosie," Jan, Monica, Gina, and Christie all spoke together.

"So, this is where you come to meet your friends for lunch every week?" Manny raised his voice looking at Christie. "This is awfully pricey for a lunch."

Christie looked sternly at her husband. "May I remind you whose family firm you work for?"

"It'll be the fifth time today, but sure, go ahead," he teased.

Christie smirked and sat back in her chair.

"So, Michael. Nice ploy you played on me last week," Jan pointed at him.

"I had to do it, Jan. You know how relationships are. Please forgive me?"

"I'll forgive you this time, because I'm still getting your company's residuals."

"Yes, that's right—residuals. And, there's more where those came from whenever you want to come back."

Gina elbowed him.

"But the more money she makes for Goodson and Associates, the more I can spend on you, baby" Michael pleaded.

"When you coming back, Jan?" Gina teased.

Pete turned a twisted face to Monica. "Do you have an assburn?"

"Whaaat?" Monica blared turning a shocked expression to him.

He leaned back in his chair surprised by her response.

"What do you mean 'what?' Do you have an assburn?"

Monica stared at him through squinty eyes, studying his

expression. "Honey, do you have a headache?"

"Yes. That's why I want an assburn," he declared.

"It's as-pir-in. Aspirin." She huffed. "Not assburn, Mr. ESL." Monica shook her head as she laughed.

"Well, excuse me for not e-nuc-iat-ing better, but I'm in horrific pain." He looked at Monica with a pleading, contorted face. "So? Do you have an as-pir-in or not?"

"Yes." Monica dug in her handbag and withdrew a small, bejeweled pillbox. She took one oval-shaped blue capsule out and handed it to Pete. "Here you go."

Pete looked at it in the palm of his hand. "Are you sure this is a pain reliever and not an ED treatment?"

"No, I'm not. But either way you'll be feeling much better in no time."

"Okay, time for the gift exchange," Christie said as she brought out a small brown paper handle bag with gold embellishments on it. She withdrew three sachet bags holding faux diamond initial brooch for each of her girlfriends.

"These are beautiful. Thank you," the other women exclaimed.

"I'm next," Jan said. She withdrew miniature paper gift bags each containing an oval-shaped, tree ornament with each of their names in a heart.

"Aww, this is so sweet," the others admired.

"Now mine," Gina handed each of them a small box containing a heart shaped charm with their birthstones in the middle.

"This is lovely," they said.

After a few minutes of ohhing and ahhing over the gifts they had already received, three of them turned their gaze to Monica.

"Well, I hope I got everyone's cup size right," she said as she brought out three pink ribbon handled store bags. She peeked in each one before handing them over to the other women.

"Oh my," Gina said. "I'm not sure I want to open this

here in front of all the men. Should we go to the women's room?"

"Don't be shy," Monica teased. "It's not like these guys haven't seen one before.

The men started leaning over their partners gifts trying to get a glimpse of what was in the package.

"Well, let's do this, girls." Christie led the action removing a large hard, tissue wrapped object.

Jan started laughing. "Coffee mugs with our names on them. How clever." She threw her friend a kiss. "And, it is the right cup size."

"Well, sorry guys. But I didn't bring you a gift. So, how about I just buy the next round of drinks?" Michael offered.

"Best gift ever." Pete nodded.

Jan watched as Rob checked his phone for a text message. He immediately replied then put his phone on mute and slipped it into his sport coat pocket.

"Who was that," she whispered to him as the others carried on sidebar conversations.

"Nothing," he shook his head and took a sip of his beer.

"Was it Denise? What are you two planning now? A special gift for me to make up for the second Thanksgiving?" Jan teased.

"It was nobody," he said turning away and throwing back the last of his drink. "I'm gonna step outside for a minute."

"Should I come with you?"

"No, no. I just need some fresh air," he said as he left the room.

"Rob taking a phone call outside? It is a little noisy in here." Michael said.

"You don't need to worry. He'll come back," Christie teased.

Jan laughed, but then started to wonder what her husband was up to now. Regardless, she recognized the opportunity in front of her. With everyone's attention going in different directions, she inconspicuously switched beer glasses with her husband's.

Jan placed her knife and fork side by side on her nearly empty plate and pushed it away. "What a great meal," she complimented about the food to the others.

"Are you gonna eat that?" Rob reached over and speared the half of chicken parmesan she had left on her plate.

"I was going to get a box," she said defensively. "Oh, fine. I should know better by now."

"You never eat your leftovers anyway. I'm just saving you the trouble of carrying it home."

"Shall I bring boxes for the ladies?" The waiter asked looking around the table. His gaze stopped at Jan's plate and he displayed astonishment.

"Yup, that's my wife. She has a veracious appetite," Rob remarked good-naturedly.

"I'll be back with your checks," the waiter hastened away still expressing astonishment.

Manny leaned back in his chair. He stretched his neck to hear the table next to him. The serious look on his face signaled the others to pause the fun and listen.

"It's all over the news that there's illegal contract connections with Detroit," one man said to the other couple and his wife.

"Not surprising. They're trying to push this revival thing to fast. It takes time for a city to rebuild. Sometimes decades," the other man retorted.

"I don't care what they do as long as I can still go downtown to shop and dine," one of the women said.

"And, don't forget the sporting events," the first man jumped back into the conversation. "I can't live without my Detroit teams."

The group at the other table all laughed together.

Jan looked around at the somber faces as the awkward silence hung in the air. "Well, my glass is empty. Anybody else?" She asked trying to change the mood.

"Yes," Manny robustly shouted. "We're here to celebrate Christmas aaand . . ."

"And, our adopted family," Gina added.

"Good times," Christie said.

"Come on. Who's next? We're on a roll here. Pete, say something," Manny ordered.

"Aaand . . ." Pete sputtered, "our businesses," he cringed as he said it.

The corners of Jan's mouth turned up as she watched the enthusiasm come back into the group.

"Michael, you're up." Pete pointed at him.

"What I'm best at," Michael grinned, "wealth."

Gina turned to him with a sly grin.

"I'll take my turn," Monica injected. "Love," she said with an eyebrow flash to Pete.

He put his arm around her shoulders and kissed her. "Good one, babe," he said softly.

"Marriage." Rob looked at Jan.

"I'll drink to that," Manny said as he picked up his glass with one hand and gave Christie a gentle hug with his other arm.

"Jan, you're the only one left," Christie said.

Jan opened her mouth to speak, but no words came out.

For several seconds everyone stared at her.

"Okay, okay, okay. I got one," She said. "You're really going like it," she said with a wide grin.

"Oh so much drama with you," Christie laughed.

"Just tell us already," Michael moaned.

"Booze."

"Booze, good one," Michael said as he held up his drink. "Cheers everybody."

"Cheers!" They resounded.

Jan took her husband's arm as they walked out of the restaurant. Her steps were much swifter than his just so she could keep up.

"So," he looked at her with a big grin, "drank everybody else under the table during your college days, huh? I wish I had known you back then." He moved his arm around her waist and pulled her tight.

Jan laughed. "It wasn't quite like that. My friends were exaggerating."

"I don't know about that. I think I'm inclined to believe them," he said. "When you make your mind up to drink, you drink. It's hard for me to keep up."

"True. But on those rare occasions I'm usually at home so I don't take any risks."

They stopped at the truck's door on the passenger side. As Rob reached for his keys in his pocket, Jan stopped him by gently placing her hand on his arm. "You better let me drive."

"Why? I only had two beers," he said giving her a surprised look.

"Actually, you had four beers." She smiled innocently at him, hoping he wasn't going to be offended.

"No, I had two," he said holding up two fingers.

"No, you had four. Because you drank my two beers. And, two plus two equals four."

"How'd I drink your two beers?"

"Because I set my glass right next to yours and when you finished your beer, then I switched glasses letting you think you still had more beer to drink."

"But I saw you drinking your beer."

"What you saw was me putting my glass to my mouth." She grinned. "But I never drank anything. Well, other than water." She watched him process what she just said. "Clever, huh?"

He squinted as he tucked his chin to look at Jan. "So, is that how you drank the others under the table in college?"

She snatched the keys from his hand. "Yup, pretty

much," she said walking around to the driver's side.

"That or pouring it into their glass when they weren't looking. It's amazing how quickly drunk girls respond to '*hey, look over there*.'"

They both laughed as their car doors closed with a thump.

Jan adjusted the seat, mirrors, and steering column before starting the truck.

"Oh no, now I'll have to reset everything for myself tomorrow. I knew there was a reason why I don't like it when you drive."

Jan smirked. As she made a left turn onto Rochester Road she started thinking about the conversation they overheard involving the dealings with Detroit contract negotiations. "Rob, do you think all those media reports about Detroit have anything to do with Nichols Construction Company?"

"I'm not sure. But Manny seemed concerned that it could. He spoke to me on the side and said he's going to be a little proactive and see what he can find out from his friends at the district attorney's office."

"I'm not sure if you want to hear this or not, but I've got my concerns after reviewing the company books," she said as she made brief glances at him while driving, hoping to get a read on his expression. "From what I can tell, the company should have been showing substantial profits all along. I'm going to have to do some more digging to see where it's been syphoned off to."

"I hope my bookkeeper is having a good time, wherever she is," Rob said resentfully resting his head back.

22 GIFT WRAPPING

"This had better not be some bullshit supplies Denise has for us," Monica barked as she sat down in the passenger side of Jan's roadster. "I'm used to department store quality gift wrapping and I'm not going to settle for less." She slammed the door.

"I know. I know." Jan tried to calm her friend's concerns. "I feel the same way."

"I'll throw that shit away if I have to, then take my gifts back to the store to be wrapped." Monica shook her head. "How the hell did I get roped into this stupid gift wrapping party anyway?" She turned an icy glare toward Jan. "You." She pointed. "She's your stepmother-in-law. Why do I have to go?"

"Listen to me. Denise assured me that this is going to be a top-notch event." Jan looked over and blinked twice at the expression on her friend's face. "Look at it this way. You'll be making Denise happy and you'll be on her good side."

"Good point," Monica snarled.

"Hey, girls," Denise greeted Jan and Monica at the

door. "Come on in. You know the way."

Ed walked into the living room mumbling.

"Girls what do you think? Doesn't Ed's hair look good?" She gave a front lock a tousle.

"Don't do that," Ed growled. "I wish my Barbershop was still open. It closed when the owner, my barber," he stuck his finger into his chest, "retired and moved to Florida."

"Well I like it," Denise said admiring Ed's new do. "So what if the stylist used a product that made your hair a little fluffier. You need the height because I think you lost a couple of inches since the eighties were over," she teased.

Ed put his head down and hurried to leave the room.

"Well, that was awkward," Monica said expressing embarrassment for both of them.

"Setup wherever you like, girls. There's many others coming today, so it's good you got here early." Denise continued to put finishing touches on all the tables.

Ed thumped back through the room wearing his jacket.

"Where are you going?" Denise followed him to the door.

"To Rob's. To Pete's. To the pub. Doesn't matter to me as long as I get the hell outta here."

Denise looked down and breathed in. "Probably better that way," she murmured.

Monica carried her many shopping bags over to one of the gift wrapping tables. The tables were setup with an assortment of paper, foil, tulle, ribbon, gift bags, tags, scissors, assorted boxes, and tape. After setting her things down, she reached into one small bag, brought out a black felt box, opened it, and admired a beautiful diamond bracelet.

"Wow, who's that for?" Jan asked as she snuck up alongside her friend and set down her two ruffled store bags.

"Nobody." Monica slammed the box closed.

"Yourself?"

"No. Now get to work."

"*Meee?*" Jan displayed a big toothy smile.

"Wouldn't you like that?" Her eyes crinkled at the corners.

"Well, who then?"

"So, what did you bring for gifts?"

"Coupon books."

"Coupon books?" Monica snapped. "For everyone? Me too?"

"Uh huh. That's what this family loves the most," Jan said as she fiddled with some tissue. She rolled up the first book in the thin wrapping, then pressed her hand on it to make it hold its creases. "Come on." Making a fist she hammered it down. "Tape. Quick."

"Shhh, here she comes."

"Thank you, ladies, for coming to today's gift wrapping event," Denise said as she strolled over to greet them. "I see Monica's all in with her gifts. But Jan must not trust me enough yet to get all her wrapping done here." She leaned in and gave Jan a brief hug. "That's okay. Some relationships take time," she said gently patting Jan on the shoulder. "So, I'm guessing you two will be gift wrapping buddies throughout the day? You know, help each other tie knots, hold the paper's edges, and so on."

"Well . . ." Monica started to say.

"Yes," Jan chimed in.

"Great. We'll be having wrapping demonstrations throughout the day. Of course, help yourself to food and drinks in the kitchen any time."

As Denise walked away to greet other women, Monica turned a frowned face to Jan. "I kind of wanted a different wrapping buddy. You're not exactly the creative type."

"Too bad." Jan shot back as she leaned against the table with one hand. "Now, who's the bracelet for?"

"The person I want to win over the most right now."

"Pete?" Jan scrunched her face.

Monica laughed. "No. Pete's step mom." She proudly grinned at Jan for her strategic idea.

"Denise?" Jan said loudly.

The others in the room turned to look at her.

"Shhh." Monica grabbed her arm and turned her toward the table. "Yes, Denise," she whispered. "If Denise likes me and I have her approval, then that's one more that I have on my side during family, let's say," Monica cleared her throat, "discussions."

"But what about me? What if she likes you more than me and we're pitted against each other?"

"I don't see a problem. I'll win and you'll lose." Monica smiled and returned to work with the paper and ribbon. "Hmm, this stuff's not too shabby. This may turn out to be a good day after all." She selected a glossy red paper and measured off the gift, folded over the paper lining up the edges, and creased it. "Scissors." She held out her hand. "Well, then what are you getting Rob for Christmas?" Monica asked.

"A coupon book."

"Oh come on. A coupon book and nothing else? Seriously?"

"Yes, he likes coupons, he's getting them for Christmas. I'm making it for things like his favorite meal, one ironed shirt, backrubs, you know stuff like that."

"What about your side of the family? What are you getting for your parents? When will you open presents with them if you're at the cottage?" Monica held out her opened hand and sympathetically nodded.

"I'm not sure. It might have to wait until after New Year's. I've never been away from my parents for Christmas. This is new territory for me, for all of us."

Monica grinned as she nodded. "Well, since your husband is a big shot CEO now you should buy him a private jet for his company."

Jan took a step back. "What do you think I am? A millionaire?" She shook her head. "I wish."

Monica half suppressed a laugh. "Were you able to make any changes or get any more information about salaries?"

"Yes." She looked sternly at her friend.

"What? Why didn't you tell me?" She leaned into Jan and threw her hand in the air. "So, how much do they each make? Is Rob keeping most of it for himself?"

"They all make the same amount," she replied dryly.

Monica squinted. "That's not what I was expecting. Are you sure? Did you check for secret accounts?"

"Believe me. I've been all over the Nichols Construction Company books." Jan stared off as she reflected on all the bookkeeping work she had done. "All over them."

Monica wrinkled her nose. "That's not a euphemism is it?"

"Huh?" Jan turned to her and smirked. "No, of course not. It's just the numbers don't quite add up. The previous bookkeeper did something and I haven't quite been able to figure it out yet."

"I see. Wasn't she a fifty-something-year-old lady with a high school degree? You have an MBA from UM. And, you're stumped by her work?" Monica taunted.

Jan turned around and leaned against the table to watch the other women wrapping their gifts.

"Aren't you going to finish wrapping your gifts?" Monica looked at her curiously.

"I did. I'm all done." She pointed at a pile of crumpled tissue paper globs tied up with crimped curling ribbon.

"You have all these beautiful supplies and that's what you're going with."

"Yup. Rob doesn't want me to spend money on department store gift wrapping, so I'll show him how good I am at this stuff."

"Again? Rob wants this. Rob doesn't' want that. Why don't you just think for yourself and do what you want to do?"

Jan puckered sideways and silently looked away.

"Let me ask you this. Does Rob consider what you want before he makes a decision?"

Jan crossed her arms and shifted her feet. She took a deep breath. "It's not that easy being married. You have to make compromises."

"If that's what you want to call it," Monica said as she looked through her shopping bags and picked out another box to wrap.

"Ladies, if you look over here, please. Jeanette is going to demonstrate how to wrap this beauty." Denise held up a medium sized box with a three-dimensional shape on top. "And, if you like it, then you have all the materials you need at your stations."

"Wow, that is cute," Jan exclaimed.

"Why don't you rewrap some of that crap you call gifts and use that idea?" Monica asked.

"If Rob sees that I can—" Jan paused and turned away. "Never mind."

"Hi, honey," Rob ran over and kissed Jan when she walked through the door. "Did you have a good time?" He cringed as he looked curiously at the shopping bag she was carrying. "What's all that?"

"My Christmas gifts for everyone in the Nichols family." She set the bag down next to the counter on the floor and gave it a kick to keep it from falling over. "Well, it was another one of Denise's top-notch parties. Great supplies, great food, and—

"Did Denise send anything home with you for me?" Rob excitedly waited for the answer.

"Yes," Jan moaned and handed him a large paper bag. "Here's your dinner."

"Oh, this looks good," he said peeking inside the sack rubbing his hands together. He set several containers on the island next to a plate he had waiting. He turned slightly to his wife. "Would you like some?"

"No. I ate already."

He took a deep breath, dropped his head back, and turned around to face Jan. "Now what's wrong?"

Jan plopped herself into a chair. "I'm just tired. That's all." Her lips started to quiver. "Tired of all the additional work from Marjorie. Tired of the late nights for Nichols Construction Company. Tired of my so-called friends picking on me." She looked at Rob. "Just tired, tired, tired," she said breaking down into sobs.

He looked over the containers of food and picked a meatball out of one of them and tossed it into his mouth. Quickly he grabbed some paper towel and wiped his hands and mouth. "I'm sworry," he said still chewing. "Whad yo friends do thos time?"

"Oh just finish eating before you choke," she growled.

He swallowed hard, then took a deep breath. "Okay, but only because you say so. But if you want I'm ready to talk when you are."

"Eat," she shouted. Checking her email on her phone, she was relieved that nothing needed her attention from Hedge. She took a deep breath, set it down, and started to watch her husband. Denise's food is so good, Jan pondered. I understand why Rob loves it so much. I'm not sure I'll ever be able to cook like that.

Jan yawned and stretched. "Is there anything for me to do with the company books tonight? If not, I'm going to bed."

Chewing, Rob looked at her putting his finger to his mouth before swallowing. "There is one little thing."

"One thing?" She tilted her head.

"I think so. Just one. But . . ."

"But?"

"I don't know. When you look at it you might think differently."

Jan's eyes narrowed skeptically. "Let's take a look."

23 RUN-IN

On Monday with Christmas only three days away, Jan scribbled in her planner and then smacked her pen down. "Who has a meeting on the last day before Christmas vacation," she grumbled. "I've got so much to do and I feel like my breakfast is fighting back." She walked into the conference room and picked out a seat furthest from the door. Sitting down she rested her head back and felt her forehead.

"Feeling okay there, Jan? Or, just being a little dramatic?"

She opened one eye to look at who was talking. "Oh, hello, John. Just trying to rest my eyes before we begin. Putting in some long nights." She sat upright and clasped her hands on the table. "Will Mr. Albright be here for the last directors' meeting of the year?"

"No. He gave this place the one finger salute and walked out. He's probably in his new home on the Gulf already. And, I do mean *on* the Gulf."

Jan smiled. "I know. He told me about his new beach home. I wish him well." She wrapped her arms around her stomach to muffle the noise.

John looked around, puzzled, before stopping his gaze

on her, and then abruptly turned away.

"Let's begin folks. Christmas is around the corner and we all need to get out of here." The senior director swiftly walked in and planked himself at the head of the table.

Oh, I shouldn't be here, Jan thought. The more she squirmed in her seat, the more her temperature went up. "Excuse me," she abruptly jumped up with her notebook and headed for the door. *Uh oh, I'm not going to make it.* She knelt down by the door and grabbed the waste basket. She heard the moans and groans as she heaved guttural noises. She paused, then wiped her mouth with the back of her hand before lifting herself up. She opened the door to leave the meeting, stopped, then took a step backward and picked up the waste basket. "I'll just take this with me," she said never turning around as she left the room.

Jan returned to her desk and dropped herself into her chair. "I can't believe I just did that. There's no way I'm going back in there now," she muttered. "I wonder if I can get fired for that?" With her arms around the waste basket sitting on her lap, she leaned forward and peered into it. "Oh bleah." Quickly she tied up the ends.

"Are you coming down with the flu?" Tracey stood in the doorway with her index fingers crossed in front of her.

"I'm afraid I am." Jan felt her forehead again. "I'm not feverish, but you better stay back."

"That stinks. You're going to be sick through the holidays only to be feeling better when you have to return to work after the break."

"I know," Jan moaned realizing her Christmas break would be wasted away lying in bed.

Tracey grimaced. "Um, Jan, I'm supposed to be leaving here soon to catch a flight home to my parents. But if you need me to stay, I will."

"No. You're not staying. You go and enjoy your holidays." Jan mustered a smile.

"You sure?"

"Yes. Absolutely." She tilted her head. "Merry

Christmas, Tracey. I'd hug you but—"

"I appreciate the thought. Best Christmas gift ever." Amused, she expressed relief. "Merry Christmas, Jan." She turned to leave.

"Oh, Tracey, just one more thing."

The young assistant slowly turned around.

"Would you . . ." Jan lifted the basket toward her.

"No. Absolutely not."

"But—"

"John sent a video out and it went viral in the office."

"Oh no." Jan cringed.

Tracey took a deep breath. "Listen, just put the whole thing in the larger trash bin in the breakroom," she whispered. "Nobody's here to see you now."

Jan grinned and nodded approvingly as her assistant left the doorway. She laid her head back in her executive chair, contemplating the long list of things she wanted to get done. Looking at her watch it was already eleven-thirty. *Hmm, maybe it was my breakfast. I'm starting to feel a little better.*

She stepped into the aisle outside her office. "Where is everybody?" She looked through the cubicles and everything was quiet. She checked her emails one more time, but nothing new arrived. "Time for lunch." After disposing of her trash, she returned to her office. Grabbing her handbag, she left the office.

"Could I see those earrings with the red stones," Jan asked the store associate behind the department store's jewelry counter.

"Here you are," he said handing them to her.

Jan put the earrings up to her ears and looked in the mirror on the counter. Gasping, she dropped the jewelry, ducked down, and snuck to the other end of the display cabinet.

"Is something wrong," the associate ran within the glass display cases following Jan to the other end. He leaned over the cabinetry and watched her scooched down out of sight.

"My husband is heading this way," she whispered looking up at the store associate.

The young man grinned and turned around when he heard another customer.

"Excuse me. Can you help me out here?" Rob asked. "I don't come to these places very often. Is this jewelry any good? Is it real or the fake stuff?"

"Well, it depends. Who you're shopping for?" The store associate replied trying hard to suppress his amusement.

"Is that for me?"

Jan recognized the woman's voice and she peeked around the corner. It was Marissa. Jan watched as she approached Rob like she's always known him. But how could that be, Jan wondered. Her curiosity took her mind off her uncomfortable, awkward posture.

"What the hell! Are you stalking me again?"

"Stalking you? Don't flatter yourself. I was looking for Jan when I saw you. I thought you might know where she is."

"Yeah, sure you were. Well, that text message you sent me the Saturday night made Jan think that Denise and I are conspiring some surprise for her. So, now I have to buy some expensive bullshit to give her for Christmas. Thanks a lot."

"You always were a romantic, Rob. I guess I'm not missing anything after all."

"What's that supposed to mean? I was a good boyfriend to you. Dinners. I think one time I bought flowers or candy or some shit like that. That's romantic. What more can a guy do for a woman?"

"Nothing, Rob. You're a model boyfriend, er uh, husband now. Jan's a lucky woman. God bless her for taking you off the market."

Oh no, my leg is cramping up. I'm not sure how long I

can stay in this position, Jan thought. I'm losing the feeling in my legs. Uh oh, I think I'm starting to attract a crowd.

"Mommy, look. That lady fell down. I'm going to help her." A little boy dropped his mother's hand and rushed from her side.

"No. Nooo," Jan shook her head as she whispered and wagged her finger at him.

"Come on lady, get up. I'm a boy scout. I can help save you."

Jan pushed his little hands away, but he was insistent. She looked up and saw Rob, Marissa, and the store associate watching her struggle against the young man. Feeling embarrassed, she stiffly lifted herself off the floor while grabbing onto the glass display case. "Thank you, young man. You saved me," she sneered.

"You were here the whole time? Listening?" Rob questioned, a shocked look crossed his face.

"I saw you coming this way. And, I thought you'd only be a few minutes and leave. I didn't know all this was going to transpire." Jan leaned back while waving her hand up and down in the air toward Marissa.

"You make it sound like it's my fault," he shot back. "I was here to buy you a present."

"Or some bullshit," she sneered and turned to face Marissa. "And, why are you always following us?" Jan looked around. Her hands dropped by her side and her shoulders slumped. She turned her glare back to her husband and drew her hands to her hips.

"Okay, okay. I should've told you the first time Marissa showed up at our house." Rob took a step toward his wife with open arms. "But it was such a shock to see her. I couldn't believe she would come back after all these years."

Jan relaxed her jaw. "Do you still love her?"

"No, no. Of course not. She's a psycho. Can't you tell?" Rob drew circles on the side of his head. "It hurt me when she ran off with another guy. But I got over it." He raised his eyes to the ceiling. "And, man, am I glad she did. Just seeing her sends creepy chills up-and-down my spine."

"It was pretty shocking to find out that a woman I thought was going to put our house on the map, turns out to be your ex-girlfriend. I need time to process all this."

"Jan, I came here to buy you a gift, not because I thought you were expecting something. But because I really love you. You're the best thing that's ever happened to me. Everything else I said to her was just to be an asshole so she'd get away from me, from us." Rob moved his arms around his wife's waist.

"Okay, we'll talk more tonight. I need to go back to work now."

Rob leaned in for a kiss.

Reluctantly Jan reciprocated, then embraced her husband's affection.

"Awe!"

Jan and Rob startled, and turned to see an audience of store associates and shoppers standing around them applauding their display of affection.

"I saved your wife, mister," the little boy shouted.

"Yes, yes you did," Rob gave him a thumbs up.

With smiles, blushing faces, and their heads down, they walked away holding hands.

Before stepping back into her office, Jan heard some paper rustling. She took a deep breath and marched in.

"I know, I know. I was gone longer than an hour. Just don't fire me. I'll stay late before starting my Christmas vacation," Jan snapped at her.

Marjorie's face dropped from a smile to a frown. "I have a gift for you."

Jan grabbed the door frame on both sides to steady herself. "A gift? For me?" Jan shook her head. "Why?"

Marjorie sniffled. "I know you think I'm too hard on you. But I think of you as the daughter I never had."

Jan shivered at the thought.

"Are you cold? I can have maintenance turn-up the thermostat," Marjorie offered.

"No, no," Jan quickly waved her hands. "That's not necessary." She slowly stretched out her arms to accept the gift from Marjorie's outreached hands holding the beautiful, albeit tiny package.

"Marjorie, this . . . this is incredible." She shook her head and couldn't believe her eyes. "Thank you. Thank you so much. This gold-plated key to the executive room is just what I needed. Um, do you go in there a lot?"

Marjorie sniffled again and wiped the corner of her eye. "You're welcome. Merry Christmas, Jan."

Jan lifted her eyes from the gift to look at her boss. "Merry Christmas, Marjorie." She smiled as she opened her arms.

Marjorie came in for a gripping hug, then let go and stepped back. She straightened her jacket sleeves and smiled. "Well, Christmas or not, it's back to work for me," she said as she left Jan's office.

Jan dropped into her seat, held her head with one hand, and the tiny gift in the other, contemplating the day's events. She jumped when her phone vibrated.

Can you meet me at the pub? The text message stated.

Jan squinted at the message. Is she kidding me, she thought. She quickly entered her reply and sent it. *Why would I?*

Because I want to give you somethings. I need closure.

Curious, Jan agreed. *What time?*

7 okay?

See you then. Still holding her phone in both hands, she dropped them in her lap and sighed. What is this about now, she wondered? Rather than wait, Jan left immediately.

Jan's eyes adjusted to the darkness of the mahogany wood paneling and dimly lit seating and booths. She took a step back. Then, composed herself and walked to where the other woman was already seated.

Marissa looked up at Jan as she approached. "I came back to Michigan thinking Rob might still be available" she said defensively.

"So, what now? Where are you going?" Jan questioned.

"To Florida first. My parents live there. I'll visit over the holidays, then go back to California." She laughed softly. "I was living with a guy who owns a small ranch in Northern California."

"He was crazy about me, but I broke it off." She sighed and picked up her purse removing a small object. "Fingers crossed, he'll take me back. My life is a series of bad decisions."

Jan listened and started to feel compassion for the woman who sat across from her.

"I wanted to give you this," she said and brought out a small diamond ring. "Rob gave it to me shortly before I ran away." She shook her head. "I think it scared me. When he showed it to me, in my mind I saw a jail cell." She laughed. "How stupid is that?"

"Well . . ." Jan paused.

"I know I hurt him deeply. And, I'm glad that he was able to get on with his life. I'm happy for the two of you."

"What made you think he wouldn't get on with his life?"

"Denise was constantly contacting me. Telling me he was a mess. Rarely coming out of his room. Just . . . hurting." She shrugged. "But I couldn't bare the idea of settling down. Life is short. You know?" She held her hands up with a smile.

"Thank you for this. I hope you'll find what you're looking for. By the way, what made you come looking for us at the grocery store on a Saturday night? Why did you think we'd be there of all places?"

Marissa snickered. "You're not the first date he's taken out to dinner by feeding you free samples at the local market."

The two women shared a laugh.

"Well, my flight leaves soon. So, I'll get out of your way." She laughed. "Forever. Merry Christmas, Jan."

She watched her walk out of the restaurant and stood up to leave herself. As Jan drove away from the pub, she smiled, happily knowing that the ghost of Christmas past is gone forever.

24 FIRST NIGHT

"Come on, let's get packing," Rob said as he plopped his duffel bag onto the settee at the foot of their bed. "I want to make sure we get the east side bedroom so we can look out onto the lake."

Jan came out of the bathroom after feeling sicker than ever. "Honey, I'm sorry, but maybe I shouldn't go. I'm pretty sure I have the flu."

"Hah, you're still trying to get out of this aren't you?"

"What?" Jan gave her husband an incredulous stare. "No, seriously, I just threw up. I have the flu. You can't fake that."

"The flu's not so bad. I'm surprised you didn't come up with something worse that would have kept you in bed."

"The flu is bad. And, I don't want to get everyone else sick. I feel terrible. I really do."

Jan stared at her husband as he looked back her. "Fine. I'll go."

Rob jumped and did a fist pump in the air. "Yesss!"

"But can't we just stay in a hotel?"

"A hotel? Are you kidding? Do you know what a hotel costs in Caseville? Two hundred dollars a night times three days equals Rob's broke."

"But if everyone else gets sick, then it's your fault not mine." She noticed her husband's travel bag was much fuller than when they went on their honeymoon, almost splitting at the seams. "What do you have in there? When we went to Barbados you hardly packed anything."

"When we went on our honeymoon all I needed were shorts and swimsuits. Now, I need long johns, battery operated heated socks, plenty of thermal, long-sleeved t-shirts—"

"Okay, okay, I get it. It's cold up there. But what did you take so we can go into town for a drink? Or by chance," Jan said with a pleading look, "go visit Busha and Jaja?"

Rob looked disheartened at her, then came over and hugged her tight. "Don't be a spoiled sport. This is gonna be fun."

Jan laughed as she sat on the edge of the bed with her hand on her forehead checking her temperature. "I have to say, just watching you is entertaining enough for me. You're acting like a little kid. I never saw you this happy and excited." She went over and wrapped her arms around him. "I'll make the best of it, even if I do have the flu."

"Right," Rob said as he backed away. "I got my flu shot, but still I don't want to take any chances."

"Really? Well, can you at least make me some toast?" She requested of him.

"I can do that." He swiftly walked over to Jan and kissed the top of her head. "Roooad triiip," he shouted springing away from her, grabbing his bag, and heading downstairs.

After minutes, Rob abruptly came back into the room.

"Where's my toast?" She sadly looked at his empty hands.

"Can I take your suitcase now?"

"Wait." Jan stared at the bag. "Um, okay I guess," she said as she slowly zipped it closed.

"Are you sure you're okay? I know you're not upset anymore. But you just don't seem like yourself."

"This flu is really taking it out of me. It'll be nice to get some extra sleep during our holiday break."

He looked at her suspiciously. "Sure it will be." He lifted her bag. "Not too much in here. You really aren't feeling well. You're not bringing half the closet with you including two dozen pairs of shoes."

Jan gave the mere hint of a smile.

"Come on, let's hit the road. I'll make your toast and you can eat it in the truck." Rob carried Jan's bag. "Last chance. Are you sure you packed enough? This is much lighter than the bag you took on our honeymoon." He teased.

"Well, for Barbados I needed sundresses, shorts, capris, tops, shoes, sandals, sneakers, swimsuits—"

"Mmm, you in your swimsuits." He paused a moment closing his eyes recalling the memories. He set the suitcase in the truck bed, barely able to find room for it. "That's an awful lot of presents. Is all that necessary?"

"I stayed within my budget. In fact, I had plenty of money left over," Jan said proudly as she entered into the truck cab.

"Good. We can put it back in the budget," Rob laughed.

"You really are excited," she said. As they started down the road, Jan pulled the visor down to check her makeup. "What?" Paperwork, cocktail napkins with drawings and notes, and pictures, all came tumbling down onto her lap.

Rob tried hard to suppress his laughter knowing he caused the catastrophe that fell onto his wife.

"Why is that stuff tucked up there. Is that your secret hiding place?" She shoved all the items into the glove compartment. After using the mirror, she flipped the visor back to its resting spot. "There, now I won't get dumped on again."

"The weather stations are predicting winter storms

combined with lake effects for Christmas day for the entire Thumb area," Rob said solemnly. "Snow can get pretty deep even for a truck. I just want to warn you in case you get bored and want to leave earlier than planned." He glanced over at her.

"Let's hope not, for snow or boredom," Jan replied. She remembered the Christmases when she was a kid and how the lake effects made huge snowbanks. She and her cousins had fun playing, building snow forts, and Jaja brought out the sleigh and pulled it behind the tractor.

"This is nice, this road trip," Jan said. "It'll give us a couple of hours to talk to each other." Her face became serious. "Rob, don't you think you should let your brothers have a say in how the corporation is structured?"

"Again?" He said indignantly. "They don't put in the same amount of time as I do. And, besides I'm the oldest and had to get it up and running."

"Yes, you started it. But Pete and Brian have been in the trenches while you're out there drumming up more business."

"What are you talking about? I'm in the trenches."

Jan took a deep breath. "Yes, you are. But you also spend a lot of time, the majority of your time," Jan searched for the word, "selling." She saw Rob was contemplating her arguments against his brothers and thought it would be best to give him time to think about it. She hurried to finish her explanation. "And, rightfully so. Because without more business, there's no company. I'm just saying, you saw them talking with potential customers at the Christmas party. Don't you think they can handle it now?"

Rob drove without saying anything, eyes on the road, straight ahead.

"I'm just saying—"

"Saying what? I don't do anything for the company besides party?"

"Selling is a huge part of any company. But you—"

"But what? Whose side are you on, anyway?"

"Side? Rob, there are no sides. These are your brothers and this is your family's company. If you don't start listening to your brothers there won't be anything to fight about." Jan laid her head back and looked out the passenger window. Watching as the woods and farms passed by, she wanted to go to sleep. But instead she felt restless without being able to convince Rob that he needed to recognize his brothers' participation in the family business. He needed to see them as being more than worker bees. She tried fighting the tiredness she felt, but her eyes started to close.

Jan stirred when Rob went into a turn. She sat up and stared at the homes as they drove along M-25. "Wow, these homes are beautiful."

"This is a nice community. You'll like it." He pulled into a long driveway.

Jan leaned forward, pushing against her seatbelt looking out every window. "Where are we?"

"The cottage."

She saw the house and took in a deep breath. "Wow! That's the cottage?"

"Yeah," Rob said as he looked at her with furrowed brows. "Why? What were you expecting?"

"Um, something, um, smaller. I guess."

"Cottage means house on a lake." Rob snickered. "It doesn't mean small house. Did you think it was going to be a run, down shack? This is supposed to be Ed and Denise's retirement home."

"Supposed to be? Aren't they retired already?"

"Not officially. They're still a little too young to retire. But neither one has had job in quite a while."

Jan turned a bewildered look to Rob. "What do they live on?"

"Why do you think Denise clips coupons?"

Jan couldn't help but laugh at her husband's insinuation.

"Seriously, they have some savings and investments. I guess they're doing okay." Rob shrugged.

"From the looks of this house, I would say they're doing better than okay," Jan said as she peered out the truck window for a better look. "You know, sometimes when people act like they're poor, they're actually rich with millions of dollars hidden away."

Rob expressed his amusement at the notion. "Ed and Denise are comfortable at best. But certainly not millionaires," he said as he exited out of the truck. "Now, let's hurry up and get inside before the others get here." He grabbed the suitcases, one by each hand and one smaller bag under his left arm. "I'll come back for the presents. Come on in and check out the house—and the view from our bedroom."

"I'll help with the presents," she shouted to him as he went into the house. Jan was amused at her husband's enthusiasm for the holidays. She realized that whatever Ed did to make those boys love Christmas seems to have worked. Grabbing several, light weight gift bags with one hand, she clutched a large box with her other arm and headed toward the house. As she walked up the sidewalk to the front door, she admired everything about it. She studied the shrubbery arrangements, brick work, and windows. Nice work, you two, she thought. Inside the house was quiet except for some heavy thumping sounds from upstairs.

"Rob? Is everything okay up there?" Jan asked as she set the gifts around the Christmas tree. With the inside and outside decorated so nicely, she pondered when did Ed and Denise find the time?

"Everything's fine, honey. Just doing some last minute rearranging."

"Ouch," Jan backed away from a branch that scraped her hand. Getting on her hands and knees she crawled back and looked closer, then slightly touched the needles feeling the prick on her fingertip. Taking in a deep breath she closed her eyes and memories came flooding back. "A real Christmas tree," she enamored. "That natural pine aroma. You can't fake that—"

"What the hell is going on here?"

Jan turned around, jumped up, and ran to look out the opened front door to see Ed, Denise, Pete, and Monica, all standing on the front lawn with suitcases thrown around them. She went out to see what the commotion was about.

"Rob, are you insane?" Pete shouted while looking up at the house.

"What's going on?" Jan asked the others.

"Like you don't know," Monica sneered.

Denise looked at her strangely. "Did you put Rob up to this?"

"Up to what?" Jan shrugged unknowingly.

"That," Denise and Monica said in unison as they pointed up at the house.

Rob's head was sticking out the second-floor, open window. "Don't worry, Pete, Monica. I'm just changing your room to the west side of the house for the sunset view. You'll love it." Rob tossed another piece of luggage out the window onto the lawn.

The front yard was littered with luggage and gifts. Jan's heart sank at the sight of what her husband was doing. My husband, his brother, my best friend—fighting, she thought. *What a mess. He's ruining all their belongings and gifts.* Another gift flew out the window. "Rob stop it!" She screamed.

"That's it, damn it," Ed muttered as he marched into the house.

Jan's eyes overflowed with tears as she cautiously approached Pete and Monica. "I'm so sorry. I don't know why he's doing this."

Pete looked suspiciously at Jan.

"I swear this wasn't my idea. I didn't even know you

were here."

"I know why he's doing this. Because he can't stand the idea of me and Brian being as good as he is at running Nichols Construction Company. He's so full of himself."

"I thought you were going to talk to him?" Monica glared.

"I did. But he's not listening to me. I don't know what else to do." The tears continued to stream down her face.

Brian pulled up in his truck and with an astonished expression, walking around the yard. "What the hell happened here? Wait, don't tell me." He closed his eyes and nodded.

"Let's start picking this up and get inside," Denise ordered as she hauled a couple of suitcases back into the house.

Carrying as many suitcases and presents as they could, they cringed as the boisterous sound of Rob and his dad arguing upstairs resounded throughout the house.

"Get your ass out there and clean that shit up off the lawn before the neighbors complain," Ed shouted.

"Fine. I will. But Pete should've—"

"Who gives a shit what Pete should've? Now move!"

Rob sulked as he stomped down the stairs and outside.

Jan cautiously slipped by him to return into the house. Surveying the room for place to sit and be alone, hide. *I just want to get away from all this craziness.*

Brian picked up a suitcase. "Can I help?" He gave a sympathetic look to Monica.

"That would be great," she said as she surveyed the room for other belongings.

Rob stepped into the house and watched as Brian went up the stairs. He stomped his foot on the floor. "Whad'ya doing? Your taking their side now too?"

"There are no sides, Rob," he shouted down the stairs. "We're a family. We're a family owned business. You don't own it. You don't own me. I'm not your employee. And," his voice was louder, "you don't tell me what to do."

"Jan. Monica," Denise said from the archway leading into the kitchen. "I could use some help in here."

"Okay. What do you need me to do?" Monica snidely remarked while reluctantly, slowly, strolling into the kitchen. "Stuff a turkey? Churn some butter? Gut a moose—"

Denise stuck her hand in front of Monica's face stopping her in her tracks. "Drink."

Monica's crossed eyes widened at the sight. "Okay," she said and smiled. "I can do that." She plucked the jigger of brandy from Denise's hand and tossed it back. Pressing her eyes closed as she licked her lips. "Mmm, that is smooth."

Denise held her arm out with another drink in Jan's direction.

Jan covered her mouth and belched, causing her cheeks to puff out. She stared at the small glass of liquor. "Oh yuck, that's making me feel sick just looking at it. I have the flu. I can't possibly drink that."

"That's just what the doctor ordered," Monica admonished. "You need to drink your way through the flu. After a few days, you'll wake up feeling good as new."

Jan's jaw dropped. "After a few days? Christmas is one day away." She wrapped her arms around her waist, bent slightly as she walked over to the chair and sat down. "I can't sleep through or be passed out during Christmas."

Monica walked over to the table.

"Don't get too close," Jan said as she held her hand up. "I don't want to contaminate you and make you sick with the flu too."

"Drinking is the best way to treat the flu," Monica laughed. "If you're going to be sick anyway, might as well make it fun." Monica placed her hand on her hip and leaned onto the table with her other hand, slightly forward toward Jan. "Besides, not a problem for me because I got a flu shot."

"Me too," Denise said as she poured two more shots.

"Jan, you sure you don't want to take your medicine?" She turned from the waist looking back at her from under her eyebrows.

Jan's eyes darted back and forth from Monica to Denise. Their aggressive push to drink alcohol and glaring faces were frightening remembrance from college days.

"Drink, drink, drink, drink . . ." the students shouted nonstop as each took a turn for the college drinking contest. Jan put the bottle up to her lips, but the smell of spicy, bitter whiskey made her gag. The room began to spin before she blacked out. The next day she went to class feeling embarrassed. But instead, her friends claimed she won since they thought she passed out from drinking too much.

Jan tightened her arms around her waist, hunched over she belched as she carried herself toward the great room.

"Where is she going?" Monica questioned as she ran to Denise's side. "Is she really sick? She's going to throw-up, isn't she?"

Denise ran after her. "Jan, wait. Can I get you something? Tea? Ginger ale? Toast? I'm sorry I didn't mean to make you sick."

"Stay away from me. I've got the flu," Jan screamed as she led the trail of women through the great room past Rob, Pete, Brian, and Ed.

They stood there watching the women chasing each other up the stairs.

"I got a flu shot," Pete shouted after her.

"Me too," Brian said with a shrug.

"Why the hell didn't you take her to get a flu shot?" Ed yelled at Rob.

Denise followed her through their bedroom and pounded on their bathroom door. "Jan, honey? Open up, please? Let me help you?" She pressed her ear on the wood panel with her hand on the knob.

"No, Denise it's not your fault. Please, I just need to be—"

"What was that?" Monica and Denise stared questioningly for moment, then rushed back down the stairs.

After several minutes Jan peeked out from behind the door. Cautiously she treaded down to the great room where the front door was wide open and everyone gone.

25 KING OF THE HILL

"Just because you're older doesn't mean you get to tell us what to do," Pete said as his hands were clenched in fists by his side. "Rob, you're not the boss," he yelled at the top of his lungs.

Jan couldn't believe what she was seeing. Her husband and his brothers, all circling each other, ready to fight. She slowly stepped down the sidewalk next to where Ed, Denise, and Monica were standing. "Why are they doing this? What's wrong with them? It's Christmas for crying out loud."

"This pretty much happens every Christmas," Denise said to the other women as they watched the men in action.

"What?" Jan and Monica turned their scrunched faces to look at Denise, then turned swiftly back to watch the brothers as the arguing and maneuvering around continued.

"That's right, baby," Monica shouted to Pete. "You're better at running this company than he is. You should be the CEO."

"Seriously, Monica, you're not helping anything," Jan said quietly in disgust.

"When you do the same amount of work that I do bringing in the same number and value of contracts, then maybe I'll think about it."

"I don't even want to work for Nichols Construction Company," Brian yelled back at his two brothers. "I've been accepted at Michigan and I'm starting college for the Winter Semester."

"What?" Rob dropped his fists, stood still, and stared at his youngest brother.

"Good for you, bro," Pete complimented. "Get the hell out of here and make a better life for yourself."

Denise continued her explanation. "Yeah, every Christmas and maybe once or twice again throughout the year these boys go at it."

"Because of this same subject?" Monica asked not taking her eyes off the action.

Denise and Jan kept their eyes focused on the men, stepping out of the way when they drifted to close to them.

"Brian, you can't leave," Rob countered. "You're second in command."

"No, there's been other reasons," Denise continued to talk focusing on the action. "The causes have ranged from a favorite toy, to a girl, to who's Ed's favorite, to who drank the last beer, to who's going to the store to buy more beer." Denise turned a pressed frown to the other women. "The thing to remember is that the boys have always been this way and you shouldn't blame them or yourselves. You'll just have to get used to it and learn to live with it. I did." She sighed.

Jan and Monica exchanged frightened glances, then quickly turned their attention back to the brothers.

"There's no second in command, dumb ass," Pete scorned. "This is a family business," he shouted as he shook his fist at Rob.

"You tell him, honey," Monica cheered for Pete. She covered her mouth to the side so only Jan and Denise could hear. "Incredible. A psychologist would have a field day with this bunch."

"Uh oh, where's Ed going?" Jan said as she pointed at him going into the house. "He's not leaving it up to us to stop this fight, is he?" She grabbed Denise's arm.

"Most times he uses the garden hose, but that's not in the house," Denise stared at the open front door with a puzzled look on her face. "So, I'm not sure what he has up his sleeve this time."

The brothers stopped arguing when they realized their dad went back inside. Their fists dropped relaxing their hands and their jaws relaxed.

The six of them stood outside staring at the front door to see what was going to happen next.

"Where did he go?" Jan took a couple steps forward and leaned over to look into the house. "Is he okay?" She looked back at Rob and the others. "Should we check on him?" She turned fully around with her back to the door and opened her arms to the others. "The stress of something like this could cause him to become seriously ill."

"Watch out!" Rob shouted as he ran to Jan and scooped her up out of harm's way.

Screaming she held onto her husband.

Ed stomped out of the house with his hands raised high above his head holding a set of papers. He stopped and scowled at Rob, moving his hands to the center of the sheets, ready to rip them in half.

"What are you doing?" Rob shouted as he fast walked toward his father.

"I'm sorry, son, but family comes first." Ed swiftly ripped the papers in half and threw them up in the air. The loose ends scattering all over the ground and the stapled clump landed with a thud.

"*Nooo!*" Rob fell to his knees, trying to catch the pieces as they rained back down to the ground. He gathered up what he could of the papers and tried to align the jagged edges. "Do you know how much this cost me?"

Jan, Monica, and the others all looked at each other, not knowing what to say.

"Now let's go inside and have a family Christmas drink." Ed led the way, stopping to let Denise go into the house first.

Monica, Pete, and Brian followed them, stopping to take a brief look back before going inside.

Jan walked over to her husband and stood quietly.

"Aren't you going with them?" Rob mumbled.

"Are you going to be okay?" She asked softly as she gently placed her hand on his shoulder.

"This was the only copy and it cost me, uh, the company a lot of money. I can't believe my dad did this." Rob's chest heaved and he dropped his hands on his lap, still holding remnants of the papers. "I was just trying to make this family business something better. I started having visions of a large corporation. Maybe even with some fancy offices like the ones you have at Hedge." He sighed and from his kneeling position looked up at his wife. "I was drunk with power. Guess I kinda got a little out of control."

"You were a lot out of control," she said as she held her hand out for him to get up. "But your family loves you and I'm sure they're anxious for you to go inside and celebrate Christmas with them."

"I don't know," Rob said as he shook his head. "I think they're probably—"

"Are you gonna get your asses in here and celebrate Christmas with your family?" Ed shouted standing in the front doorway. "Or, stay out here and mope?"

Rob looked up at Jan with a hint of a smile. He accepted her hand as a gesture while getting up off the ground. He leaned over a couple more times to gather up the last few pages. With both hands he carried the messy stack pressed against his chest up to the house.

Jan put her hand threw the crook of his arm and they

walked in together.

Ed grinned as he stood by to let them pass, then closed the door to the outside.

Pete walked up to Rob and handed him a beer. He raised his beverage to his brother. "Merry Christmas, bro."

Rob held his bottle and clanked it against Pete's, and Brian's. "Merry Christmas."

The guys put their arms around each other for a group hug, patting each other on the back.

Rob held his hand out to Pete. "How about we'll be equal partners?"

"Sounds good to me," Pete said as he accepted Rob's gesture.

Rob held his hand toward his youngest brother.

Brian quickly raised his hands in the air. "I'm going to college. Remember? I'll come back and work for the company after I graduate."

Rob nodded. "I don't know how we're going to get along without you."

"Second that," Pete added.

Ed shook his head as he walked over to Denise and put his arm around her shoulders.

"Anybody hungry?" She headed into the kitchen.

"I could eat," Brian said as he followed behind the group.

"Maybe we can all go into town and have some cheeseburgers," Rob said.

"That'd be great," Brian replied anticipating eating something delicious. "There's nothing better than a burger in Caseville."

"Well I don't have hamburger, but I've got lunchmeat. Anybody interested in a fried bologna sandwich?" Denise looked around the room.

"Uh, no thanks. I'll pass," Jan moaned as she placed her hands on her upset stomach and hunched over.

"What is a fried bologna sandwich? I'm not sure I would like it." Monica scrunched her face in Denise's direction.

"Who doesn't like bologna?" Excitedly she retorted. "It's one of the B-gifts from God." She held up her hands and counted off with her fingers. "You know, beer, bacon, bologna." She threw her up hands and slapped them down on her thighs.

There was a quiet pause from the others. The guys looked at each other and acted like they wanted to say something.

"What?" Denise asked.

"Boobs." Pete offered up. "Another B-gift?" He grinned.

"Boobs!" Denise shouted, grinning as she put her hands on her own and squeezed. "There you have it. Boobs. These are a gift." Turning back to the counter, she lined up a half dozen paper plates and placed two slices of bread on each. Taking the hot frying pan, she used the spatula and placed several slices of fried bologna on the bread. "Come and get it," she said to the others.

Brian picked up a plate and went to sit down at the table.

"Why don't all of you go and eat your sandwiches in front of the TV," Ed suggested waving his arm to get them out of the kitchen.

"Okay, okay. We're going," Rob said dodging his father's arm, following his wife into the other room.

Jan quickly turned around to go back into the kitchen to ask Denise for some soda crackers. "Oh no, I'm so sorry," she blurted out, witnessing Ed and Denise kissing and groping each other pressed up against the counter.

Ed took a step back, then spanked Denise. "Let's go upstairs." Taking Denise's hand, he led her out of the kitchen brushing past Jan. "Excuse us, Jan. Help yourself in the kitchen. We're gonna be awhile."

Her wide eyes fixated across the kitchen, feeling stuck in place. Oh no, I can't undo what I just saw. Like if it's not bad enough that I have the flu. I had to see that? Now

I really am sick, she thought.

Gradually, Jan pulled herself together and searched the cupboards. Finding the crackers, she went back to join her husband in the family room.

"You look like you're getting worse," Rob flashed a concerned expression to his wife.

"You have no idea," Jan whined.

"I hate these news updates during the game," Pete complained. "It's like you're all happy enjoying some sports, and then, bam. They tell ya some depressing news and ruin everything."

"The FBI continues their investigation into the alleged illegal contract dealings with the City of Detroit. More tonight at eleven," the news reporter announced.

Jan and Rob looked at each other with worrisome expressions.

"Let's get through the holidays, then we'll work with Manny and Christie to get some answers. I'm sure it's something else the news is referring to," Rob said putting his arm around her shoulders, trying to ease Jan's concerns.

"Oh, you have got to be kidding me," Brian said throwing his hands in the air. "Well, we know who's going to win that game. Anybody interested in playing a few hands of euchre?"

"I'll play," Rob said going to table in the other room along with the others.

"Losers buy the beer for tomorrow," Monica challenged. "Deal 'em up."

Jan sat next to her husband at the end of the table, keeping her distance so she wouldn't spread her illness to the others.

"Aww, look at that Ed. The boys do know how to play nice together," Denise said, snickering as she walked back into the kitchen followed by Ed. They pulled up a couple of chairs to watch.

Jan yawned and laid her head on her husband's

shoulder listening to Monica and Denise talk about what they have planned for next year's vacations, parties, and birthdays.

"Where's a calendar," Denise said jumping up from her chair. "Ed, didn't you throw one in the drawer that you got from the pharmacy last time we were here." She pulled open a drawer and withdrew a glossy, picture-filled tablet. Pulling her chair closer to Monica, she flipped the pages to June.

Calendar, Jan thought as she sat back, wide-eyed staring at the document in Denise's hands. Oh my gosh, I haven't checked my calendar in a couple of weeks. I've just been so busy and pulled in so many directions that I forgot to check my . . . uh oh. Jan's eyes moved around the room. "I'm going back to bed," she said as she ran upstairs.

"I'll bring you some toast in a little bit," Denise shouted to her then continued her conversation.

Alone in the room, Jan removed her phone from her handbag and opened the calendar app. She scrolled through the last two weeks of appointments, then four weeks. She pressed her lips and took a deep breath, then climbed into bed. She laid awake listening to the noise from downstairs for over an hour. Thinking about how she needed to focus on herself better and not react to the demands of work, family, and friends.

Goodnight everybody. Jan listened to the others as they made their way to their rooms.

"Honey? You sleeping?" Rob asked as he slipped into bed. "Feeling any better?"

"Uh huh," Jan mumbled sleepily.

"I'm sorry I didn't take you more seriously about being sick. I'll make it up to you." He kissed the top of her head. "I still can't believe what my dad did to my, uh, the company's corporation papers," he said rolling his head on his pillow.

"Yes, it's terrible," she said smiling wrapped up in her husband's arm. No point in me telling him, she thought.

I'll let Manny take the brunt of his wrath when he explains that those were only a copy and the formal papers were filed with the Michigan state licensing and regulatory department.

26 SHOPPING FOR ONE

"I'm going to run into town for a quick shopping trip. I need some medicine and I forgot my shampoo," Jan said as she slung the strap of her handbag over her head and onto her shoulder. Dramatically she felt her forehead. "Need anything?" The smell of bacon and pancakes hung in the air. She scanned the table and counters in search of leftovers.

"I'll go with you," Denise said as she reached for her purse and started thumbing through a few coupons.

"No," Jan blurted out and held up her hand. "I mean," she dropped her arm, "You have so much to do here. I'll get whatever it is you need and you don't have to waste your time shopping." She tried smiling, but the apprehension in her voice was sending a different message.

"Oh, I get it. Monica's going, but I can't? The two young, cool girls don't want the old lady around?" Denise turned away and walked to the sink resting her hands on the rim. "That's fine. I'll just stay here and continue to slave away so the rest of the family can enjoy *themselves*."

"Monica's not going." Jan shook her head desperately.

"Monica's not going." Denise quickly turned around to face Jan. "Do you want me to go for you, since you're sick?"

"No. No, no. I'm very particular about what medicine I take. And, my shampoo."

Denise looked at her suspiciously. "And, you're sure Monica's not going?"

"She's upstairs in the shower." Jan cleared her throat and walked closer to Denise. "You know, I'm just not used to being around so many people all the time." Jan rolled her eyes for effect and waved her hand through the air. "I just need to get away by myself for a little while and breath. You know what I mean?" Jan asked with a pleading look.

Denise sighed and softened her stance. "I know exactly what you mean. That's why I was thinking I'd go with you. But that's okay. I do have a lot of things to get done here." She pulled a long list from her purse and a thick, paper-clipped bunch of coupons, then shoved all of it into Jan's cupped hands. "Thank you for doing the shopping for me."

Jan stared at everything in her hands for a moment, then slowly straightened the items together and placed them in her purse. She chuckled softly. "Good thing I'm much better at grocery shopping than I used to be."

"You've learned well." Denise gave her a forceful pat on the back, compelling Jan to take a step forward.

Quickly Jan moved to get outside, but paused to observe the guys acting like silly, little boys, playing touch football. "Huh," she thought, "Yesterday they wanted to tear each other apart. And today, they're all patting each other on the butt and having fun. I'll never understand it."

"Hey, where you are going?" Rob shouted from across the yard running toward his wife.

"Oh damn. Now here he comes." Jan sprinted toward the truck then started to climb in. "I'm going to help Denise out by running some errands for her," Jan said when he caught up with her.

"Well, that's nice of you," Rob said as he closed the

door for her. Reaching into the open window, he clasped her face in his hands and pulled her over for a kiss. "Thank you for being such a good sport about this," he said looking deeply into her eyes. "I really appreciate it and I'll make it up to you. I promise."

"Denise is good to me and I'm happy to be able to help her for once," Jan said as she pulled his cold, clammy hands off of her face and held them tightly. *But I have to get out of here now before Monica finds me leaving. She'll be mad as hell.* Jan smiled back at him.

"Love you," he said through the driver's side open window.

She blew him a kiss. Driving down the road, Jan shouted out loud. "Holy crap! What does it take to escape this family?"

Jan drove up and down Main Street in Caseville looking for a place to park. Busy time of year even for a small town, she thought. She turned down the side street and nearly rear-ended another car that was leaving their spot. "Whew! That was close, but I'll take your parking space." Taking a deep breath, she exited the truck. As she walked to the pharmacy she looked around and admired the small town feel. People waved and passersby wished her a Merry Christmas even though they didn't know her. Christmas music streamed through the air as she walked down the sidewalks. *So, this is what they mean when they talk about a hallmark moment.*

Jan entered the pharmacy and slowly studied the aisle signage. She fumbled with the strap on her purse as she looked around.

"Can I help you?" The woman behind the counter asked.

"Thanks, but I know what I'm looking for." When she observed the aisle she wanted, she walked swiftly to the location. As she studied the product selection, she pulled out a tissue and dabbed her nose. "From the cold outside to the warm inside air, the runny nose never stops," she mumbled. Pressing her lips together, she picked up one box after another and examined them. This one has the cutest indicators. But this one has the easiest instructions, she thought as she picked up the product, turned around, and headed toward the checkout counter. Anxious to get this over with, she set it down and smiled at the store associate. She sniffled and withdrew her tissue from her pocket to dab her nose again.

"Oh honey, it's not that bad. There's worse things in life," the store associate said as she patted the back of Jan's hand as it rested on the counter.

"What? No. You don't understand," Jan said trying to clarify the situation. "I'm just—" She noticed her left ring finger was bare beneath the clerk's hand. Of all the days how could she have forgotten her wedding ring.

"It's okay. I understand better than you'd think." She scanned the product and set it back on the counter. "That'll be ten dollars and fifty-eight cents." She waited for Jan to get the payment out of her purse.

"Wait. I have a coupon." Happy that she remembered the discount, Jan withdrew the glossy slip of paper from her purse, pressed it against the counter to straighten it out, then held it out for collection.

The woman behind the counter stared at the piece of paper. She looked at Jan and next slowly removed the wrinkled sheet from her hand.

"Okay then, one dollar off. That'll be nine dollars and fifty-two cents."

"Here you go." Jan nodded handing her a ten dollar bill.

"Out of ten and here's your change." She dropped the coins into Jan's hand. Leaning against the counter she looked closely at Jan. "You know, there's a women's clinic down the road just outside of town if you need help." She studied Jan's face.

"I'll be okay, but thank you for that information."

"You'd be surprised how many young women like

yourself come in here for those kits." She nodded her head slowly. "You'd think it was an epidemic or something."

"Could I have a bag?"

"For one item?" The woman frowned. "Okay. Suit yourself."

Jan left the store walking as quickly as she could, clutching her purchase as she went back to the truck. She threw her purse and purchase into the passenger seat and quickly jumped inside, locking the doors. Laying her head back against the headrest, she sighed. After giving herself several minutes to relax, she picked up her purse and rummaged around in it. "Okay, now that that's done. What's next?" She pulled out Denise's lengthy shopping list and stack of coupons. Taking a deep breath, she started the truck. Well, let's get this one over with too, she shook her head as she backed out of the parking spot nearly missing another truck that honked at her. Jan looked in her rearview mirror and saw a man shake his fist at her. She innocently shrugged and gave a friendly wave back to him as she mumbled, "Merry Christmas to you too."

Less than a quarter of a mile down the road, Jan turned right into the grocery store parking lot. Inside the store she set her handbag in the child seat and removed the list with coupons.

"Hey, aren't you the girlfriend of one those Nichols boys?" A store associate called out to Jan.

Startled, Jan turned to see who was talking. A tall, thin man with Manager for a store name tag.

"Oh, uh, girlfriend? No. I'm Rob Nichols wife."

"Rob got married? Wow. Well, I'll be darn. Guess I lost that bet." He laughed.

Jan looked at him quizzically.

He cleared his throat. "I mean, I'm so happy for you. And, Rob." With a nervous smile, he took a step back. "Is there anything I can help you find?"

Jan withdrew Denise's list and shook it out. The lengthy piece of paper waved in the air. In her other hand

Jan showed him the coupon stack.

"Ah, you must be shopping for Denise. I'm surprised she let you. She's very particular."

"She trained me herself. It's just that her shopping list is all over the place. She has a dairy product up at the top and butter at the bottom of the list. It's inefficient. At this rate it's going to take me all day to get through this." Jan shook her head as she looked up and down the sheet of paper, holding it so both her and the manager could view it.

The manager leaned over and stared at the paper. "Looks to me like she writes an item down as she needs it. Maybe she should make a new list before going to the store and organize it by department."

"That's exactly right." Jan looked at him and beamed. "I can teach Denise a thing or two as well." She gave a firm nod.

"Well, good luck with that." The manager smiled kindly and slowly stepped away.

Jan dug in her handbag for a pen, but didn't find one. "Great," she complained. "Any other time I have a dozen of those that I carry around with me." She went to the stationary aisle, grabbed a six pack of pens, opened it, took one out, then tossed the rest of the pack into the cart. Using a cereal box for a surface, she immediately started to draw arrows, circles, and scribbled on the shopping list.

"Ah, that's better," she said as she held the list up giving it a close review. "Hmmm, or maybe not." She held it further away, then up close. "It's the overhead light. It's glaring off this glossy paper. Where in the world did she get this paper from anyway? It's too shiny. Too blinding." She shrugged. "Albeit pretty."

Jan set the writing materials down in the cart. Looking over the shelves, she spotted several notepads. She picked several up, checked the thickness of each, and the number of lines per page. Then she spotted a lengthy, narrow tablet, nice and thick with a hard, cardboard backing. "Oh yeah, baby, you're the one," she said as she started writing a new list. She figured she add the tablet to Denise's gift once she returned to the cottage.

Jan placed the last product into the shopping cart that was filled to capacity. She checked her watch. Having been gone for over two hours she started to have concerns that Rob would think she wasn't coming back. She laughed a little at the idea. Removing her phone from her handbag, she opened the text app. *Almost done shopping. Will be home soon.* She hit send and held onto the phone as she pushed the cart. She immediately removed it, when she heard it buzz.

That's great honey. See you when you get here.

"Wow, Rob must be having a great time. Usually it's stop spending money, get out of the store, and come home right now," she said quietly.

She pushed the cart into a checkout aisle with only one customer ahead of her. Waiting her turn, she saw the Detroit paper on the media stand. *Suspected illegal contracts with the city have federal agencies turning over every stone.* The headline annoyed Jan. Why don't they just get to the point and get it over with.

Some room opened up on the counter and Jan started taking her items out of the cart and placing them on the conveyor belt.

"Hello, ma'am. Did you find everything you need?" The young man asked.

"Yes, but I have a lot of coupons for you too," Jan held up a handful of slips of paper for him to see.

The manager walked up next to the store associate. "Make sure you take extra special care of this young lady. She's Rob Nichols wife."

"Rob got married. I have to tell my dad. He'll be surprised."

Huh, Jan thought, everyone is surprised that Rob is married. Is there something I should know?

27 CHRISTMAS EVE

"Oh good, you're back," Denise exclaimed. She dropped the potato she was peeling and went to sort through the groceries. "Jan, did you get the corn starch I had on the list?"

"Yes, it's here somewhere," Jan said as she peeked into each bag.

"What about the browning sauce?"

"Yup, that too." She found that item and handed it to Denise.

"Perfect," Denise said as she walked over to Jan and hugged her. "You're a life saver. Ed would've gone through the roof if we didn't have gravy with the mashed potatoes tonight."

"Why do you put up with that shit from him?" Monica demanded.

"Her gravy is really good," Jan said shaking a finger at Denise.

Monica continued to stare at Denise and ignored Jan.

Denise turned from the sink and was startled when she caught Monica's glare in her peripheral vision. She composed herself and glared back. "It's none of your damn business." She placed her hand on her hip. "Now, if you plan on eating here tonight, you'd better start helping."

Jan's eyes widened as she watched.

"What can I do to help?" Monica softened her stance and walked over to the stove.

"Here's the stuffing recipe to get you started," Denise said as she stood close to Monica and placed her arm around her waist. "Pretty simple, pour the broth over the bread cubes, add the seasoning, and mix." Denise patted her on the shoulder. "Any questions just ask." She returned to her potatoes.

Jan realized that Monica hasn't even looked at her since she returned to the cottage. I can only assume she is really pissed, she thought.

Monica turned suddenly toward Jan. "Well, what are you going to do to help?" She lashed out.

"Whoa! Weren't you ready to let me have it?" Jan fell back in her chair.

"Damn right. What the hell was the big idea taking off without me today?"

"I needed to get some medicine and shampoo. And, since I was out, I helped Denise by getting the groceries," she shouted her alibi.

"What the hell is going on in here?" Ed entered the kitchen and looked at each of them. "We can't even hear the game, you girls are so loud." The kitchen was silent and he left the room.

The women busted out laughing and felt the tension leave the room.

Jan's phone buzzed. She picked it up and saw a picture of a huge diamond ring and a text message from Gina, *Michael proposed!!!*

Monica was looking at her phone, then turned to Jan.

They both smiled acknowledging their friend's happiness.

That's great! I'm so happy for you two! Can't wait to hear the details. Congrats!!! Jan hit the send button and set her phone down.

"Looks like there's going to be a wedding next year," Monica said.

"Wedding?" Denise frantically turned around. "What wedding?"

"Gina and Michael. She sent a picture of the ring. Look at the size of that rock." Monica showed her phone to Denise.

She took a deep breath. "Oh, my goodness. Thank God. I thought that maybe you and—" Denise stopped what she was about to say and looked wide-eyed at Monica.

"Thought that me and who might what?" Monica gave her an inquisitive look.

"Not you . . . I didn't mean you exactly . . . or Pete. I mean. Not Pete, but—"

Monica laughed so hard she fell back against the counter.

Denise started laughing with her. "Hoo boy," she exhaled.

Their phones buzzed again.

"Now what? She got the earrings and necklace to go with it?" Monica bemoaned.

Jan moaned when she saw the picture in the next message. A sunny beach with Christie and Manny standing knee deep in ocean water. *Congrats, Gina! Happy Holidays from our resort to yours!*

"What's with these two women showing off to us?" Monica looked at Jan then Denise. "We need a picture and a damn good message to send back to them," Monica said as she started walking into the great room followed by Jan and Denise. "Oh, I know what the message can be. 'In your faces, bitches!'"

"I'm not sending that," Jan replied.

Denise shook her head. "What are you going to do for a picture?"

"All I can think of in a moment's notice is the

traditional family by the fireplace photo. But I'll have all year to plan for next Christmas," Monica said with a devious tone. She paused the TV and motioned with her hands. "Everybody, up. Over by the fireplace and strike a pose."

Ed looked angrily at her and opened his mouth.

"Quiet." She pointed at him. "You can fast forward during commercials. You won't miss a thing. Now get over there."

"This is a first for the Nichols family," Brian said.

"You're kidding," Jan replied. "You never had a family Christmas photo before."

"Oh, is that what this is?" Pete teased stretching as he walked to his place by the fieldstone wall. "I thought it was a lineup for the police department."

Ed and Denise cooperatively stood at the far left and waited for the others.

Jan was surprised by the affectionate way Ed placed his arm around Denise. Whatever it is between the two, it seems to work for them, she thought.

"Rob next to Denise. Jan by Rob. Then Pete. Leave room for me. And, Brian."

Monica setup her phone's camera with the timer and ran over to the others. "Say Merry Christmas," she said through her teeth.

"*Buuull shiiit*," the men almost simultaneously said together.

Laughing, Jan asked, "Are you sure this is your first family Christmas photo?"

"Wow! This picture is perfect," Monica shouted. "We make a great looking family."

Rob flashed an irked look to Jan.

She tilted her head giving him a warning look back.

Monica projected the picture on the television screen.

"That does look great," Denise commented. "Can you share that with me?"

"Yeah, me too," Brian said as he removed his phone

from his back pocket. He noticed his brothers' sneers. "I guess. No big deal."

"Sounds like college boy is getting soft already," Rob came over and wrapped his arm around Brian's neck and mussed his hair.

Brian wrestled his way free. "That's the nicest thing you've ever said to me," he said laughing.

"On the count of three we press the send button together. One, two, three." Monica set her phone down. "Did you send it?"

"Yeah, did you?" Jan replied.

"You sent it ahead of me, didn't you?"

"Because I thought you were going to send it before me," Jan argued.

Monica laughed. "I did."

"Denise said let's eat," Brian called to the rest.

"I'm stuffed. Another great meal, Denise," Rob said as he slid his chair away from the table. He grabbed Jan's hand and pulled her along. "Come on, honey, we have to go."

"Go? Go where?" Confused, Jan went along with her husband to see what he was leading up to.

Leading her into the family room, he pulled her down next to him on the sofa. "We need to get our seats because this is when we open the gifts," Rob whispered.

Jan cuddled up with her husband. She showed him the picture of Christie and Manny on the beach.

"Nice."

"Can we do that some Christmas?" Jan whispered.

"Maybe someday. But today our families are here and we're fortunate to have them. We need to spend time with them while we can. Would you really want to be away from your parents this time of year?" Rob kept his voice quiet.

Jan smirked. "My parents would come with us."

"No, they wouldn't. Your grandparents are still here

and *they* are going to be with them."

"Okay. But I'm not with them. So, why can't we go to Mexico?" Jan spoke softly questioning her husband.

"We'll make plans to be with them the day after Christmas. And next year, when it's your turn you'll, uh, I mean, we'll be with your parents on Christmas Day."

"Not the same." Jan slipped into a comfortable position, resting her legs over the arm of the sofa and leaning back into her husband's arms.

Rob sighed and squeezed her tight. "I'm glad you're here with me. Because, I'm excited about sharing my family Christmas with you. Did you ever think of that?"

Jan squirmed. "Well, why didn't you put it that way in the first place," she scolded. "You were all," Jan lowered her voice, "me man, you woman."

"What are you talking about?" He leaned forward to look at her. "I told you that from the beginning, when this whole thing started in the grocery store may I remind you."

"You said that," Jan lowered her voice again, "We're the Nichols family—"

"Okay, cut it out with the impressions of me. I get it." Rob leaned back and rested his free arm on the back of the sofa.

"Listen, I don't want to fight on Christmas Eve of all things," Jan spoke softly. "I'm here with you. And, this is the Nichols family Christmas." She stretched her neck to kiss his cheek. "Okay?"

"Better than okay," he replied as he kissed her passionately.

"Coming in," Denise warned Jan and Rob as she carried her coffee. "Time to open gifts."

Everyone found a seat and settled in.

"So, who's going to pass out gifts?" Denise looked around the room.

"I'll pass out, but not gifts," Pete joked. "Last year you did it."

"We have more members in our family this year. So, it's not going to be me again," Denise countered.

"I'll start, but I'm going to need help," Monica said as she looked at Jan then the others. She picked up several handle bags and slipped them over her wrist, and carried a boxed gift in each hand. "Let's see here. And, this one goes to . . ."

"I'll help too," Brian said as he walked over to the decorated tree and looked underneath. "This is a lot of stuff to get through and there's only a few days left in the year to get it done."

Ed tore off the wrapping from a gift box and lifted the lid. "What the hell?" He picked it up and thumbed through it, then started to read each one. "Thank you, Jan. This is a very thoughtful gift. Unique too."

Jan went over and gave her father-in-law a kiss on the cheek.

"Do I need a coupon for that?"

"Nope. That one's on me," she grinned as she picked up a similar package and handed it to Monica.

"For me? It's not the same thing you gave Ed is it?"

"You have to open it," Jan provoked.

Monica hurried to the tree and picked up a beautifully wrapped box in a pattern of gold and silver. She ran back to where Jan was sitting on the couch. "Let's do this together."

"Wow! Those gift wrapping skills really took off with you," Jan said grinning at her friend.

"You like it? That's it. That's the gift," Monica teased.

Jan smirked at the idea that the packaging was the gift and held it tight. "This is a beautifully wrapped gift, Monica. But I thought you said it was for—"

Monica quickly put her finger to Jan's mouth to shush her. "She didn't open her gift yet." She looked at Denise, but she was busy removing red and green tissue paper from a shiny red bag.

"You got us the same thing?" Jan gave her friend a

strange look.

"How will we ever know unless we both open our gifts?" Monica asked with her finger tips ready to pull off the bow on her gift.

Together, the best friends eagerly tore off the wrapping paper.

Jan lifted the top off the box and her jaw dropped. "Monica, this is too much. It's beautiful. But it's too much."

"You know I'll do what I want to do. You're the sister I never had."

Jan smiled as she reflected on where she last heard those similar words. "And, you're the sister I never had. Thank you."

"Well, this is a nice little package. Let's see what I've got," Monica grinned. She lifted the box lid and squinted at the contents. "Are you kidding me?" She looked at Jan's eyes. "You know I know how much you make, right?"

Jan laughed. "Do you like it?" She continued to smile at her. "Aren't you going to check out what the coupons say?"

Monica huffed and picked up the clipped construction paper slips. "Oh!" She grinned as she looked at Jan. "How clever." She lifted the bracelet out of the box and placed it on her wrist. "This is too much," she said as she held out her arm and admired the gift.

"Still friends?" Jan asked.

"No." Monica turned to her with a sinister look. "Sisters," she said as she wrapped her arms around Jan.

"Sisters," Jan said as she tightened her arms around her best friend. Over Monica's shoulder Jan saw Denise pick up her gift. "Hey," she whispered. "Look over there."

Monica turned around in her seat and watched as Denise peeled away the shining paper. She removed the bow and set it with the pile she started from the other gifts already opened. "Oh my," she said as she stared at the contents. She looked up and saw Monica's eyes on her, smiling.

"Do you like it?" Monica asked.

"It's beautiful," she said closing the lid and putting it down.

Monica's face dropped with curiosity. "Aren't you going to try it on?"

"Maybe later. I don't want it to get ruined while I'm working in the kitchen." Denise picked up another gift.

"Uh oh. That's me," Jan said excitedly.

She removed the tissue paper and felt deep into the bag. She withdrew a pack of colorful, construction paper coupons. Denise read the top one and quickly examined the others. She reached back into the bag and pulled out a stack of glossy sheets, all neatly held together with ribbon. "What a wonderful gift," she said as she came over and gave Jan a hug. "This is so thoughtful. And, you better be ready," she said as she laughed, "because I'm gonna take you up on every one of these. And, the manufacturers coupons, well that's like giving me cash or gift cards. What a great idea." she said shaking her finger at her stepdaughter-in-law. Denise returned to her chair and continued with the next gift.

"That's amazing," Monica said to Jan as she watched Denise. "I give her a diamond bracelet and she couldn't care less. You give her a bunch of paper and she loves it. What the hell did you write on those things?"

Jan couldn't help but laugh at the irony. "I'm sure she'll come around to liking your gift too. The thing is, she's not about glitz and glamour. I honestly think she likes the chase of a buck or two. You know, kind of make a game out of it by combining sales with coupons with store rewards and so on." Jan sighed. "Mmm, the thrill of the chase. I have to say, I think I'm getting some of that myself."

Annoyed with her friend's chatter and Denise's reaction to her gift, Monica turned her glare to Jan. "You were working two jobs. When the hell did you find time to make all those stup—, um, I mean those adorable coupon books?"

"I started keeping a list for Denise in October, when I read about it in a home magazine. Then I thought, what the heck, I'll share the wealth with the entire family."

"I'm going to the kitchen for a drink."

"I'll join you," Jan said as she followed. "For a drink of water."

Jan sat down at the table and cracked open the seal on a fresh bottle of water.

Monica sat down and took a long drink of beer. "I don't get it. I just don't get it."

Jan shrugged and sat quietly commiserating with her friend.

Ed walked into the kitchen with Denise. "Girls, sorry to interrupt but Denise has something to say to Monica."

"It's okay, Ed. I thanked Monica in the other room for the beautiful," she stammered as the words came out of her mouth, "diii-a-mooond bracelet." She smiled at Monica. "Didn't I?"

"I guess. If you want to call it that."

"Denise," Ed said sharply.

"Okay. Monica, I absolutely love the new bracelet and will cherish it and wear it often. I'm just not used to getting gifts like that. I used to dream about it, but eventually gave up. So, when I first saw it, well, I was blown away," she said with a slight laugh. "Will you forgive me? I'm sorry. I didn't mean to be rude."

Monica jumped up and grabbed Denise into her arms. "There's nothing to forgive. You just made my Christmas."

Ed smiled. "My work here is done." He left the kitchen.

Jan admired the two women as she watched them come to terms with each other. This can only get better with time, she thought.

28 MERRY LONELY CHRISTMAS

Christmas morning, and Jan snuggled closer to her husband on the loveseat in their bedroom to stay warm and enjoy his childhood story.

"My dad did the best he could after my mom died," Rob spoke softly as he held Jan in his arms. "He didn't know what to buy a bunch of little boys for Christmas gifts." Rob squeezed Jan tight. "So, he bought some equipment for each of us and taught us the one thing he knew how to do well so we wouldn't be disappointed. He took us ice fishing." He paused with a smile, turned his head to look at Jan's expression. "And, that's how the Nichols family Christmas tradition got started."

"Ice fishing!" Jan sat up and turned to look at her husband. "Ice fishing! I can't believe that this is the big reveal everyone was so excited about." Jan wrapped her arms around her knees and sat sideways to face Rob.

Still smiling, Rob leaned back and crossed his legs.

"You thought I was going to cry, didn't you?" Jan asked after an awkward pause.

"I was kinda hoping for something." Rob nodded as he moved to the edge of the seat. "You talked about your family traditions and this is mine."

"Yeah, well, we're not at my grandparents' farm now, are we?"

She rolled her eyes and stood up. "Rob, it's our first Christmas together. And you're going ice fishing? While I what? Wait for you?" She challenged.

Rob shook his head and walked to the door. "I'll be back when we're done ice fishing," he said as he left the room and the door slammed behind him.

Jan listened from her room as the guys fought over the best thermal attire, grabbed some fishing gear, and headed outside. She heard Denise and Monica trying to talk them out of it, but their objections didn't seem to matter to the men.

Jan checked her watch. Eight fifteen, not time yet, she supposed. She went back to sit down on the loveseat. She felt it would be safer to stay upstairs and suffer through the flu, if it was the flu, alone rather than face Denise and Monica's questions about how she was feeling and how they could help.

Jan jumped at the sound of knocking on the door.

"Jan, sweetie, can I bring you something to eat or drink?"

"Thank you, Denise, but I'm okay. I just need to sleep through this."

"Can we come in? We'd just like to see that you're okay."

Monica actually sounds sincere, Jan thought. "No, you better stay away from me. I don't want you two to get sick and ruin your Christmas too."

"It's not going to be any fun without you," Monica sighed.

Jan listened as the two women went back downstairs. She went to the door and cracked it open enough so she could her what they were saying.

"Want a drink?" Denise asked Monica.

"Why miss Denise, I like the way you think."

Glass was clanging and the long pouring sound of

liquor traveled up the stairs. Jan couldn't help but smile as she listened to the two very different women share one thing in common—a love for alcohol.

"And what a nice, generous drink you pour. Cheers!"

"Cheers!"

Jan listened as the glasses clanged.

"So, the guys really have gone ice fishing every Christmas?"

"Oh yeah. I used to do all the cooking and, you know, holiday crap by myself. Then I figured what the heck, it's my Christmas too."

"Absolutely. To your Christmas and mine."

"It's nice to have you and Jan with me this year. Although I feel bad for Jan, but we'll make it up to her next year."

Jan smiled at the thought. Right now, the idea of liquor at eight o'clock in the morning just added to her nausea.

"Another round?" Denise asked as her chair screeched as she stood up.

Jan's eyes opened wide, surprised by her stepmother-in-laws behavior. Hope the guys won't be too hungry when they come back in, she thought. Oh, who am I kidding, they're going to be hammered too.

"What about dinner?" Monica asked.

Denise started laughing and there was the sound of her falling against the counter bumping the pots and pans.

"That's the best part." She laughed with a snort. "I bought a prepared meal from the grocery store." She continued laughing. "I just put everything in the oven on low. And, when they return it's ready to serve."

Some pots fell to the floor. Jan was starting to laugh herself.

"Aren't you the cleaver one. Denise, I'm seeing a side of you I really like. You should be this way more often."

"Well, now with you and Jan in my life, I just might." Her voice rose louder as she trailed with her laughter.

Reaching for a pillow, Jan pulled it over to use as a

cushion and sat down on the floor by the door.

"How's your drink?" Monica asked.

"Give me a second. Gone."

They were both snort-laughing now.

"So, how long do the guys stay out there on the ice? Do you worry?"

"Naaah. They've been doing this for years. They know what they're doing."

"Hmm, but we're having a bit of a warm up in the weather. Should we check on them at some point?"

"Oh, you can check on them anytime. Just look out the kitchen window to your left."

There was the sound of Denise bumping up against the counter again. "Can you see that shanty over there? It's kind of hard to see with all the snow coming down."

"All four of them in that tiny, little thing?"

"Yuuup. That's them."

"That's hard to believe. Are you sure there's not a bar open in town that they go too?"

"Weeell, I just know that . . . I checked out the shanty one time and, and surfries," she chortled, "sur-pris-ing-ly" she garbled her words, "it is quiet . . . I mean quite spacious." she pressed her eyes closed, laughing.

"Okay, so you don't think we should go into town looking for them?"

"Oh, no. It's snowing too hard nows anyways." Denise took her time talking as the words were getting more and more slurred. "Besides, that storm that's coming our way, we're also getting some reee-ally bad lake effects."

Jan woke up and stretched out the stiffness in her body after lying on the floor for so long. The clock on the nightstand indicated it was noon. She listened for sounds from downstairs, but didn't hear anything. Slowly she made her way down the stairs, quietly so she wouldn't draw attention to herself.

Peering around the corner, she had to cover her mouth to keep from laughing out loud. Denise was propped up in the corner of the kitchen on the floor and Monica had her head on her arms on the table. Her hand still clutching her drink.

Jan went to the mudroom and withdrew her phone from her purse. Back in the kitchen she opened the camera app. "Smile ladies," she said softly. Grinning she slipped the phone into her pajama pocket. Leaning against the counter, now she was starting to feel hungry. She sighed and decided to make herself a sandwich from yesterday's leftovers. Quietly moving around the kitchen, she put the ingredients together and carried her plate to the table. Taking a bite, food has never tasted so good, she thought.

She remembered what Denise said earlier that morning about looking at the shanty from the kitchen window. She walked over and was surprised to see how much snow had accumulated in several hours. Then, she saw the tiny construction that the men used for ice fishing. There was no activity outside of it, so she assumed they must still be inside.

She went back to her food and thought about what a day it's been. But like Denise said, it was her Christmas too. So, why shouldn't she do something she wanted to do. Jan dropped the sandwich and stared straight ahead. She quickly chewed then swallowed the food in her mouth. *And, what I want to do is go to my grandparents for Christmas.*

She became excited at the thought. Only forty miles from here and she could be with her family. Starting her plan, she could take Rob's truck so she would make it through the snow. She'd take the cheesecake too, so she wouldn't be emptied handed. As quietly as she could, she ran upstairs to get herself ready.

"Wow, it's windier out here than I thought," Jan mumbled as she struggled to get to Rob's truck while carrying her dessert and handbag. She brushed off the chrome handle and inserted the key hoping the locks weren't frozen. The door swung wide open with the help of the wind. She reached over as far as she could to set down the cake and purse, then climbed inside. She forcefully pulled the door against the wind before it slammed closed.

"Oh, great." She sat in the gray, dim light that barely shown through from all the windows blanketed with snow. Reaching for the ice scraper, she opened the door, slid off the driver's seat, and went back outside. Once clean enough to see the road, she threw the tool on the rear floor and climbed back in the cab. Shivering heartily in the truck, she started down the driveway. She glanced back just in case, to see if anyone was coming after her. No one was.

"Stay in the tracks. Stay in the tracks," Jan said as she gripped the steering wheel tightly. Jan talked to the truck as it fishtailed going out of the driveway. "Thank you," she said as it straightened out. She took a deep breath, but still felt tense, arching over the steering wheel.

She hummed some Christmas music trying to stay relaxed. "Okay, so it's only forty miles and I only went five in fifteen minutes." She sighed. "This is going to be a *looong* trip." Squirming in the driver's seat, she forced herself to be positive and alert. "Dum, da, da, da . . ."

I need to get away from the water, she thought. She knew that getting away from the shoreline might diminish the lakes effects. She turned off M-25 and onto Van Dyke Road heading south believing that the inland roads were probably a lot better. "Oh God, please." She swiftly turned the steering wheel right, then left, then right again. Another deep breath and the truck did what she needed it to do, straighten up and settle back into the tracks.

The visibility was severely limited. Jan turned up the speed of the windshield wipers hoping they would throw off the ice buildup. But it just seemed to smear the glass even more. She turned up the defrost and it helped to reduce the ice accumulation. Driving through a town she looked for an open gas station. "It's Christmas day. Nothing is open," she mumbled as she continued to drive.

"I never want to see white again," she mumbled as she looked at the time on the truck's dashboard. "Two o'clock and finally here's County Road 142. Getting closer," she said turning the truck heading east. She peeled her hands off the steering wheel one at a time and shook them to let her blood circulate through her fingers.

Mesmerized by the gray everywhere she looked, Jan grappled with the radio knobs trying to find a station with some Christmas music. Static noise filled the truck from the AM frequency that Rob listened to for traffic reports. Fearful to take her eyes off the road for too long, she made quick glimpses at the display. "Satellite radio, finally," she murmured. "Christmas classics, they're the best. I remember singing this one in grade school." She smiled at the thought and hummed along with the music.

Slowing down to make a right turn, Jan pressed lightly on the brake. "Finally, it's starting to feel like home. Parisville Road. Almost there." She breathed a sigh of relief until the road seemed to disappear. "These north-south roads are so much worse. The winds are blowing the snow across the road," she whispered. "Why aren't there tracks up ahead," Jan said as she squinted and blinked trying to make out the road. As she drove through the open fielded area it was hard to tell where the sides of the road were. The drifts turned it into one large patch of white. "Oh no . . ." She felt the front right wheel drop off. "*Shit* . . ." Stepping on the gas a little harder she steered left but the truck went right and stopped.

"Oh my God. How am I ever going to get out of this?" Jan wanted to panic, but she knew it wouldn't help.

She took it out of automatic and put the truck in 4HI. She gradually feathered the gas pedal. For a moment there, she thought she was going to inch her way out, but the tail-end of the truck slid sideways, further into the ditch. She started to rock the truck back and forth, but eventually it stood still with the wheels spinning in place. "Oh, come on," she screamed pounding her fists on the steering wheel. Stopping to catch her breath, she looked around the area. Not a farmhouse in sight. She held the steering wheel tight and leaned her forehead at the top, mumbling between sobs. "Oh God, please get me out of this."

29 RESCUE

Jan watched for any sign of another vehicle coming down the road. The snow was coming down in thick, large flakes. Visibility was minimal. She prepared herself to jump out of the truck fast enough to signal it to stop. But with the snow blowing and coming down so hard it would be risky.

"So now what do I do? I forgot if I'm supposed to keep the truck running so the battery stays charged up or shut it off to save fuel." She took a deep breath but could still feel the anxiety rising up inside of her. "I'm a smart person. I can figure this out." She fiddled with the keys dangling from the ignition. She shut it off, but within minutes the cold infiltrated the cab. "Be strong. Be strong. I'll run the engine for more heat in a few minutes." "Be strong," she said as her voice started quivering. "One more minute."

She looked at her watch. Two-thirty, her mother's family would be starting dinner by now at Busha and Jaja's. She felt an aching in her stomach thinking about the food, but mostly wishing she were there with them, in that spacious loving farmhouse, warm and safe.

"Well, let's pass the time by seeing what Rob has in his

truck," Jan said as she opened the glove compartment. She pulled out all the items she shoved in there just a couple days ago. "Hmmm, this is interesting. A truck manual. Maybe it will have some safety instructions for when you're stuck in a ditch." She continued rummaging through the contents. "Insurance and registration. Seriously? That's it? He really is R-squared." She shuffled through more paperwork. "Note to self. Make sure I have my insurance and registration in my roadster when I get home." She took a deep breath. "If—no, when I get home," she piped out.

She lifted her legs over the center console and leaned back against the driver's side door. "What time is it?" She picked up her phone, took a deep breath, and sighed. A cloud of condensation floated away.

"Huh," She watched it dissipate into the air. Taking a deep breath, she formed an "O" with her lips and pushed a short puff of breath out forming a smoke ring. Smiling at her creation, she tried several more times but the results diminished. She relaxed back in the seat and breathed naturally.

"Okay, one more time. I'm going for the gold." Inhaling to fill her lungs to capacity, she sat up and held her breath for several seconds, then again pushed out a short breath. "Poof . . ." she let the rest of her pent-up breath out of her lungs. "It's a ten," she feigned.

"Maybe this was a bad idea," she mumbled and laid back against the door. Her chest rising and falling from a deep breath.

She looked around, out all of the windows. There was a fence line in sight that she hadn't seen before. Trees further out in the fields were starting to appear. She could tell that the storm is slowing down. The visibility was improving a little. But it would be a long time before road crews and tow trucks would be coming around.

The cheesecake was starting to look pretty good as she listened to her stomach growl. Jan checked her phone again. There was no connection, but for all she knew no one tried calling her anyway. She tapped the photo app. Scrolling through pictures of her and Rob when they first met, remembering how he looked so good and why she fell in love with him.

Not wanting to run down her phone's battery, she set it back in her purse, and turned to check out the rear window again.

Yawning, Jan stretched out her arms and legs as far as she could in the contained area. "I'm getting sleepy." Tears streamed down Jan's cheeks. "This is it? This is how I go out? By freezing to death. On Christmas day of all days." She swiped her face with her gloved hand and sniffed. "I think they call it hyperthermia. I'll have to look it up when I have a better connection." Tears continued from her eyes. "If I make it."

"What's that?" She swiveled in her seat to look back out the driver's side window. "I see something." She excitedly prepared herself to jump out. The car was slowing down. Jan grabbed the keys, threw them in her purse, and clutched the cake as best she could. Throwing the door open, she waved her free hand to signal the vehicle.

The car stayed in the tracks on the road, stopping alongside the truck. The passenger side window lowered.

"Jan? Is that you?"

"Who's in there? I can't see you," Jan shouted back.

A man stepped out of the driver's side and came running over to her. "Here, let me help you."

"It's me, your cousin Cindy," the woman shouted back.

"Oh, Cindy. Thank God you're here. You won't believe what happened."

"Let's get you inside the car and then you can tell us all about it," the man shouted over the wind before closing the rear door.

Jan relaxed in the backseat of the driver's side of the car. She leaned forward and placed her hand on her cousin's shoulder. "Thank you." Choking, she held back the tears.

Cindy nodded. "This is good. Great. We've got a lot of catching up to do."

Cautiously, the man slowly started to maneuver down the road.

"What about the truck?" Jan asked.

"It'll have to wait until tomorrow. Even if you could get a tow truck out here today, it would probably take hours and it's not safe for us to be out here that long," the man replied.

"Marvin, you remember my cousin Jan. Right?" Cindy asked.

"Yeah, we were at their wedding in June. You probably don't remember me, though," he said looking in the rearview mirror. "You must have talked to what seemed like a million people that day. That was one big ass wedding," he stressed.

Cindy turned to face the back of the vehicle as much as she could with a seatbelt on. "Well then, Jan, meet my husband, Marvin."

Jan laughed at his analogy. "Yes, it was. Between the families and friends on each side, we didn't realize we knew so many people." She shifted in her seat and pointed at Marvin. "But I do vaguely remember talking to you. One thing is for sure, I'm definitely happy to meet you today." She raised her folded hands in front of her.

"Were you going to Busha and Jaja's?"

"Yes. Is that where you're going?"

"Uh huh. Looks like this was a bit of kismet."

Jan nodded. Curious, she decided to do a little research on the couple. "Do you mind if I ask? When do you celebrate Christmas with Marvin's side of the family?"

"We just left his mother's house in Kinde. Their family celebrates in the morning giving everyone a chance to see their other sides in the afternoon."

"That's a good idea. Rob and I struggled with the

decision. Needless to say, I lost."

"Where is your husband? Is he okay with you being out by yourself in this kind of weather?" He asked.

"Marvin!"

Jan chuckled. "That's okay, Cindy. You two are my heroes. You can ask me anything you want," Jan said removing her gloves and rubbing her hands together. "My husband's at his parents cottage in Caseville. There's a lot of history with it, but the guys have a family tradition they do each year. So, I thought I would go to Busha and Jaja's by myself for a while." Jan grimaced. "But I didn't realize the roads were so bad."

Cindy turned her head to Jan. "We considered just going home. But I've never missed a family Christmas yet."

"That's a good size truck you have there, but with the icy layer underneath the snow it doesn't matter how many wheels you have." Marvin adjusted the defrost, then looked in the rearview mirror at Jan. "How'd you end up in the ditch?"

Jan smiled and looked out the window. "Well, for starters, I left the cottage," she said trying to be funny. She looked down at her hands in her lap. "I hit a drift going across the road a little too fast and lost control." She looked at the gloves in her lap and picked at some of the lint stuck on the lining.

"So that's how I was able to get through. You blew the pile of snow right off the road," Marvin said with a laugh. "See, it's the other way around, you're my hero," he said trying to make light of the situation. He focused on the rearview mirror. "Uh oh. I'm sorry about this Jan, but your truck's lights are still on."

Jan spun around to look out the back window. "Oh."

"We can't go back. It's too risky."

Jan sighed. "I know." She turned in her seat facing forward and looked out the side window.

Jan listened to her cousin recalling memories from their

childhood and her thoughts drifted to a conversation her parents had in the car one time on their way to Busha and Jaja's for Christmas. She remembered how hard it was snowing, like it was now.

"Beth, I told you we should've stayed home, just this one time. We're putting ourselves and our child at risk being on these roads right now."

"Charles, I'm sorry. I didn't realize it was so bad."

She recalled that by the time they arrived at the farm, her mom and dad were pretty shaken up.

Busha quickly pulled her aside to the table with all the deserts so she wouldn't hear the adults argue.

"Go ahead, pick one, my dear *wnuczka*."

She picked the fluffiest, most covered in powdered sugar cookie and Busha hugged her.

"Do you know what they're called?"

Jan shook her head.

"*Chruściki* or Angel Wings. You picked out the best Angel Wings. You have good eyes. Good angel eyes," Busha said giving her granddaughter another hug.

Jan realized now that for adults sometimes Christmas memories aren't always so good.

"So, what does your husband do?"

"What?" Jan snapped out of her memory. "Oh, uh, Rob and his brothers run a family business called Nichols Construction Company. They do commercial building. It's pretty cool stuff."

"Sounds like it. Do they ever need help with excavating? Because, that's what my family and I do. In fact, we do quite a bit in the city right now because of all the interest in rebuilding Detroit."

"We live in the Thumb so when we have children we can raise them in a small town." Cindy turned in her seat again to talk to Jan. "But we also have a place in Washington Township so Marvin has a place to stay closer to work."

"Two homes, that's a lot of upkeep. But I like your idea

about a small town." Jan complimented. "Some of my best memories are the times that I spent with Busha and Jaja and going into town to do the shopping. Talk about where everybody knows your name."

Marvin and Cindy laughed softly at Jan's reference.

Jan's phone bleeped. She felt a tightness in her stomach as she read the message. *Where are you?* She moaned, fearful of telling her husband what happened.

"Everything okay?" Cindy asked picking up her phone. "Looks like the service is backup."

"Oh yes. Just friends sending their Christmas wishes."

Holding her phone and resting her hands in her lap, Jan paused and stared out the window contemplating her reply. After a deep breath, she feverishly started typing. *Hi honey. Since everyone was busy celebrating Christmas in their own way, I decided to make a quick trip to Busha and Jaja's. I'll be back at the cottage later.* I'll worry about when to tell him about the truck after a few hours, she supposed. She felt bad for the others in the house. Assuming he's probably blowing a gasket after reading her message, Jan reexamined her decision.

"Speaking of rebuilding Detroit, did you hear about all that investigating that's going on now about some suspicious agreements? Boy, the city just can't get a break."

Jan contemplated whether to discuss it further. "I've been reading about it. And, it seems like it's all anybody can talk about wherever you go in the city. But I agree with you. I hope it can be resolved quickly. So, we can put a positive spotlight on Detroit again." Jan shrugged and held her hands open in the air. "If there's any substance to it all."

"We're here, but where we gonna park?" Cindy asked as she looked around the snow covered yard.

Jan sat upright, leaning and turning in both directions, looking to see if there was any available space.

The car swerved as it pulled into the driveway. "Not parking in the ditch, I hope," Marvin replied to his wife's question as he maneuvered the vehicle keeping it in the tracks. He pulled up to the front porch.

Dozens of large cars, trucks, and SUVs were parked throughout the yard and a few were lining the road near the end of the long driveway leading up to the house.

"It's hard to tell whose cars these are," Jan said. "I can't tell which one is my parent's." Jan glanced around the yard. "Look, there's the tire swing. "

"Yeah, Busha and Jaja had to put that swing up so all us kids would stop fighting over the porch swing."

Jan smiled as she recalled the memories. "Then we started fighting over the tire swing."

The two women chuckled at the irony of their grandparents attempts to appease them.

"Let's unload, then I'll find somewhere to park the car." Marvin stepped out and kicked off the built-up snow from the tire wells.

"This is a good place to park," Cindy joked as she lifted herself out of the passenger seat.

"Cindy, you're expecting." Jan marveled. "I didn't notice from the back seat."

"This time of year makes it easy to camouflage," she said as she slowly took small steps in the snow.

"Let me help you," Jan held her hand out for her cousin.

"Marvin will help me, but you better get inside before the tracks fill-in."

Jan rushed up the farm house steps, her gloved hands full with a dish and her handbag. She knocked on the door and stomped her feet waiting for someone to answer.

Marvin held his wife's arm and with his other hand supported her back as they followed the footprints through the snow.

The front door of the large farm house opened wide and a tall, elderly man held out his arms. The smell of a homemade family meal and desserts floated out from the kitchen with the sound of chatter and laughter booming in the background.

"Jaja, I've missed you," Jan said as she gave him a hug.

"Come in, come in, *dzieci*. Get out of the cold and get some food and drink in you. You're too skinny." He smiled at Cindy. "But only soft drinks for you," he teased. "Let me take those heavy coats."

"That sounds good, Jaja," Cindy said as she removed her boots. "The ride to get here was much longer than expected and we're starved." She placed her hand on her protruding belly.

A slender, mature woman came over.

"Busha, Merry Christmas." Jan kissed her grandmother's cheek.

"Jan, you look good. Marriage agrees with you," Busha held her granddaughter by her arms and looked her over. "Where's that big, strong husband of yours?" She moved closer to Jan and tilted her head as she whispered. "There's not trouble in paradise, is there? Do you want your Jaja to talk to him?"

Jan chuckled as she gave her grandmother another hug for the gesture. "No, no, Busha. Everything is fine in paradise. Rob has this manly tradition he does with his father and brothers on Christmas day. So, I thought I would come alone this year." Jan choked as she spoke. She cleared her throat. "Maybe next year though."

Jan saw her mother forcefully managing her way through the maze of tables and chairs. Beth grabbed her daughter and hugged her tightly. "I'm so glad you're here."

"Thanks, Mom. Merry Christmas. I love you." Jan held tight, not wanting to let go. "I didn't bring your gifts with me though. I thought maybe we could get together later on in the week and celebrate just the four of us."

"That sounds wonderful." She looked inquisitively at her daughter. "So? What is the secret Nichols family tradition? Do you like it?" Her smile turned to a frown. "Wait. You're here. You must really not like it to leave your husband and come here in this weather."

Jan held her mother at arm's length. "Ice fishing."

Beth stared blankly at her daughter for a moment. "Ice fishing? Ice fishing is their family's Christmas tradition." She grimaced. "No, it makes sense that you're here."

Jan nodded. "But there's a lot of heartfelt history behind the tradition, so I can't be too judgy about it."

"Understood. I see you brought the cheesecake. Let's set it over here."

Jan followed her mother to the dessert table. And, stopped to talk with a few cousins, aunts, and uncles on the way.

EPILOGUE–THE GANG'S ALL HERE

Jan finished her plate of food while sitting with her cousins and sharing stories. She relaxed back in her chair, turning to take in a look at all the family having a good time.

"Somebody's at the door," Beth said directing her husband to assist with the family duties.

"Okay, okay, I'll get it," Charles said as he wrestled his way between chairs and people blocking his path.

"Charles, are you thinking about playing football again? Those was some pretty good moves," Jaja complimented.

"It's the coach." He winked back. "She's the best at telling the team what to do."

"I can tell you where to go to," Beth teased.

"Well, look who it is." Charles put his hand out to welcome them. "You made it. Jan said you guys have some tradition you do on Christmas and couldn't be here."

Jan's eyes widened when she heard her father's comments.

"Well, we finished our tradition and are ready to celebrate Christmas with family."

Jan heard her husband's voice and immediately turned around.

Once he spotted her, Rob smiled at Jan as he stepped

further inside the farmhouse.

"Can I help with anything?" Charles asked as he held the door open for the rest of the Nichols family.

"I think we've got it. Thank you," Rob replied. "Busha and Jaja, do you remember my parents and brothers from the wedding?" He asked as they all squeezed inside the door, stomping their feet to get the snow off their shoes.

"Of course, we remember," Jaja snapped. "I remember everything. Come in. Come in," he said. "I've got the mind of a steel trap." He grinned.

"Rob, you made it," Busha said as she held his face in her hands. "That's good. You need to be with our Jan on Christmas day. Family needs to be together."

He nodded and grasped Busha's hands to hold them tight. "And, I guess you know Monica," Rob added. "Without her we probably would have gotten lost."

"Monica is family. She's been here many times." Busha took her hand to lead her further into the kitchen. "Denise come, come. There's plenty to eat and drink."

"Oh, as good as that sounds," Denise grimaced, "I may need to take a rain check on that."

"Woah," Jaja exclaimed looking out the farm house window. "So, that's how you got here. The county should pay you to clear the roads with that truck."

"Thanks," Pete replied. "I just put the blade on yesterday. Pretty righteous, huh?"

"Pretty what?" Jaja looked at him quizzically.

"Oh, nothing," Pete stammered.

Beth grasped Rob's arm to bring him closer. "I'm glad you're here."

"Me too, Beth. Me too." He looked around. "I can see what Jan was talking about now."

Beth nodded. "Family."

"Ed, whad 'ya drinking?" Charles called from across the room.

"That bottle on the top shelf looks good," he said pointing.

"Everything's top shelf here, my friend" Charles said as he reached while looking back at Ed. "It's Busha's homemade rye whiskey. The recipe is from the prohibition days."

Busha laughed and covered her mouth with one finger. "Don't talk so loud. They'll come and arrest me."

"That damn Rosentowski isn't gonna arrest you. He just wants you for himself. He's still mad at me because I got the girl." Jaja put his arm around his wife, kissed her on the cheek, and smiled to the others.

"Ah, *szalony dziadek*," Busha said as she threw her hand at him.

"Merry Christmas, Jan," Ed said as he walked over to greet his daughter-in-law.

"Ed, I'm so sorry—"

"Don't be." He cleared his throat. "I'm your Secret Santa. And, I saw going to your grandparents' farm was number one on your list. And, I wanted to bring you here." He pressed his lips sideways. "But—I was waiting until after the boys and I finished ice fishing. Guess that was pretty insensitive of me, huh."

"Ed, thank you. It's the thought that counts. It's nice that we're all here together now." Jan gave him a curious look. "How did you get the others to come with you?"

"Jan? It's me, Ed, you're talking to."

She laughed with her father-in-law. "Best Secret Santa ever. Merry Christmas, Ed." Jan moved closer and gave her father-in-law a hug.

"Oh, well," Ed mustered and awkwardly patted Jan on the back. "Merry Christmas," he said stepping back, smiling at her.

"Hey, Jan. You have to come here." Rob waved his wife over. "Your cousins are giving me your backstory."

She squeezed between the tables and chairs, and then stood side by side next to her husband.

"Merry Christmas?" Jan said as she stood next to him.

"Merry Christmas." Rob embraced her which drew

some adoring sighs from the ones sitting nearby.

"Did you see your truck?" Jan bit her bottom lip and lovingly laid her hands on his chest.

"Yeees, yes I did." He turned his serious face to smile at his wife. "I called a tow truck, but it'll be tomorrow before they can get to it. They're really backed up."

"I'm sorry." Jan's forehead creased. "But I—"

"Hey, it's okay. I'm just glad you're here now, safe. I tried calling many times, but the towers were out, covered with ice."

"Do either of you know how to play Euchre?" A family member asked sitting at a nearby table.

"Brian, that guy over there, is an expert. You should ask him." Rob redirected their attention.

"Thanks. Brian, you said."

"Yup."

"Hey, Brian?"

Rob's brother looked over at them.

"Not me. This guy. They want you to play Euchre."

"Yeah, sure," he said walking toward them. "Get ready to be crushed."

Rob looked at Jan. "Is there someplace we can go for a little privacy?"

"Yeah." Jan smiled. "Around that wall is the stairs to the loft. I'll go up first and you follow in about five minutes," she whispered.

"Why can't we go together?"

Jan gave him a funny look. "Because it'll look like we're sneaking away." She inconspicuously made her way through the family stopping only for brief conversations.

"Wow. What took you so long? I feel like I've been sitting here for hours," Jan said when her husband finally arrived upstairs.

Rob had a big grin. "Well, many of your cousins, aunts, and uncles wanted to share their stories about you with me." He continued grinning at her. "You were a very interesting child, as one of them put it."

"Whatever they said isn't true, unless of course it's something good," Jan defended her reputation.

"Uh huh."

"So, what do you think? This is the room I stayed in when I would spend time here with Busha and Jaja. Pretty nice, huh?"

"This ol' farmhouse has a lot of character," Rob said as he looked around at the slanted walls and recessed dormer windows. "You can tell there's a lot of love here."

"You're the first boy I ever had upstairs." Jan giggled.

Rob smirked. "Really? A good looking, sassy little girl like you didn't have a line of boys at the door waiting to be with you?"

"Well, I did get to know some of the locals. Nice boys too." Jan looked up as she hugged her knees to her chest. "I wonder what they're doing today?"

Pulling her closer, Rob held her tight. "Don't even think about other boys. You're mine. You're the best thing that's ever happened to me."

"Oh, that reminds me. I have a present for you."

"You brought my present here? You didn't know I would be coming."

"I know. *Buuut*, I didn't want you to find it. So, I brought it with me." She smiled, then fumbled around in her handbag. With both hands hidden in the purse she waited. "Okay. Close your eyes and hold out your hands."

"Oh, come on. We're adults. Just give it to me."

"No, you have to close your eyes and hold out your hands or no present," she taunted and kept her hands hidden.

"Okay," he moaned. "I'm guessing it's a set of keys to a new truck."

"Ha-ha, that's really funny. You ready? Hold still." Jan giggled as she placed the object in her husband's hands. "Okay. You can open you're eyes."

Rob stared at the long, thin stick in his hands. "A really tiny fishing pole?" He squinted as he pretended to cast a line.

Jan laughed at the suggestion. "Keep guessing."

"A mix drink thermometer? It looks like a thermometer. Doesn't it? It does to me." He said as he pretended to stir a drink. "See it's got that little display there."

"You never saw one of those? You really don't know what it is?"

"A battery operated straw? A new invention you came up with to make us rich? Your lips touch it and you don't even have to suck. The liquid just automatically comes up the straw into your mouth." He continued to turn it over and over again, examining the item. "I give up."

"It's a pregnancy test." She waited for his reaction, softly smiling.

Rob snorted. "A pregnancy test. What do we need that forrr—" He looked at her. "A pregnancy test? You . . . Me?"

"Uh huh." Jan nodded. "We're pregnant."

Rob stared at the object in his hands, motionless.

"Are you okay?" Jan nudged her husband's arm.

"What did you say this is? I thought you said pregnancy test." Rob stared at the object in his hand.

"Yes," she said with amazement spreading across her face. "I took the test this morning. I don't have the flu. It's morning sickness."

Her expression changed to concern with her husband's lack of enthusiasm. "Are you okay?"

"So, let me get this straight," Rob said as he stared at the pregnancy test stick. "You don't have the flu. Me and you," he turned to look Jan in the eyes, "we're pregnant?"

"Yes," she said as her smile widened. "I'm pregnant. I can't believe I'm saying that." She took a deep breath. "I can't believe I'm pregnant."

"We're, you and me," Rob pointed at Jan then himself, "are gonna have a baby," his mouth dropped open. "A child. Do you know if it's a boy or a girl yet?" He looked closer at the stick, turning it over and over, examining it. What's this little pink plus sign mean? It's a girl?"

Jan laughed gently. "No. That just means I'm pregnant. But I haven't even been to the doctor yet. So, we better keep this between us for right now," she whispered.

"Okay, you're right." He pulled her closer and kissed her hard on the lips.

"Can you believe it? Our lives are going to change forever." Jan looked into her husband's eyes.

Moving back slightly to look at his wife he whispered, "Best Christmas gift ever." He smiled.

"I know we didn't plan this. We didn't even talk about having kids."

"Talking's not what we do best," He said with a thoughtful grin. "And, yes, I'm okay. In fact, I'm great. I'm gonna be a dad, an Ed." He laughed.

"Well, we'll have to talk about our parenting skills." Jan squinted. "Probably have to take some classes or something. Read some books." She shrugged.

With pressed lips, Rob slowly shook his head in agreement as he looked off into the distance. "You know, this," he held the pregnancy test stick in the air, "would be a great gift for your parents who have everything. We can regift it, return the present you bought for them, and save a few bucks. Whatd'ya think?"

Jan started laughing at the idea. "Okay, but not here. When we get back to Shelby, we'll have them over. But maybe we should wash it first?" She choked back her laughter as she waited for his reaction.

"What do you mean? You mean you didn't wash it yet?" He questioned as he dangled it in his hands.

"Maybe I did." She continued laughing. "I can't remember."

"Well then, I'm regifting your gift to you," he said as he grabbed Jan's hands and lovingly struggled with her to return the gift.

"Coming upstairs," Monica shouted halfway up to the

second floor.

"This house is cool. I want one of these," Pete's voice followed. "There's all kinds of different rooms and cellars."

"Quick, where's my purse?" Jan scrambled with the stick in her hand.

"Here. Here drop it in," Rob said as he held her handbag open for her.

"What are you two doing up here?" Monica teased. "Jan, did you put another notch in your bedpost?"

"What? You're crazy," Jan's jaw dropped and she stood up and stared at her friend.

Rob gave her a curious look and raised his eyebrows. "Another notch, huh?"

"There are no notches. No bedposts." She scoffed. "Besides, what are you going to do if there was?"

"Count them so there won't be any more the next time we come here," Rob said shaking a finger at her.

Jan sat back down next to her husband. "Not to worry. You're the only boy for me." She said wrapping her arms around her husband's neck. She whispered in his ear, "Merry Christmas."

ॐ

Next Book in Series Preview

Maternal Instincts

Friday night and Jan Nichols tapped her fingers on the steering wheel of her roadster as she drove home from Hedge Corporation. Her favorite music was on the radio and she moved her shoulders to the beat. Her boss was on vacation. And, she hadn't experienced morning sickness in over several weeks. So, with looking forward to the baby shower on Sunday; this was the most fun she had had in a long time.

Turning into her subdivision as she approached her house, she saw a black sedan parked on the street not far from where she lived. She laughed softly. "Mr. Daniels, are you dropping off my husband again," she said, parking the roadster several yards away. After getting out of her car, she walked over to the other vehicle. She opened the door and shook her finger at the man inside.

"Mr. Daniels, really? Why don't you just come into our home—"

Two men startled, shifted in their seats, then quickly shuffled papers and equipment around.

"Lady, you're not supposed to be here," the driver yelled.

"What the hell?" The passenger shouted. "What do you think you're doing? Mick, hurry. Close the door."

"Hey, you're not Mr. Daniels." Jan's eyes scanned the interior of the car. A camera sat on the dash, and paperwork, files, and listening devices were strewn about. "I'm sorry, but I thought you were . . . hey, who are you, and why are you watching my house?" Her eyes focused on the folders and labels on their equipment. "FBI? You're the FBI?" She held onto the door, starting to feel weak. "Why are you watching my house? What do you want from me?" She screamed.

"Lady, get outta here." The driver slammed the door shut, nearly clipping Jan's arm as he did.

They sped off, and Jan watched as the car disappeared. She stood in the middle of the street, watching the backend of the sedan until it was out of sight around the corner. She was breathless and trembled uncontrollably. "FBI," she sputtered, taking deep breaths. "Oh my God. We're the ones being investigated. It's us that the newspapers won't reveal."

She tried to raise her right hand to brush back a strand of hair that blew across her face. But she trembled so hard she couldn't control her movements. Finally, after several deep breaths, she slowly stepped back to her car, placed her hands on the hood, and leaned against it. After several more breaths, she was able to get back into her vehicle and drive up to her house.

She realized now that the FBI were the people in the dark cars following them around during the holidays and the past several months. She felt so stupid, so naïve, thinking or maybe wishing it was only Mr. Daniels in those cars, like during the first few weeks of her marriage to Rob. She hated how every time he stepped out of the house, Mr. Daniels just happened to miraculously appear. And Rob would give him all the attention he wanted. But he was the customer. And her husband's company had a very lucrative contract to prove it.

Her breathing returned to normal. Sitting in her car, she stared straight ahead at the garage wall. She thought about how much she would give anything to have it be Mr. Daniels again in those cars now instead of the FBI.

She started to feel anger rise up inside her. She wanted answers, and she wanted them now. "What in the hell did that woman do?" Jan snarled, getting out of the car and yanking her handbag and portfolio from the passenger seat. Carrying them into the house from the garage, she quickly set up her laptop on the island and opened the Nichols Construction Company file.

Jan scrolled through to the earliest contracts Rob had given to her. These were the ones she used to start their company's financial database. She went to the library and grabbed the stack of original paperwork to do one more sanity check on the calculations.

Adding another field to the data, she entered a formula to back out the difference between the cost of materials plus labor and the overhead.

"The management reserve. What Rob wrote down and what she took out were two different amounts." Jan covered her mouth and stepped back from the island for a moment. "Oh my God. The Daniels Technology Center contract is almost a billion dollars."

Jan quickly shuffled through the stack of papers for the contract. Not finding it, she picked up the stack and slapped it back down on the island. "Where the hell is it?" she yelled.

Angrily she picked up her phone and pressed Rob's number. "You had better pick up this time," she mumbled. The third ring sounded, and she was just about to hang up.

"Hi, hon. What's up?" Rob said casually.

"Do you have the Daniels Tech Center contract with you? Because I need to see it. Now," she demanded.

"I think I left it in the library."

"It's not there."

Rob paused. "Okay. Well, it's got to be somewhere. What's going on? Why do you need that contract so badly right now?"

"Jan, what's going on?" Rob asked when he entered the house from the garage. He set his briefcase on the mudroom bench and kicked off his boots.

"Where did she go?"

"Who? Who are you talking about?" Rob scowled.

Jan took a deep breath, realizing she needed to slow down and explain from the beginning.

"Glenda. Your former bookkeeper. Where did she go? We need to find out because we're the ones being investigated by the FBI. Nichols Construction Company is the name they won't release because they haven't charged us yet." Jan's voice started to crack.

"What? You don't know that."

"Yes, I do. When I came home, a black sedan was parked near our house. So, I thought I would get out and surprise Mr. Daniels." Jan's face turned grim, and she covered her quivering lips with her fingertips. "But instead, I surprised the FBI. They've been sitting outside our home all this time watching us. Spying on us. Possibly even listening to every word we've said." Jan expressed the pain on her face. "Our intimate moments."

Rob gazed off. Jan knew he was as shocked as she was. They were the ones in the news. They were the ones being investigated by the FBI. Making all the headlines. But not the kind of news you want to be known for.

Rob walked to the island and placed both hands on it to support himself. He took several deep breaths. Reaching up in the air, he then brought his hands back down to the back of his neck and pressed. "Why? Why us?" He turned to Jan and gave her a pressing glare. "Why would the FBI be investigating us, of all people? We didn't take the money. It doesn't make any sense."

Her husband's rejection made her feel like she had just received a huge blow to the gut. "Because your bookkeeper embezzled the company's money. A rough estimate is several million dollars. Gone, out of the country. Cheating yourself and your clients out of millions of dollars. The Federal Government out of who knows how many tax dollars." She took a deep breath. "Is that enough reason for you now? Does it make sense now? Who the hell was this woman?" She angrily raised her voice. "I just spent the last half-year of my life trying to figure out her bookkeeping methods. Now, I meet the FBI in front of my house. So, you don't ask the questions. I'll ask the questions. Who the hell is she? And why did she steal money from our family company?"

Rob sat down on a café chair and stared off quietly. After several minutes, he turned to his wife. "I don't know. I don't have any answers for you."

Jan sat down and placed her head on her crossed arms to rest. The baby pressed against her side, and she rubbed her hand on the sore area.

"Are you okay? And the baby? I'm sorry. I didn't mean to turn this against you. But somehow, we'll figure this out." He softly placed his arm over her shoulders.

"We need to tell your dad and brothers. Now that I've exposed them, it's probably only a matter of time before the FBI issues a statement. Better they hear it from us than from the late-night news."

"We should let your parents know too. And what about our friends?"

"Right. All of them." Jan cringed and slightly pressed her hand on her protruding belly. "I think the baby's foot is kicking my ribs."

Rob leaned forward and placed his hand on his wife's pregnant stomach.

"Do you think Manny will be able to get any information from the district attorney's office? We'll need to schedule a meeting with him. What should we have for dinner?" Jan walked over to the refrigerator and stared inside at the contents but never selected anything. She wiped below her eye, then pressed her lips. Slamming the refrigerator door shut, she leaned against it and sobbed.

"Jan, are you okay?" Rob ran over to her and pulled her into his arms.

"It's not supposed to be this way," Jan said as she tried to take a breath. "We work hard. So hard, and all we get is bad publicity instead of a thank you for doing something good." Her body shook from the emotion pouring out of her.

"Shhh, shhh. Honey, try to relax. Remember what the

doctor said. Let me help you. Let's take some deep breaths together, okay?"

Jan held onto her husband, quietly slowing down her breathing until it was normal. Finally, she lifted her head and looked at him. "I'm okay now. Let's sit down."

Rob helped his wife to a chair at the breakfast nook table. He supported her back with one hand and held her arm in the other as she slowly sat down.

"Are you okay now? Comfortable?" He pulled out a chair for himself and sat down.

"Yes, I'm okay now." Jan grabbed his hand. "But Rob, we need to talk to our family and friends. Now." She gave him a stern look before closing her eyes and taking a deep breath. "Do you think you can make something for dinner tonight? I don't think I can be on my feet long enough to prepare a meal."

Rob parked his truck and jumped out. He quickly ran to the passenger side to assist Jan in stepping down from the large vehicle. He put one arm around her back and used the other to support her arm, helping her to the front door.

"Are you okay? You'll be able to sit down in a minute," Rob said as he brushed his hand on his wife's back.

While waiting for someone to answer the door, Jan looked back at her husband. "I'm just tired and hungry." She turned around and stared into the front door. Holding onto the doorjamb to support herself, one at a time, she stretched her legs, pulling her heels toward her backside. She breathed and softly counted each time.

The door swung open. "Jan, come on in. How are you feeling?" Denise put her arm around her stepdaughter-in-law's shoulders and directed her inside.

"Don't worry about me. I'm okay," Rob said, following the two women into the house.

"I'm just tired and hungry."

"She says for the millionth time," Rob grumbled under his breath. He sat down on the recliner and stretched into it, getting comfortable.

"Rob, get up," Denise ordered. "Jan, honey, come here and sit down. You should put your feet up. Can you reach the handle?"

"Yes, I got it, Denise. Thank you," Jan said with a sigh.

Rob rolled his eyes and walked over to sit on a straight chair next to his dad. He leaned forward, resting his elbows on his thighs, and watched Denise pamper his pregnant wife with attention.

"Everything okay, son?" Ed asked with a curious side-eye glance.

"Not really. I used to be Denise's favorite. Now look." He pointed across the room.

"Don't worry. When the baby gets here, nobody's gonna care about either one of you."

Rob turned to his father, his eyes opened wide, and he took a deep breath. Clasping his hands, he looked back at the two women sitting across from them. "More importantly, what did Denise make for dinner?"

"Pete and Monica are bringing pizza."

"Pizza? That's it? Denise didn't make dinner?" Rob leaned back on his chair and threw his hands in the air. "I could have had pizza at home."

"You said that you and Jan have something you need to tell us, and it's important." Ed looked curiously at his son.

"Oh yeah. I guess I'm hungry too. When are they getting here with—"

"Ed, can you get the door?" Denise said with a sideways glance toward her husband.

"Why the hell do these kids keep knocking and ringing the doorbell? Why the hell don't they just walk in? This place is frickin' grand central station," Ed said as he got up to walk to the door.

Pete and Monica bolted in without waiting, bumping

into Ed as they entered. "Hey everyone, we got pizza," they announced together.

"Oh, hey, hello, dad," Pete said, pulling the door back after nearly slamming it into him. He handed over a pizza box.

"Thank you. And, from now on, don't bother knocking."

Pete and Monica looked at each other and shrugged. "Okay."

Jan flung the recliner to its upright position and jumped to the edge of her seat. "Rob, can you get Brian on the phone, and I'll call my parents. This will be easier if we tell everyone at once."

"Tell us what?" Pete looked curiously at Jan, then at Rob.

Rob took a deep breath before looking at his wife.

"We're the ones in the newspaper headlines. We're the ones being investigated by the FBI. Us, the Nichols Construction Company," Jan explained, holding her arms open. She turned her attention to her phone. "Oh hey, dad. Is mom with you?"

"Hey, Brian. Do you have a few minutes? Okay. I'm putting you on speakerphone."

Monica elbowed Pete and quietly instructed him.

He removed his phone from his back pocket and pressed a favorite.

"I'm getting Gina and Michael on the phone, and Pete will have Christie and Manny," Monica said.

"Good. Okay, here it goes," Jan took a deep breath and looked around the room at everyone.

"The FBI has been watching our house. And, from what I can tell, it's been going on since about late last fall. I thought it was Mr. Daniels always in his dark transport cars. But apparently, it wasn't."

Ed jumped up from his chair and pushed his hands in the air. "Jan, what makes you think that? Why would the FBI investigate Nichols Company when we didn't do anything wrong?"

"We didn't, but the former bookkeeper, Glenda, did. She embezzled several million dollars of the company's money when it was awarded the Daniels Tech Center contract." She looked at her husband. "Rob, where's the paperwork?"

"I'll get it. It's in my truck." He left the room momentarily, returning with a thick stack of papers, and handed them to his wife.

"Hey, Jan. This is Manny on the phone. As your attorneys, we need to advise all of you before you say anything more. Could somebody go take a look outside, up and down the street, for any parked cars?"

"I'll do it," Pete said as he jumped up and went out of the house, leaving the front door open. He came back. "It looks like the coast is clear from what I can tell," he said, returning to his seat.

"Okay, Jan. You can continue, but Christie and I may caution you about your statements," Manny directed.

Jan opened her laptop, sitting on the arm of the chair. She entered her husband's written numbers in the newly created data fields. Covering her mouth, she gasped at the sight.

"How bad is it?" Rob said as he walked over to her and looked over her shoulder.

He took a deep breath and cupped his forehead in his hand. "Six and a half million."

Gasps sounded around the room and from the guests on the phones.

Ed paced back and forth several times, then turned his attention to Pete's phone. "Manny, Christie, what immediate advice do you have for all of us? And when can we meet to start planning our defense?"

"For starters," Manny spoke, "don't talk to anyone, and I mean anyone, about this. No relatives, friends, no one. Christie and I will meet with all of the Nichols party first thing tomorrow morning. I know it's not exactly what you wanted to do on a Saturday, but this can't wait."

"I agree," Jan said. "Thank you, guys, for being here for us."

Everyone on the phone said their goodbyes while the others went into the kitchen for dinner.

"I'm not sure I can eat after all that," Pete said, staring at his empty plate. "I bet the FBI's been monitoring the Daniels construction site too. Probably all of our sites. If only we had paid more attention to what was happening around us."

"Come to think of it, you guys were pretty clueless given all the signs," Monica alleged.

"We had no reason to think that we were the ones suspected of illegal activity." Jan pounded her fist on the table. "We didn't do anything wrong."

&0C&

Continue reading *Maternal Instincts*

Spread the love! Leaving your review on Amazon, Goodreads, or your favorite bookstore helps others discover new stories and authors they'll love too. It helps fellow readers find their next great read.

Amazon   Kobo   Goodreads

READING GROUP GUIDE

These reading guides are for book clubs and individual readers who want to gain a clear, meaningful understanding of the purpose of Jan's journey through love and marriage. Additional printable guides for each book in the Happily Ever After Series are available on Deborah's website.

These reading guides have discussion questions for you and your fellow readers to consider and debate. It is designed with the reader in mind and allows them to relate their own life experiences when contemplating their conversation topics.

Readers can also add their own questions for discussion. We'd love to hear what you add to your reading guide. Send an email with your suggestions

Christmas Runaway Discussion Questions

1. Jan expresses to her husband how important family holiday traditions are to her. Were you able to relate to her feelings? Are any of your family traditions similar to Jan's, e.g., family farm, large multigenerational family, other traditions?

2. Can you think of a better way for Jan to get Rob to share Christmas between their two families other than making a bet? How would you write the story differently?

3. Should Jan have known better than to stick to her "fair weather fan" attitude? Is that a worthy ideal for her or anyone to have?

4. Why do you think Monica wants to win over Denise's favor? She was described in Moonlighting Bride as being a woman who was "aggressive with men." Do you think she'll stay with Pete or drop him to go back to playing the field?

5. Rob expresses disdain for his brother, Pete, repeatedly throughout the story. He claims it's because Pete is incompetent. Yet, Pete has proven himself to be very capable. Why is Rob so hard on his brother, Pete? Why does he favor his youngest brother, Brian?

6. Throughout the story, a black sedan continues to show up wherever they are. If it's not Mr. Daniels, then who could it possibly be? Did it bother you that there wasn't closure about who's in the sedan? Will you read the next book, Maternal Instincts, to find out?

7. Rob's former girlfriend, Marissa, returned. Why do you think he wasn't honest about her with Jan in the first place? Should Jan feel like she can still trust him?

8. Beth, Jan's mother, was very upset that her daughter wouldn't be with her family on Christmas day. Do you think she had a right to feel that way? Should she have respected the decision Jan and Rob made and kept her nose out of it? If it was your daughter, what would you have done?

9. Is the story of married couples arguing over where to spend the holidays a common theme? Have you read similar books on the subject? Did this author do a good job of writing the story depicting the two extreme views of the wife and the husband?

10. What feelings did the book bring out in you, e.g.,

sadness, happiness, frustration, holiday spirit, others? Did the story measure up to your expectations given the description? Why or why not?

11. Would you recommend Christmas Runaway as some good holiday reading? Would you read it again next holiday season? Would you give it to someone else as a Christmas gift?

12. What is the main plot of the story? What are the subplots? Did the author do a good job of intertwining the plots throughout to the end of the story?

13. Did the main character, Jan Nichols, demonstrate any growth or change throughout the story? Did her husband or any of the other characters change?

14. Did Jan react appropriately when she learned that her former boss, whom she disliked, was returning and her current boss, whom she adored, was told to leave? Did her former boss change, and does Jan give her a chance to demonstrate this?

The Happily Ever After series is one woman's journey in love, business, marriage, motherhood, and gracefully aging. And, just like everyone else, she can't go back and rewrite her story. Follow Jan Nichol's love story with the entire series of books; *Life Changing*, *Moonlighting Bride*, *Christmas Runaway*, *Maternal Instincts*, and *Age Related*.

Continue Reading Happily Ever After

All books include free reading group guide and next in series book preview.

Read the entire Happily Ever After Series *Life Changing - Moonlighting Bride - Christmas Runaway - Maternal Instincts - Age Related*

Life Changing
Happily Ever After Series Prequel

Jan Brooks is young, ambitious, and ready to fulfill her life's dreams. When she meets the handsome stranger, can happily ever after come true for her?

With everything checked off her life's to-do list, it was time for Jan Brooks to look to the future. She was accomplished with an MBA degree and a thriving career. Being an independent, rational woman, she normally did not react so impetuously, especially when it comes to matters of the heart.

But when it was love at first sight for the handsome stranger, Jan finds herself questioning everything she thought she ever wanted.

Will Jan have the courage to rewrite her life's checklist and embrace the possibility of a future she never imagined? Or will fear and doubt keep her from the love she never saw coming? Jan Brooks must navigate the complexities of romance and find out if she's willing to risk it all for a chance at her own happily ever after.

Moonlighting Bride
Happily Ever After Series First Novel

When rich meets middle class love ensues. But will it be enough to keep newly married Jan Nichols from creatively financing her high maintenance lifestyle?

Jan Nichols is a newly married woman who has to give her paycheck to her dominating husband. Instead of her money going to support her high maintenance lifestyle, she now has to pay for things like electricity, insurance, groceries—and stay within her budget.

This comes as a complete surprise to her. How did marrying the man of her dreams suddenly turn her world upside down?

Jan has to figure out how she's going to maintain her standard of living at any cost. She can't let him know what she's up to, and she still wants to make her husband happy. But when Jan realizes that her husband may be playing her for money—even at the expense of her life—she needs to find safety fast.

Christmas Runaway
Happily Ever After Series Second Novel

*For Christmas, all Jan Nichols wished for was a
celebration with her husband they'd never forget. But
when her idyllic celebration takes a dramatic turn, will
her husband reach her in time to save their holiday
magic?*

Jan Nichols always cherished a traditional Christmas with
family on her Grandparents' farm. But this year, the
newlywed excited about sharing this tradition with her
husband faces an unexpected twist and spending the
holidays with his family.

As the holiday season approaches, Jan is overwhelmed by
her husband's growing demands, her friends' sharp
accusations, and the pressures of her career. And when a
mysterious woman shows up in their lives, it cast doubts
about everything Jan thought she knew about her husband
and her marriage.

On Christmas day, still determined to have her own way,
she faces a heart-pounding dilemma. Will Jan discover that
sometimes the most incredible challenges come not from
the world around us but from the choices we make in our
hearts?

Maternal Instincts

Happily Ever After Series Third Novel

Caught between a thriving career, family drama, and a looming threat to her husband's livelihood, Jan Nichols must navigate a storm of challenges—just as she's about to have a baby.

With a great career, married, and pregnant, Jan Nichols felt like she was living the dream. And with so many family and friends to help support her through a risky pregnancy, she was excited to start a new chapter in her life—motherhood.

The last thing she imagined was that her husband and his family company would come under attack. So, when threats against them escalate, she has to find out who is behind the accusations. Determined to uncover the source and save the company, Jan dives in and discovers just how far she'll go to protect her own. What she didn't expect was to have to choose between her career or her family, to play referee between her mother and stepmother-in-law.

With her family's livelihood hanging in the balance, she must uncover the truth behind the attacks before it's too late. In a story where love, loyalty, and resilience are tested, can Jan stand the fight for her family's future?

Age Related
Happily Ever After Series Fourth Novel

In a world where power and love collide, Jan fights to save her family's multibillion-dollar company from a hostile takeover. Will she confront her own shortcomings and decide what truly matters in her life, her legacy, or her heart?

Jan Nichols has turned her husband's family business into a multibillion-dollar empire. But when a ruthless corporate takeover looms, everything she's built is at risk, including her marriage. With the weight of generations on her shoulders, Jan must confront her past and prove she's more than the spoiled woman she once was.

Twenty-five years after the honeymoon, Jan juggles a high-stakes corporate career, the demands of three young adult children, aging parents, aging friends, and a husband whose loyalties are in question. Just as she thinks she has it all under control as the chief financial officer, an outsider arrives and opens her eyes to new possibilities. Now Jan is torn between preserving the Nichols legacy or pursuing something or someone else new. Can Jan transform herself into the leader her family needs? Or will her ambitions and personal desires lead to their downfall?

ABOUT THE AUTHOR

Deborah Kulish wants to share her family humor with others in her Happily Ever After series. For most of us, marriage is a life-changing event and for Jan Nichols, it was no exception. Throughout the series, Jan encounters one difficult situation after another; money issues, a little weight gain, a new baby, sharing the holidays, and, running a family business. These are just a few examples of what can happen after the words, "I do." Torn between her love for her husband and her love for a high maintenance lifestyle, Jan comes to realize that most importantly, love can overcome the conflicts.

Deborah resides in Metro Detroit enjoying the surrounding arts, culture, sports, and entertainment. She holds a degree in management and has a wide range of experience writing for businesses and media. In addition to reading, writing, and dabbling in technology, Deborah enjoys cooking her favorite family recipes. And, when not dining at home you'll often find her at one of the local pubs or taverns having a great time with family and friends.

deborahkulish.com

CONNECT WITH DEBORAH

Sign up for Deborah's newsletters for special offers.

Email
deborah@deborahkulish.com

Website
https://deborahkulish.com/

Amazon
https://www.amazon.com/author/deborahkulish

Barnes & Noble
https://www.barnesandnoble.com/s/deborah+kulish

Facebook
https://www.facebook.com/authordeborahkulish

Instagram
https://www.instagram.com/authordeborahkulish/

Pinterest
https://www.pinterest.com/deborahkulish

Goodreads
https://www.goodreads.com/deborahkulish

BookBub
https://www.bookbub.com/authors/deborah-kulish

Deborah Kulish website
https://deborahkulish.com

From Book To Market website
https://frombooktomarket.com